BLACK WATER

CORMAC O'KEEFFE

BLACK & WHITE PUBLISHING

First published 2018
by Black & White Publishing Ltd
Nautical House, 104 Commercial Street
Edinburgh, EH6 6NF

1 3 5 7 9 10 8 6 4 2   18 19 20 21

ISBN: 978 1 78530 162 9

Typeset by Iolaire Typesetting, Newtonmore
Printed and bound by CPI Group (UK) Ltd, Croydon, CR0 4YY

To my amazing wife, Jacinta, and our three children,
Adam, Quinn and Fay

PROLOGUE

I've killed the boy.

Shay ground his teeth at the realisation.

The side of his head throbbed from the impact of the explosion and, with his nose split and swollen, he struggled to breathe as he ran.

Orange flames danced against a canvas of black. On the other side of the perimeter wall, he heard the canal waters hiss as crackling debris hailed down.

If the gang was inside the building they were blown to pieces, Jig with them.

A sheet of corrugated roofing slammed down in front of him, searing his shin. He winced, but forced himself on.

So, this is how it fucking ends: risking my life searching through rubble for bits of the boy. After everything I've sacrificed.

Somewhere behind, the detective shouted at him to come back. But, ahead, Shay thought he could make out screams. Distant sirens echoed along the warren of Dublin's streets.

The remainder of the warehouse heaved and groaned. He was out of time.

Fuck it, I've nothing to lose.

He stumbled forward, his face bubbling with the heat. His ankle twisted over something loose on the ground, tipping him off balance. Spitting blood from his lips, he looked down and followed the forks of yellow light.

Something small was smouldering.

It looked like a runner.

A child's runner.

1

Jig liked the word SNAP. The sound the wipers made when he ripped them off the car. And when he wrote the letters on the page, his tongue curled against his lips.

He took the path in jumps, inches from the canal's black waters. But when he saw the swans, he stopped. They were clustered here and there, asleep, their long necks curled into their backs, their heads buried under layers of thick white feathers. Like little soft icebergs, lit up by streaks of yellow from overhead lights and the silver haze of the moon.

He had slipped out of his gaff no bother. When the bottle fell from his ma's bed onto the floor, and the snorting started, that was the green light. He had kept on his tracksuit and runners so he was ready to go. He remembered to put on his gloves before taking the wipers and the note out from under his Man U pillow.

The canal was still. A gust of wind wrapped around Jig's face, carrying a waft of roasted sweetness from the brewery. He checked the time on his phone: 2 a.m.

He ran, the wipers in his gloved hands and the note in his pocket.

He had a job to do for Ghost.

Mary heard a noise at the front door, then footsteps running off, light, like that of a child. She swung her arm to turn on the bedside

1

lamp and knocked something over. Easing herself out, she placed the double picture frame back up, her eyes drawn towards the old photograph on the right. A fine big man, chest puffed out, a mop of black hair brushed to the side, eyes looking into the distance. It was her favourite of James.

She couldn't help but glance at the photo next to it, taken years ago. Leo leaning forward, grabbing a friend's head at his nine-teenth birthday party, beaming a wide and wet smile.

Frozen images melted in her mind. James, sitting at the front window, watching and waiting for Leo to come home. James, on his deathbed in hospital, refusing to let the cancer hollow him out without seeing his son one last time. And Leo, when he did visit that time and looked for ten thousand euro.

'Da, I need it, Da. They have a bullet for me...'

But James was lost in a nightmare world of pain and sweeping tides of morphine. Mary had roared at Leo to get out. It was the last time she heard from him. But not the last time she heard from the lowlifes who wanted their ten thousand euro.

She put on her slippers and reached for the dressing gown. At the tiny landing, she turned on the light for the bottom of the stairs and peered down. There were long black rods or something inside the door.

Instinctively she went to grab the railing, but stopped, remembering the top fitting had come out completely from the crumbling wall. She pressed her two hands against the walls either side and stepped down.

The black things were wipers. Her heart jumped.

Oh God, they must be from the car.

As she neared, she could see a piece of paper on the ground. A voice inside told her not to, but she picked it up, her hands shaking. She dragged a short breath.

SNAP. TALK TO COPS AGAIN UR NEK WIL B NXT.

Blood drained from her body. Her legs buckled.

As she fell, her head smacked against the edge of the hall table. The force of the blow twisted her head and shoulders around and she went crashing onto her back.

The note sailed into the air.

Her eyes fixed wide open, blinked once, then twice.

Jig ran his hand through the reeds. They were swaying and rustling now. He tingled at the sensation. The wind had grown teeth.

Lampposts rattled as he sprinted. The water was flowing stronger, spilling over the locks onto the chambers below.

He wondered what Ghost would say about the job. He imagined bony fingers tossing his hair and Ghost saying, 'Good job, little man.'

I'll be in big time with Ghost now, I will.

A swan stirred. It unfurled its neck and shook its tail.

Jig knew from the brown feathers it was a young swan. That was what his granda had said. A cygnet, he'd told him, was what they were called. He thought he could see a sprout of white feathers. Jig stopped and stared for a moment.

Then he karate-kicked the air and ran.

2

The blows rained down. White fists and red-raw knuckles crunching on bone. Shay shuddered at the pummelling to his arms and hands, tossed at his moans for mercy.

Noise was dragging him away from his dream.

Bang. Bang . . . Yang. Yang.

Shay peeled back the sheets and flexed his wrists. They often throbbed with the memories.

The intrusion was the scream of an alarm from outside.

He eased himself out of bed and shook his head, the racket aggravating his tinnitus. He stood up, his feet arcing at the touch of the cold floorboards. He loosened his tight boxers and stepped silently to the window. Opening a blind, he tried to pierce the darkness, but he couldn't determine the source of the siren.

He curled back into bed behind Lisa, warmed his feet and fixed on her hair. For a moment he expected to see the ripples of long blonde curls. He moved to push them out of his face, away from his nose, like he used to, a few years ago. When his vision focused, it revealed short straight brown hair and a pale thin neck. He remembered the day she arrived home from the salon. He knew why she did it, but never brought it up. Nor did she.

The scumbag grabbed her hair and licked her neck, the fucking animal.

That, and what Shay did afterwards, had landed them here. To this life.

The sense of being fucked over, of being trapped, of trying and failing to get his life – their life – back, scratched at his skull and clawed at his stomach.

The walls and windows began to shudder. The Garda helicopter must be overhead, he thought.

Red lights flashed behind the blinds. He got up and looked out again; a fire tender was coming to a stop. Away to his right was the source of the noise: a car, now ablaze. Thick yellow flames curled into the night.

Ghost and his crew at work again, he thought.

He would see Ghost at the next match, as usual. The boys nearly shat their arses if he even looked at them, they held him in such awe.

I know what Ghost's game is. Digging his nails into some of the boys. Like Jig.

He strained his neck to try and see the helicopter, it seemed that close. But then the vibrations subsided as it pulled away, towards the canal.

The noise from the car became more tortured, screeching one second, then receding. Two firemen pulled hoses, like long, bulbous snakes, and extinguished the flames with bursts of foam. Massive plumes of smoke puffed up.

Upright on the edge of the bed, he pulled at the skin under his eyes, then glanced down at the thin frame curled tight under the sheets.

He fretted over her reaction, once the sleeping tablet wore off.

'You see that?'

The morning light pained Shay's eyes as he blinked them open.

Lisa had her back to him, hands pressed hard against her hips.

'Yeah, a car went up on fire,' he said, keeping his tone measured and slipping out of bed. 'You were out for the count.'

He started at the sight of the smouldering shell, bare and black in the bright morning sunshine.

'What a lovely thing to have on your doorstep,' Lisa said, casting a look in his direction. 'I bet you it will be there into next week before those useless lumps in the council remove it.'

She scrunched up her nose at the smell of molten metal which had infected the room. Shay knew she was being pulled down. His stomach tensed.

'Brilliant,' she said.

Shay watched three kids running from different directions to the car, whooping with delight. They circled the wreckage, kicking at it. Another boy, around six or so, emerged screaming, dragging a golf club behind him, the head of it scraping and slapping off the road. As he neared the car, he arced it up over his head and slammed it down on the bonnet, greeted by hoots.

Lisa recoiled at the noise, her face tightening.

'Why car all burnt, Daddy?' came a little voice from below.

Charlie had crept past them. Molly followed. They put their hands on the window sill and stood up on their tiptoes.

'They're bold boys,' Molly scolded, pointing her finger at them, 'they shouldn't be doing that.'

Lisa turned her back on the window, and the kids. Shay saw the moistness in her eyes as she shuffled towards the door.

'Listen, Lisa ...'

Shay wanted to say something more, but couldn't find the words. Lisa turned, her features tight against her pale skin.

'What?' she said.

Shay sensed the kids stiffen, looking up at them.

'Well?' she said. 'What were you going to say? That we'll be out of here soon?'

'We will, Lisa. It can't be much longer, won't.'

'Can't or won't? Which?'

Shay moved forward to hold her shoulder, to reassure her, but she shrugged him away. The kids jumped now at the banging outside. The hammering was getting more frantic.

'You've been saying the same thing since we were dumped here,' Lisa said. 'A lot of our stuff is still in boxes. We've nothing up on the walls,' she said, swinging her thin arms around. 'We barely have any shelves. We're half-living here.'

She paused. But he knew what was coming.

'You said it'd be a year.'

'I know,' Shay replied, his stomach clamping. 'But what can I do? It's not my fault.'

Her face strained again at the clang of metal on metal.

'Isn't it?'

3

Crowe sprinted over the bridge, her runners crunching on scattered shards of glass. She turned right and down the other side of the canal. She dipped her head to an oncoming gust, her black ponytail brushing her shoulder.

She was stressing about the sergeant exam. Her second interview was just yesterday. She thought it had gone well. That's what she told the doubting voices in her head. Now it was up to how the bosses would write her up.

Recommended. Better still, highly recommended. That's what I want.

The run was doing the trick.

A swan splashed onto the waters, rousing her. It pushed its chest up, unfolded its great wings and flapped them. In the distance, the gentle 'jing jing' of the Luas tram chimed.

Crowe pushed herself down the path as Canal Road Garda Station loomed into view from behind the flats. She watched a blade of sunlight cut across its facade. The station didn't look like a bastion in the war against gangland: a long, dull yellow block, peppered with aluminium windows, fastened with mesh grilles. It could be a forgotten office building, she thought – save for the communication mast towering behind it. Coming to a stop, she eyed the latest graffiti scraped into the thick wooden entrance doors.

Rats Out.

She heard male voices behind the frosted glass at the public counter, laughing. She thought about saying hi, but her hand hesitated at the door. She felt too self-conscious in her running gear. Knowing the guys, they would be twisting their big heads to have a good gawk at her.

She strode towards the shower, hoping it wouldn't splutter as usual between hot and cold.

'Calling Detective Crowe. Come in Crowe.'

She smiled on recognising Grant's chirpy voice. She hadn't heard her behind the screen. The lads had probably been laughing at one of her stories.

'Hey there, girly,' Crowe said, swinging around.

'You know I hate landing stuff on you, and you in early, all fit and sweaty,' Grant said. 'But there's a possible suspicious death on Larkin Road. Number 36. Elderly woman. Peters is already there. I can leave it for someone else?'

'No. Duty calls, Garda Grant,' Crowe said, smiling. 'Just let me have my luxury power shower first.'

Crowe processed what Peters said as they walked through the house next door to Ms King's. She climbed over the rusted low railing separating the back gardens, pulling up her trouser belt to counter the weight of the Sig and shoving her bag around her back.

They stepped through the door into the kitchen. She glanced at the wooden units, dull green and with a shiny metal strip along the border. A tea cosy sat up on top of the fridge.

It reminded her of her grandmother's kitchen. She felt a sudden pang for the woman inside.

With the curtains closed, the sitting room was in semi-darkness. The room felt cramped. A rickety coffee table jutted out in front of a sofa. Scraps of paper and bills lay scattered on it. An old portable gas heater was lodged in one corner, a bulky television in the other. A Sacred Heart painting dominated the chimney breast, its red light encasing a small white cross at the bottom of the frame.

Crowe coughed at the thick air and moved towards the front door. She halted when she saw bare white legs, parted at awkward angles, the hem of a dressing gown thrown back. She eased closer, pulling out latex gloves from her bag and slapping them on.

The woman's shoulders were twisted away from Crowe, while her face tilted towards her. Dark eyes stared out. Crowe twitched at the sight, then resumed her observations. There was a matt of congealed blood and hair on the left side of the woman's head, circled by black bruising.

Nasty bang, she thought, looking around for the cause. The edge of a hall table was blunted, revealing pale wood under the dark veneer.

All of which drew her to what might have been the cause of the woman's fall. The broken wipers looked odd lying near her head, right under the letterbox. The note Peters mentioned had landed on the woman's chest, opened out.

Crowe pulled out her phone and took some photos: of the blow to the head, of the table's edge, and the position of both. She stepped carefully over the body and took photos of the wipers and, lastly, the note. The writing was clearly visible.

Her heartbeat quickened as she read the message; she glanced at the wipers. The words were all written in capitals. There was something about the unevenness of the letters and the text-spelling that suggested the work of someone young, a child even. The paper looked like a page torn from a school copybook.

So they've got kids to do their dirty work now.

Crowe tightened her lips at the thought.

She continued her observations. The locks of the door and chain were untouched.

No forced entry. The wipers must have been shoved through the letterbox. That will give forensics something to work on.

She visualised the woman's shocked reaction as she read the note and fell, hitting her head off the table.

Once outside, she got Peters to bring the cordon out further, boxing off the small two-bed terraced houses and the road. She walked over to an old Renault Clio parked in front of Ms King's house.

The wipers were gone, broken off.

Jig had a stick in his right hand and the bars of a flicker scooter in his left. He crouched down, bouncing slightly.

'And they're off,' he shouted, cracking Bowie's behind.

The Staffie took the strain of the rope tying it to the flicker and pushed forward into a run, right down the middle of the road.

Spikey cycled beside, doing the commentary.

'Jig Time's made an early lead. The jockey does be riding the bollix out of him.'

A car screeched to a halt to avoid them.

'Jig Time has jumped Becher's Brook and the jockey's still on. He has the bit between his teeth today, the mad bastard.'

Dizzy Dylan ran towards them, his hands waving in the air.

'Some woman's dead,' he shouted, panting. 'Coppers outside a gaff on Larkin.'

Jig pulled up.

'Who?'

'Dunno. Missus someone.'

Crowe watched Tyrell's dirty Mondeo slam over a kerb and park on the corner. He walked towards her in looping strides, his shoulders stooped, glancing furtively around him without moving his head. She could see the DI was sucking on his mints.

'Hey, mister? What happened?' a girl in tight shiny leggings and false eyelashes shouted up to Tyrell, but he didn't notice her.

'She's dead,' a little boy beside her said.

'She been shot?' the girl asked, chewing, her mouth open.

'No one's been shot, now move back,' Crowe said, as Tyrell approached.

'Crowe,' he said, looming nearly a foot over her, 'what have we got?'

'A woman in her sixties died from what looks like blunt force trauma to the head,' she said, looking up at him.

She pulled up the images on her phone. 'It appears she may have fallen and hit a hall table in the small front porch. As you can see, there are suspicious aspects ...'

'What's this?' Tyrell snapped.

Crowe looked up and down at her photos.

'You know if there's a prosecution out of this and the defence looks for disclosure, this is evidence,' he said, with a nod at the images. 'They could argue the scene was interfered with by you taking these photos. That's why we leave it to the scenes of crime people. You're going for sergeant. You should know better.'

'Sorry, DI,' she said, curling a stray strand of hair behind her ear.

'Don't apologise. Just be careful.'

Crowe was still holding the phone in the palm of her hand. She felt both awkward and stupid.

'Here, show us anyway,' Tyrell said.

He stretched out a yellow-stained finger but the screen suddenly went black.

'Sorry, it turns off quickly.'

He looked at her, she knew impatiently, as she tapped in her code and held out the image again. His blue eyes narrowed.

'There's two broken wipers inside, most likely pushed through the letterbox,' Crowe said. 'And this car here,' she said, pointing back to the windscreen, 'looks like it had its wipers ripped off.'

Crowe had secured brown evidence bags over the ends of the wipers for further tests. Tyrell nodded ever so slightly when he saw them.

She tapped on another image.

'And then there's this note.'

Tyrell leaned in, cracking the mint in his mouth.

'They knew, or suspected, she was talking to us,' Crowe said. 'Looks like a threat that went wrong. Also, the writing looks like the hand of someone young, a child even.'

'Who's the deceased?' Tyrell asked.

'Mary King, the neighbour said. She lived there alone. Her son is Leo King. She reported him missing three weeks ago.'

Crowe saw the lines on the DI's forehead rise slightly. In a man who gave little away, she was learning to spot any tell-tale signs.

'DI, did you deal with Leo before?'

'Little fucking weed,' Tyrell replied. 'Caught with a load of gear a while ago. He wouldn't spill who he was holding for. Got bail, of course, and did a runner.'

She could see he was still thinking.

'How was she discovered?' he asked.

'The neighbour, Ms Mulligan,' Crowe said, pointing to the house with Grecian plaster casts of reclining women in both the living-room and upstairs bedroom windows. 'She called in to Ms King and became concerned when she got no answer. She looked through the letterbox and saw the deceased's body.'

'Great,' Tyrell interrupted. 'So her prints and DNA are now on the letterbox.'

'Yes. The ambulance crew went through Ms Mulligan's house and gained entry to Ms King's through the back door.'

Crowe could see Tyrell's eyes rise slightly to his right and she figured he had recalled something – he didn't look pleased.

'DI?'

'She met Flynn a few days ago,' he said.

Crowe scrambled her brain for information, trying to impress Tyrell.

'Isn't Detective Sergeant Flynn the new liaison for locals being intimidated by gangs?'

But Tyrell was already heading for the neighbour's house, taking in the distance in a matter of steps, barely acknowledging Ms Mulligan at the door.

'Missus. Are ya a detective, a lady one?'

Crowe looked down at the boy from earlier, peeping up from under the cordon.

'Ya ever kill anyone?' he said excitedly, pointing at her gun. 'Ya ever shoot a woman?'

'No, little fella,' Crowe replied, pulling her jacket across her holster and zipping it up. 'Now, please step back.'

'I live there,' he said, pointing to a house where a large woman leaned against a door, smoking and chatting to a neighbour, who was in her pyjamas.

Crowe scanned the swelling crowd. Children in their school uniforms jumped and shaped as if they had pins and needles. Many were on their mobiles, texting, taking photos or listening to music. A young girl pushed a buggy towards the scene, a big teddy strapped in the front. Kids clambered up on walls, with packets of crisps and cans of Coke, to watch the drama. Teenagers with hoodies and baseball caps looked on darkly, some of them cycling around in loops, phones pressed to their ears.

'Bet ya someone's been shot, gunned down like a dog,' Spikey shouted back, making a gun gesture with his hand. Jig crouched low on the flicker, Bowie panting beside him. 'Here, let's go over to the others,' Spikey said.

Sharon, Taylor and little Bill were there. The girls were sharing earphones, swaying to music. They smiled at the boys in between shouting out the words from the song. Crouched behind them, Jig's mind was all fuzzy.

How the fuck is the woman dead? Am I going to be locked up for years, like me da was?

He twitched around to see if anyone was looking at him.

I needs to talk to Ghost.

'I'll ring the coroner and the pathologist,' Tyrell said, coming back out. 'We'll organise a house-to-house and harvest any CCTV. We'll need to get a handwriting expert on the note. See what you can find out about the deceased and who was hassling her.' He nodded to the massing kids. 'And keep those fucking ants back.'

Crowe looked behind her, halting at the sight of a kid taking a piss against the wall of a house. She turned back to Tyrell, thinking about what he had said earlier.

'DI, how did the people behind this know she was talking to us? You said the deceased had spoken to Sergeant Flynn just days ago. You think it could have come from inside?'

Tyrell clenched a piece of mint between his teeth. Crowe lowered her eyes, silently cursing herself.

'Did I say that?'

She shook her head.

'No, I didn't.'

'Sorry,' she said, curling a hair behind her ear.

'What did I tell you about apologising?'

Crowe felt her cheeks warm and bowed her head, hoping Tyrell wouldn't notice.

But all she heard was him stride away, crunching on his mint.

4

Jig scrunched his nose at the stink from her mouth.

'I don't know where yer fucking jumper is,' his ma shouted. 'Do I?'

He pulled open the fridge. Bowie barked at the sound. There was a lump of butter, the dregs of milk and that onion cheese spread he hated. A bottle of vodka lay flat along one of the ledges, a thin film of liquid sliding from the force of the door opening.

'And don't be moaning about no food neither,' she continued, shouting over Bowie and the chatter of morning TV.

'Welcome back. Now, with the days getting longer and the weather, fingers crossed, I know, getting better, we have the lowdown on the coolest garden furniture.'

'There's cheese spread and butter there, and here,' she said, throwing a squashed bag of sliced bread onto the table.

'Shut up, will ya,' she shouted at Bowie, moving to hit him.

Jig wanted to tell her to fuck the fuck off, but knew better. The TV presenter broke his ma's concentration, giving him an opportunity to slip away. Bowie followed. He picked up his Man U scarf from the mound behind the door and wrapped it around his face.

'Cunt,' he said, closing the front door. The scarf muffled his curse. But he still looked over his shoulder to make sure she hadn't followed to land him a couple of slaps. He hated her smacking him around the head outside, in front of people.

He grabbed a bicycle pump off the ground and swung it around, aimless. He kneeled over one of the bikes and gave it a good beating. Bowie barked with each slap.

Wonder how she'd like it if I gave her a smack in the gob with this.
He lashed into the bins.

The red mark on the back of his hand pained from all the hitting. He squirmed at the memory of his ma, blitzed off her tits on vodka and tablets and trying to make tea, swinging a boiled kettle. She tripped and spilled steaming water over his hand. He fucking roared the house down and lashed around the kitchen. He thought his bones were cracking. She smacked him one and told him to 'give over' and 'stop his moaning' over a drop of hot water. 'No fucking way' would she call an ambulance and have some 'snooty staff' at the hospital asking questions.

Jig held his hand under the cold water tap all night. But it still roared red after. All the while, she snored in the sitting room, in front of the TV.

Shayo had asked him about it, but he just told him he spilled the water on himself. He knew Shayo didn't believe him. But he couldn't give a fuck. That fella could be a nosy bollix.

Jig flung the pump at the bins. He stood on the bars of the gate and swung on it back and forth, listening to it protest at the strain. He kept doing it, hoping the rusted joints would just collapse out from the wall.

What else can I do? Not going up to school now.
He picked up a few stones and threw them onto neighbours' roofs and listened to them rattle and bounce back down. Bowie barked and Jig tapped him on his wide head.

'Let's run to the canal,' Jig said.

He sprinted down the road, Bowie zigzagging in front of him, looking back every couple of seconds, his big tongue lolling about.

As he stopped running, Jig heard the deep growl from behind. His hair prickled. He turned to the road. His eyes bulged as bull bars passed before him, silver and gleaming. He could see his face distorted in the reflection, like melted plastic. Huge shiny side mirrors and massive silver wheels, wrapped in jet black tyres as high as his shoulders, cruised past.

17

The jeep hummed to a halt.

Jig stood back and looked up at the tinted windows. He gaped in awe; his cheeks sweated behind the scarf.

The jeep vibrated from the bass inside and Jig tried to recognise the rap artist that was playing. The passenger window glided down with the smoothest of sounds.

'Alright?'

Jig got on his toes, but the seat was so far back he couldn't get a proper look at Ghost's face. A hand rested over the window, a smoke lodged between blackened knuckles. Jig stared at the tattoo on Ghost's long, bony hand. It was a grim reaper, coloured in black and white, a flowing tattered cape revealing the side of its face: a large black eye, a sharp nose and a slit of a mouth. Two scythes above its head arced down either side to a sharp point. Ghost had loads more on his arms and his legs and a huge one of a skeleton's head all over his back. Jig had heard about that, but hadn't seen it, yet.

He looked back up and squinted. He could make out Ghost's shadowed head. His eye sockets were dark, like deep holes in the grass.

'Ya off to rob a bank or something?'

Jig didn't get it at first, then pulled down his scarf, and smiled up at Ghost.

'Good man,' Ghost said. 'What ya up to?'

'Not much,' Jig said, scuffing his runners on bits of glass. He heard a crackle and saw the light of the cigarette creep around Ghost's pale mouth.

'No school, no?'

'I hates that place,' Jig said, kicking the ground.

'No matter,' Ghost said, taking a drag and then pointing at the road. 'This is where ya learn, Jig. On the street.'

Jig nodded and gave Bowie a pat.

'Ya down training the other night?' Ghost asked.

'Yeah, practising some frees, I was.'

'How's the Shayo? Still getting all stressed at youse keeping him late?'

Jig laughed and nodded. And waited.

'So,' Ghost said, lowering his voice. 'Did ya hear what happened?'

Jig barely heard him with the music, but his tone had switched. Jig called it the 'no fucking messing' voice. He didn't reply. He didn't know what to say.

Ghost leaned forward and glanced at the side mirror. His cheekbone looked sore, pressed against his skin.

'Ya thinking about it?' Ghost said to him.

He nodded. That woman dying was scratching away inside his head okay, but he kept telling it to fuck off.

'I'm gonna have to keep ya closer now,' Ghost said, pulling on his cigarette.

Jig smiled at that.

I'll be in Ghost's crew soon, proper like.

'Cos it's a bit of a fuck up,' Ghost muttered. 'It's gonna cause some heat.'

Jig's stomach shrivelled. He was confused now.

I done what he told me to do.

'There's gonna be a price,' Ghost continued, his voice nearly drowning under the music. 'It will have to be worked off.'

Jig twisted on his feet, looking up at the shadows.

What price? What's he on about?

The cigarette butt flew past him. Ghost slapped a hand on Jig's head and shook his hair.

'But that's good, little man,' Ghost said with a grim smile, the tips of his narrow teeth showing, 'cos, ya be, like, my man.'

Jig smiled back as Ghost's window glided up. He loved that sound. The jeep growled. Jig stared at the four exhausts as the jeep accelerated down the road and swerved around the corner.

Jig looked around, waiting for someone to salute him or give a nod of acknowledgement. Bowie jumped up against him.

'Ya hear that, Bowie,' Jig said, putting his arm around the dog's head, getting a big lick in return, 'Ghost said I'm his man.'

5

The thud of the toddler's head against the window dragged Shay away from his thoughts.

The child swayed on his mother's lap as the Luas snaked around the hospital. She leaned against the window, her eyes half closed, her mouth open. One hand clasped a roll, the other was curved loosely around the boy.

Shay stared absently at them as a familiar record played in his mind.

How the fuck am I going to get my life back? And how much longer is it going to take?

Another thud. The mother moved, her loop earrings jangling. She took a bite out of her roll and slumped back, chewing slowly like a camel.

Shay was on his way back from college. He went to the meeting, as usual, and gave his report. He was told he was doing well. But, he knew they wanted more from him.

The Luas stopped and he watched two girls in roller-skates clatter on.

This was all part of his rehabilitation, he told himself; the long payback for what he had done.

Yes, it's taking fucking ages. Yes, it's wrecking Lisa's head. But there's no other way.

Another thud, louder this time.

Shay looked over at the child. The boy cried, twisting his head around for attention.

For fuck's sake.

He reached across and tapped the mother on the shoulder, slipping back before she roused.

'Whaaaa?'

The word sounded like it had been pulled out of her mouth by a rope. Her eyes opened, her vision trailing behind.

'What is it, chicken?' she said to her son. She pushed the sagging bread against the child's mouth. 'Here, have some roll.' The boy struggled to cry, breathe and take the roll all at the same time.

The girls on the roller-skates rattled past, slapping off the sides of the seats on the tram.

He looked at the time on his phone. He had to collect the kids. Their ages tumbled around his mind like a lottery machine. Molly was four, Charlie a year behind.

They were soaking up everything the area had to offer, like proverbial sponges.

I'm running out of time. If I don't deliver the goods, the kids will end up being stuck here.

As Shay approached with the kids, seagulls flapped and squawked over a man scattering bread into the canal, snatching what was meant for the swans.

'Daddy, who put that there?' Molly asked, pushing her long blonde hair away from her face.

Shay squinted at the canal. A child's high chair had been dumped; the top half of it stuck up out of the waters. The canary yellowness of the plastic chair added to the incongruity of the sight.

'Bold boys?' Charlie asked, looking up at him.

Shay nodded. You couldn't step out the door without being confronted by 'colour', as he called it.

A loud rev and shouting from behind caused him to turn around. A boy racer was leaning forward in an old banger bombing towards a roundabout. A young fella on the path shouted at him and rolled his fists in the air.

'Daddy, it's like a butterfly.'

Molly had run down the path and stood staring at a tree. She pointed to a blue plastic bag flapping against the trunk. A smile opened across her face. The wind puffed the bag in and out and made it dance against the bark, until another gust sent it off. The kids screamed after it.

'Ah, isn't it me favourite children.'

Shay recognised Ms Moore's raspy voice. The Hugging Mama, the kids called her. They ran to her and wrapped themselves inside her layers of coats. Shay looked down at her white runners as they adjusted to take the force.

She had a rollie balanced between fingers bent with arthritis. She rummaged deep into assorted pockets with her free hand. The kids inched closer, all quiet now. She looked up and gave Shay a wink.

'Let's see if I have anything here for youse.'

When they moved into the area, Ms Moore had dropped a card through their letterbox, a bright vase of flowers on the front. Inside were the words 'welcome to the area'. It was such a nice thing to do, and seemed to be a good omen.

'Now, there youse go,' she said, digging out a crumpled bag of jellies. Wine gums, Shay could tell.

She pressed Molly in against her with her smoking hand and rubbed Charlie's mop of black hair with the other. She mumbled a few words. It was a quick prayer, which she often did. Then she waved goodbye.

The kids devoured the jellies, sharing glances at each other, their eyes sparkling at the surprise treat. Shay motioned forward, throwing the kids' bags up over his shoulders.

As Molly and Charlie scampered off, he looked across the canal at the massive crane looming on the skyline on the far side.

It hadn't moved since they came here. It hung like a metallic spectre over the remains of James Connolly flats.

Modern apartments were to replace the flats, a mixture of social and rented housing, Shay recalled. A model of public–private partnership, everyone was told. The developer would build the apartments, the council would rent them and the tenants of the flats, after decades of neglect, would at last have a decent place to live. But it was a lie. The developer, owing the banks millions, went under. He was fine, Shay reminded himself, if the photos in the papers of him and his wife out shopping in New York were anything to go by.

The flats had almost all been knocked down when the builder went belly up, apart from one solitary tower. Boulders and rocks from the demolitions lay in mounds, half protected with broken railings, separated by filthy pools of liquid. It was a popular play area for kids.

Dealers had scattered from the flats. Many set up base up and down the canal, along the greens and parks, all fighting for a patch from those who controlled it: the Canal Gang.

'Look, Dad, a goldfish,' Molly said, pointing into the waters.

But Shay could only see cans and plastic bottles bobbing amid all the other rubbish.

He looked over at a group of young fellas at the next lock, gathered on the other side of the canal. One of the crews at work, he thought.

He watched thin shapes approach, one of them struggling on a crutch.

He knew the routine. The buyer would text the crew leader in advance what they wanted. He'd get his mate to go to the stash, hidden in a bush or behind the block of a wall, get the deal and leave it on the ground. The buyer would arrive, hand over the cash, go to the allotted area, pick up the drugs and scurry off. All in broad daylight.

As he neared, Shay took a mental note of who was there. He knew most of them, their faces and nicknames at least. There was a smaller figure leaning against the lock gate, looking down into the waters.

The boy had his back to him, but Shay knew exactly who he was.

6

Crowe cut the engine. She took in the grey concrete walls, the narrow windows with rusted grilles and the broken boundary fencing. The Oasis Centre looked anything but that.

She opened the door and slung her bag over her shoulder.

As she crossed the potholed tarmac, a man stepped out from behind a large metal door. He lit up a cigarette, crumpled the box, lobbed it in the air, and kicked it a good ten feet, so it landed just in front of her.

'Like Aguero that. Back ... of ... the ... net.' A smile spread across his face and he pulled deeply.

Crowe was not in the mood for senseless banter, particularly about football.

'Lynn in there?' she asked.

The man's smile evaporated.

Crowe was used to it. She was dressed in a zip-up jacket, dark blue jeans and black runners, but still she was regularly clocked as a detective. The locals had that sixth sense when it came to a garda, plain clothes or otherwise. The bulge on the right side of her hip did tend to be a giveaway.

He nodded to the door.

She pressed a black button and the door cranked open. There was a basic room inside, bright, with a battered sofa. She nearly hopped when the door clanged shut behind her.

'Thought ya were Marco.'

The voice came from a woman in a glass-partitioned room to her left.

'I'm looking for Lynn Bolger.'

Lynn was close to Ms King. That's what the neighbour had told Crowe earlier.

'She's with someone,' the woman said, nodding to the room beside her.

Crowe stood there for a second, before copping the woman wasn't going to say anything more. She shifted awkwardly and moved to the sofa.

She placed her bag beside her and sat upright. She tried to look composed.

Her right hand came to rest down the edge of the cushion, which was torn and frayed. She grabbed a thin line of material and began wrapping it around a finger, undoing it and wrapping again. When she realised what she was doing she took her hand up, placed it on her bag and inwardly chastised herself.

Next, she busied herself studying the noticeboard on the wall opposite. One note was emblazoned 'Centre Rules'.

'No *dealing, no using on premises. Show respect to each other and staff. No verbal or physical abuse. Remember, you're not an addict, you're a human being. Act like one.*'

Crowe pursed her lips, impressed.

A while later, there was a motion from behind a door. The handle creaked and voices spilled out. A hard-looking woman – squat, with short brown hair – glanced at Crowe as she walked another woman to the door.

Must be Lynn.

The woman turned to face her, but said nothing.

'Lynn Bolger?' Crowe asked, holding her belt as she stood up.

The woman nodded, glancing at Crowe's hip.

'Would I be able to talk to you, in private?'

Lynn raised her right eyebrow, then stepped towards her room. Crowe pulled her jacket over her holster and followed.

The room was bigger than she expected. There was a large table with six or seven chairs around it. In the corner were kitchen units, with a sink. They were shiny orange, seventies style. They looked like something that had been ripped out during a house renovation and stuck in here. To her left was a desk, with a heap of paper and a packet of John Player Blue resting on top.

'I'm Detective Garda Tara Crowe,' she said, rooting out her badge from her bag.

Lynn stood there, impassive.

'I'm here in relation to Ms King,' Crowe said, putting her badge away. 'I believe you knew her well.'

No response. Lynn just eyed her.

This could be a waste of time.

But she persisted.

'Do you know why I might be here?'

'Yeah,' Lynn said, walking around her desk, 'to find out who killed Mary.'

Crowe reared back.

'Why do you say that?'

'Why else are ya here?'

'Well, we're investigating all the circumstances of . . .'

'What? How come she died a couple of days after meeting youse?'

Crowe couldn't hide her reaction. She wasn't expecting this.

This woman is going to lash me out of it.

She berated herself for not being better prepared.

'I shouldn't be even talking to ya,' Lynn continued, pointing her finger towards the door. 'Do ya know what could happen to me if they find out I'm talking to the garda?' She leaned forward to emphasise her point. 'That even cross yer mind when ya just walked in here for anyone to see?'

Crowe wanted to apologise, but fought the urge.

'No,' Lynn said, 'didn't think so.'

Crowe thought about taking the typical garda approach: throw her weight around and demand some fucking answers. That's what the lads in the unit would do. But she knew that all it would do was rub someone like Lynn up the wrong way.

'Can we just sit down for a moment?' she suggested, after taking a breath.

Lynn hesitated. The muscles in her face and neck flexed. With a sigh, she dragged a chair out from her desk. Crowe sat at the table and took out a notepad from her bag.

'Did Ms King tell you about who was hassling her?'

Lynn shifted in her seat, giving Crowe another once over.

'Couple of heavies came to her door a while ...'

'She give a description?'

'Foreign lads, Eastern European. But they're just goons, paid by the Canal Gang to intimidate.'

'When was that?'

'A month or so ago.'

'Thanks. You were saying?'

'They wanted to know where Leo was. She doesn't, didn't, know. They said, "Okay, ya owe ten thousand."'

'For the drugs that were seized off Leo?'

Lynn nodded. 'Told her if she didn't pay up, they'd light up her house, then track down Leo and chop him up. She was in bits. And ...'

Crowe looked up from her notes; Lynn was shifting in the seat again.

'A couple of days ago she told me her wipers were broken off,' Lynn went on, emotion stealing into her voice. 'I tried to play it down, told her it just be kids messing. But now I knows it was part of the intimidation.'

Lynn turned her face to the side.

'Ms Bolger,' Crowe said gently, 'none of this is your fault.'

'Damn fucking right,' Lynn shouted, rearing off her seat, jabbing a finger at Crowe. 'It's bleeding youse that are at fault.'

Crowe grabbed at her notepad as it slipped off her lap. The sides of her neck warmed.

'What do you mean?' she asked, cursing the timidity in her own voice.

'I told her about this new garda system,' Lynn waved her finger about, 'confidential system – well, supposed to be – for families terrorised by gangs. She met that Sergeant Flynn fella from the drugs unit in town last week. Now she's dead.' Lynn looked straight at her. 'Ya telling me they didn't find out?'

The palm of Crowe's hand went all sweaty. She wiped it on her jeans and avoided making eye contact.

'They did,' Lynn pressed, 'didn't they? The pricks.'

Crowe pushed a loose hair behind her ear and looked up at her.

'Ms Bolger, there's no evidence of that. We are only at the early stage ...'

'Ah here, if yer going to waste me time, just get out.'

Crowe watched Lynn shove the chair in with a slap.

I have to salvage something from this.

'Ms Bolger, we will be thorough, that's all I can say.'

Lynn walked over to the sink and poured out a glass of water. She leaned her thickset arms against the units and swallowed large gulps.

'Did you tell anyone else?'

'What do ya think?' Lynn uttered between gasps.

'Would Ms King have?'

'Not a chance,' Lynn said, refilling her glass. 'Well, except Pat.'

'Who?'

'Pat, Father Keogh. Mary was religious. Fat lot of good it did her. Ya must know Pat. He knows everyone, and everything; at least he thinks he does.'

'Would he have told anyone?'

'Pat? No,' Lynn said, turning to her, the redness in her face receding. 'He's a bit sanctimonious, interfering, but not stupid. He's had his own share of run-ins with the gangs.'

Lynn walked back to her desk. She looked more composed now and Crowe thought she might get more out of her.

'Ya best go,' Lynn said, grabbing her smokes and looking up at the clock. 'It's late and I have to check in on a few people.'

Typical. Never get your hopes up.

But still she pushed.

'What can you tell me about the Canal Gang?' Crowe asked. 'I'd like to know more about them.'

Puzzlement jostled with annoyance on Lynn's face. She tapped the packet of John Player a couple of times, leaned back against the desk.

'Nothing does move around here without Ghost either knowing about it or in the thick of it.'

Crowe knew the name as she scribbled her notes. The lads in drugs were kept busy by him. But he'd never been caught or charged with anything major, as far as she knew.

'Cracko is Ghost's debt collector,' Lynn said. 'Nasty bastard. Ghost and him rule this area. Ghost does be getting kids to do all his errands.'

Crowe felt she was getting somewhere. There could be a connection between Ghost and a kid being used to threaten Ms King. But, she knew Lynn could stop any second.

'Kids?' she asked.

Lynn passed the cigarette packet from hand to hand.

'Ghost recruits them,' she said. 'Picks kids from bad homes and no homes. He gives them a purpose, throws them a few bob. I'm talking as young as eight, nine, ten year olds. He does have them running and hiding stuff, harassing families, all that. The garda can't touch them kids, because they do be under the age of criminal responsibility. Then Ghost has the teenagers doing the dealing on the canal, in the parks, outside the shops, on the Luas, each with their own little patch. They all work for themselves, their own crews. But Ghost owns the patches and he controls the supply.'

Crowe scratched down her notes while trying to listen.

'People around here keep their heads down and eyes closed,' Lynn said. 'They don't feel safe – safe from the gangs. And Mary won't be the last one to suffer.'

Lynn pushed herself off the desk. Crowe thought she was heading for the door, but Lynn stepped right square up to her face.

'Mary's death doesn't matter to youse.'

Crowe was about to say something, to defend herself and the force.

But Lynn wasn't finished.

'It'll take something awful, something fucking terrible, before youse lot, before society, does wake up to what's going on in areas like this. And, I tell ya what,' she said, jabbing a finger at her, 'I have a bad feeling that's going to happen pretty fucking soon.'

7

Shay drummed his fingers on the steering wheel, half listening to the radio.

'Garda Commissioner John Harte has told the Oireachtas Justice Committee that gardaí have not lost control over parts of Dublin to gangs ...'

Shay scoffed as he checked the time again. He removed the keys and took a deep breath.

I'm going to be late. What's keeping the little fucker?

As he approached Jig's house, a television boomed from an open window. The gate grated as he shoved it back. He heaved two overflowing bins apart and stepped over battered plastic garden chairs and assorted bicycles to get to the door.

A wire hung from where the doorbell once was. He rapped on the door twice. Broken shouts came from inside, in between blasts of the TV and Bowie's barks. No one answered. He hit the door with the side of his fist.

It pulled back.

Shay looked at Jig's dad, who went by the nickname Hunter. The clamour of separate televisions collided: one from inside the front room and another from down the kitchen. He tensed as they yammered at his eardrums.

'Well, well, Marco Tardelli.'

Shay smirked at the jibe.

'Hunter.'

A bright bare bulb swung over Hunter's head, as if it had just been given a smack.

Shay wasn't sure when Hunter had got out of prison. A career stroker he was, Shay had learned, who spent as much time behind bars as in his own home.

'Big match today, Shayo?'

A cigarette dangled between Hunter's fingers.

'Just training.'

'Training. Ah, Jaysus. Here, why didn't ya say?'

He turned towards the stairs.

'Jig man. Fucking training today. Get them skates on. There could be scouts around.'

Shay smirked again.

He thinks he's such a smart fucker.

'He got his touch from the auld man,' Hunter said, doing a mock-shimmy in the doorway. 'In the blood it is, handed down from me da, to me, to Maggot and to Jig.'

Shay nodded. He hadn't seen Hunter play. Jig's older brother, Maggot, had genuine skill, but was unstable, both on and off the pitch. A bit like his auld man.

'I'll wait in the car,' Shay said, hoping it would speed things up.

'Ya do that, Seamus. Tell them scouts Jig can kick the bollix out of anyone. A real Roy Keane he is.'

Shay got in and hit the ignition.

Another ten minutes passed before Jig hopped into the seat next to him. The kids' car seats in the back gave whoever he was collecting no choice but to sit up front. Better chance of a conversation that way.

'You're taking the complete piss, having me wait for ages,' Shay said, looking at the boy.

Jig blanked him. He was playing some game on his phone. He looked pale, strained. There was the familiar smell of unwashed clothes and dog, but at least he had his gear.

Shay's eyes were drawn to the dull red blotch on the back of the boy's right hand. Jig had spun him some yarn about what happened.

'You know we have to set up?' Shay said.

'Don't ya be wrecking me head as well,' Jig snapped, keeping his eyes on the screen.

'What's up with you?'

'Saw yer face, that's what.'

Shay just shook his head and swung the car off the kerb.

Shay reminded himself, again, why he bothered collecting boys like Jig. It did them good. It put a bit of structure in their lives, basic things, like having their gear ready and being picked up at a certain time. He also got them to help set up and carry all the stuff – balls, corner flags, cones, nets, spades and rubbish bags. And to help him get rid of the crap – the broken glass and crumpled cans, the fire debris and the dog shit.

Not that Jig was of much use this evening. He was just moping around.

Shay felt he was only ever scratching the surface with that boy.

He emptied dregs out a can, shoved it into a plastic bag, and wondered what lay ahead for Jig. Could he actually reach him, influence him in any way?

'Jig, help me mark out the drills here,' Shay called, pulling the poles and ladders out.

But the boy was busy kicking balls inside the bag.

'Would you not be better taking one out?' Shay said, putting the stuff down. 'Tell ya what,' dragging a ball out of the bag, 'try and get around me.'

Jig feigned disinterest, his limp arms hanging.

Shay waited.

'What? Worried you won't get around the old man?'

Jig twitched and looked over his shoulder. He jogged towards Shay, stepping over the ball with his right leg and pushing it past Shay with his left foot.

'Nice one,' Shay said. 'Now, again.'

The next two times, Jig tried the same thing. Shay got the ball off him each time.

'What are you, a one-trick pony?'

'Yer the bleeding pony,' Jig mumbled, but Shay let it slide.

Jig tried the roll-around, dragging the top of the ball around him and over to the other side of Shay. He was too slow.

'Fuck that,' Jig said, kicking at the air. He reached into his tracksuit pocket and took out his mobile and fiddled with it.

'Who you expecting a call from, Trapattoni?'

Shay expected the standard 'fuck off', but Jig just put his phone back in.

'There's nothing an opponent loves more than a skilful player, like you, dropping his head when the ball is taken off him,' Shay said, tapping the ball back to him.

This time, Jig pretended to go right, then nutmegged Shay and gathered the ball on the other side.

'Little Ronaldo, are ya?' Shay shouted, clasping Jig's shoulders. 'Good man.'

Shay could hear the other kids coming before he could see them. He gathered the poles and marked out a couple of drills.

Glancing back, he smiled as he saw Jig practising his moves, his head bowed in concentration.

8

Crowe sat, looking blankly at the car dashboard. Lynn's grim warning bounced around inside her head.

Only the phone vibrating in her bag distracted her. By the time she rummaged around to pull it out, the call was gone. She looked at the display.

Tom. Shit.

Two missed calls. Three messages.

'You nearly done? Want me to wait? What's the story?'

She typed in a message.

'Delayed. Heading home.'

As she steered away from the kerb, she noticed the white graffiti on the wall beside her. *RCAD Patrol*, it read. Putting her foot down, part of her tried to recall what the acronym stood for.

It was 10 p.m. by the time she entered the code to the underground car park. She liked the location of the apartment building: a stone's throw from the Four Courts on one side, O'Connell Street on the other, with Temple Bar just across the Ha'penny Bridge.

Crowe refused to live in garda ghettos in County Meath and west Dublin. She wanted to live in the city. She'd had enough of the country as a child: the isolation, the long summers sitting by her window wishing she had someone to play with, fighting with her parents to drive her to the local disco, or to anything. Okay, here, she had the smell of piss, the addicts injecting and defecating in the lane-ways, the shouting during the night and the endless clatter of traffic. But she had the Luas at her doorstep and her station was within running distance. If she got transferred to any other district in the region, she had the buses, the Dart and the Luas. She thought that all through before she and Tom bought the two-bed apartment. What she didn't think through was the timing: right at the height of the boom. That was like a boil on the sole of her foot. Now, the 'for sale' and 'for rent' signs jostled for space, adding a new layer to the outside of the building. People rattled around inside their apartments, jobless, waiting for things to turn around. Like Tom.

As she entered the apartment, Tom was in default mode: stretched back on the couch, a glass of beer in his right hand, a packet of crisps beside him, watching some nature programme.

'You're back,' he said.

Crowe put her hand on his shoulder.

'Sorry for being so late. It's been a long day.'

Her search for sympathy didn't elicit any.

She turned to the kitchenette. Dried lumps of bolognese in one pot. Soft spaghetti floated on yellow water in another. She looked back towards Tom, toyed with saying something.

Her heart sank further at the thought of all the CCTV waiting for her in the office tomorrow.

Crowe raised her eyebrows as the Luas curved past a garish sex shop. She and Tom hadn't made love in ages. He'd barely looked at her last night. There was no passion in his eyes anymore. No lust even. Not towards her anyway.

She got to her stop at Canal Works. An arrowhead shape of swans flapped over her as she strolled the short distance to the station. When she got there, a new sign had gone up at the entrance. It informed locals that the public office at the neighbouring Kilcocher Garda Station was soon going to be closed between 10 p.m. and 7 a.m. and that all public inquiries should come here. Crowe had heard the justice minister the other night on the radio saying it was about 'efficiency and effectiveness, not cutbacks'.

Some shite like that anyway.

Her mood lifted somewhat on seeing Grant at the counter, talking to a woman. She was scribbling down details on a scrap of paper.

Heads turned when Crowe entered the public office. She smiled at the male guards on duty and got a few muted hellos in return. She was used to not getting the warmest of responses. She wasn't really one of the lads. Grant, on the other hand, was very popular with the male guards. The females were cold to her when she got assigned to the station, less than half a year ago. They didn't like a good-looking garda on their patch. Crowe hated that kind of bitchiness. She'd made an effort to be friendly to Grant from the start and helped her out any way she could.

Crowe stepped over the boxes that fought for space on the ripped blue lino. A kettle balanced on a narrow window ledge.

'Hi,' Grant said, her blonde hair swinging as she closed the latch. She gave Crowe a warm smile.

'Helping the good people of dear old Dublin, I see,' Crowe replied.

'Of course. I am here to serve,' Grant said, doing a mock salute.

'You will remember to put that incident onto Pulse, won't you?' Crowe said nodding first to the loose piece of paper Grant had just taken details down on and then to a computer.

Grant feigned offence. 'What do you think I am, some blonde bimbo?'

'So how's things with you?' Crowe asked, siding closer to her. 'Did you decide between Fiachra or Noel?'

'Who the fuck is Noel,' ones of the lads shouted, 'some turnip-munching culchie from darkest Tipperary?'

'Never you mind,' Grant said, turning her back to them and leaning against the counter.

Crowe looked at Grant's trousers. Standard issue all right, but certainly a bit tight around the bum. She could sense eyes staring in that direction. Crowe reflected on her own unflattering heavy pair of jeans with large loops. She needed loops that were big enough for a thick belt. It took her ages to find jeans like that. It was all to hold up her holster, which weighed as heavy as a bag of sugar on her side. She wouldn't get the official belt for detectives until she was formally appointed as one. What a joke, she thought. She was what they called a 'buckshee' detective. She did all the work of a detective. In fact, she believed she worked harder to prove herself. But she didn't have the title, nor for that matter the same level of pay.

'Anyway, that's why I'm giving Noel a chance,' Grant said with a mischievous smile, rousing Crowe from her brooding. 'How are things with you? How's Tom?'

Crowe's mood dropped.

'Ah, grand. You know yourself.'

Catching Grant's sympathetic smile, Crowe made her excuses and left, kicking herself for being such a downer.

Crowe manoeuvred around the mound of box folders in the middle of the district detective office. She'd tried last week to organise the metal filing cabinets to make space for folders, but the others just told her to leave it.

'You're a detective, not a clerk,' her sergeant loved to say. 'Solving crime is what we do, not interior design.'

That usually got a chuckle from the other detectives. All she had in the room was a cubby hole. Her boxes and files were stuffed into the corners of other rooms.

The unit on shift must be out on a job, she thought, as she deliberated which desk to take. As a buckshee she didn't have her own desk yet and had to take pot luck. What pissed her off most about that was when a detective would stand over her, waiting for her to get off, even though she might have a shitload of paperwork to do. Sometimes she'd hear them breathing and sighing behind her. Often, she'd come back after going to the toilet and one of the guys would have logged her off and taken the desk.

She had reached for her organiser when the Chief barged in. He closed the door firmly behind him and leaned against it. The bottom of his shirt had pulled out from under his trousers, barely covering his belly. Crowe got up.

'Garda Crowe. Sit down. I wanted to ask you about Ms King?'

Crowe ran a finger over her organiser.

'Could it be a prank by some local kid that went wrong?' he asked.

'It's possible, Chief, but given the content of the note and previous incidents experienced by Ms King, probably not.'

The Chief nodded and adjusted the weight on his feet.

'Any luck with CCTV or witnesses?'

'We did a door-to-door, but drew a blank. I've collected footage from the area and will go through that in the coming days.'

'Good.' He nodded. 'Good.'

Crowe's shoulders relaxed. The Chief could be a ball breaker. But he was also what members called a 'Garda's Garda', an ordinary policeman who knew the frontline. He ran one of the busiest divisions in the city. He liked a tight ship. And didn't like nasty surprises.

'And Ms King's dealings with us?'

Crowe clutched her organiser tight.

'I have to follow this up. I understand she had been in contact with Detective Sergeant Flynn and had met him in the days before.'

She paused as she watched a muscle pulse on the side of the Chief's head.

'And are you presuming those intimidating her knew that?' he asked.

Crowe scratched the side of her neck.

'Is it not possible,' he continued, 'that she told someone else and they passed it on, or they were overheard?'

'Yes, Chief, it's possible. She was going through a family support project in the Oasis –'

'Lynn Bolger, I know,' the Chief interrupted. 'She has little time for us. They all believe their own paranoia: that we are always harassing their poor innocent junkies, as if they weren't responsible for nearly all the burglaries and robberies in the area.'

Crowe could see the side of the Chief's head pulse again.

'Yet, somehow we are the enemy,' he added. 'She give you all that bollocks?'

Crowe shifted in her seat and decided to share his views. 'Yes, Chief, I got all that, in bucket loads.'

'Anyone else that knew of the deceased's dealings with us?' he asked again.

'Ms Bolger said Ms King would not have told anyone else, apart from maybe Father Keogh.'

The Chief breathed deeply and stuffed his shirt back into his trousers.

'Another member of the Garda fan club,' he muttered. 'What has he to say for himself?'

'Haven't spoken to him yet.'

'Ah, he'll give you the same guff,' he said, waving his hand in the air. 'But, best cover all your bases.'

He leaned closer towards her. 'Sort this one out, Crowe. Nice and quick. And I'll write you up well.'

With that, the Chief left. Crowe felt a tingle down her spine.

Write you up well. Wow.

The report on her interviews was making its way up the line, she thought, grabbing the stack of CCTV disks from her cubbyhole. The Chief would have the final word on the recommendation for promotion, she knew, before it went to HR at Garda HQ. Although, with the embargo on promotions, it wouldn't happen anytime soon. But still.

9

On match day, Shay watched Jig stumble out the door, dragging his bag along the ground. He clambered into the front and slammed the door shut.

'Have you got your boots?' Shay asked, glancing at Jig's bag.

No answer, just a surly look.

'Let's go, kick-off in Blackrock is at half eleven.'

'Thought Ghost was picking me up,' Jig said, taking out his phone and tapping on some image on YouTube.

Shay bunched his eyebrows and looked over.

That's not what I want now, Ghost bringing Jig to and from games.

He shook his head.

Ghost wouldn't do it. He wouldn't put up with all the waiting around and listening to Jig's da and ma. Anyway, Ghost had his own kid to bring to the game.

But the thought lingered.

'What are they like?' Jig asked, staring at gyrating women on a hip-hop video.

Shay raised his eyebrow at the possibility of a conversation.

'Handy enough the last time we played them. They have a few skilful guys and play as a team.'

No response. Shay looked at the screen, at a woman in very few clothes and very high heels. She bent over, caressed her ass and opened her mouth. Shay had to jump on the brakes when he looked up and saw red lights.

'Little posh poofs, I bet ya,' Jig said when the video ended.

'Listen, they have guys who can play football. Like what we can do when we put our minds to it.'

'Am I starting?'

Shay looked out the window.

'Depends which Jig turns up. You going to work hard or just mope around if you lose the ball, like the last day.'

'Fuck off so, ya grumpy bollix,' Jig said, tapping on the video again.

Ten minutes into the match, Jig was sitting on the bench scraping his boots off the grass. Shay glanced at him. The home team was up 1–0 and he could do with having Jig on, but he wanted to send him a message. But it looked like it could be heading to 2–0 any moment. Their number 6 was causing problems.

'Jig,' he shouted, 'you're on.'

He called to the ref and pulled one of the lads out. Turning, he could see Ghost slapping Jig on the shoulder and end what seemed like a brief word in his ear. Jig kicked at the grass as he came towards Shay.

'We need to create some chances out there,' Shay said, a hand on Jig's shoulders. 'I don't mind you taking risks to do that, but, if you lose the ball, don't drop your head. Get it back. Okay?'

Jig ran on, shouldering the other team's number 6. Shay looked over at Ghost who was sticking his thumb up.

'I'm the bleeding manager here,' Shay muttered.

Fifteen minutes later, when the ref blew half time, it was still 2–0. Jig, after a promising start, let his head drop. Just what Shay told him not to do.

'Youse on the *PlayStation* all night, lads, or something?' Shay said as they came off.

'Playing with yerselves more like,' Ghost quipped, getting the odd snigger.

Shay gathered his team around.

'The only way we won't be four down by the end of this game is if you stay with your man, put challenges in and stop moping

42

around the place. Jig, and Sam, we need to start bossing that middle.'

He sensed Ghost moving near.

'Let their number 6 know yer fucking there, right. Hit him hard,' Ghost said smacking the palm of his hands off each other. 'That will tone him down.'

Shay put his arms around some of them as Ghost drifted away.

'The last thing we need is a sending-off. The only way we'll get back in is by scoring, so that means playing football, passing it, finding a man. Now, if I shout to you "three minutes", you have that long to wake up, or you're coming off.'

Five minutes in, their number 6 was floating around, when crunch, Jig flew in and took the legs out from under him, sending him up into the air. Shay knew that if Jig's feet had been any higher, he could have caused a serious injury.

The boy screamed. His manager protested. Shay could see the ref pulling Jig in. He was giving the ref lip. 'Shut up, Jig,' Shay roared. The ref was reaching for a card. It looked like a red one. Ghost let out a roar. The ref looked over and for the briefest of seconds hesitated. He seemed to adjust his fingers in his pocket and took out a yellow.

'Ref, that has to be a sending-off,' shouted the manager for the other team. 'That's a disgrace.'

The score remained the same at the final whistle. Shay heard Ghost congratulate the kids coming off, a bit louder than needed. He did it just to aggravate the home team. Their manager came marching over. Ghost, munching on an apple, blocked his path.

'You should be ashamed of yourselves,' the man said, looking away from Shay to Ghost. 'You know it was sheer blind luck his leg wasn't broken?'

Ghost stood there, taking noisy bites and chewing with his mouth open, his bony jaw rubbing against the inside of his skin.

'Nice little team of scumbags you're building here?' the man said.

Ghost stopped his chewing and Shay thought he was going to box the man. The kids inched forward in expectation of seeing

Ghost in action. The silence was split only when Ghost's munching resumed. Shay could see the man's expression switch, from anger to anxiety. He turned and strode away. The boys broke out laughing. Ghost winked at a few of them.

Shay watched Ghost saunter over to a parked car. A BMW powered up.

Shay gathered the balls and gear together. Jig came over and muttered something about having a lift.

Jig scraped with his knife as quietly as he could, glancing up at the windows. He was buzzing. The cool night air ran up underneath his hoodie.

He stood back and admired the 'Fuck U' scratched into the car's bodywork. He held the rock in his gloved hands. Before he threw it, he went over to the porch and took a piss all over the door and flower pots. Then, he ran up and lashed the rock through the sitting-room window. As the alarms blared he took out the apple and lobbed it through the hole in the glass.

'Ya got style,' Ghost said, slapping Jig on the shoulder after he jumped into the jeep. 'Leaving yer mark on his poncy flowers.'

Jig loved the soft brown leather of the huge seats and the array of vents, switches and digital displays across the vast dashboard.

Ghost tapped his iPhone as the jeep powered away.

'These guys are massive,' he said to Jig. 'Local hip hop crew. Downloaded the fuckers from YouTube.'

Jig was beaming from ear to ear. The passenger window was down. He stuck his head out. The smack of the wind against his face made him tingle.

'I'm a bad nigga!' he shouted, pumping his fist in the air and nodding to the beat.

Ghost laughed. Jig said it again. He felt dizzy with excitement. Ghost turned up the volume.

'I'm fuckin mangled on drugs and tangled in debt. Mangled and tangled, drugs and debt.'

Jig sang the chorus as Ghost slammed the dashboard to the beat.

This was some buzz, Jig told himself.

I've done jobs for Ghost, but not with him, like together, in his jeep and all.

He'd showed Ghost what he was made of. That the Jigster was the real deal. That he was paying back that price Ghost was on about, like a man.

Ghost tapped his nails on the steering wheel, while he lit a fag. He rested a long bony arm out the window. Jig looked at his yellow-grey fingers under the flare of the cigarette.

'That fucker had it coming,' Ghost said, handing Jig the fag. 'No one calls my boys scumbags. Those rich pricks are always looking down on our type, Jig.'

Jig clasped the smoke between his finger and thumb and inhaled out the window, coughing. Sensing Ghost was looking at him, he turned around.

'Yer a right little soldier,' Ghost said, 'aren't ya?'

Jig's face flowered into a smile.

'Here,' Ghost said, pulling something out of his jacket pocket. 'Ya still have that debt, but ya deserve a little treat after that.'

It was three €50 notes.

Jig's eyes nearly popped out of his head as he held the crisp cash.

This is the best night ever.

He shouted the chorus out the window, punching the air some more.

'I'm fuckin mangled on drugs and tangled in debt. Mangled and tangled, drugs and debt.'

10

Crowe pinched the corners of her eyes. She had spent seven hours in the Imagery Office, looking at tapes and disks. The council tapes drew a blank, so did the cameras outside the chippers and the off-licence. She slid in the final disk.

The camera angle was good on this one. It captured the front gate and the low front wall and a bit of the road outside. She checked the address. Not far from Ms King's.

'Give me something,' she muttered.

Detectives hated this job. Except her. Not that she didn't hate it, she told herself – just she was good at it. She had the patience and the eye for detail. 'You don't cut corners,' Tyrell told her once. Though there were times she wished she did.

The clock on the tape crawled towards 2 a.m.

She thought about the backlog of cases she had on: burglaries, assaults and a rape trial that was coming up. She was struggling to focus on them all.

There was movement on the screen. A figure walked past the gate. It looked like a kid. She noted the time: 2.10 a.m. She rewound. She kept playing it back until the gait of the boy sunk into her mind. She brought it back to the best image of the boy. The face was blurry. Definitely young, no more than twelve, if even that, thin build.

Her phone beeped. It was a reminder of something she had put into her calendar. 'Priest,' it said. She had arranged to meet him up at the Parish Centre. She rooted through her bag to check she had all her stuff. She marked the time on the film, ejected the disk and left it in her cubbyhole.

Crowe buzzed. She loved assembling the building blocks of an investigation.

The New Beginnings Centre was a mismatch of single- and double-storey buildings at the rear of the church. Crowe saw guys working as she approached: men painting, raking up leaves. Some looked vaguely familiar. She caught a few glances and knew they clocked her.

She pulled back double doors and entered a surprisingly welcoming space. There were two comfy sofas, and a shaded lamp in the corner emanated a soft yellow light. Fresh flowers in a glass vase decorated the table. Faint incense burned near by.

The walls were covered with photographs of activities and awards of one sort or another. Voices and noises circulated from different parts of the building. There was a clatter of knives and plates and an arresting smell of baking. The whole place had a nice vibe about it.

'Garda Crowe, I take it?'

She turned to see a man with glasses and a balding head. He had kind eyes, which narrowed slightly as he studied her.

'Father Keogh?'

'This way,' he said, smiling, stepping quietly down a corridor. He gestured to a door that was ajar. 'Please.'

There was a hush on entering. A thick carpet softened her step and dimmed lights cast the room in shadows. A hum of Gregorian chanting played from speakers that she couldn't locate.

Father Keogh upped the dimmer and pointed to one of two seats in front of an altar, which was adorned by a smooth white cloth and a fat church candle.

The surroundings reminded her too much of the claustrophobic prayer room from school.

The priest positioned his seat in front of her and folded one leg over the other. He leaned forward, as if the two of them were about to resume a conversation.

'Father ...' Crowe began, taking out her notepad.

'Please, Pat. No one calls me Father, unless it's to do with a funeral, or wedding maybe.'

Crowe smiled.

'As I explained on the phone,' she said, 'I wanted to talk to you about Ms King?'

Father Keogh took a deep breath and held his hands out towards Crowe in a gesture that seemed a bit overdramatic.

'God bless that dear woman. Mary had a heavy burden to bear and paid the ultimate price.' He stopped for a moment and looked at Crowe intently.

'Did she talk to you in the weeks before her death?'

'Oh, yes. I saw her nearly every day; either at mass or afterwards or here in the centre. She sometimes helped out.'

'Did she tell you about the people who were intimidating her?'

'Garda, the dogs in the street know who they are.'

'Father, there is a difference between what the dogs in the street know and evidence.'

He nodded, sympathetic. 'Of course. Well, I don't know the actual people who threatened her, but they would have been working for Ghost and Cracko.'

His voice hushed as he mentioned their names.

'They have the whole community intimidated,' he said, leaning forward again, clasping his hands on his knee. 'I am concerned about this community, detective. I don't need to tell you the problems it faces ...'

Crowe brought advice Tyrell repeatedly gave her to mind. Don't get sucked in. Focus.

'Father, I need to concentrate on this investigation.'

The priest took a breath and nodded again in the same patronising way. She could see what Lynn had meant about him.

'I encouraged Mary to go to the guards,' he said. 'But they – those who were intimidating her – appear to have found out. She told me about the wipers when they were broken off and I tried to comfort her.' He paused, stopping to clean his glasses with a neat tissue taken from his trouser pocket. 'Now there seems to have been some note, with a threat . . .'

Crowe knew he just let that drift out as he cleaned his glasses methodically.

'What do you know about a note, Father?'

'I'm her priest, garda, I hear things. And I do read the papers.'

She shifted in her seat. She hadn't seen any of the news-papers.

How the Jesus is this information getting out?

'I can see you're irritated, but I am conducting her funeral tomorrow and I have been dealing with Detective Inspector Tyrell. A hard man is the detective inspector,' he said, folding his tissue and putting it away, 'but, a good man, I feel, when it comes down to it.'

He stared at her for a moment, as if making a point. What exactly it was, she wasn't sure.

Is he letting me know he knows the DI? Is he suggesting the DI gave him the information? Or is he telling me the DI is a good man? And why?

'This is another funeral, Detective Crowe, I have to preside over which, in one way or another, is caused by gangs or drugs,' he said, as he inspected his glasses and slid them on to his nose. 'You know how many suicides and drug overdoses I've had in the last eight years or so? I'd say about seventy to eighty, young people mostly. That's this church alone. That's not even including the murders. And in the last two years, with the recession and all that, I am seeing more despair than ever.'

She felt the sermon had started. She put her hand out to inter-vene, but the priest continued.

'We have already lost a generation of young people to these gangs,' he said, the cloying tone gone, replaced with a bit more bite. 'I feel we are now losing a younger generation. Kids are left to run wild on the streets, all day and all night. They're afraid of no one; they grow up without any structure, without discipline. They look up to the teenagers out dealing on the street and treat their bosses, driving around in their top of the range jeeps and BMWs, like football stars. Where are the guards building up relationships with these kids? It's too late when they are twelve . . .'

'Father, I'm here to investigate Ms King's death, not save the local community. I can't do that.'

Father Keogh closed his eyes.

'Of course,' he said after a few moments. 'You are not here to listen to one of my sermons.'

After a protracted pause, he rose from his seat. 'There's something I would like to show you. It might assist.'

He led Crowe back out to the reception area and stood in front of the panels of photographs on the walls.

'Look at all the smiling faces, at the innocence of childhood,' he said, surveying those faces like a proud school principal. 'There are good people in this community, garda. No one of us can save it. Not on our own. But the more of us the better.'

Crowe nodded, irritated at his attempts to recruit her to the cause.

'The sports clubs do a wonderful job,' he said, gesturing across the wall, 'the GAA, the soccer, the boxing and the rest.'

He pointed to a picture of a soccer team.

'See this man here,' he said. 'He's just one of the people doing his bit. He tries to help these kids; he encourages their talents, gives them structure.'

Crowe looked at the face, but didn't recognise him.

'Shay,' the priest said, tapping the image. 'He runs some of the kids' teams.'

Then he tapped on the photo again.

'Of course, there are others, with different interests.'

The trademark black eyes and the deep sockets struck her first. Then the pronounced cheekbones and the long tattoos snaking down his arms.

'He's involved in the kids' soccer?' she asked, incredulous.

'What better place to identify vulnerable boys,' the priest said, his voice hardening, 'and groom them.'

Crowe ran her eyes across the kids' faces; they all looked so alike. The priest was gesturing towards the door.

'I wish we could speak for longer, detective, but I have a Lourdes pilgrimage meeting to prepare for.'

She took out her phone and photographed the team.

'Where can I find this Shay?' she said, following the priest out to the door.

'Shay trains the teams on different days, Tuesday and Thursday evenings, either down at the pitches or in the community centre.' He raised his eyes up, thinking. 'He's probably in the centre today. You might be in luck.'

They stepped out into the light. Crowe adjusted her bag across her back and looked at the men, down on their haunches, pulling out weeds.

'I give them odd jobs to do around the grounds,' the priest said, following her eyes. 'This is a religion of Christ, garda. We believe people can change.'

The youth centre was bright and airy. Drawings and paintings covered the walls, jostling with colourful posters for different events. Crowe zipped up her jacket to cover her holster and turned to the woman in the reception office.

'Is Shay here?'

'Shayo? He done something?' the woman said, with a chesty laugh. 'Jaysus, have to hear this.'

Crowe sighed.

Have I got 'garda' stamped on my head?

'I just want to speak to him,' she said curtly.

'Only messing with ya, love. He's in the sports hall with the lads, on the left.'

Crowe could hear the skid of rubber on timber and the echoed shouts as she neared a set of doors. A man passed in front of a window as she peered in, shouting at the boys. He spotted her. She nodded to him to come to the door.

He poked his head out, his tanned head glistening with sweat.

'Shay?' she asked, noticing bags under his eyes then surprising herself with a glance at his fit body.

'Yeah?'

'Detective Garda Tara Crowe. Have you got a moment?'

'I'm a bit busy here.'

'I can wait.'

He looked her up and down, narrowed his eyes.

'I'll wrap up here in a while. You can wait down in the art room,' he said, pointing to the end of the hall.

She went into the room he'd indicated. It was filled with large metal tables, full of paints, brushes, pens and pencils of all types. Up on the wall were charcoal drawings – some quite good to her eye – of local scenes, an arcade of shops, trees in the park, BMWs, the canal and bridges.

Crowe had liked art in school, particularly drawing structures, like buildings and bridges. Her teacher thought she might go on to study architecture at college. Her parents didn't put any stock in that. Teaching, they said. Or nursing. Or the Guards. Secure jobs. Good pensions.

She picked up a pen and doodled on a sheet of paper.

Some ten minutes later, Shay came in, dumped his gear bag on the floor and closed the door.

'Thanks for talking to me, Shay,' Crowe said, looking at him. 'I can see you're busy.'

He nodded. 'What can I do for you?'

'This is confidential, Shay, so I'd prefer you didn't say any of this to anybody.'

'You don't have to worry about that, detective,' he said, his smile forced.

'What do you know about Ghost?'

He raised his eyebrows as if to say, 'Ah, here.'

'Well?' she asked.

'As little as possible.'

'What do you mean?'

Shay stood there, silent.

'You know about him? What he does?'

'I concentrate on the football, detective. And the kids.'

Crowe scribbled on her page. 'I'm told you're a good influence on the kids.' She looked up and caught a glimmer of pride in his face. 'Unlike Ghost.'

He shook his head, laughing.

Crowe looked up at one drawing, a guy slumped on the ground, a man with a gun standing over him and cash floating around them.

'You know of any kids Ghost is close to?'

Shay seemed to study her, and still he said nothing.

He's a careful fucker. I'll try a different approach.

'You really want to help these kids, then what are you doing allowing Ghost near them?'

He took the bait.

'Spare me the juvenile psychology, detective,' Shay replied, some steel now in his voice. 'I coach football teams. I do the best I can with the lads, but I can't fix their lives. Anyway, his son plays on the team and sometimes he comes to matches, sometimes he helps out. There's no ban on that. He has a long involvement in the club.'

Crowe didn't respond.

This guy could be of help. No point pissing him off.

'I would just like to know if there are any kids under the influence, so to speak, of Ghost.'

'I can't help you, I'm afraid, detective.'

'Can't or won't?'

He didn't react to the provocation this time, smiling faintly at her attempt.

'There is a specific reason I'm asking you, Shay. This is not just a general trawl.'

Shay nodded, but, again, said nothing.

Crowe decided to leave it for now, not to force it. She had an odd feeling about this guy, as if there was a lot more to him than he showed.

'Tell you what, Shay. Think about it. Here's my card. Just in case you decide to help.'

He escorted her down the corridor. There was a clatter behind them. A couple of kids were messing and made a point of barging between them. They gawked at Crowe.

'This the bit on the side, Shayo?' a scrawny kid, with a big gob on him, said.

'Go on, Spikey,' Shay said. 'See you on Saturday. On time.'

'Ya done well, Shayo,' a second boy said, laughing. 'Not sure what the missus would say though.'

Crowe couldn't get a good look at the boy as he passed, but noticed a red blotch on the back of one of his hands as they swung at his sides.

'Have your gear ready, Jig, when I call on Saturday,' Shay said. 'I'm not hanging about. Okay?'

The kids jumped up in the air and smacked the ceiling. The boy with the blotch glanced back. He had a pasty sort of face, Crowe thought.

She watched the kid walk towards the exit. His build. His gait. His face.

The CCTV image popped up in her mind.

What did Shay call him? Jig. That was it.

11

Jig leaned on the railing of the bridge, captivated. The swan stretched up out of the water and pushed out his chest. He opened his huge wings and gave them a great, loud flap. Then he folded them behind him into a heart shape. Or, maybe, it was more like a diamond shape. At least Jig thought it was a 'he', remembering what his granda had told him.

'The males are bigger than the females, most times,' his granda had said. 'But only they know for sure which is which. Apart from mating season,' he told him, when the male had a black ball on the end of its bill.

The swan adjusted his wings, lifting them up and angling them down at the dark waters of the canal. His soft feathers blew in the wind. Jig peered into the water and saw webbed feet pushing backwards every few seconds, giving the swan a gentle jolt each time. Behind him, his mate glided silently, wings folded in tight and her long neck scooped down in an arc.

'Isn't it mad them are so white?' Jig said, turning to Spikey.

'They should be black from all the shite in there,' Spikey said, flinging stones at apartments on one side.

'They do be grey and brown when they're young, and go white,' Jig said.

'How come their shite is all green?' Spikey asked. 'Ya see big piles of it on the path.'

'Dunno,' Jig replied, trying to remember if his granda ever talked about their shite.

The swan and his mate passed under the bridge and Jig ran over to the other side. Spikey had a stone cocked in his hand and pretended to throw.

'Don't, ya cunt!' Jig shouted, grabbing his arm. Spikey pulled away, laughing and gave Jig a clatter. The two of them wrestled, falling onto the bridge.

A slow clapping noise disturbed them. Jig looked up and pushed Spikey away. Two swans, their wings outstretched, flapped just feet above them, with that 'woo' sound they make. They slowly dropped down towards the canal, their long necks jutting out, like pencils Jig thought, and their wings shaped like a coat hanger, bent in near the tips. They stretched their dark grey feet out, angling in. They bounced onto the water, once, twice, three times, before splashing to a halt.

'Hey, they're jet-skiing,' Jig shouted, a big smile on his face.

He heard feet pattering on the bridge and looked over. The girls approached, Taylor wearing pink plastic platform heels and Sharon holding a hurley up against her shoulder and clasping a sliotar in her other hand.

'What youse up to?' Sharon asked, smacking the sliotar up in the air and catching it.

'I'm heading into town to get a pair of runners,' Jig said, taking cash out of his pocket and waving it in the air.

'Where did ya get that?' Sharon asked, her eyes suspicious.

'Doing a few jobs,' he said, shrugging and shoving the cash back in, 'ya know yerself.'

Jig could see her frown easing. She sneaked a smile at him. The hair on his arms tingled.

'Here, give us that,' Jig said, grabbing the hurley from her. 'Pull on it,' he shouted, swinging the hurley and smacking Spikey in the arse. 'Go on, pull on it.'

The two of them burst out laughing. Sharon reefed the hurley off Jig and tapped the sliotar in the air.

'Later,' she said, walking off, clasping Taylor in an arm-lock.

'See youse after,' Jig shouted, looking at Sharon's ass. He waited, and gave Sharon a big smile when she glanced back at him.

Jig stepped down Grafton Street like he was Wayne Rooney, with his new blue adidas runners all shiny in the sun.

This is as good as it gets.

He could see Spikey eyeing them, like he did in the shop. He told him he'd have the cash too if he worked with Ghost. Anyways, he said he'd get him something after. Then he spotted the ice-cream shop.

Jig threw himself at the counter, the palms of his outstretched hands banging off the plastic. He was almost drooling at the rows upon rows of treats from heaven itself. Cones of all shapes and sizes. Tubs too. And waffles and pancakes. He ran his finger along as he read the flavours. Toffee Dream. Strawberry Delight. Cookie Dough. Whipped Lemon. Behind were counters of sweets, drizzles and sprinkles.

'A big fuck-off cone with Toffee Dream and Cookie Dough, my woman. And loads of drizzle,' he ordered, waving a €20 note in the air.

'I'll be with you in a moment. This lady's first,' the woman said.

'What ya having, Spikey?' Jig said, turning to him. 'My treat.'

Jesus, that's some buzz saying that, 'my treat', and having the cash to do it.

'Waffle, with vanilla and cream and sprinkle stuff all over the bad boy,' Spikey said, beaming.

Their purchase made, they strutted down Grafton Street. Jig took lumps out of his ice cream, his teeth jarring at the soft mounds of sweet coldness.

'Ah man, this is it,' Jig said, through a stuffed mouth. 'What's the waffle like?'

'Nice. Warm. Ice cream is soft,' Spikey managed to say, before he bit off a big chunk, cream oozing across his mouth.

They finished their delights sitting near the Molly Malone statue, laughing their heads off at a man dressed up as a leprechaun and looking to get his picture taken with tourists. Beside him was a little stereo, playing diddly-eye music.

'Beegorrah and bethehokkee,' Jig shouted, jumping down.

'The Jigmaster, ladies and gentlemen,' Spikey said, clapping his hands to the music. 'Go for it, Julia, feel the rhythm. Go on, Julia. Now, Julia. Now.'

Jig danced faster and faster, hopping up and down like a madman, his mouth covered in ice cream, snot and sweat. A crowd of bemused tourists gathered.

When he stopped, exhausted, Spikey held out his hands. 'For the babie. A few coppers for the little babie.'

Jig heaved and laughed as the coins dropped, the guts of four euro as it turned out.

He couldn't remember the last time he had so much fun, and wished it could stay like this.

12

Lock Man stepped into the mid-morning sun. He shoved his hand into the pocket of his black and silver dressing gown and pulled out the smokes.

He tapped out a fag as a neighbour came along, carrying a scraper and a plastic bag. He eyed her jeans and tight white top. He licked his lips as she bent down and scraped the cobble lock.

'Bleeding weeds, eh?' he said, putting the smoke to his damp lips.

The woman turned around, adjusting her position.

'Yer better off just spraying them bad boys,' he said, lighting up.

'Oh, right. Thanks.'

He caught her face, scrunching ever so slightly as she noticed his dressing gown.

Snobby bitch.

All of them were round here, he thought. They had been that way since they moved in years back. He grabbed the cord and tied the knot tighter and enjoyed his smoke, giving his metallic blue Audi A7 Sportback an admiring look, but grimacing at his wife's gleaming white Kia Sportage SUV parked up beside it.

He glanced at his watch. Inhaling a final drag he went to flick the butt between the cars, but stopped. He grumbled at the fucking annoyance of it all. He walked over to the little ceramic bowl Tina had placed behind one of the large flower pots and stubbed the butt out. Leaning back up, he smacked the top of his head off a hanging basket, sending it into a swing.

He grabbed the basket and brought it to a stop, water dripping onto him. Cursing, he squinted at the mess of colours – yellows, oranges and purples – suffocating the basket. It was bad enough, he thought, having two large flower pots on the outside of the sitting room window and two more at the front door. Then she goes and puts up bloody poncy hanging baskets. Right in the way of his top-spec CCTV system.

'I don't want people thinking we're some sort of dodgy crime bosses with all them cameras,' she'd said.

'Too late for that, love,' he'd told her.

He sensed a presence and looked through the bulletproof window into the sitting room. There was the slight frame of his missus, her arms folded across her chest. Whatever way the light was, all he could see was her pink lips and matching nails. He looked down at the poxy white sculpture of a reclining woman on the window sill. Tina had insisted on bringing the two of them with her to their new home. She'd put the other at their upstairs bedroom window. He'd told her the women in this area didn't have them yokes in their windows. But she insisted.

Tina's lips moved and she pointed a nail up to the basket, which, when he looked up, was ever so slightly at an angle.

He waved her off. 'Yeah, yeah, the fucking flower basket. Jaysus.'

Lock Man was back out an hour later, sporting new tracksuit bottoms, a white Lacoste top and clutching a brown leather holdall. His top was a bit tight over his belly and his thighs chaffed as he swayed towards the Audi, dangling his keys. The car clicked smoothly and he lowered himself in. He pressed a button on the keys and the reinforced gates, which he got from a specialist firm in England and paid a truckload for, slid to the side.

Some ten minutes later, he purred his beauty into a spot in a secure, monitored car park. Anyone approaching his motor would be picked up on the cameras. And they'd have to get past the security first. He strolled the short distance to the Luas stop, throwing on his shades as the sun squeezed back out between the clouds.

He liked the Luas. It was good to keep his feet in the trenches, he told himself – and he got a buzz from the colour and madness on the Red Line. But more than that, the Luas was a handy way to shake off unwanted company. When the Luas got the lights, cars were left behind and he could sneak off at the next stop. Either that or he could exit the stops along the canal and take any of the various footbridges over to the other side. Or he could stay on as the Luas curved over the canal bridge, where no roads followed.

All in all, he reckoned, the garda would need at least three teams in place to cover most of their bases. And with all the austerity and axed budgets that wasn't going to happen anytime soon. Even during the height of the Celtic Tiger the guards didn't have the numbers or overtime to monitor every major criminal twenty-four/seven. And that was exactly what they needed to do, he told himself, as he was a proper slippery fucker.

Lock Man enjoyed his counter-surveillance stratagems, even if no one was watching him. He prided himself on not having a single charge to his name in ten years, not since his armed robbery days. Okay, the Criminal Assets Bureau busted his balls years ago, when he was more hands-on. They issued a tax demand and he made a settlement, which lobbed a chunk off the final bill. In effect, it legally laundered the rest of his cash.

He had stepped back from the game since. The CAB wouldn't come knocking again, as long as he was careful. Which he was.

The Luas rattled down along the canal and over the bridge. Lock Man got out at the next stop and slipped into a BMW X6, parked up on a quiet road.

He looked over at Slammer, who nodded at him, but said nothing. Lock Man never discussed business in cars. Not that that was a problem for Slammer. Slammer was a hulk. He had small eyes, which skewed inwards, and big thick eyebrows. He had a dent in the side of his head, the result of a hammer attack when he was younger. Lucky to survive, but he did. Got his revenge, though. Lock Man couldn't help but bring up the image. Slammer had entered his attacker's gaff and jammed the man's head against a doorframe. Then he slammed the door again and again until the head pulped. The nickname stuck after that.

Fifteen minutes later, the BMW cruised into the Canal Plaza car park. The driver stayed with the car. Lock Man, Slammer and a helper got out and walked across the 'Plaza'. Large banners partially covered the facades on two sides. But they had loosened over the years and now flapped dejectedly at the edges, revealing rusting metal and naked concrete boxes.

The third side of the Plaza was The Sanctuary, the so-called 'anchor' tenant. Apart from a Chinese takeaway it was the only fucking tenant, Lock Man grinned to himself.

He nearly skipped when he saw Sorcha totter behind the front doors.

Her head cocked slightly as the door pulled back.

'My favourite customers. How are you today?' she said, with her beaming smile.

Lock Man always laughed at her attempt to cloak her strong Dublin accent with a gushing D4 voice. She stood there, a folder clasped in her arms, long curly blonde hair and a tight pink dress and yellow heels.

Those platform heels triggered a momentary fantasy of her straddling him.

'Alright, Sorcs,' he said. 'Story?'

He knew she didn't like him calling her Sorcs. That's why he enjoyed saying it so much.

'Good, yeah,' she said, swinging her body slightly, showing him her curves. 'You using the pool today or the gym, boys?'

God he loved the way she said 'boys', her lips all pouty and red.

'The steam room, Sorcs. Sure, yer welcome to join us.'

He watched her mouth creak into a nervous smile.

'Your, ah, your friend is in there,' she said. 'I'll make sure you're not disturbed.'

She walked behind the reception counter. He stared at her as she leaned over the desk. He rubbed his tongue against his teeth. God, he'd love to ram it into her.

He inhaled deeply and motioned the others to the changing rooms. The helper stayed at the door.

The pool was empty, save for a dad and his kid. No lifeguards. He'd thought pools needed lifeguards. But when he was checking out this place he'd looked into it. They didn't. He thought that fucking odd, but was grateful. Fewer observers. The leisure centre was also suffering, which meant it was usually quiet, particularly during the week. He gave Sorca a fat wad of hundred euro notes to cover all his associates well enough for privacy and discretion. He slipped her extra for not fixing the cameras.

Ghost was in the steam room. Lock Man liked that. He hated being kept waiting. Slammer sat by the door. Everyone wore a towel with nothing underneath. That was his rule. Though looking at the jangle of tattooed bones that was Ghost, he often thought twice.

'Story with the goods?' Lock Man asked Slammer, adjusting his weight and freeing his balls from between his legs.

'Day after tomorrow,' he said.

'Storage?'

'A new lock-up that Ghost sourced. Being rented by a furniture guy whose son owes us.'

Lock Man nodded. Slammer and Ghost knew what they were doing, he reassured himself. He was glad he was able to step back from all that years ago. But he had to keep a tight control of everyone in his click. If he didn't, what fucking use was he?

'Any more news from those Provo fuckers?'

'Don't worry about them, boss,' Ghost said. 'We'll teach them a lesson when our toys arrive.'

Lock Man pushed a sheet of sweat away from his chest. There was something about the RCAD crowd that niggled him. They hadn't looked for a cut of profits like the other republican pretenders. He could handle those pricks. But this outfit was different. They were driven by something else. Egos. Grievances. Beliefs maybe. They had a few older heads in there. He hadn't seen their likes since the mid-nineties.

'Don't underestimate this crowd,' he said, pointing at Ghost. 'That would be a mistake.'

Slammer gave a slight nod.

'Just so ya know,' Ghost said, 'they are putting up posters and doing graffiti, advertising themselves and trying to get people to join their fucking cause.'

Lock Man bristled.

'We can't have that go unchecked,' he said. 'Makes us look weak. I'm sure Cracko and yerself can handle that.'

Ghost nodded.

'We'll meet next Monday, after the delivery,' Lock Man said. 'Who ya going to use?'

'I'll have Jobs and Shop on it,' Ghost said.

'Give them this number,' Slammer said, and repeated it a couple of times. 'We'll have something on standby in case they need to get out of dodge quick.'

'Alright,' Lock Man said, making himself more comfortable, 'anything else?'

'No, boss,' Ghost replied, standing up.

'I didn't say to leave.'

Ghost sat back down.

'What happened to that woman wasn't in the programme notes,' Lock Man said.

'No, boss,' Ghost said. 'It was an accident. She wasn't getting the hint, so we tried something else.'

'And it went pear-shaped. I hear some cop bitch is sniffing around.'

'She won't find anything,' Ghost said. 'The boy wore gloves. And there are no cameras where that woman lives.'

But this is messy, Lock Man thought. Grand, Ghost using kids to run drugs and scout. But for threats. Too risky. After years of building a tight ship, the last thing he needed was a fucking leak. Just as well he had his own bitch in the cop shop.

13

Jig yanked at the lever. It clunked but nothing came out. Bowie looked up at him, his small tail wagging. Jig stood back and kicked his heel against the machine. The dog barked. Still no gobstopper.

'That's it, Jig, kick the shite out of it.'

Jig turned around, but the man looming in front of him was all shadow with the sun blazing behind him. Jig inched forward and looked up, his arm over his eyes. The chipped front tooth told him who it was.

'Alright, Cracko.'

'Story, little man.'

Cracko was holding a kid in his hands. His son, Jig copped. He was munching on a bag of crisps.

'Dodging school, yeah?'

Jig nodded.

'How's that cool dog?' Cracko said, leaning down to Bowie, who crouched low. 'Must introduce him to my bull terrier.' Cracko smiled. 'See who's boss.'

Jig eyed the back of Cracko's hand, as he patted Bowie hard. Across his knuckles ran a tattoo of barbed wire and the word STREET. All in plain black ink. Jig looked up at Cracko's left hand, which was clutching his son. The same barbed wire across the knuckles and, above it, the word JUSTICE. The I was in the shape of a dagger, a red tip at the end.

Cracko's a seriously cool fucker, Jig thought.

Cracko leaned back up. The toddler kept munching. Jig's

stomach rumbled as he eyed the bits of crisps falling from the kid's mouth. The boy looked down on him and clutched his bag tight.

'What's the little fella's name?' Jig asked.

'Seb. A right little bollix he . . .'

Jig saw Cracko's face tighten, like someone had twisted a screw. The scar along the right side of his face twitched. Cracko turned around to face the path. All Jig could see was some guy sticking a poster to a lamp pole outside the shops.

The guy walked towards them, one stride bouncing up more than the other. He was too busy looking at a bunch of posters in his hand to see where he was going.

Cracko positioned himself right in the middle of the path. He coiled his back. Jig glanced down at Bowie; he had curled in behind the sweet machine.

Jig watched as the guy walked right into Cracko's outstretched hand, forcing him to stumble back. When he looked up his expression was like he had just walked out in front of traffic. The kid's munching punctured the silence.

'Ah, what's the story?'

Smack. Cracko slapped the guy across the face, forcing him to land hard on his right foot to stop himself from falling over. The posters flew away under his arms and scattered across the path and the road. Jig judged he was weighing up the risk of doing a legger.

'Ya fucking move,' Cracko said, 'and I'll kick yer balls up yer fucking windpipe.'

Deadly line, Jig thought.

The man's face was like his blood had scarpered down his legs and out into the gutter. He was a skinny fucker. One kick from Cracko and he'd break apart.

'What the fuck?' the man said, trying to grasp some of his posters.

Jig laughed.

This guy's about to get creamed by Cracko and he's picking up his posters.

He tried to read the posters. Something about republicans and a meeting.

'Don't fucking touch them,' Cracko growled.

'I'm on community business here,' the man said. 'Republican business. Who the fuck are –?'

Jig looked at Cracko.

This guy doesn't know who Cracko is!

Cracko lunged. Seb's head swung back at the jolt. Cracko grabbed the guy's jacket with his right hand and swung him off the ground onto the bonnet of a car. A few more posters slipped out of the man's hand. His head banged hard against the bonnet. He roared in pain and disbelief.

Jig could see Cracko's teeth bite down on his lip as he leaned forward and went to grab the man by the neck. But his grip weakened as Seb slipped out his left hand and dangled over. Cracko had to grab him with his right hand. The kid screamed. The man leaned up from the bonnet.

'Who the fuck am I?' Cracko said.

He rose his big fist up into the blue sky and drove hard into the man's chest. Jig twisted at the crunch. Seb's head bobbed from the impact, like one of those nodding dogs in the back of cars.

The man's roar ran the length of the row of shops. Jig looked around. The street was empty. No one came out of the shops to see what was going on. The man held his hand to his chest and grimaced as he tried to breathe.

Cracko pulled himself back up, spit and saliva on his lips. A gold chain tipped out from under his top.

'Da, why hit man?' Seb said, snuggling into his dad's heaving shoulder.

Jig looked at Cracko as he adjusted his feet. The thick muscles on his arms flexed. A green vein bulged against his skin like a cable. His arm shone with sweat.

Cracko reefed the man up from the car with his right hand. Seb's neck and head swung back and forwards sharply, hitting off his dad's shoulder. He roared.

'Let me introduce myself,' Cracko said.

Jig watched Cracko pull back his head, his chain catching the sun as he headbutted the man smack in the middle of his face. Jig twitched at the noise. Blood spurted from the man's nose onto Cracko's top and Seb's bare legs. The kid slipped out of his da's grasp again and Cracko hopped to keep him in. The crisp bag fell to the ground and Seb's little arm stretched down to it. His face was all red and puffy, his roaring hysterical.

The man half stood against the car, dazed. He stared down at his hands, which were covered in blood.

At that moment, music from an ice-cream van blared from a road nearby. Jig thought how it made the man seem like he was swaying to the tune.

Cracko leaned towards the man, spit and blood spraying from his mouth as he spoke.

'I see ya again, ya Provo cunt, I'll shove those posters down yer throat with a pole.'

The man jerked and slid down beside the wheel of the car.

Seb was leaping out of Cracko's grip in pain and agitation.

Jig banged back against the sweet machine as Cracko strode away, his eyes bulging.

The gobstopper dropped.

14

When Crowe discovered that Darren, or Maggot as he was known, was Jig's brother, she had a good idea what she was up against.

As she drove towards their home, she recalled the info from the Garda Pulse computer system.

Maggot had clocked up sixty charges in his fifteen years, the most serious, and the most recent, a firearms charge. He ran with a crew on the canal. She saw that he came from a good lineage. His dad had serious form, mainly for armed robberies and burglaries. The mother was a serial shoplifter and had carried out a number of nasty assaults on staff.

She'd managed to grab Sergeant Flynn at the station and asked about his meeting with Ms King. He said the meeting was short because the woman was just too nervous. She'd made her excuses and left, which, he said, was not uncommon. He said there was no way information about that meeting could have leaked out from the station. He was adamant about that. The information was known only to himself, the DI and the Chief. Ms King must have told someone, he said. Perhaps the gang had followed her on the day of the meeting, but he doubted that. He agreed that Ghost was the most likely person behind the threat and didn't seem surprised that a child might have been used to send the message. But he doubted that Crowe would find concrete evidence. The Canal Gang were too good at covering their tracks.

Crowe wasn't going to let that stop her.

She slowed over the speed ramps. The road teemed with kids. A girl was pulling a big holdall on wheels. She stopped and unzipped it and out popped the head of a toddler. He laughed and the girl pushed his head back in. Crowe smiled. You could never predict what you'd see around here, she thought.

She scanned the house numbers and recognised Maggot's. There was a gang of kids, little ones, on the other side of the road. They were hitting a lightpole repeatedly with bars or something.

She sized up the house as she got out. There were big bins blocking most of the path to the door. One of them had tipped over a railing; bits of rubbish had fallen into a neighbour's garden. The windows of the sitting room were wide open. Noise blared. A tattered, dirty curtain hung inside, looping in the middle.

The front door slammed and she looked at Maggot. As he tried to root out a bike from behind the bins, she felt for her holster, probably because of the most recent charge Maggot had against him. Outside the firing range, she had yet to discharge her Sig P226. But with fifteen rounds in it, including one in the breech and another magazine with fifteen bullets in a holder on the left side of her belt, she was well prepared for madness. Though why detectives were obliged to carry so much ammo she had yet to understand.

'Well, garda,' he shouted on seeing her, 'what the fuck do ya want?'

'You want to watch your mouth there, Darren. I'll add being abusive to a garda to your charges.'

He laughed as he pulled out his bike.

'How many charges have you got now before the Children's Court?' she asked.

'What, the joke shop?'

'Well, your firearms charge is no joke.'

He pulled his hoodie up and shrugged his shoulders in contrived nonchalance.

'You won't be smiling when you get serious time in St Pat's.'

'Be no bother,' he said, doing a wheelie on his bike. 'I knows half of them fuckers in there anyways. It be like a camp.'

She watched as he stuck his finger up back at her and allowed her thoughts to come to the surface.

Little scumbag. Chances are he'll have a short and nasty life.

She turned to the door, but couldn't see any buzzer or knocker. She gave it a rap.

'Ms Hunt? Can you open the door please?'

No response. She stood there for the next couple of minutes knocking and calling out her name. There was a light noise behind her, like little stones hitting a car. She turned around and kids looked at her, laughing. In a fit of frustration, she gave the door a kick.

There was a roar from the bowels of the house, as if she had awoken something. Feet stomped down the hall.

'Who the fuck done that?' the voice came, as the door was pulled back.

Crowe expected to see a huge battle-axe of a woman, but this woman was average height, shorter even, and skinny. But wiry. She had red hair tied back into a severe ponytail. A white vest hung off her and a black and gold belt was tight around her narrow waist. She had a big black tattoo across the top of her chest, visible above her vest. Another smudged the side of her neck. Before Crowe could take out her badge from her bag, the woman pointed to her unmarked Mondeo.

'That yer car? Come on, let's go and kick the shite out of it.'

'Ms Hunt, calm down. I am –'

She pushed past her, stormed out of the gate and kicked the side of the car. The kids across the road roared and slapped the pole.

'Ms Hunt,' Crowe shouted, holding out her ID, 'I'm a garda and that's a garda vehicle. Now calm down.'

She swung around and marched back, her face sweating, her eyes bulging. The muscles on her arms were sinewy and taut.

'Ya kick me door,' she said, gesticulating wildly with her finger, 'I'll kick yer fucking car.'

Crowe could smell booze. The woman looked like she'd downed a handful of tablets too.

'Ms Hunt, I'm looking to talk to Jig.'

'Ya mean that other useless prick,' she said, pointing in the direction that Maggot went.

'Not Darren. Jig.'

Ms Hunt stood there, swaying slightly, as if something was taking effect, or wearing off, Crowe wasn't sure.

'Yer not dragging Jig down to any cop shop. He'll come back all battered, like Maggot does.'

'I just want to talk to him. I can wait inside.'

'He's gone up the shops for smokes.' She turned and swayed down the hall, leaving the door open behind her.

Crowe followed and put her badge back in her bag. She winced at the noise from the front room. An enormous TV was bolted to the wall. Some children's programme boomed. A baby lay face down on the floor, its neck straining up towards the flashing images.

Layers of smells assailed her: damp clothes, cigarettes and the remnants of takeaways. She walked after Ms Hunt into the small kitchen. She was plonked at a table, staring up at another TV, up on the wall.

'After the break. False nails. We have the latest fashions.'

A thought bubbled inside Crowe's head.

'Can I use your toilet?' she asked, 'while Jig comes back.'

Ms Hunt lit a cigarette and pointed upwards.

There were clothes dumped along the stairs and on the tiny landing. A bright bulb dangled from a long wire, illuminating dark spots and blotches along the edges of the ceiling. The front bedroom had been crudely partitioned into two rooms. One of the doors was splintered as if someone had kicked through it. The door to her right was to the toilet and the one ahead was ajar. She pushed that door back and glanced in. There was a football poster up on one of the walls. She reckoned it was Jig's.

The room was cramped, just a narrow gap between a single bed and bunk beds on the other side. Light poured in through a curtainless window. A school bag was dumped on the bed.

Crowe reached into her bag and put on her latex gloves. She stepped carefully and zipped open the school bag. She pulled out a copy book and flicked through the pages. There were pages of homework and scribbles, of team layouts and drawings, quite good ones she thought, of the canal and swans and the Luas. Then a page opened out and she grabbed it. She nearly let out a cry. The page had bits of paper attached to the staples. She recalled the note and the tears where it was stapled. It looked like a fit. She took out her phone and took a picture of the page and shoved the copybook back in.

She stepped back out and opened the bathroom door. The smell of urine and used wet towels hit her. She held her breath, leaned over and flushed the toilet. She took her gloves off and allowed herself a smile.

Got the little fucker.

Crowe glanced around at her three colleagues as they waited. Tyrell sucked on his mint, but was otherwise expressionless. Such a cool fucker, she thought.

The door opened.

Instead of stepping back at the intimidating presence of four guards in front of her, each wearing anti-stab vests, Ms Hunt pushed her face towards Crowe.

'That's the fucking thanks I get for helping ya.' She jabbed her finger into Crowe's vest. 'I let ya in,' she said, swinging her right hand back into the house. 'I was all hospitable. Ya barely said goodbye and now ya come back with the heavies.'

'Ms Hunt,' Crowe said, 'we have a warrant to search the house. Here is a copy.'

Ms Hunt crunched the sheet into a ball, turned around and pretended to wipe her arse with it.

Crowe blinked at the sight. 'Ms Hunt, this will be a lot easier if you just let us proceed and we will be out of here as quickly as possible.'

Ms Hunt leaned back on the wall, laughing to herself. The two uniformed guards headed for Jig's bedroom.

'Well, if it isn't Garda What's-his-fucking-name,' Ms Hunt said to Tyrell. 'Not seen yer miserable head in a while.'

Crowe watched Tyrell bite down on his mint. 'Well, if you attended some of your son's court dates you would,' he replied.

Tyrell had told her on the way he wasn't surprised Jig was one of the Hunts. 'The apple doesn't fall far from the tree,' he said to Crowe. He said it was already too late to save Jig. 'Their lives are like the Luas tracks, Crowe, heading in one direction.'

Crowe went up to Jig's room to see how the search was going.

There was no sign of the boy, or the bag.

Two hours later, Crowe slumped into the passenger seat.

'I don't get it,' she said, as Tyrell drove off.

'He copped it somehow,' Tyrell said, speeding down the canal. 'Or his ma did. She's smarter than you might think, under that mad fucking exterior.'

'Or someone tipped them off,' Crowe replied, curtly.

She expected a rebuke, but none came.

'What about we arrest the boy?' Crowe said, watching a huge seagull hovering over the canal, its right eye, it seemed, glaring at her.

'On what grounds?'

'I saw the copybook. The tears on the page matched the note. I have a picture of it in my phone. The bag has since disappeared. We quiz him on that.'

'How are you going to explain to the judge the photo you have of the copybook? An image you acquired from searching his room and going through his property without a warrant.'

Crowe had that sinking feeling, one she had yet managed to deal with: of a case, which she thought she had built up nicely, suddenly collapsing.

'What about the CCTV?' she asked, in desperation.

'I already told you,' Tyrell said, careering into the station. 'A, the picture is not clear enough and B, even if we could show it was him, he could be just out acting the bollix. And the forensics from the scene drew a blank. So did the note. We have nothing linking the boy to the scene. You know that.'

Tyrell exited, leaving Crowe sunken in her seat.

She waited till he was gone inside, then lashed out hard with her feet.

15

Jig kicked at the top of the cans as they bobbed against the lock. He tried to stretch his leg down further, but nearly lost his grip on the bars. Clasping them tighter, memories flowed in.

'Respect that water, Jack. Might be shallow, but a little boy like ya could drown in seconds. Many's a boy round here have died in them waters.'

'Why was the canal built anyways, Granda?'

'The boats moved cargo and people on them, from Dublin to the country and back. This canal,' his granda said shoving his big long arms out, 'goes all the way to the River Shannon. The brewery in James's Gate,' he said, pointing his arm back the other way, 'used barges to transport all those lovely barrels of porter to the country people. And loads of turf came back from the bogs for firesides in the city.'

'Did ya help build the canals, Granda?'

'Hah!'

He loved his granda's throaty laughs.

'But ya does make things, Granda.'

'I'm a carpenter, Jack. I can make ya a table, chairs and jigs.'

'What's a jig?'

'A frame, like a border and a machine cuts out that shape. Kind of like a copy of the frame. Here show me yer hand. Look, it fits snugly into the palm of mine.'

Jig looked at his granda's huge shovel of a hand. His fingers were like big thick screws. His skin was lined, rough and dry, like the sandpaper he kept in his shed.

'Am I a copy of ya, Granda?'

'Ya know what?' he replied, grabbing the boy's face hard, 'I think ya might be. Yer called Jack, like me. Ya look the fucking spit of me when I was a nipper. And, yer hand does fit into my palm. I thinks we have yer nickname: Jig.'

He wanted to stay with the memories, but a familiar voice was dragging him away.

He looked up at Maggot. He was sipping a beer. Shop stood beside his brother, tapping away on his phone.

'What ya got a big grumpy head on ya for?' Maggot asked.

'Nothing,' Jig mumbled, starting to kick at the cans again.

He was thinking about the call earlier from Ghost, telling him to get out of the gaff as the coppers were coming. He told him to bring his schoolbag with him and not to head back home till that night. Then he just hung up.

'Yer turning into Ghost's little helper, aren't ya?' Maggot said, lobbing a bottle over his head. It splashed into the water, sending a couple of ducks scurrying away. He opened up another.

'Who bought ya those?' Shop said, glancing up from his phone and nodding at Jig's runners.

'Ya not hear, Shop?' Maggot answered. 'Ghost gave him a wad of cash. For some job he done. What ya think of that?'

Shop hocked a big phlegm and went back to studying his phone.

'Three score,' Shop said to Maggot.

Jig watched his brother walk over to behind some trees and pull a brick from the wall. He took out something and dropped it on the ground.

A guy approached. His jeans were all baggy and his coat sagged.

'Story?' he said to the lads.

They just looked at him.

He opened his fist, revealing a crumpled note and gave it to Shop.

'Can ya not get any fucking clean fifty-euro notes, Bones,' Shop said, 'ones that ya don't wipe yer streaky arse with?'

But Jig could see Bones wasn't listening. He was swaying on his feet. Maggot nodded over towards the trees. Bones skipped over and scoured the ground, picked up a little bag and was gone.

'Not going to make much money on score bags,' Shop said, looking at his phone again. 'That's more like it: a half garden.'

Maggot went back to the trees.

Jig watched a skinny little woman bounce towards them. Her hair was tied tight back. She wore a blue jacket over a T-shirt. Jig remembered what weight half a garden was after asking Maggot before. It was half an eighth of an ozzie or an ounce, he told himself proudly.

'Ya do some old dear down at the post office, Taby?' Shop asked.

The woman jumped around, laughing to herself.

'Nah, not doing that any more. Well, not today anyways.'

She looked at Jig. 'Ah, what's the story, little man? Ah, deadly runners. Nice one.'

She dug into her front jeans pocket and pulled out a couple of notes and handed them to Shop.

'Now that's more like it. Nice crisp cash,' Shop said, rustling a fifty, a twenty and a ten euro note in his hands. 'Maggot, throw in a few yellies there for Taby; keep her nice and chilled.'

Taby broke into a big smile.

'Thanks, Shop. Yer a star.' She nearly sprinted over to the trees.

Jig looked at Shop; his face was all puffed up.

'Sniffers,' Shop said to Maggot, a few minutes later. 'Get a onner bag,' he added, looking at his text, 'and ten yokes as well.'

Jig recognised them a mile off. They were students living in the new apartments built to replace the hellhole that was De Valera Mansions. A college was renting one of the blocks, Jig recalled, of what was now called Pembroke or some other poncy name.

What was a onner bag? he asked himself.

Well, a onner bag is one hundred euros' worth. The weight is, is 1.3 grammes.

He nodded to himself in satisfaction.

'Right, lads,' Maggot said, walking back, 'another party on tonight?'

Jig had a good look at them. They had Converse runners and thick-framed glasses.

Shop spread his legs and put his hands down his tracksuit bottoms.

'Listen, lads, youse want the good stuff?' Shop said to them. 'Not the shit we give the junkies? One hundred fifty, but fucking worth it.'

The students shuffled and looked at each other.

'None of that headshop substitute muck in this,' Shop said. 'No fucking lignocaine neither. This is pure fucking cocaine, Premiership quality. Youse could cut it down yerself and make a killing.'

'Okay,' piped up one fella, with a skinny beard running around his face.

'Lads, we have some deadly yokes in too,' continued Shop. 'Genuine MDMA. Straight from Holland, not some pit in Poland. Youse be banging tonight. Get the bitches all lovey-dovey on the Es, then give them a few darts of coke and they'll be sucking yer cock in the jacks before youse know it.'

Jig smiled at the image. He could see the students' eyes nearly jump out of their heads.

'For youse, fifty euro for ten,' Shop said, spreading his arms out, 'youse can't get fairer than that. Not for quality product.'

The students huddled together and gathered the notes.

'Youse need any green?' Shop asked. 'I've got grade A grass as well.'

One of them shook his head.

'Suit yourself,' Shop said, as he counted the cash.

Maggot sorted the guys out.

'What number are youse in again?' Maggot asked.

'Eh, what?' the guy with the skinny beard said.

'What number? For the party later.'

The students looked at each other, their faces pale.

'What, youse don't think those college girls would fancy getting their mouth around prime beef?' Maggot said, grabbing his balls.

They looked at him, nervous as fuck.

'No matter,' Maggot said, taking his hand off his balls and waving at them, 'I knows where youse live anyways.'

Jig joined in as Shop burst out laughing.

'Not too smart them college boys,' Maggot said, as the students sped away. 'Shoving the same shit up their noses for one hundred and fifty as the junkies plug in for one hundred.'

He turned to Jig. 'Economics, little man. That's what this is about. One thing those college types love is thinking they are getting something special. And Shop here is the pro,' he said. 'He doesn't touch the shit. Look, he's not even drinking. Watch him, Jig, and learn.'

Maggot had been bitching about some fella for ages by the time Shop closed up. Jig watched Shop roll up two bundles of cash and push one in each sock. He thought that was cool.

'That sulky cunt,' Maggot continued. 'He just said "No" when I asked him could I ride the horse. He fucking blanks me now every time I see his ugly hunched-up little face. Bobby Sands is the fucker's name.'

'That's the horse,' Shop said, as they headed for the Luas.

'Nah, the horse is, hold on, yeah yer right. What's his fucking name? That sulky bollix.'

'Dunno,' Shop said.

'Anyways ...' Maggot droned, dropping his bottle onto the floor of the Luas as they got on. Jig looked around but none of the passengers raised their eyes. '... let's go up to O'Donovan flats and pay him a visit.'

Jig saw from Shop's face that he didn't think this was a good idea.

Maggot leaned towards a woman, who was busy staring out the window.

'Going home, love?' he said, all nicey.

Jig looked at her. She was an office type: white shirt, grey skirt and white runners. A large handbag rested on her lap, which she clutched tightly.

'Did ya take yer heels off after work?' Maggot said, one hand down his tracksuit bottoms. 'They in yer bag?'

Jig laughed. The woman shook her head, glancing around nervously.

'Bet ya put them heels on when ya get back to yer fella and ride the bollix off him,' he said, his hands moving under his tracksuit. 'Bet ya, yer a little minx, alright.'

Shop gave a shout when they reached their stop. Maggot leaned down to the woman. 'Make sure ya wear them heels on the Luas the next time, yeah?'

He clapped Jig on the shoulder as they got off, Jig joining him in the laugh.

As they headed up the road, Maggot looked over at a garage and stopped. He told them to wait.

He came back carrying something. As they approached the back of the flats, Jig saw movement in the gloom.

'There he is,' Maggot said, dropping what he was carrying. He ran up to the horse and gave him a heavy kick in the stomach.

Jig laughed in shock. He glanced around; Shop was shaking his head. The horse reared in pain and yanked hard at the rope tethering him to a fence. Maggot picked up a big stone and lobbed it at the horse, hopping off the side of his head. The horse was pulling and heaving and making a racket.

'Better get going, Maggot, or there'll be a field of angry sulky fuckers here,' Shop said. 'The RA are in these flats, so we better move sharpish.'

'Fuck them. I'm not afraid of no Provos,' Maggot shouted. 'Anyways, they'll be in time for a little spectacular of my own.'

'I've a fucking job on tomorrow, for Ghost,' Shop said to him. 'If ya want to come, let's fucking go.'

But Maggot wasn't listening. He got the container he was carrying and poured dark liquid all over the horse.

'Yer a feisty fucker, aren't ya. Well, this will quieten ya down.'

Maggot took out a box of matches from inside his pockets, lit one, then the box. Giving Jig a wink, he threw the box onto the horse's back.

It looked to Jig as if it happened in slow motion. He saw the flames curl around the horse and down his tail. The animal reared up in agony.

'This will make fucking prime time viewing this,' Maggot said, taking out his phone.

The screeching sawed through Jig's head. He put his hands over his ears. The horse pulled and heaved. The rope vibrated from the strain, but did not snap.

The flames crackled and hissed. The scorched air stank, of petrol and hair and flesh. The shrieks from the horse became more terrible, more desperate. Jig couldn't block out the noise no matter how hard he pressed his hands against his ears. He could see the white of the horse's teeth, clenched in agony. The animal's eyes bulged and popped. His legs folded and he collapsed with a thud.

Jig fell to his knees. He put his head between his legs; his hands still clamped to his ears. Someone grabbed him clean off the ground. It was Shop.

Jig looked back. Maggot was falling around laughing, shouting, 'Boom! Ride yer horse now, ya fucker.'

16

Shay brooded over Lisa as he did his stretches. She didn't even reply when he said he was off for a run. She just sat there at the kitchen table, hunched over her laptop, scrolling through sites. He could never figure out what she was so engrossed in. From the few glances he caught, they seemed to be various mum sites. She'd never tell him much when he asked.

The warmth of the sun rolled across his face, lifting his spirits. He pulled his shades down and headed for the canal. On days like this, it looked its best.

Crowe entered the station and headed straight for the stairs. Before she got any further, Grant called out to her from the public office.

'Any plans for the weekend, Detective Crowe?' Grant said, with a mischievous smile, greeted with groans from behind her.

'Not really,' Crowe replied, moving towards Grant. 'Dare I ask why?'

'Spring Session's this weekend in Cork – the full three days, baby.' Grant did a little sashay.

'Any chance of those lazy banners doing any work,' joked one of the lads in the office, to a few guffaws.

That still got up Crowe's wick – being called a 'banner', their slang for a ban, a female garda. Grant didn't seem to mind, though.

'Thought you said you were working Sunday?' Crowe asked, deciding to ignore the remark.

'I was, but did a swap. Doing a double today.'

Crowe looked at her and wished she could be as carefree as Grant.

'You know what?' Crowe said, 'you were born under a lucky star.'

Grant smiled and faked a smug nod of the head.

'Peters and I are going on patrol now,' she said, 'so I might give you a wave when I cruise past as you hang out with the scrotes.'

'I'm beginning to dislike you,' Crowe replied. 'Enjoy the weekend. Easy on the sex, drugs and rock 'n' roll.'

That attracted loud hoots from the lads.

'What you mean rock 'n' roll?' Grant shouted, to cheers and whistles.

Grant opened her window and crooned quietly as the warm wind caressed her face.

'Who's playing anyway?' Peters asked.

Even with her eyes closed she knew he was eyeing her body up and down.

'Ane Brun, Lisa Hannigan, Agnes Obel –'

'Who the fuck?'

Grant opened her eyes at the sound of a car screeching hard in front of them.

'Fucking hell,' Peters said, leaning forward.

A BMW swung across the junction from the bridge, well after the lights had gone red.

'We could let it slide,' Grant said to Peters, 'and just cruise around.'

Peters sped towards the BMW and gave the siren a couple of whirls. No response. He flashed the lights. Eventually the driver began to slow down and pulled in at the entrance to a disused factory.

'What is this festival anyway, some lesbian gathering?' Peters said, stopping and turning to Grant. But she was already half way out, the door clunking behind her.

'Shop, what the fuck are ya doing?' Maggot roared, almost jumping into the front seat. 'Don't fucking pull over.'

'What do ya want me to do?' Shop shouted back, glancing at Jobs next to him.

'Ya tore through the fucking lights back there, ya dope,' Jobs said. 'I told ya to take it handy.'

'We get searched we're fucked,' Maggot said, leaning forward.

'Youse want me to take off?' Shop said. 'Then we'll definitely get done.'

'They saw us breaking a red,' Jobs said, holding his hand out to calm things. 'That's all. They'll give us a telling-off or slap us with a fine.' He turned to Maggot. 'They won't search, unless we give them a reason to fucking search.'

'I'm already facing a gun charge,' Maggot shouted. 'I'll get the ten year if caught again.'

'No ya won't, yer a juvenile. Now, keep yer cool,' Jobs said. 'Say ... fucking ... nothing, right? Leave the talking to me.'

'There's some blonde bitch walking towards us,' Shop said looking at his side mirror, as he kept the car in gear.

Jobs typed a text and sent it to the number Ghost gave him. Maggot pulled his hoodie up.

Jig wheelied down the path, enjoying the breeze off the canal running up the arms of his top. Bowie bounded beside him.

He had been out of his house all day, ever since he woke up screaming, from all the images, of red flames, of that horse screeching and Maggot laughing.

There was still a stink of petrol and burning stuck inside his nostrils even though he threw loads of water up them.

He slammed the front wheel of his bike down when he saw Taylor walking towards him with her dogs. She was with her big sister Megan.

'Hiya, Jig,' Taylor said, pulling the lead on one of the dogs as Bowie went over for a sniff.

'Hey, Tay. Story?'

'We have to get back home,' Megan said, pulling Taylor along.

Jig knew her sister didn't like him. She had that look on her face. He was used to it.

'How old are them dogs now?' Jig asked.

'Nibs here,' Taylor said, pulling the lead on a Jack Russell, 'is thirteen months. Joxer the boxer,' she laughed, 'is two years old and the cocker, Diana, is six.'

'She's a year older than Bowie,' Jig said.

'Bowie is such a deadly dog,' she said. 'Sharon wants him ya know.'

'Well, she not getting him,' Jig snapped, but warmed at the thought of him and Sharon hanging out with Bowie.

'Come on,' Megan said. 'We told Ma we'd be back in half an hour.'

'Hold on,' Jig said. 'I'll head back with youse.'

Grant was still smiling at Peters' lesbian remark as she approached the car. The Luas cables near the canal jangled with a passing tram. Everything looked so good in the sun, she thought. If it held for the weekend, she'd be able to wear that new summer dress she got.

She shook off a little shower of white cherry blossoms from an overhanging tree as she approached the BMW. She pulled her anti-stab vest down on her short-sleeved uniform top and glanced in the back window. There was a young fella with a hoodie in the rear. She slowly walked up to the driver's side and rapped on the window. The window zoomed down.

'Story, garda?' the driver said, a bit forced it seemed to her.

'Story is you breaking a red at the bridge and taking the junction at speed.'

'Ah, garda, it was yellow as we were going through it,' came another voice.

She looked in at the front seat passenger. A fella with a cap on. Must be their spokesman, she thought. She noticed Peters walking around casually to the front of the car, his hands buried in his pockets, studying the disks on the dashboard. He made a point of taking out his notebook.

'So?' Grant said, speaking to the driver. 'What's the rush?'

The spokesman answered. 'Just want to park old Betsy here

and get a few cans and kick back in the garden. Want to make the most of the day, before the fucking sun goes in. Ya know what I mean? Yer welcome to join us, if ya want?'

Cool customer, Grant thought. Probably why he was doing the talking and not the mute lump driving. She looked at him again; he looked like he was holding in a shit.

'You okay?' she said to him.

'Grand, yeah. No problem. Have to get a car with some AC though for the summer. Fucking boiler this thing.' He managed to smile at Grant, but his face glistened with sweat.

She turned her attention to the hoodie in the back.

'And what's the story with you?'

No reply.

Grant took off her shades and studied him.

'It raining in there?'

'He's not feeling well,' the spokesman said. 'And he's short on charm.'

Grant smiled. She kept her eyes on the hoodie. She had planned to just give them a telling-off, being in good mood and over half way through her second shift. She wanted an easy end to the day. But something about the situation unsettled her. She turned to the driver again.

'Why don't you knock off the engine there?'

'Back off, bitch.'

Grant turned to the hoodie, and saw a Glock pointing at her. As he shouted, the engine shut down, but it was still in gear. The car jumped forward. One shot went off.

Grant felt a fire on the side of her cheek. She saw blood spurt onto the driver's face. She staggered and banged onto the ground. The car shunted back, then forward, catching Peters on the bonnet, smacking him hard against a metal pole. The car reversed towards her, and she saw no more.

'Christ, get out of here,' Jobs roared, slamming the dashboard. 'Out!'

Shop careered onto the road, struggling to control the car. He glanced at the side mirror and saw the legs of the female garda splayed on the ground. He turned away before he could see any more. Her blood was on his face. He could feel it. The fucking enormity of what he had done was hitting him like a bat.

'Ya total cunt,' he roared at Maggot, reaching round to box him.

'Eyes on the fucking road,' Jobs shouted, pulling Shop's arm back.

Jobs' phone beeped. He read the text.

'Right. Here we go. Rear of shops on Philip Road.'

Jig ducked at the loud clap. He fell sideways off the bike, hit his head off the edge of the path and splashed into the canal. Water poured into his ears and his eyes. The weight of his clothes dragged him flat to the bottom of the canal. He could hear warbled noises and screams above. He saw someone in pink, Megan it was, shouting on the path, but the sound was all worbly. He pushed himself up and spat out water. Megan was jumping, shaking her hands and her arms wildly. Her pink top was sprayed with red dots. The dogs spun and barked. There was a body on the path. From the school uniform he knew it was Taylor. He roared when he saw her face.

Shay jumped when he heard the loud crack. It came from further down the canal. A fucking gunshot, he told himself, running towards the sound. A car was tearing up the road towards him, screeching heavily. It was a BMW 3 series, 95 reg. There were three men inside, but he couldn't make out who they were. But there was something about the guy in the back, or the hoodie he was wearing, that seemed familiar.

Terrible screams splintered the air. There were people on the path ahead, moving in different directions. He made out a girl in a pink tracksuit jumping up and down screeching, her hands and arms flailing as she turned in circles, roaring, 'Ma, Ma.'

Dogs jumped and barked around her. A mother with a buggy was running towards them from the other side. There were some men across the road, where Shay could make out two other bodies, uniform gardaí, one with a massive injury.

Jig was standing in the canal, transfixed by the slumped body.

'Have you got a phone?' Shay shouted to the woman with the buggy. 'Ring 999. Police and ambulance.'

Shay moved to hold the roaring girl, but she pushed him away. A Jack Russell was licking the face of a girl on the ground. He stepped around, to see her face, unable to avert his eyes. The bottom half of the girl's face was gone. What was left was a mound of twisted bone.

Jig stood trembling in the water and hadn't noticed Shay yet.

'Jig, you okay?' Shay shouted. 'Jig?'

The boy didn't respond, motionless where he stood in the canal, his eyes stuck on the girl.

Shay heaved Jig out and pulled him onto the path. He turned Jig's face away from the girl.

He had to adjust his hold as Jig collapsed into his arms.

17

Crowe tensed as she approached her car; the radio, muffled, was crackling intensely. As she opened the door she caught words between the noise and the shouts.

Shooting ... Multiple injuries ... MacBride Road ... All units.

She rammed the keys into the ignition and pulled away. She threw the dashmaster up against the windscreen and plugged it into the cigarette lighter socket. The blue lights flashed out to other motorists. The radio kept spluttering out a call to all units to descend on MacBride Road. Crowe sucked in air as she heard the words 'member shot'. Her body shook with raw adrenaline. She held her concentration and whipped around bends and roundabouts, her stomach swishing at the sensations, her mind fighting off blurred images of horror.

The five minutes it took to get to MacBride Road seemed like an hour. She could hear the blare of sirens. She dumped her car up on a kerb. Her eyes, squinting in the strong sun, strained to see through the trees as she ran around a corner, her Sig pulling at her side.

An ambulance sped away; another was parked in the middle of the road ahead. But it was the stance of the uniformed officers and detectives that squeezed her heart. Some stood stationary with their hands up to their mouths, others paced the road randomly, their heads bowed.

A patrol car stood out from the other vehicles as it was parked up neatly, half on the footpath and half on the road. Ahead, there was a shape on the path, crudely covered over with sheets. Crowe halted, as if she had walked into a pane of glass. A man walked towards her. It was Tyrell, his face drained of colour.

Christ, what is it?

She ignored petals from a blossom tree landing on her face. She stepped towards the body, but Tyrell closed her off.

'You don't want to . . .' he said.

'Who?'

Tyrell put his hand on her shoulder. The caws of seagulls over the canal cut the silence.

'Peters has suffered severe back injuries,' Tyrell said. 'He's just been taken to hospital.'

Crowe's mind raced.

Peters? Grant was going out on patrol with him. Oh my God. It must be her.

She looked up at Tyrell.

'Grant?'

Tyrell looked into her eyes, then nodded.

Grant's smiley, carefree face popped into her mind. Crowe looked again at the sheet on the ground.

She couldn't be under there. Not Grant.

Movement on the far side of the Luas tracks, along the canal path, intruded. She glanced over.

'A bullet hit a girl on the path,' Tyrell said. 'She's been taken to hospital too, but it doesn't look good.'

Crowe's mind was swirling.

'What?' she asked, beseeching him. 'What happened?'

'We don't know,' Tyrell said. 'Grant and Peters must have pulled in a car. There's tyre marks over there,' he said, pointing towards the body. 'Witnesses said they heard a shot. It hit the girl.'

She held onto Tyrell's outstretched arm as her stomach bent. As she contorted, Lynn Bolger's warning, that 'something awful' was going to happen soon, slipped into her mind.

Crowe straightened up and let go of Tyrell's arm. She looked around.

Tyrell seemed to read her mind. 'It's all derelict buildings and closed factories on this side.'

'Cameras?' she asked.

'The Luas stops have cameras, but they just look down on the stops, not out on to the road. There are cameras down at the junction, which we'll have to get. A Luas may have passed around the time, so we'll put out an appeal. We'll organise the jobs at the conference in a couple of hours.'

Crowe tried to take it all in, but images of Grant swaying in the station, beaming at her, ebbed and flowed in her mind.

'Jesus, if she wasn't doing a double, this wouldn't have happened to her,' she said, holding her hand to her mouth. 'Just so she could go to the festival, with her boyfriend.'

She looked into Tyrell's face for some solution, explanation even, for the madness, but all he could do was hold her gaze.

Crowe watched as scenes of crime officers arrived and began erecting a blue tent and a tarpaulin around the sheets covering Grant. She couldn't believe it. Her head was spinning. She felt Tyrell's strong hand clasp her shoulder.

'You okay?'

She nodded.

'Any witnesses?' she asked, clearing her throat.

'Reports of a car with a couple of men inside. Some description of a BMW. Command and Control have sent out the alerts. They're trying to cordon off the area now. We've spoken with some of the witnesses. There's another at the hospital. That's where I'm heading now.'

'Me too.'

18

When the clamour subsided, the whimpering and wailing became unbearable. Shay's mouth was stuck together like gum when he tried to breathe. The noise was coming from Megan, Taylor's sister. She was sitting on a bed. All he could see was part of her back. Jig had told him who the girls were. He'd said Taylor was a friend. That's all he'd managed to say.

He went with Jig in the ambulance, leaving all the dogs behind, barking frantically. Shay told a passer-by the boy's address and asked her to tell the parents what had happened.

He looked down at Jig. He was trembling under the sheets. Shay recoiled as images of the girl elbowed their way into his mind: her small body contorted on the path, her legs twisted, her jaw and mouth ripped apart, replaced by a mess of bones and blood.

He watched a nurse and a doctor as they walked over to Megan. The nurse threw her arms around the girl; the doctor placed her outstretched hand on the girl's shoulder. Shay's chest crunched at the sound from the girl: it was like that of a dog run over by a car, lying on the cold ground waiting to die. The staff held the girl up and brought her down to a side room. She was bent over, her feet dragging on the polished floor. Some of the gardaí in the ward held hands to their faces. Others shuffled their feet, their heads bowed. Their colleague had been brought to surgery when they all came in. Still no word yet on him.

Shay felt a presence behind him. Turning, he saw that female detective, Crowe. Her face was a grey-white colour, her lips a watery red. She looked anxiously along the corridor, then back to him and down to the bed. Behind her was a tall, lean man. Her boss, he guessed. After giving Shay a cursory glance, he walked down to one of the uniformed officers. The silence dragged, before Crowe spoke.

'So, you're one of the witnesses?' she asked, a hint, it seemed to Shay, of disbelief in her voice.

'I was running along the canal at the time,' he replied.

'And?'

'I heard a loud bang and sprinted down.' He turned towards Jig. 'And he was in the water beside the girls there and . . .'

Shay looked at her boss as he came back.

'This is Detective Inspector Tyrell,' she said. 'This is Shay. He coaches a local football team. He's the witness you were talking about.'

'We need descriptions of those in the car,' Tyrell said, his voice betraying little, but his eyes now scrutinising Shay.

Shay turned to Jig and nodded to the doors. He was still in his running gear. His legs, chest and arms felt stiff and groaned when he moved.

As they walked out the doors, Tyrell's phone went.

'Where? . . . Yeah, go on.'

He turned to Crowe.

'You deal with this,' Tyrell said, striding away. 'Anything you get, ring me straight away.'

Crowe nodded after him and turned back to Shay.

'How are the guards?' Shay asked, before she could say anything.

Crowe blinked, then shook her head.

'One is,' she coughed, 'dead, the second is –'

Shay nodded. 'He was already in surgery when we arrived.'

Crowe flexed her shoulders, steadying herself.

'Shay, we need any description of the car you can give us, and the people inside.'

Shay watched her root in her bag and take out a notepad. Her hands were shaking.

'I couldn't see much,' he said slowly, conscious that she was struggling to write. 'The car was tearing up the road as I was running down. But it was a BMW 95 reg, 3 series maybe, red. It looked fairly battered.'

Crowe scribbled away. Shay paused. She nodded for him to continue.

'Looked like three males. Guy in the back was wearing a green hoodie. Other two, I couldn't really see. The driver seemed to be a big fella, but youngish. Front passenger had something on his head, a cap, I think.'

Crowe noted the descriptions.

'Good. You ever see any of them around?'

Shay bunched his mouth. 'Don't think so. Didn't get a good enough view.'

He knew she was studying him for any sign he was holding something back.

'Where they go?'

'Didn't keep track. I was running down to the bodies. Think I heard a screech as if they might have turned off the road.'

'Anything else?'

He thought hard, looking for something more to give her.

'Afraid not, sorry.'

Crowe took out her phone and walked away a bit. He saw her reading out from her notes. She came slowly back towards him.

'Who's the boy inside?'

'Jig.'

'You're joking me,' she said, her eyes jumping. 'What the hell was he doing there?'

'Don't know. He was in the canal when I got to the girl. He must have been beside the girls.'

'Bit of a coincidence he was at the scene at the time of this?'

'Not really. He's always hanging out on the canals.'

She's stretching here, he thought.

'He suffer any injuries?'

'He banged his head falling in. They're keeping him overnight for observation. He's in shock.'

'Is he?' she said. 'Where are his delightful parents?'

'On their way.'

Crowe walked back into the ward; Shay followed her.

'Jig?' she said, as she got to the bed.

The boy didn't stir.

'Did you see who was in the car?'

Nothing.

Crowe walked around to the other side to face him.

'We need to find them. You see them?'

Jig shook his head.

Crowe straightened up and smoothed down her clothes. She took a short intake of air, and pulled loose hair back behind her ear.

'We desperately need any description of the car or who was inside,' she said. 'Jig?'

No response.

'Detective, maybe …' Shay said gently, trying to reel Crowe back.

'I'll repeat myself: did you see who was in the car?'

'Detective,' Shay repeated, a bit firmer this time. 'You need to ask the doctors first if it's okay to talk to him. And his parents should be here as well.'

Crowe shot him a look. The look cops give when someone has crossed a line in their eyes. Shay had seen it before. She took out her pad.

'Shay, what's your full name, address and contact numbers?'

He filled her in. She took out her wallet and handed him two cards.

'Give one to Jig's parents when they stumble in here. Tell them to ring me. I know I gave you one already, but take another.'

And with that, she left.

Shay held the cards for a while, considering his options.

There was a commotion from the corridor. A woman burst through the doors. She rushed forward, arms up in the air, keys jangling from one hand, a mobile clasped in the other.

'Where's my baby?'

Nurses emerged and took either side of the woman. They held her up as her legs began to buckle.

'She was supposed to be home by half six for dinner,' the woman said, her eyes pleading at the nurses in desperation.

The door at the end of the corridor opened. Shay looked at Megan: she was a pitiful sight. The front of her pink tracksuit was blotched in blood. Brown curls hung limply by her puffy red face.

'Ma!' she roared, holding out her hands.

'Megan,' her mother cried, half running to her, 'where's Taylor?'

The girl collapsed before her mother could get to her, her fall broken by the nurses.

Shay stood there motionless as the staff carried them into a room and shut the door. But they couldn't block out the terrible sounds from within.

He turned to Jig, who was now facing him. He saw tears on the boy's face before Jig had time to turn away. Shay leaned over and placed his hand on Jig's shoulder.

'You alright?'

He expected Jig's shoulder to tense, to pull away, but it didn't. He was shaking again.

He held his shoulder for a while, swiping his hand away when the doors swung open.

'There he fucking is.'

'And what the fuck are ya doing here?' his mother said, scowling at Shay.

Jig turned onto his back. Shay could see he was putting on a brave face.

'He helped me out of the water, Ma, and came with me.'

She twisted her head dismissively.

'He okay?' Hunter asked, looking at Shay.

'He banged his head. He's in shock. He was beside the girl, a friend of his, who was shot. She's dead.'

'It was Taylor, Ma,' Jig said. 'She got shot. In the face.'

'Yer okay. That's what matters.'

Shay looked at her.

What a fucking horrible woman.

96

'Cops were here,' he said, after a moment, 'talking to Jig, and me.'

'What the fuck about?' his mother demanded.

'They wanted to know did we see the guys in the car involved in the shooting.'

'And ya let them do that?' Hunter said. 'They're not supposed to talk to a kid without their parents. That's abuse of power, that is.'

Shay felt like telling them to go fuck themselves.

'He told her that, Da,' Jig piped up.

'Anyway,' Shay said, 'Jig said nothing. Here's the garda's card.'

He handed it to Hunter, but the mother grabbed it.

'That cop bitch,' she said, flinging the card away, 'she can go fuck herself.'

Shay nodded to Jig and left. As the doors closed behind him, he heard Jig's ma.

'I don't trust that fucker,' she said. 'There's something about him.'

19

Lock Man pressed his fingernail deep into his thumb. He stood in front of the fireplace, grimacing at the sight of it. The white marble monstrosity jutted out from the chimney and invaded the sitting room. Tina had insisted on it.

He placed his beer on the gleaming mantelpiece, in between the neat line of four family photographs, equally spaced apart and each in matching Waterford glass frames. They sparkled as a slate of sunlight cut across them. Lock Man glanced at the images to his right: Las Vegas, Florida, Torremolinos.

He touched the final picture: his daughter, Shania, at a gymnastics competition, beaming at the camera.

He ran his finger along the top of the mantelpiece. Not a speck of dust. The noise from the hoover upstairs moved across the floor: from the bedrooms towards the landing. Tina had reached the stairs. She was going over the cream carpet, making her way methodically down to the porch.

Lock Man shifted his feet in his slippers and looked at his watch. Slammer should have called round by now.

Better not have been some cock-up. I'll fucking take a pliers to someone if there was.

He turned around and looked past the red leather sofas at the dining-room table. His nerves were all jangled and the whole place was pricking at him. Tina had the bottle of wine in its usual place, in the exact middle of the mahogany table, on top of a silver coaster. She insisted on having a bottle of wine there all the time. Not for actually drinking. No. It fitted in with the area, she said. Which she said was Terenure. But it wasn't. It was Walkinstown. It said it clearly on the map. No, it was Terenure, she said. When he showed her it was fucking Walkinstown, she folded and contorted the map into all sorts of shapes to disprove him.

He turned back around and reached for his beer. The fifty-inch television, bolted to the wall, was his sole stamp on the room – in the whole fucking house, the more he thought about it. She said it was too big. Vulgar, she said. Didn't stop her from watching all her fucking soaps though, he thought. He could see the red light on the box, glaring at him as it recorded.

Where the fuck is Slammer? What the fuck is going on?

He flexed his arms as the sweat massed. He reached for the glass and emptied it.

Tina and the hoover were getting closer. He could hear his wife humming each time she turned it off for a second as she pulled it down the stairs. He felt like grabbing the hoover and fucking it out the door.

He walked through the 'music room' as Tina called it, complete with a piano that no one played, into the sparkling kitchen to grab another beer. The hoover erupted in the front room. He could see his wife's eyes surveying the carpet, brandishing the hose of the hoover like a half-cocked shotgun. Adjusting the power level, she began the swoop.

Lock Man leaned back against the island, which was the size of a giant concrete slab, and pressed the cold bottle against his forehead and the back of his neck.

Slammer was never late. If it wasn't safe for him to come he'd have some kid drop by or something. Slammer knew no mobiles on a day like this, not until they knew it all went to plan. He felt in his bones it hadn't. He gulped, and grimaced as the hoover closed in on the music room. He was gearing up to let rip at Tina. He couldn't fucking think with the racket. But he stopped himself, given the row after lunch, when she did round two of cleaning. He'd told her she was a fucking cleaning freak, spending more time with that fucking hoover than at her own tanning shops. He'd told her she was 'obsessed with bugs'.

That was where he'd made the mistake.

'Yer the one who does be obsessed with bugs,' she said. 'How many sweeps have ya done, guys trampling all over the place trying to find them? Ya won't allow any cleaners in here cos ya think they'll plant bugs for the garda.'

She was right there. He did. He looked at his watch again: 8.30 p.m.

He turned on the radio.

The presenter's sombre tone sent a bolt up through him. 'Turn off that fucking hoover!' he roared in at his wife, who looked up at him, her orange face wrinkled with annoyance.

'*A shooting incident in Dublin ...*'

He pointed at the hoover. 'Off.'

The hoover whimpered to silence.

'*We are getting unconfirmed reports of multiple injuries on MacBride Road. A massive operation is underway. Gardaí are not commenting at the moment.*'

Lock Man grabbed the bottle and fucked it against the wall.

20

The groans from Shay's stiff legs eased as he ran. The garda helicopter circled overhead. Lightpoles and railings vibrated when it
hovered low; the pressure eased when it swerved away.

Shay approached MacBride Road. The area was cordoned off.
Screens and a blue tent had been erected where the garda's body
still lay. He noticed the vans of the Technical Bureau and watched
the white-clad figures. Some were crouched low, studying the area
where the bodies were found and placing numbered markers at
intervals. Others took detailed photographs to map the scene. The
movements were careful, deliberate, methodical. Their profession-
alism, to Shay, was reassuring. To him, they seemed to operate in
a slowed-down version of time. It was at odds with the hopping
and jostling of the local kids. Some of the younger ones gathered
at the flapping garda cordon, while older boys huddled in groups,
clasping cigarettes and phones. Shay spotted a few mobile TV
units parked up. Reporters traipsed around despondently, trying
to find someone willing to talk to them.

Good luck around here, he thought.

When he got home, Lisa gave him a big hug. It caught him off
guard. He melted at the warmth of her body, the closeness of her,
a sensation he really missed.

'Jesus, Shay, you okay?' she asked, looking at him, her face
etched with concern and shock. 'It's just awful.'

He stepped into the sitting room, just as the ad break finished
on the television and a news programme came on.

'This place is going to hell,' Lisa said.

The presenter was outside Garda HQ, looking grave.

'A shocking new low in gangland. A ten-year-old girl and young female garda are dead and a second garda is fighting for his life after a shooting along Dublin's Grand Canal. In a joint statement, just released, the Justice Minister and the Garda Commissioner pledged that no stone would be left unturned in bringing the perpetrators to justice.'

The presenter took a breath and deepened his tone as he continued.

'Tonight, in what has already been called a Veronica Guerin moment ...'

Lisa pointed to the mantelpiece, where Shay had left his mobile.

'Your phone rang,' she said, 'several times.'

21

Crowe pushed through a swarm of reporters, photographers and camera crews outside Canal Road Garda Station. They cast fleeting looks in her direction, their eyes betraying a desperation for some scrap of information.

She took the steps in twos, drawn by the noise and sounds coming from the incident room upstairs. There was no way she was not going to be at the heart of this investigation. She knew she should have been more professional with that boy, to get whatever information he had. But her emotions got the better of her.

Her phone vibrated as she approached the open door. She glimpsed at the mass of bodies gathered for the case conference. A third text from Tom, asking her, again, was she okay. She hadn't replied to the others. She punched in 'fine' and squeezed her way through.

The room was packed. Detectives from nearby stations and national units swelled the numbers. She scrunched her nose at the smell of sweat the further she pushed down.

Faces were hard and tense, ready for action, but, Crowe sensed, needing direction. She neared the top table, halting at the line of rank sitting there, facing her. There was Commissioner Harte in full uniform, flanked by the assistant commissioner for Dublin and the senior divisional officers. Tyrell met her eyes and gave a brief nod.

Silence descended as the Chief stood up. He shoved his thick arms out for attention.

'The commissioner will lead us in a minute's silence.'

The commissioner rose. He bowed and clasped his hands. All the officers stood. Crowe sensed sinews tighten. Background noises, of the street and the reporters milling outside, sharpened then faded. She scanned the faces of the top brass: the lined foreheads, the furrowed brows, the tight lips.

The commissioner coughed, ending the silence. Then he spoke.

'This is the worst of days,' he intoned. 'Some of us have seen these times before. For many of you, this is the first.'

Crowe swallowed the lump in her throat.

'This division has the finest of reputations when it comes to solving serious crime, including murder. I remember being here when young Garda Murphy died, ten years ago now. The gang who did that were caught, and prosecuted. I have no doubt the same will happen on this occasion. And every resource will be made available to ensure that.'

And, with that, he sat down, upright in his chair, staring forward resolutely at some invisible spot.

The senior officers sat back down too. The Chief nodded to Tyrell, who stayed on his feet, to take over. Really, on a case this big, the detective superintendent should be the senior investigating officer, Crowe thought. But that post had been vacant for months and there was no sign of any replacement. Which meant an even greater strain on the DI.

'This is what we know so far,' Tyrell said. 'At 8.02 p.m. Garda Grant and Garda Peters pulled over a car on MacBride Road, just past the junction with Canal Bridge.'

Crowe scrambled through her bag and pulled out her little notebook and pencil.

'Why, we're not sure,' Tyrell continued. 'We believe a single shot was fired. The post-mortem may tell us if that shot hit Garda Grant.'

Crowe tried to focus on writing, rather than think of Grant being shot.

'The preliminary post-mortem suggests that Garda Grant died from catastrophic head injuries suffered as the result of a moving car.'

The point of Crowe's pencil snapped with the pressure she put on it.

'Sweet Jesus,' she muttered.

Gardaí shuffled on their feet, brushing against each other. Crowe twitched at images of Grant's head under the wheel of the car.

'I know this is difficult,' Tyrell said, looking across the room, 'but you need to know. Better you hear it from me than the press. In relation to Garda Peters, he has suffered severe spinal injuries which we believe was the result of being hit by the car and driven against a metal pole. He is in a coma.'

Crowe rummaged for another pencil in her bag.

Fucking bastards.

'We do know the bullet that was fired struck a girl, Taylor Williams, in the head across the road, on the path along the canal. Those injuries were fatal. She was just ten years old.'

Crowe halted as she finished writing ten. She was so obsessed with Grant, and Peters, the full horror of the child's death hadn't registered yet. She was Jig's friend, Shay had said.

'The car sped off up MacBride Road and a 999 call came in at 8.05 p.m. We have a partial description of the suspect car. It's a BMW, 95 reg, possibly 3 series, red in colour, pretty battered, according to a witness. Sightings of three males inside: a guy with a green hoodie in the back, a big lad driving, described as youngish, and another in the front, possibly wearing a cap. I've allocated tasks from the Jobs Book for all the detectives.'

He looked down at the book on the desk.

'There are thirty-five jobs. I'll give them out at the end of the conference. Command and Control blocked off the main routes within ten minutes of the shooting being reported,' he said, looking up. 'These fuckers,' he said, sharpening his tone, 'either slipped out before then or are lying low.

'We have a blank page on suspects,' he continued. 'We have

several gangs in the general area, but it could also be an outside gang on their way to carry out a local hit. We need to tap each and every source we have. This is bad news for local gangs as it means heat on them. Tell them if they don't cooperate on this one, we will bring them down. I want names of suspects nominated for tomorrow's conference.'

Crowe liked keeping her notes clean, but struggled at the speed Tyrell was speaking.

'Anyone not cooperating, tell them you'll be bringing them down to the station for withholding information, through the front door, past all the cameras. That might concentrate their minds. Dust off what charges they have coming to them and tell them we'll be going hard on them in court. Intelligence will work the covert informants. We have colleagues from the national units here to assist us. Security are doing checkpoints and patrols. A lot of people we're looking for will have gone to ground. We need to dig them out.'

Tyrell sat back down. There was a collective exhaling of breath. People wanted to get their job and go to work. The Chief stood up and stretched his arms out again, as if to gather his gardaí in and calm the restlessness.

'Garda Grant was special,' the Chief said, letting the words penetrate. 'Those of us who worked here know that.' He nodded solemnly as he said the words. 'She was a bundle of positivity. Her loss will be great.'

Emotions welled up inside Crowe. The fact it was the Chief, the rock of authority in the station, the father figure, saying these words hammered it home. She pulled out a tissue and held it to her eyes.

'Our thoughts are with Garda Peters and we desperately hope for the best. And while they are our colleagues, our friends, we must also remember a child has been murdered. A girl just out walking her dogs, her life brutally robbed from her.'

The Chief heaved a long breath.

'There will be time to mourn the deaths and unburden ourselves,' he said, his voice strengthening, 'but now is not the time. Now is the time to focus on the job at hand. And to do that, we must set our personal feelings and emotions aside.'

Adrenaline surged through Crowe.

'You all know how important the initial hours and days are,' he continued. 'There are no overtime restrictions. We will work round the clock.'

Crowe glanced at the commissioner. His tight face twitched.

'We need information, accurate information quickly on the bastards who did this,' the Chief said. 'But I need your brains as well as your balls. No point running out there and kicking seven shades of shite out of every scrote on the street.'

He paused, his cheeks turning ruddy. 'I do not want to be wasting time responding to allegations of police brutality.' He spat out the last word as if it was poison. He looked around the room. 'Let's get to work.'

And with those final words, the mood changed. Faces sharpened with determination and purpose.

Crowe put her notepad and pencil into her bag. She stepped over to Tyrell, his hands spread across the big register on the table. Each job was numbered on its own page, with a copy of each page. Tyrell pulled out her copy. She nearly dropped it when she read the job 'Harvest CCTV' with her name on it and date.

'You must be,' she said, leaning in closer to Tyrell, 'joking.'

She glanced furtively around in case anyone heard. Tyrell spoke as he handed out the other jobs, his eyes on his task.

'This is too close for you, Crowe,' he said, quietly. 'There are detectives here who don't know Grant, or Peters. They will handle the scrotes, the raids. Some of it may be a little unpleasant.'

That felt like a slap in the face.

What, I can't handle it? Fuck you.

She felt her neck grow warm.

'I need the best person I have on cameras,' Tyrell added. 'You don't cut corners. You have a sharp eye and a good instinct on what to follow up. I can trust you on this.' He looked at her. 'And that car could be key.'

But Crowe wanted to be in on the action.

'What about Jig, his mother, Shay and Father Keogh?' she pleaded. 'I have an in with them.'

But she knew the DI had made up his mind.

'You have five uniforms to help you,' Tyrell said. 'Find something.'

22

A huge green horse passed by, its belly shaped like an arc. His head was all swollen and padded, like it was made of hard foam. Jig knew it was weird. The horse bowed its head and exhaled long tubes of steam from its nostrils. A rider, wearing a red racing hat, stooped forward. The horse began to limp. The rider turned towards Jig, but all Jig could see were rows of square white teeth. The horse reared up and kicked out its front legs. The rider hit him hard with a big whip. The more Jig looked at it the more it looked like a long gun. The rider's teeth ground with each whipping. Something was pulling Jig away. He could see the rider's face now. It was Maggot. Then there was a bang. And an image of Taylor's mangled face exploded in his mind.

Jig jumped up out of bed and let out a roar. He punched his duvet to get rid of the images and smells assailing him: the shattered bones of Taylor's face and the stink of the burning horse.

He lay back on the bed, his eyes pulled right back as the event came at him. One second he was cycling beside Taylor, then went past her. The next second there was a bang and he fell off, clattering his head. When he got up out of the water, she was in a heap on the path, the bottom of her face cut away. Megan was screaming; the dogs were going mad. He didn't remember Shay or getting out of the water.

He stared at the damp blotches on the ceiling until the sound of the television from the kitchen roused him to get out of bed.

He rooted around for his school uniform. His trousers were behind the door. The shirt was on the bathroom floor.

He wanted to go for a dump but there was no loo roll.

He couldn't find his school jumper and slumped down the stairs. He found one shoe in the hall and the other under the sofa in the front room.

Opening the door to the kitchen, he adjusted his eyes to the harsh light and his ears to the booming TV.

'After the break – how to bake a coconut meringue. And later, some DIY super-luxe pampering.'

Bowie bounded over to him. His ma was at the kitchen table, holding his baby sister Leanne in one hand and a bottle in her gob. A fag smouldered on a plate. His da sat on the near side, with his back to him.

'That shirt's manky,' his ma said.

'Where's the other one?' Jig asked.

She squirmed her face: 'Up me hole. I don't know.'

'And me jumper?'

'Wherever ya fucking left it,' she snapped.

'Is there anything to eat?' he asked, giving his da a quick check over his shoulder.

'Look,' she said, throwing a bread pan across the table.

Jig picked it up and went over to the counter. He grabbed butter from the fridge. Bowie shadowed him. Jig tried to spread the butter on the bread.

'It's too hard,' he muttered, as the thin bread ripped apart.

'Fuck it,' he said, throwing the knife into the sink.

His head hopped from the smack.

'Ow, ya bastard.'

'Watch that mouth, boy,' his da shouted, an inch away from his face. He could feel his short breaths against the side of his head. He braced for more. 'And stop moaning like a little girl.'

Jig ran for the front door, holding his head.

He slammed it shut, stood outside and kicked the bins. He could feel the heat from his ear. Bowie barked and scratched behind the door. Jig grabbed a hammer from the railing and swiped at anything and nothing.

'Fucking bastard.'

He smacked the bin. Then he took on the front wall. Chips of it flaked and flew.

I'd love to drive this into his rotten head.

'Bastard,' he shouted. 'Prick. Bastard!'

His ear was still stinging and he could feel his face was all puffy. He swung in the air. He missed the wall and hit himself.

'Ah, me fucking knee.'

He dropped the hammer and hopped around with the pain. Tears rolled down his cheeks.

His da and ma hadn't even asked him how he was since they got back from the hospital. All they seemed to talk about was Maggot, and where the fuck he was, snapping at each other.

When Jig looked up, a dad was pushing a bike up the road. He was chatting to his son, who was balanced on the saddle, all chuffed looking.

Jig blinked and twitched at the memories from years back.

'Don't just stare at it, get up on the fucking thing,' his da shouted, lifting him up and banging him down hard on the seat. 'Hold the handlebars. Put yer feet on the pedals. Yeah, the fucking pedals.'

The saddle was too high and Jig couldn't push the pedals all the way round. His feet slipped off.

'Don't slip. Get up. Push. Steer.'

But he couldn't.

'Fucking steer,' his da roared, clipping him across the head.

Jig held his head and shouted back, 'I can't push the pedal all the way.'

He could see people on the paths either side of the canal glancing in their direction. His feet slipped off again.

'Jaysus, ya on the gargle last night or what? Stop fucking slipping.'

His da slapped him, harder this time, around his ear. His ear throbbed and he started to cry.

'Da, that hurt.'

'Ah, stop yer sobbing and yer moaning.'

A man with a dog approached them.

'Story, Hunter. Out with the little fella?'

'Yeah.'

'What ya doing, training him for the Olympics?'

'Fucking Special Olympics more like.'

They both laughed.

'I'm heading down to the Docker for a few scoops after I bring the dog back, if yer interested?' the man said.

'I'll be fucking gagging after this. See ya down there.'

The man headed off, laughing to himself.

'Da, why youse laughing at me?'

'Cos yer a joke. An embarrassment. Fucking six today and ya can't ride a bleeding bike.'

'I'm five, Da.'

'Is that fucking right? Well, I'll count to five and if yer still acting the bollix I'm heading to the Docker.'

Jig wiped sweat from his forehead. He grabbed the handlebars, but his grip was greasy now.

His da was counting.

'One.'

Jig put his feet on the pedals.

'Two.'

His legs shook as he tried to push them.

'Three.'

His feet slipped.

'Four.'

He scraped his shins against the pedals.

'Five.'

Terrified, Jig looked over his shoulder.

His da straightened up and glared down at him. He swung his arm right back and smacked him so hard he flew clean off the saddle.

He landed face down on the path, whacking his nose and mouth off the rough tarmac. He roared at the pain and shock.

Tears blurred the shape of his da storming off.

The rev of a car roused him; the memory drifted away. He felt himself shaking where he stood.

He heard a noise at the door and jerked. Tensing, he darted a look over his shoulders, but it was Bowie whining inside.

His ear throbbed afresh. Jig clenched his teeth, picked up the hammer and attacked the wall.

23

The headlines screamed out from the news stand.

Canal Carnage, roared a tabloid. Underneath were three decks of large photos. Taylor Williams, 10, holding a camogie stick. Ciara Grant, 22, smiling, with striking blonde hair, pictured at her graduation. Garda Sean Peters, 23, dressed in the Galway county jersey.

Gutted Mum Says Killers Should Hang, trumped another tabloid. It carried a photo of Taylor's shattered mum, being held up by family members outside the hospital the previous night. *Declare War Now*, hollered another red-top.

Shay surveyed them quietly, before crossing to an anonymous office block. A small sign read CBLCS, College of Business, Language and Computer Studies. He punched a code to open the set of doors and tackled the stairs to the fourth floor, the headlines jumbling around in his brain.

He stood at the door and knocked. Feet shuffled from behind. The door clicked and swung back.

Shay nodded to Hall and stepped in.

His handler locked the door behind him.

'Shay,' Hall said, gesturing for him to sit down as he took the other side of the desk. 'There's a meeting at twelve with Number One, so let's get to it.'

Shay flexed his fist.

'Tell me more about Jig,' Hall said, leaning back on his chair.

'It's pretty much all in my reports,' Shay said.

'I want to get more of a feel – to see if there is leverage there,' Hall continued. 'You have built up,' he paused, 'a relationship with the boy. I see you accompanied him to the hospital yesterday. You stayed with him, even when questioned.'

Shay nodded, noting Hall's usual knowledge of his movements.

'What I want to know is: can he be used somehow to prise open the Canal Gang? Every single detective in the city wants to be in on this, squeezing these fuckers. But you are in situ, close to the players. You're a member of the community. A respected one even.'

Shay noticed the curl of Hall's mouth as he said the final words.

'No one is going to talk to the guards,' Hall went on. 'Already, no one is talking. Can you believe it? I see from the reports that you are the only one who has actually given any decent witness info. The rest have crawled back under their rocks.'

Hall always had a way with words, Shay thought.

'When I look at Number One today, Shay, I want to tell him that our units have an inside track here.'

'I want to get my family out.'

Shay immediately berated himself for blurting it out.

Hall looked at him as if he had just stood up and pissed against the desk. Hall creased back his hair and composed himself.

'You want what?'

'We're in that hole for years,' Shay said. 'My kids are growing up in that place. My wife's had enough. We can't see a way out. For what?'

He said that last bit, again without meaning to.

Hall's face darkened, but he kept his voice controlled.

'Did you say, for what?' Hall said, standing up and turning to face the window.

Shay braced himself.

'We threw you a lifeline, Shay. That's what.'

Shay's stomach tensed.

'You faced a criminal prosecution for assault, causing harm if the investigators got our intel reports on you. A stretch in prison. As a garda. You wouldn't have lasted long.' Hall paused, glancing back at him. 'Particularly with those rugged good looks of yours,' he said, with a smirk.

Hall turned back to face the window. 'That's unless one of those McCabes got to you first and sliced you in half with a fucking scythe. This,' Hall said, turning around again and pointing downwards, 'was your ... only ... fucking ... option.'

Shay watched Hall pull his neck back, pat down his silk blue tie and survey the damage.

You are a complete cunt. You have my balls in a vice-grip. You know it. I know it.

'Garda Grant is dead,' Hall said. 'Garda Peters is in a coma with a suspected severed spine. Both in their early twenties. Two of our own, Shay.'

Shay looked up when he heard the words 'our own'.

'Not to mention that little girl,' Hall added, 'what's her name ...'

'Taylor,' Shay said. 'Taylor Williams.'

'You know that Grant was like a tonic in the station,' Hall said. 'Full of life. Great craic. Members loved her. The young Peters lad, intercounty footballer, decent fella by all accounts. Colleagues are devastated. They are fucking gunning for blood.' He stopped for a moment and touched his neck. 'I don't have to tell you, Shay, what can happen to good guards when they are steaming for revenge.'

Hall let the warm knife cut deep. Shay felt it open up his chest.

'We have a national crisis here,' Hall said. 'Gangs have kicked us in the balls and given society the finger. The government is blowing spit and fury. The media is crying war. The minister has summoned Number One today. He, in turn, is shouting down the phone at us. The commissioner will be hopping at the meeting if we are not on top of this.'

Shay watched Hall sit down, with what looked like a satisfied face.

He recalled when Hall recruited him into Intelligence, straight from Garda College. He left Templemore before everyone else. His classmates thought he just dropped out. He never wore a uniform. Apart from some officers in Intelligence, no one ever knew he was a garda.

He recalled how much he loved working for the Intelligence and Security Division. Until it all went pear-shaped.

Hall saved him, or snared him. He wasn't sure which.

Hall had been his handler since he resigned. He was his only direct connection with the force. He knew DI Slavin was part of the set-up and that Hall answered to ISD boss Deputy Commissioner Nessan. But he had no idea if either of those two men knew he performed this role or that he was doing it to get back into the force. All it would take would be for Hall to cut the rope and he would be cast adrift. No way back then.

'Shay, you listening?'

He nodded.

'I was looking through your reports,' Hall said. 'Your reports are good, thorough. Details of gang members, associates, addresses, car regs, girlfriends, ex-girlfriends, where they drink, where they bet, their movements, any ailments or disabilities they have, a couple of mobile numbers, dealing locations, street dealers, rows, rivals, addicts. Deep intel we've never had before. Years of it. Every cough and splutter.'

Shay thought how he should have felt pride in his work, but he couldn't shake off a feeling they had him on a spinning wheel.

'When I set up this little unit,' Hall said, leaning back in his chair and indulging himself, 'I knew it was a long haul operation. It was going to work differently to our undercover unit. They can operate for short bursts. But you and other community intelligence sources have to be bedded in; left to take root in local areas. I've had to explain to those above me that the investment would take time to show a return. Not an easy sell, even in the Celtic Tiger years. But I explained that the relationships, the connections you build are priceless, nothing a standard UC can do, certainly over the long term. And, in time, with the right work, you can place yourself within the circles of a crew, like that of the Canal Gang. That work can take years to bear fruit. I understand you want your life back, Shay. I do. You want your family – your kids – to have as good a life as possible. Yes?'

Shay twisted inside at the patronising tone of Hall's lecture.

'I want my family out,' Shay said, 'and I want to be back in the force. Official. My past . . . forgotten. A fresh start.'

Hall tapped his fingers on the table, as if doing a quick calculation.

'You deliver the goods here, on this one,' he said, leaning forward, 'and I'll make the recommendation myself to DC Nessan that you are allowed to rejoin the force. Fair enough?'

Shay felt lighter. Relief poured through his blood, eased out the knots in his muscles. It was the closest yet he'd ever got to something like a commitment.

'We know from your reports,' Hall said, 'that Ghost and his associates recruit armies of these little shits through the football club and from the street to do their dirty work.'

There was a venom in the way Hall described them as little shits that Shay didn't like, but he shrugged it away.

'We know Ghost works for Lock Man. But Lock Man's a clever fucker. That's why he's survived when a lot of other gangs have imploded or scattered. This is our opportunity to crush this gang once and for all.'

Shay wasn't clear where this was going.

'What's the connection between these murders and Ghost?' he asked. 'Why are you sure it's them?'

'We can't be sure,' Hall said, 'but I have a strong suspicion it is. We might know a bit more at the meeting later. But every unit will want to keep as much as they can to themselves. Particularly us. Few in the organisation even know about this little detail, let alone what we do.'

'Has the car been found?' Shay asked.

'No,' Hall said. 'Speaking of which, I saw what you told that female detective. You remember anything more about the three scrotes in the car?'

'I didn't get a good enough look,' Shay said, 'but I did think for a second there was something about one of them, but I don't know for sure.'

He felt Hall's eyes studying him.

'Keep digging around that brain of yours,' Hall said, standing up. 'If it turns out to be the Canal Gang, this is a mammoth fuck up for them – for a gang so, untouchable, as they like to consider themselves. They will not want this heat. They will erase any links between them and this. It wouldn't surprise me if the three scumbags in that car have been disappeared.'

'Is the government giving us the resources on this?' Shay asked. He was buzzing now, being at the heart of a covert garda operation into the murder. He bristled with adrenaline. It was the sense of purpose he loved, that he longed for.

'The minister is making all the right noises,' Hall said, dismissively. 'It will last three weeks, a month maybe, possibly longer if the commissioner bangs the table enough. But after that, there'll be no more money for overtime or surveillance. The media will drift away from this when the next financial drama comes along. This will take longer to crack. That's why we need deep assets like you.'

Shay felt more of a connection now with Hall.

Maybe he's not as bad a fucker as I make him out to be.

He watched Hall take something out of his pocket – a ziplock bag. There was a phone inside.

'We'll be having more regular contact from now on,' Hall said. 'Use this phone to ring me.' He pushed a sheet towards him. 'Ring this number every day to give me an update, say at 10 a.m. But don't write the number down and delete the call history every time you dial. And keep the phone somewhere offside. Keep your other phone on you, but don't ring me on it.'

Shay memorised the number and placed the bag in his pocket.

'We'll still meet here every Monday, as usual. And, another thing,' he said, his tone sharpening.

Shay knew he wasn't going to like this.

'We will need you to get into situations … where you can place surveillance devices.'

24

Lock Man shifted his arse on the wooden bench. The side of his temple pulsed the more he ate through his thoughts. He had built up his life with great care over the years. He had put distance between himself and the daily operation of his little empire. People were in place to do the heavy lifting, to take the strain.

He slapped his hand against his forehead and wiped a film of sweat away. He tried to picture which of the fucking muppets had managed to shoot dead a garda and a little girl, and land another garda in a coma.

The frosted glass door swung back. In stepped Slammer. The bench creaked as he sat. The heavy squint in Slammer's eyes meant Lock Man could never read much from them. He studied the crevices and lumps in the man's big head. He knew him long enough to sense he was feeling the strain from the heavy lifting.

'Talk,' Lock Man said, as calmly as he could.

'Jobs, Shop and Maggot were pulled over.'

'Maggot. What the fuck was that headbanger doing there?' Lock Man uttered, the pieces of the how-the-fuck jigsaw rapidly assembling in his brain. 'Bet ya that fucking prick caused this.'

Slammer nodded. 'Shop said he let him come along only because he had been wrecking his head to go.'

'Stupid cunt,' Lock Man said. 'Anyways, what the fuck happened?'

'Shop said this copper was nosy, asking loads of questions, but he and Jobs reckoned she would have left them go. But Maggot got itchy and pulled a gun, one he had on him.'

Lock Man shook his head and cursed the new generation of gobshite gangsters.

'Shop said he had the car in gear when he knocked off the engine – cos the copper had told him to – and the car jumped. That's when the shot went off.'

'Fucking abortion this,' Lock Man said, the pulsing in his head going techno. 'How did they get out?'

'In the artic we had on standby. Gave instructions to Jobs by text. The Romanian lads had the ramps out and they drove right up into the container. They were gone in minutes.'

'Dosser's Field?'

Slammer nodded. 'I was there, waiting for them. On my way down I texted Dosser to go to work.'

'Talk me through how ya cleaned up.'

Lock Man knew the wiser thing might be ignorance on his part, to leave it to Slammer. But he needed to know everything. His brain wouldn't give him rest until he digested every detail and was satisfied of a clean repair job.

'The truck came and Shop reversed the car down the ramps onto some industrial sheeting Dosser put out. I squared with the Romanians and told them to head for the border and the ferry to Scotland. The lads fell out of the car, gasping with the heat and dehydration and all. I had my hands by my side, a T-shirt on, to let them think I didn't have a piece. I had me nephew up on the balcony on the second floor. He took Maggot and Jobs out as they were half-sprawled on the sheeting. I went over to Shop, who was shaking like a lump of jelly. He told me what happened. I got Shop to get the mobiles off the two lads, Maggot's Glock, and his own mobile and put them into a bag. They've been smashed up and scattered. I had Shop put the two lads back in the car.'

Lock Man smiled. Even though this was a shitstorm, he knew Slammer had taken care of this, down to a T.

'I got Shop to take the firepower out of the boot.'

Good man. I don't want to be losing that arsenal, after forking out for it.

'Disposal?'

'I told Shop to ease the car out and head for the JCB. I walked beside the car all the way. The spot is by the woods, where no one can see. He pulled up by the section Dosser had just finished excavating. I plugged Shop as he sat in the car.'

Lock Man sniffed, impressed as fuck.

'The JCB tipped the car in and banged it down flat. And filled in the soil.'

Slammer ended his story.

No sign of Slammer playing the fucking hero, thought Lock Man. Just did what he's an expert at.

'Slam, if I had more of youse, I wouldn't need an army of muppets.'

Slammer tilted his head in acknowledgement. 'Dosser even sprayed grass seed over the patch. It being the growing season and all.'

At that, Slammer allowed himself a rare smile.

Lock Man couldn't help but laugh. But the paranoia kept scratching the side of his head.

'Any CCTV that could have picked up the artic at the shops?'

'No,' Slammer said. 'I done a scour of that area day before. It was clear.'

'That leaves any fucking camera footage of the car and any eyewitnesses.'

'If they can ID one of the lads, they'll know they're ours, yeah, but they won't find them or the Glock or the phone now, so they won't have evidence linking this to us.'

Lock Man gave his belly a slap, the sweat spitting out in an arc. The techno in his head had eased to a dull throb. 'Right, we need to be extra fucking careful. They'll be watching us and pulling us over wherever we go. Give them nothing to hang on us. So tell Ghost to lay off resupplying the crews and put Cracko on a tight lead. We have to expect that the Provos will seek advantage in this, but we'll have to wait till things die down. In the meanwhile, we stay visible, act as normal. Don't give the filth any reason to suspect we're behind this.'

He looked at Slammer and flung another layer of sweat off his forehead.

'We've been around long enough, Slam, to know the avalanche of shit this will mean if they get the slightest bit of evidence linking us to it. The filth will make it their life mission to nail us, now or in the future. That Tyrell fucker, for one, won't let this go. He'll be like a dog digging for a bone. And now he has his little bitch too.'

25

Shay left through the back of the building and took a moment at the top of the steps. He needed a strong coffee. With sugar.

He walked down an alleyway, one that led through a car park and onto the street. There was an Insomnia on the corner.

If I do deliver on this, I'll be back in – Hall said as much – and Lisa and the kids will get out.

But part of him knew he couldn't trust Hall.

'Americano and a Danish,' he said to the assistant.

He took a stool at the window. He placed his coffee and plate on the counter and watched the traffic and the pedestrians stream by.

He knew Hall controlled his future, no matter what way he cut it. He took a chunk of the Danish and slurped down a mouthful of the steaming coffee, nearly burning his throat. He exhaled in satisfaction. Memories of Hall popped into his head, from a few years ago, after the assault, when he was working in Cork and Waterford. Hall had met him one bracing morning along the strand in Tramore.

'You have one option,' Hall had told him. 'You resign from the force. You leave all this to quieten down. You hope you haven't been spotted and that no complaint is made against you – that you do not become a suspect. After a couple of years you should be able to get back in. In the meantime you can continue to work for us, as a community intelligence source.'

'This a joke?'

'No joke. You remember a light flashing at you? Just as you were about to drop a block on that scrote's head? That was a surveillance team we had on the McCabes. They couldn't ID you for certain as you were well covered and it was dark, but we know it was you. You were seen shadowing the scrote the weeks beforehand.'

Shay remembered the flashing light. He thought he had planned it all perfectly. He'd conducted surveillance on Jamie McCabe, established his movements at night and when he might be on his own.

Then one night he jumped Jamie from behind, on a quiet road, and forced him onto the ground. He kneeled onto his shoulder and rained down blows on the back of his head. His fists felt like they were splitting with the impact, but he kept slamming him, left and right. Jamie's teeth grated on the rough tarmac. Before he knew it, he was dragging over a big slab of rock lying against a wall. That he hadn't planned, but a dark rage had consumed him. He lifted the block. That was when the light flashed in the distance, small, but bright like a torch. He couldn't tell where it came from. He threw the slab to one side and ran.

But he'd kept to his plan. He got to the old factory, pretty sure no one had followed him. He found the bag where he had left it and emptied the clothes out. He pulled the double layer of latex gloves off his hands, caked in blood and hair, biting his lips at the pain from his fists. He stripped completely, including the snood, hoodie and cap, and dumped everything into the bag.

He rubbed himself down with a towel, put that in the bag too. He threw on another set of clothes. He poured accelerant on the bag and set it alight. He got to the B&B about half an hour later – again checking for anyone tailing – and went up to his room. He shed that set of clothes and put them into another bag. He had a long shower, washed his hair and face and hands over and over. He scrubbed the inside of the shower with a brush and Dettol and steaming water.

He put on a new set of clothes and took everything in his bag. No one saw him leave. He had already made sure there were no cameras in the B&B and, as far as he could see, on the road outside. He dumped the bag in a bin put out for collection the next morning.

He got home about an hour later, taking a complicated route by foot. Lisa was still sound asleep. He'd seen her taking a sleeping tablet before he left, on top of the anti-anxiety medication. He soaked his fists in ice bags for hours. He covered them with antiseptic cream and collapsed into bed, and a fierce sleep.

A bang on the café window pulled Shay from his thoughts. Two drunks were arguing and pushing each other, thumping against the pane. Shay realised he was still holding the coffee cup in his hand. He took a sip. It was lukewarm.

He rose suddenly and swayed, feeling dizzy. The tinnitus in his ear rang clear as a whistle. Then he dropped.

'Sir, you okay? Sir?'

Shay felt something cold and damp against his head and cheeks. He opened his eyes and saw a cloth over his forehead. The assistant looked at him, concerned. He dragged himself up, feeling weak and embarrassed.

'You okay?' the assistant asked.

'Yeah. Did I faint?'

'You fell on floor hard. Lucky you not bang head.'

Shay took the cup of water she offered, nodding in thanks. His fist throbbed. His knuckles resisted when he flexed them. He stood there for a moment, pressing his left arm against a counter. He needed fresh air.

As he left, a red BMW cruised past, not unlike the one used by the shooters at the canal. What was it about the fella in the back of that car, he asked himself again, knowing there was something. Then it hit him.

It was a green hoodie, but it had dark green stripes along the shoulders and arms. The same kind of hoodie he often saw Maggot wearing.

26

Tyrell took his mints out his jacket pocket as he pulled up outside Harcourt Square. It was 11.30 a.m. and he was already half way through a packet.

He'd arrived at the Garda Dublin HQ early to organise his thoughts. They'd all been working straight through the night. But they hadn't found the car. And they had limited descriptions on the culprits.

He opened his car door, stepping over a splatter of vomit. Bottles and shattered glass lay strewn along the footpath, the usual morning debris from the clubs dotted along Harcourt Street. He walked along the perimeter wall of the police complex, his nostrils assailed by the stench of piss. Combined with a lack of sleep and of appetite, he felt a bit weak. A Luas click-clacked beside him as it curved down towards St Stephen's Green.

Admitted into the conference room, he circled the massive thirty-foot table. Three glasses of water were positioned on one side and some ten glasses on the other. As he came to the far side, he peered out through the tall sash windows onto the unkempt courtyard, absently studying the grim fountain that never seemed to function.

He turned to noises from the direction of the door. In strode the Chief, his hat under his arm. His suit looked freshly dry cleaned and pressed.

'Anything more?' the Chief said.

'No update,' Tyrell replied, noticing the cluster of red veins that always sprouted on the Chief's cheeks when he was anxious.

'I'll give an intro and you'll take over,' the Chief said.

He pulled back the chairs and placed his heavy frame down. The Chief put his hat in front of him, adjusting its position slightly. Tyrell took his place beside him and waited, disturbed only by the metallic twang of the trams.

As the minutes passed, other senior officers streamed in. The chiefs and supers of the various specialist crime bureaus: organised crime, drugs and a couple from Intelligence and Security. They greeted them with nods and hellos, taking positions either side of them.

Tyrell eyed Detective Superintendent Hall. He tried to recall exactly what he did in the shadows. He knew he was a leading light in the revamped intelligence structure that was set up a number of years ago. A judicial tribunal had called for an overhaul in the garda structures in the area to separate intelligence and security from operational policing. The result was a new expanded section, the Intelligence and Security Division. It brought together various intelligence sections – both criminal intelligence and subversive intelligence – and all the security, counter-terrorism, surveillance, undercover and covert units, as well as policy and analysis units and IT under its command. ISD was no longer headed by an assistant commissioner, but a deputy commissioner, next rung down from commissioner and officially, if not traditionally, equal to the rank of deputy commissioner operations.

Commissioner Harte swept in, rousing Tyrell from his thoughts. He checked his watch. Bang on midday. Accompanying him were Deputy Commissioner Ops Archibald Brady and Deputy Commissioner Intelligence Raymond Nessan. Everyone else stood up as the force's top three officers positioned themselves at the other side of the table and took off their hats.

'Gentlemen,' Commissioner Harte said dramatically, taking his seat, the rest following suit. He looked directly across at the Chief.

'Commissioner,' the Chief said, with a cough. 'Firstly, the situation with Garda Peters is unchanged. He is in a coma. His spine is severed and the injuries to his brain remain the same.'

The commissioner nodded. Tyrell noticed others either dropping their heads or adjusting themselves in their seats. Except for Hall, who remained impassive.

'I spoke with the families of Garda Grant and the little girl, Taylor Williams, last night, as well as Peters' parents,' the Chief went on.

The commissioner closed his eyes slowly and opened them again.

Then the Chief filled everyone in on the details of the shooting. Tyrell kept his eyes on the commissioner. Number One was nearing retirement, he mused, in less than a year. The rumour was he wanted an extension. And was likely to get it. Apart from the Smyth Tribunal report into Garda intelligence, he had a fairly unblemished record. Harte got good press in media circles and was seen as the good guy, against government efforts to push home austerity plans.

'The early indications from the Technical Bureau and the State pathologist are that, from where the bodies were found and the tyre marks, Garda Grant was at the driver's side. Garda Peters was at the front of the vehicle. Garda Grant suffered catastrophic head injuries. The PM this morning confirmed her injuries were from the wheel of the car.'

The Chief stopped to take some water. The top button of his shirt was too tight, Tyrell noticed; it dug into his neck, adding to the strain in his face, already clear from the thick bags under his eyes.

'One shot was fired from a 9mm Glock,' the Chief continued. 'The shot may have glanced the side of Garda Grant's head, then travelled across the road and hit the girl in the face.'

Tyrell looked around and noticed faces reacting in some way. Again, apart from Hall.

'The Technical Bureau believe the car hit Garda Peters and rammed him against a metal pole inflicting traumatic injuries to his back. As the car reversed, he fell, hitting his head against the ground.

'Detective Inspector Tyrell will fill you in on the investigation,' the Chief said, sitting down, the chair groaning with the strain.

Tyrell was startled at the sudden announcement, but didn't show it. He was well prepared.

'According to witnesses the suspects were in a red BMW, 3 series, 95 reg. There are three suspects, with partial descriptions. We have no pictures of the actual shooting from cameras. As I said, we have only partial descriptions of the shooters.'

He could see the commissioner's eyes narrow as he spoke and could sense his shoulders tensing. But he kept his composure.

'We got some description on the car, which one of our teams is tracking from Phoenix Park, where it was captured on camera beforehand. We got a partial reg. We suspect the registration is cloned. So, unless we get an actual hold of the car, we can't trace its owners or where or when it was stolen. We are trying to follow the car since the shooting. One 9mm shell was found at the scene. The firearm hadn't been fired before and we haven't located it yet. We're getting limited assistance from witnesses, so far.'

Tyrell stopped, and judging by the looks from across the table, a bit too abruptly. He sat down.

'I see,' the commissioner said, drumming his fingers on the table. 'So, who do you think is behind this?'

The question shouldn't have caught Tyrell off guard, but he took a second to compose himself.

'Too early to say, sir.'

He immediately realised it was not the answer the boss wanted. He continued. 'If we can get a better description of the suspects in the car, or if the car turns up or the gun –'

'A lot of ifs there, detective,' the commissioner interrupted. Tyrell was getting the heat. He noticed the Chief bow his head.

'Given where this happened, it's possible that it was one of the local gangs,' Tyrell said. 'However, it could have been a hit team from elsewhere. We are trying to locate all known gang members, to see who is turning up and, more importantly, who is not. That might give us a lead. We are examining what threats are out there against gang members. We have teams turning over every scrote in the area. Our colleagues in Intelligence,' he said, glancing briefly at Nessan, who returned him a blank face, 'are examining phone traffic in the area at the time and checking their own, em, sources.'

The commissioner turned to Nessan, who nodded to Hall.

Tyrell leaned forward and watched Hall, who remained bolt upright. He looked impressive in a dark grey suit and blue tie.

'Phone taps are showing up some noise, commissioner, but very little of any use, so far. We are also examining what calls or texts were made in that area at that time through mast dumping. We are monitoring the movement of known mobiles at the time.'

Hall paused briefly, for effect, it seemed to Tyrell.

'We have some assets in the area and, as we speak, we are gathering information from them. This could yield results.'

Tyrell shot a look at the Chief, who pulled at the collar of his shirt. Tyrell glared back at Hall.

'Our intel would suggest,' Hall said in a measured voice, 'that a criminal network run by Ghost and Cracko is worth examining. The Canal Gang as they are known, or *click*, as they like to call themselves.' He looked towards Tyrell and nodded. 'I'm sure the investigation team are already on to them. We are examining further use and deployment of our assets.'

Hall tilted his chin, signalling an end to his contribution, and patted down his tie. The commissioner's complexion seemed to lighten a bit.

'I would suggest, Detective Inspector Tyrell, you bring yourself up to speed with what ISD has.'

Tyrell couldn't avert his gaze much, but spotted Nessan eyeing Hall, a satisfied look on his face.

'We are not going to allow whoever did this to get away with it, nor the gang bosses they work for,' the commissioner said. 'No fucking way. Not on my watch. I want to see suspects nominated for our next meeting. And I want to know how we are going to nail them.'

He paused as he placed his hands on his hat. 'I have to meet the Justice Minister now. He intends to speak to the media at the Department and wants me at his side. Then I'm travelling to meet the parents of that Williams girl and Garda Ciara Grant, and will then go to the hospital to see the family of Garda Peters. There will be a full State funeral for Garda Grant later in the week, once the pathologist is finished and the family confirm their intentions. I expect to see doors kicked in soon after that.'

He rose, setting off a ripple effect around the table.

As soon as the three commissioners left, the Chief walked over to Hall, followed by Tyrell. Hall could see them coming, but showed no anxiety.

'Any particular reason you didn't tell us last night what you had?' the Chief said, his belly almost touching off Hall he stood so close.

Hall smiled at him. 'Our information has only crystallised in the last couple of hours. This was our first opportunity.'

'You could have told us before the meeting, not in front of Number One,' Tyrell said.

Hall looked at him. 'Don't worry about how you look. As I said, this was our first opportunity. I've asked the National Criminal Intelligence Unit to supply you with any relevant information.'

'What about these assets?' Tyrell asked, knowing he wasn't going to get an answer. 'Crims or undercover or what?'

'In my area, the slightest bit of information one way or the other could be misinterpreted,' Hall said, doing up the button of his jacket. 'Better there is complete separation between intelligence and investigation. Leave us to gather the intel and let you get on with your job, which is to investigate.'

Hall walked leisurely to the door.

Tyrell disliked him even more now. Hall had a reputation. For arrogance, deviousness, even ruthlessness. But he was also smart.

27

Shay summoned his courage as he opened the door and peered into the sitting room. Lisa walked into view. She had a yellow glove on one hand, a second was draped over her other arm. Her hair was wet and sweaty.

She must have been cleaning all morning, he thought.

'Well?' she asked.

He took a breath. Best not exaggerate things, he told himself. But the desperate look on her face unbalanced him.

'We could be on the way out of here,' he said.

'What?' she said, the tension in her face easing. 'You mean it?'

He smiled tentatively and headed for the kitchen.

What the fuck did I say that for?

Turning on the radio, he awaited the questions.

'How will we be out of here?' Lisa asked, a slight doubt in her voice.

I need to recover this.

'I do my job on this one and they'll recommend that I get back in, with a clean slate, and us out of here.'

He opened the fridge, took out the water container and poured himself a glass.

'What do you have to do?'

'You know I can't say too much, Lisa. There's a national crisis here. Those guards were just in their twenties. And that little girl.'

Lisa dropped her eyes.

'I know,' she said, looking at a photograph of their children on a kitchen shelf. 'The parents of that poor girl.'

'Lisa. This is my chance, our chance.'

She placed the loose glove on the table and reached out a hand, holding Shay's arm softly. He relaxed.

At least we're talking, not shouting.

'The kids heard on the radio about a girl being shot dead,' Lisa said. 'Charlie's still too young, but Molly was all upset, asking why someone would shoot a child. How do you explain to a child why a child has been shot?'

Shay nodded, sensing the anger rising in Lisa.

'The people behind it are scum,' she said. 'But we know that. We live here.'

Shay rubbed his arm. It was still sore from the fall.

'You trust them?' Lisa asked.

Shay didn't respond straight away. The ghostly rattle of the Luas echoed through the open windows.

'Well, that's what they said.'

Lisa's eyes widened at the distinct lack of certainty in his voice. She knew him too well. But what could he say? He didn't trust them.

'Will what you have to do put us in danger ... the kids?'

Shay refused to think about this too much. It wasn't clear yet what he would have to do.

'Just the usual eyes and ears.'

He felt her probing him as he poured out more water.

'How long more do we have to stay here?'

Shay said nothing, and swallowed another gulp.

'Not long,' he said, putting the glass down.

He moved to hold her, but she avoided his touch. That coldness had returned and she stepped into the sitting room. She stood there with her back to him and stared out the window, the yellow glove still on her right hand.

'They still holding what you ... did ... over you?'

Shay flinched. Lisa had never directly referred to it since they moved here. He couldn't gather his thoughts quickly enough to respond. There was a pull and a smack. Lisa flung the other glove onto the sofa.

'I'll collect the kids,' she said, moving for the door.

Shay was nailed to the floor. His brain was firing wildly and memories came crashing through.

'Look at the ass on that. What do ye think her husband likes to do with that now? Ha?'

'Jesus, Jamie, I tell ye what I'd like to do. But it's not for, what do ye call it, public consumption, like.'

Shay glared back along the queue at Jamie and Tommy McCabe.

'Why don't you fuck off,' he shouted back at them.

'The boyfriend's got spunk,' Tommy said.

'He does alright, and I bet ye I know where he likes to put it,' Jamie said.

They broke out laughing, loud and obnoxious.

Lisa grabbed Shay's arm.

'Shay, don't.'

'I likes what you're wearing there, Lisa, tight jeans and high heels,' Jamie shouted. 'Oh, I likes that.'

Lisa pulled at Shay. His face was pale with rage.

'Just ignore them.'

'You should tell the manager of the project about those fucks,' Shay said, 'get them barred from the centre.'

'That'd just give them more attention and end up giving me more hassle out there. Anyway, they come from a horrible family.'

'So that means they can abuse community workers like you, people who are actually trying to help them?'

Shay got the tickets for the film. He was raging.

'Listen, when we get home you can let your frustration out on me,' she said, sneakily putting her hand against his crotch. 'Okay?'

Shay almost jumped when his phone rang, the memories evaporating. He held his hand against the kitchen counter, his wrist throbbing.

28

Lisa braked hard in the playschool car park, her car straddling two spaces. She shouldn't have mentioned to Shay about that night, she told herself. But now that she had, the memories of it consumed her.

She'd pulled the bins out for collection as Shay went upstairs to have a shower.

Maybe the boys were just showing off to each other, she thought. Boys were like that, all macho bravado. There was no real malice in them. Anyway, she liked her job, even if it could be difficult. She was good at it. And she did good. She wasn't going to let Jamie McCabe, or his brother, ruin it.

She heard the noise of the shower upstairs. Shay had said he needed to cool down.

The sensation of the wool against her cheek baffled her at first, until it gripped around her mouth. A finger and thumb pressed against her cheekbones. She tried to scream, but the sound was muffled. Her attacker responded by shoving her against the wall and smacking her head against it. Pain ripped across her forehead. She momentarily lost balance and felt sick. She could feel the man pressed behind her, his penis bulging into her.

'Make a sound, bitch,' he said, clasping her mouth even tighter, 'and I'll drive your head through the fucking wall.'

The voice was familiar.

The shower droned away upstairs.

She froze for those brief seconds, waiting for some horror

to unfold. Another hand slid down onto her bum, rubbing it, squeezing it.

Lisa's mind roared.

Shay, help me, please help me.

But no words came.

'Tight jeans, high heels. Always does it for me,' the voice spat into one of her ears.

Her eyes pulled back in horror. It was Jamie McCabe.

'What I don't understand,' he said, rubbing his groin against her, 'is why ye strut into the centre in those heels and that ass, knowing I be looking at ye. But ye ignore my looks. You're a community worker like, but ye kind of look down on us. The community. That's not fucking right, is it?'

He yanked her back by the hair. He opened the button of her jeans and pulled at the zip. He heaved on the jeans with his free hand, forcing them down.

God. Please. No.

Just go, Jamie. Leave me alone. I'll tell no one. This never happened.

His left hand went down her underwear, grabbing her bum again. He grunted against her. He pressed his thumb against her bum and pushed it in. Lisa felt part of her brain shut down. He pulled his thumb around roughly, took it out. She heard his zip. His gasping became frenzied.

No, this can't happen, won't happen. No.

She pulled her eyes up and to the right. The light from the narrow window at the top of the stairs shone out.

'Shay,' she tried to roar, but he just pressed his hand harder against her mouth.

He licked her neck and reefed her back by the hair again.

'You won't ignore this, you snotty bitch. Not this nasty bastard up your tight ass.'

The shower turned off. Lisa sensed him distracted. He had slightly eased his clasp on her. Her brain sparked.

Now, it screamed. Now.

She lashed wildly back with her elbows. He let out a shout and pulled his hand from her mouth. She heaved away. He grabbed her neck, catching her right earring, ripping it down and through her lobe. She screamed and half fell against the wall.

'Bitch,' he shouted, his teeth clenched.

He drove his foot into her stomach, catapulting her forward.

Lisa jolted hard as the flashback snapped shut.

She was clasping the steering wheel. Her knuckles were white. Her heart hammered against her chest bone.

She roared out and banged the wheel with her head, elbowing the door with her right arm and the air with her left. Tears poured down.

After the rage expired, she desperately looked out the windows in case anyone could see her.

She shook as she recalled the rest from that night.

She'd told Shay to bring her to the garda station. She wouldn't say any more until they got there. If she'd told him back at the house, he could have gone and done something stupid. By telling him at the station, he couldn't.

Soon after that, she went on the sleeping tablets and the anti-anxiety medication. The nightmares and the screaming were exhausting. She couldn't go around the side of the house any more, not on her own. She had panic attacks and they sucked the confidence out of her.

One day she summoned up the willpower to ring the manager of the centre. She offered her sympathies, but explained that the centre couldn't ban Jamie. He was innocent in the eyes of the law, she said. But Lisa suspected it was more because of Jamie's family. They had everyone intimidated in the area. Even still, Lisa couldn't accept that the centre wouldn't stand up for her. She felt victimised a second time. And betrayed. She had spent years in that community, doing her best to help people, working all hours, earning buttons. The bitterness of that dug deep.

Months later, detectives called her and Shay in for a meeting. They explained that the DPP had directed no prosecution against Jamie McCabe. Although the DPP wouldn't say why, the detectives said that the forensics and DNA had come back inconclusive. There were no eyewitnesses. And Jamie's family, including his mother, made sworn statements that both he and his brother had come straight home from the cinema and stayed with them all night.

Lisa felt like she had entered a thick, cold fog and night had descended.

She recalled how Shay remained unruffled during that meeting, as if he knew what the detectives were going to say.

Soon after, she realised she was pregnant, something that must have happened shortly before the attack. No matter how much she told herself that the attack and her pregnancy were unconnected, she couldn't get rid of a feeling, crawling inside her skin, that the purity of the pregnancy had been sullied, invaded in some way.

Before the year was out, she had given birth to a baby girl. Coping with Molly took over her life. Shay was working a lot, away from the house almost every day. She didn't feel she was bonding with Molly. She didn't love her as she should have, as she expected she would.

She convinced herself that having another child would change things: that by loving the second child properly she could learn to love Molly better. And things would be as they should be for her as a mother. She convinced Shay of it too.

But he often seemed distracted. Shortly after Charlie was born, she discovered why.

She had seen news reports of a violent feud that had reignited between the McCabes and another family. That's when he did something stupid. Shay had just been biding his time all along, Lisa realised. That, after all, was what he was trained to do.

He did it for her. Not that he said it in words. He was too careful for that. But she could see it in his eyes. No you didn't, she screamed back with her eyes. You did it for yourself. You didn't think of the consequences for us, our family.

Because of his actions, they had ended up here, with this life.

After all the shit, she was, at first, glad at the prospect of leaving Cork. She wouldn't have to see Jamie McCabe on the street, which she had done once. That had catapulted her into a full panic attack. She was terrified of being seen, of the kids coming face to face with her attacker. She pushed the buggy, hunched over, across the road, oblivious to traffic. She flagged down a taxi and bundled the kids in. She would have left the buggy on the path, had the driver not got out and folded it up and put it in. She cowered in the back until they were on their way.

The move to Dublin would be a fresh start, Shay had reassured her. She didn't ask too much about where they were going or what Shay would be doing. She just needed to get away.

She soon realised it was a lot different working in a community with problems and living in one with problems. And this community had fractures far deeper and wider than the one she had worked in.

Having Charlie didn't improve things. In fact, her son seemed to make things worse, as if he confirmed some flaw in her, one she never knew existed, a fissure that the assault had prised open. When that black realisation sunk in, her outlook darkened. She leaned on the pills more, and as soon as she could, got a job as a care assistant. They needed the money, but, more than that, she needed to get out of the house.

Shay kept saying they would only be there short term; they would move soon enough. But there was no time period, no plan. After a while, she felt they were stuck. At the same time, she couldn't just leave. She owed him that much. And, where would she go? Back to her parents, like a child? Move out and get a place on her own? With the kids? She didn't have enough money. And she knew she wouldn't be able to cope. Not yet anyway.

She twiddled at her wedding band as she looked around the car park. She did still love Shay. But some bone deep inside her had snapped – maybe in Shay, too – and had never healed. Having the children didn't bolt it back together.

She didn't blame Shay for their life. More, she just held it against him.

The way she saw it, there was one thing he loved more than her, than the kids. That was his life as a garda.

And, though he wouldn't admit it, even to himself, she knew her husband would do anything to get that life back.

29

Crowe squinted at the glare of the morning sun. Hopefully, the shop owner will be here soon, she thought. She kicked the back of her runner against the wall and yawned. She had been working pretty much straight through for almost three days. No sleep the first night and just a couple of hours on a sofa in the station on the second. Tyrell had ordered her home at one this morning to get some proper sleep. Not that he seemed to take any break at all.

She smiled at the effort Tom had made when she got home. Her heart pinched when she saw he had cleaned the apartment, even the bathroom. A box of camomile tea had been left out on the counter beside a cup, a spoon inside, along with a chicken sandwich, wrapped in foil. Small gestures, but welcome ones in the worst of days.

Not that it helped her sleep. She was down for a few hours when she leaped clean out of bed, images of Grant's smiling face pulping under a wheel catapulting her awake.

She was back at the station by 7 a.m. Her team had made solid progress in the three days. They had identified and gathered all private cameras on access roads off MacBride Road and main arteries out. One house camera on Dangan Road had captured a red BMW speeding by at 8.04 p.m., a minute or so after the shooting.

Crowe had assembled numbered maps on the walls in the Imagery Office, where they were based, and made copies for the incident room. One map marked known or suspected sightings of the car; a second mapped possible routes to the shooting; a third mapped possible routes after and a fourth was a blown-up map of MacBride Road. They had got an image at Phoenix Park of a similar car and a partial reg, some fifteen minutes before the shooting. Two of her team were beginning the laborious process of viewing images from there to MacBride Road. She and two others were on the roads after the shooting.

This brought her to a row of shops on Philip Road, which intersected with Dangan Road. One of them had a camera.

Back at the station, Crowe slid in the disk from the shop. Private cameras were notoriously unreliable for police purposes. Images were often poor. This was a ritual she went through, dampening expectations, so as not to be disappointed.

Images uploaded onto the screen. The quality was sharp and Crowe straightened in her seat. The shop owner had told her he'd got brand new cameras in, after his third burglary, when he had a gun pressed against his cheek. The camera only went up the morning of the shooting. Crowe raised her eyebrow when he said it, calculating the chances of that.

The camera captured the entire front of the shop, including a lane that ran beside it and a good part of Philip Road, which was a main artery out of the area. The lane went right around the rear of the shops and back onto the road again. Crowe had walked around the block earlier. There was an industrial unit at the rear. The lane was completely hidden from view from the road or any houses. There were no cameras back there. Crowe forwarded the disk to the time of the shooting. She glanced up at the clock as it hit 8 p.m. Then 8.03, 8.04, 8.05. 8.06. Nothing. She knew the BMW headed along Dangan Road and this was the most likely route, the other road bringing cars back towards the canal, which they would have avoided.

She leaned forward when a vehicle lumbered slowly out of the lane. The clock said 8.10. She sunk back when she saw the front of an articulated truck, with a blank black canvas draped over it. Coming from the industrial estate, she presumed. She wondered, wasn't it late for a truck to be heading out? She watched as the container emerged into view and swung onto Philip Road. She tilted her head and scratched down the reg as the truck manoeuvred away. The edges of the canvas flapped loose at the rear. She looked at the bolts across the back. The bars hadn't been pushed over. A thought popped into her head. A crazy one, but one that chimed with her instincts.

Crowe ran out the door with the note of the reg in her hand.

30

His sister's picture was the only family photo Jig ever saw in the house. Unlike Spikey's house: it had photos of him and his ma, and his brothers and sisters. Not of his da though. Spikey didn't seem to know where his da was.

As Jig watched his sister approach along the path, he recalled that one picture frame. It was on the mantelpiece in the sitting room. It was of his ma, his da and Donna, when she was a baby. They called her that after Madonna.

That frame ended up over Donna's head, years ago, when he was small. They were all rowing, Jig remembered. He was there. Donna pointed at the picture and said something about her still being her da's daughter. He'd called her a 'dirty junkie tramp', grabbed the frame and smashed it off her head. The glass went all over the place and there was blood on her skull. She screamed and went to kick their da. He punched her full in the face. She fell back like one of those trees being cut down and hit the back of her head against the bottom of the wall.

His ma roared and went to break her fall. His da wiped spit off his mouth and flicked it away. Some of it landed on Jig's face. His da moved for Donna again, but his ma told him, 'Fucking leave her alone.' He reached down and grabbed his ma's hair and pulled her up. He hit her with his thick, square fist right into the side of her face. He dropped her and drove a kick into Donna. His da's boots seemed like black cement blocks. His ma managed to half stop a second kick. He tried to shake her free. They were all screaming. Jig had his hands over his ears. His da kicked his foot right through a panel in the bottom of the sitting-room door. Clean through it went. And he almost took the front door with him.

Donna left after that. She wasn't going to live in a 'fucking hole' she told their ma.

Jig kicked at a wreath wrapped around the railing of the bridge as he looked down at Donna. He smiled as she sashayed down the path, her dyed blonde hair tied back. She wore a tight top, with 'Party Time' written across it. She had a small jacket with fur around the top. She wore tight jeans and platform wedges, scraping against the path as she half-ran towards him.

He felt a tug in his heart.

'Here, let me look at ya.' She landed a big smacker on the top of his head. He looked at her purple lips and her long dark nails. Bowie jumped and barked.

'Ah, Jaysus. Jig.'

Her left arm came up and she scratched the top of her other arm.

'When I see ya last? Must be six months?'

'Yeah.'

'Seriously?'

'Yeah, seriously.' Jig cracked a smile.

'Well, I don't be back much. Ya understand, chicken? But I heard about Maggot going awol, so I said I better see were youse all okay? Ya know?'

She grabbed him into a huge bear hug.

'Ah, Bowie, come here,' she said giving the dog a shake and getting a lick to her cheek in return. 'Jaysus, he's getting big. Granda be so proud of the way ya do be looking after him.'

Jig smiled at that. Donna, Bowie and Granda. His body warmed at the thought of the three of them as a family.

'Some get up,' he said, nodding at her.

'Thank you,' she said, doing a little twirl. 'What ya doing around the canal?' she asked, looking at her fancy watch. 'Ya not supposed to be in school?'

145

'Fuck school. Them teachers are a shower of pricks.'

Donna grabbed his arm, her nails gathering his bones in a clasp.

'Come on, let's go. I'll walk up with ya.'

There was no way he was going to school. But he liked walking with his sister. She looked great and all positive. And not embarrassed to be with him. Bowie hopped along beside them.

'How's the hole. Not school now,' she laughed. 'The other one.'

'I was thinking about that picture when I saw ya?'

'Ah, Jig, forget about that fucking picture.'

She scratched her cheek. Jig looked down on the ground, going back into himself. After a moment, she spoke again.

'Heard yer in with Ghost?'

'Yeah,' Jig said proudly. 'He does be treating me like, his man and all – that's what he says. And I get to go in his jeep.'

'Wow. Go Jig.' She stopped for a second. 'But, be careful, yeah? Ya know with everything that has happened.'

They walked on.

'He ever ask after me?' Donna said suddenly.

'No,' Jig said, thinking about Taylor now.

'Where's he hanging out, anyways?'

Jig knew she was thinking about something, pouting her big lips and pushing her boobs out.

'He's always driving around. He might be at football later.'

Donna scratched her face again. The sound was like sandpaper, Jig thought, looking at her nails. One of the nails was cracked and the varnish was half done on another.

'Hey, Paulie,' Donna roared at a guy across the road. 'What ya up to, ya sneaky fucker?'

Jig knew the guy from the canals.

'Is a modelling school after opening around here or what?' he shouted back.

'Go on, ya charmer. Listen, I'm meeting someone at the clinic. I'll walk up with ya.' She turned back to Jig. 'Up to school now. Don't take any shit from the principal. Tell him I'll have his bollix if he gives ya hassle for being late. Yeah?'

She grabbed his face with her nails. Jig could see dirt in behind them. She landed him a big kiss, this one on his cheek. Her teeth were yellow up close.

'Score a goal for me at football, yeah?'

He watched her skip across the road on her wedges, Bowie barking after her. She grabbed the guy and put her hand around him. He smacked her ass.

She looked back at Jig and blew him a kiss.

31

Shay followed Pat into the meditation room. He knew this was where he took people for one of his private chats. The priest had rung him earlier and asked him to call up.

Shay was struck by the hushed, carpeted quiet in the room.

'Thanks for coming,' the priest said. He was about to close the door behind him. 'Want some tea or water?'

Shay realised he was a bit parched and asked for water. He took one of the two seats as he waited. The lights were down low. A large crucifix adorned one of the walls.

'There you go,' Pat said, coming back and closing the door behind him.

'How you keeping, Pat? Tough day yesterday?'

'The toughest of days, Shay,' the priest said, shaking his head.

The funeral mass for young Taylor Williams had taken its toll on the priest by the looks of him. Not that Shay felt much better. He'd had nightmares again last night. This time Taylor was reaching down into the canal and was throwing water up onto her missing face.

Shay felt like he hadn't slept in days.

He watched Pat take off his glasses and give them a clean with a tissue before placing them carefully back on – a ritual he'd done more than once during the funeral.

Shay noticed that Jig's parents had sat the family way back in the church. There were looks in their direction. Maggot wasn't with them, an absence not lost on some people. Jig kept his head bowed for the whole mass. Shay saw him react when Sharon, his and Taylor's friend, blanked him as she walked past.

All the top brass of the force were there, led by the commissioner. Crowe sat a number of rows behind. He saw her looking in Jig's direction a number of times. Her face was ashen. Garda Grant's funeral had just been the previous day.

'You know Leo King, Shay?'

The priest's question took him by surprise.

What could the priest want with me regarding Ms King's son?

'You might have heard there were suspicions around her death. A detective was looking into it. Did you get to speak to her?'

Shay guessed the priest knew anyway.

'Yeah, Garda ...' Shay pretended not to remember, 'something or another.'

'Yes, Detective Garda Crowe, Tara Crowe,' the priest replied. 'Seems a very capable young woman. Anyway, I knew Ms King well. She was under terrible pressure from dealers about a debt her son had. He'd been caught with drugs and was ordered to pay. He was charged, but disappeared.'

Shay was nodding along, not sure where this was going and what part he could have in any of it. But the unit would want to know whatever it was.

'Well,' the priest added, lowering his voice even further, 'he's turned up.'

'Right,' Shay said, trying not to show any reaction. Inside his mind, quick calculations were being done as to possible ramifications.

The priest coughed and leaned his hands onto his knee, looking earnest.

'Now, Leo was holding drugs for ... certain well-known individuals ... and he blames them for his mother's death.'

The priest paused for a moment.

'Shay. I swore to Leo that I would not talk to the guards ... but he mentioned the people he was out to get.'

149

Shay's heart skipped a beat. He resisted adjusting his body, to keep up the pretence of disinterest.

'Who?' he said.

'One of them is Jig.'

Jig? What's he want with him?

'I see,' he said calmly.

'You're the only person I know he's anyway close with.'

'I wouldn't say close, Pat.'

'I wanted someone to know, in case we need to act, if something happens.'

'What kind of something?'

'Well, it's just vague talk. He's rambling and raving a bit. I'm mainly trying to help him and keep him safe.'

'He's here?' Shay said, finding it hard to believe the priest was sheltering Leo in the heartland of the gang out to get him.

'I swore to his mother I would find her son and do my best to help him,' the priest said. 'I did find him, although he was the one who wanted to come back. Out of the blue he rang me, just after the murders. I have to tell you, Shay, I'm worried.'

'You think Leo's capable of posing a threat to anyone?' Shay asked.

'Not at the moment. He's still got a severe drug problem. I'm trying to sort out some detox for him.'

'And who else is this Leo after?'

The priest squinted at Shay. Shay didn't show any reaction. He needed to get as much information as he could.

'Well, Ghost for one.'

Shay nodded.

'You better be careful getting mixed up with this, Pat.'

'Bit late for me, Shay. I'm already a marked man with them. What I can't get around, after being here for more than ten years now, is how everyone knows who Ghost is, what he does, yet no one says anything, let alone does anything.'

Shay adjusted his legs against the chair.

'It's the way things are around here, Pat. You know what it's like.'

He saw that the priest was still looking at him, as if waiting for more.

'I can only do what I can,' Shay added.

'I understand, Shay.' The priest nodded. 'Even good men have to make choices, compromises they're not happy with.'

32

Crowe took in a blur of faces and handwritten notes as she scanned row upon row of sheets of paper. The i2 charts covered two walls: a roll-call of the great and good of gangs in the area.

She honed in on the central chart on the wall opposite her, the principal suspect in the Canal Gang. The thumbnail picture in the middle of the sheet revealed a man with a bald head, and a smug curl to his lip. Lock Man, it said. Position: Leader.

Like a wheel of a bicycle, the other players spoked away from him, each with their own thumbnail. Slammer (Security), Ghost (Distribution) and Cracko (Collection) formed an inner circle. Crowe wasn't sure which of them looked the scarier fucker. More spokes led out to a third circle, dotted with two dozen faces, mainly young. They struck hardman poses, puffing their chests out and staring defiantly at the camera. These were members of the various street crews and associates of the network in the area. Maggot was one of these. A fourth circle contained thumbnails of even younger children, used as couriers, scouts and the like. Jig was on this circle.

Other gangs in the area were to be hit too. Each target had assigned officers.

Crowe stepped back. On either side of the main sheet were separate i2 charts for each target or linked targets being hit. The sheets listed full details: position; name; alias; addresses; Pulse Identification Number; partner; ex-partners; family; associates; car registration; mobile phone numbers; phone call activity on the day of the murders; location on the day and other relevant notes from their criminal intelligence file.

Crowe looked behind her, to a third wall, thick with maps and charts from her team. They documented what was known about the movements of the BMW that day, from Phoenix Park, where it was first picked up, to Philip Road, where it was last spotted.

There were a few blown-up photographs of the BMW, but none were clear enough to give a glimpse of the occupants.

Another map showed one sighting of the vehicle from the ANPR cameras on a traffic corps vehicle. And as well as that, local authority traffic cameras captured the truck twice, once on the Naas Road and again on the M9. After that, the trail went cold. Crowe was still working on its possible routes.

The registration plates on both vehicles were cloned and inquiries went dead.

Crowe numbered her maps and supplied text for all of them, typed up and printed. She looked at her work, and that of her investigation team, with a sense of pride. It was the culmination of two weeks of round-the-clock work. It seemed longer. It had blurred into one never-ending day. Her bones ached from the hard floors and makeshift cushions. The few nights she was home made little difference. She couldn't sleep. She hadn't spoken to Tom properly in ages. Whenever they had an opportunity, and Tom tried, her mind was elsewhere.

The incident room had filled in the last few minutes. Bodies heaved and jostled for space.

The DI pushed himself up from behind the desk. The word had come down from HQ that the commissioner wanted to see doors kicked down, soon after the funerals were over. Crowe shook herself at the images of those funerals, occurring on successive days. She still couldn't believe she'd never see Grant's face behind the public counter again.

'This is to run like clockwork,' Tyrell said loudly.

Crowe got up on her tiptoes to try and see past the men, shifting on their feet in front of her.

'We are going to hit them hard, let them know who is in charge,' Tyrell said. 'Put them on the back foot.'

This was a massive shakedown of gangs in the area, the Canal Gang in particular, Crowe told herself. They were coming in on suspicion of withholding information about the murders, not on suspicion of the murder itself. Two separate offences, two distinct powers of arrest. Arrest them for murder now, their chance would be spent. They wouldn't be able to arrest them again, unless they had new evidence. This was about sitting on them, sweating them. It would help boost the morale of gardaí too. If truth be told, it was a PR exercise – a show of strength to the public, and the media.

'Most of these lowlifes,' the DI said, waving his arms at the walls, 'have been expecting us to break down their doors. They will be prepared. Each of you knows your targets and you know which station you are bringing your prisoners to. You have been broken down into interviewing teams. Let them know before we bring them to the interview rooms that, if they don't give us something, we have clearance from the DPP to immediately press outstanding charges against them. Remind them their little drug business is going to be on hold as we continue to sit on them. And feed their paranoia about rats in the camp.'

Crowe thought Tyrell's stoop was more pronounced than usual. She didn't think he had left the station since the shooting. It was generally known there was no one at home; his marriage had broken up years ago and his daughter was grown up.

The morning chorus greeted Crowe as she exited the car. Silhouettes of birds stretched out along the wires, beaks pointing up, chirping away.

She clutched the warrant. Intelligence told them that Maggot hadn't turned up anywhere since the shooting.

Up until this morning, she was just on the cameras. Now she was in on the raids and the interviews. And Tyrell had given her charge of Maggot, if he was there, and Jig. She smiled at the poisoned chalice, but loved being in on the action.

Three ERU officers were ahead of her, all of them pictures of moving darkness, covered head to toe in black combat gear. She eyed their arsenal: a Heckler & Koch MP7 machine gun, smoke bombs, a Taser along with the standard issue Sig. Two brandished their MP7s. The third was holding the red hammer. The threat level was rated medium. They didn't expect firearms, but there could be resistance. Not least from the deranged ma.

Crowe glanced at her watch: 6 a.m. on the button.

She watched the red hammer slam just above the handle, catapulting the door back. The ERU man left the hammer down and grabbed his weapon and followed his colleagues in, firearms poised. The ERU's 'shock and awe' approach was impressive, if slightly scary, Crowe felt.

She and the others waited at the door, listening. There was shouting and roaring and a clatter of bodies.

Crowe felt the weight of the Sig on her waist, a reassuring sensation at times like this.

The birds continued to whistle as order was enforced. One of the ERU men came back down and checked each of the downstairs rooms.

He walked back towards Crowe.

'Secured. No sign of Maggot.'

She nodded. No surprise. She strode up the stairs, avoiding getting tangled in random clothes and bags.

Crowe squinted at the bright bulb on the tiny landing, no more than two-foot square. She scrunched her nose at the smell of piss from the toilet.

'Go on, point that weapon at me,' the ma snarled from inside her room. 'I fucking dare ya, ya prick.'

Crowe looked in. She and Hunter were lying face down on their beds, their hands cable-tied behind them. So, they had put up resistance and the ERU guys had to restrain them. A second ERU man stood facing them, his gun poised. In Jig's room, she could hear the third ERU guy ordering the boy to put some clothes on.

'I fucking knew ya be behind this,' the ma shouted on seeing her.

'This is the warrant to search the house and arrest Jig and Darren,' Crowe said as she stepped in and placed it beside the mother's head.

'Fuck ya, ya culchie bitch,' she shouted at Crowe. 'I'll be on to the radio about all this. This is fucking harassment, State fucking oppression, it is.'

But Crowe ignored her and went towards Jig's room, just as he was pulled out. He was dressed in tracksuit bottoms and top, his hands cable-tied behind him. There was shouting from the younger children in the room.

'Mr and Ms Hunt,' Crowe said, turning back into their room. 'When I release you, if you interfere with our search you will be arrested. Is that clear?'

She could see them biting their tongues.

She cut the cables. The ma jumped up and jostled against her.

'Back down, Ms Hunt,' Crowe said firmly, not giving ground.

The ma pushed past her and entered Jig's room.

'Mr Hunt,' Crowe said, looking at him as he sat up, 'we will need you to accompany your son for questioning. Are you going to come peacefully or will we have to arrest you too?'

Hunter looked up at her, as if he was considering ripping her head off.

'Youse are wasting yer time,' he scoffed.

The baby started crying behind him.

'Get dressed,' Crowe said, squaring her shoulders. 'And follow Jig down. Bring the baby with you.'

The dad grunted, but complied. The ERU officer escorted him down.

Crowe looked into Jig's room.

'Wayne, Crystal, are youse okay, chickens?' the ma was saying from inside.

Crowe kept an eye on her as she gathered them up.

'Ms Hunt, I suggest you take them down to the kitchen while the search continues.'

But the ma just turned to Crowe and spat at her.

'Bitch,' she said.

Crowe twisted as gob hit her on the chin. She wiped it away with her sleeve and rubbed her chin hard.

Christ, I'd love time with you on my own. Out of sight of anyone.

She battled the rage inside: part of her told her not to lower herself to their level; the other part said fuck it.

The boy, Wayne, looked at her. 'Bitch,' he said. The girl twisted her face at her.

Great, the next generation of Maggots and Jigs.

After they trundled down the stairs, Crowe realised she was shaking, but it was more adrenaline than nerves. She followed them and paused at the doorway. The birds had stopped singing.

Things were different now, she said to herself.

I'm not going to be intimidated any more. I owe it to Grant and Peters and the little girl: to stand up for them and show these scum the line has been crossed.

33

Jig slouched; his arse hung off the edge of the seat. He stretched his legs out under the desk, his blue adidas runners pointing up.

Crowe pushed open the door, followed by a colleague, Detective Spain. She walked around to the other side of the desk. She had her file in one hand and three new tapes in her other hand. She avoided Jig's eyes for a few moments as she calmly placed her file in front of her.

She looked up as Jig's dad was brought into the room and took the seat beside his son. He was like a boxer ready for a fight, flexing his neck from side to side. He turned and glared at Jig for a few long seconds. Jig leaned away, as if waiting, or expecting, an elbow into his ear.

Crowe ran her fingers around the wrapping on the tapes, savouring the family harmony.

'Right, Jig, this is how it's going to roll,' she said.

The boy tried to adjust his seating, but the chair didn't budge, bolted as it was to the ground.

'I'm the only friend you've got in here,' Crowe said. 'I can speak up for you. But if you play the fool, I can't help you. And I want to help you, Jig.'

'What's this,' Hunter scoffed, 'amateur hour at garda patrol?'

Jig glanced over at his dad.

'Once I put these tapes in, Jig, it's on the record,' Crowe continued, making a point of keeping her eyes fixed on Jig and ignoring Hunter. She wanted Jig to realise she wasn't interested in what his dad said, or what games he tried to play, she was focused only on him. 'The cameras above and in front of you will capture everything, including how you react to questions.' She took out the three tapes. 'Is there anything you want to tell me before we start?'

'As I told ya at the gaff, youse are wasting yer time,' Hunter said.

'Just to remind you, Mr Hunt,' Crowe said, glancing over at him, 'you are not allowed to interfere with the questioning. You are here only to observe.'

His mouth curled at one side.

'Okay then,' Crowe said, putting the tapes into the three decks, and hitting record and switching on the video recorder.

'This is an interview of Jack Hunt, alias Jig, aged ten, born 30.11.99, address 42 Evergreen Close. He is in the company of his father James Hunt. An offer of consultation with a solicitor has been declined. Present are Detective Gardaí Tara Crowe and Martin Spain attached to Canal Road Garda Station. The time is 7.15 a.m. and the date is 04.06.10. This interview is being recorded on video and is being conducted at an interview room at Canal Road Garda Station. Jack Hunt is detained under Section 30 of the Offences Against the State Act on suspicion of withholding information. I'm conducting the interview. My name is Detective Garda Crowe, and Detective Garda Spain is taking notes. Jack, you are not obliged to say anything unless you wish to do so but anything you do say will be taken down and may be given in evidence. Do you understand?'

No response.

'Do you understand, Jig?' Crowe repeated calmly.

He nodded.

'Jig has nodded he understands,' Crowe said. 'Do you know why you have been arrested?'

The boy shrugged.

Crowe wanted this to be by the book, nothing any lawyer could subsequently take issue with. She had to make it clear the boy understood everything he was being asked.

'Jig. Do you understand why you have been arrested?'

'Youse think I know something. But I don't.'

'Yes. You are being held on suspicion of withholding information. You understand that? I need an answer?'

'Yeah. I bleeding understand.'

She let things settle for a moment, now the formalities were out of the way.

'So, I hear you're good at football?'

Jig looked up at her, surprised at the question.

'Under-11s, isn't it?'

'Yeah, so?'

'From what I hear, you have talent. You could go places even.'

Jig's face softened and he tilted his head as if to say 'yeah, could'.

'You're a Manchester United fan, aren't you?'

'How ya know that?'

'I've seen your Paul Scholes poster.'

Jig raised his eyebrows, but said nothing.

Crowe could see he didn't expect this. She knew she was a bit out of her comfort zone, given her lack of footballing knowledge. But she needed to build up some basic level of rapport, before she even began to touch on the matters at hand.

'Close one this year,' Crowe said, recalling her googling last night.

Jig nodded.

'Last match of the season. Chelsea nosed you out by one point.'

'Yeah, shite it was,' Jig responded.

Crowe was happy so far. Now she wanted to make it a bit more personal.

'Is that who you'd like to play for?'

Jig glanced up at her.

'Would you like to play midfield for United, like Scholesy?'

The dad laughed.

She cut him a look, but wondered if she'd made an arse of her pronunciation.

'How come Rooney's not your favourite?' she asked.

Jig looked at her, then to his dad.

160

'Well?' Crowe continued. 'He scores the goals.'

'Nothing would happen without Scholes,' Jig said. 'He makes it all happen from midfield.'

'Where do you play?'

'Same. Midfield. And I score too, like Scholes.'

Good, Crowe thought. A couple of sentences. She could see his dad wasn't happy. He knew what she was doing.

'He must be due to retire soon, though,' she said. 'United will miss him.'

Jig nodded.

And on it went. Crowe thinking of anything she could to do with Manchester United and Canal United.

'The thing is, Jig,' she said, 'if you want to follow that dream, and you have the talent to maybe do it, you don't want things to get in your way, do you?'

Jig shuffled in his chair. She could see his forehead glisten. His dad was already sweating like a pig after an hour in the room. Thanks to the heating. Even in the summer it was on: one of the bizarre quirks in many garda stations. And in the small interview rooms, such as this one, with no functioning window, it could get very uncomfortable.

'What I'm saying, Jig, is – if you get caught up with people, the type you shouldn't be caught up with, are you risking your dream?'

The muscles on Jig's face tightened. She sensed he couldn't help but take in what she was saying.

'I wants to go to the jacks,' Jig said, his legs hopping up and down.

She couldn't deny him a toilet break. She glanced over at Detective Spain, who nodded.

'Tell you what, Jig. Let's break for ten minutes. You have a think about what we've been talking about. Mr Hunt, you can take a break too.'

Maggot. Maggot. Maggot. They counted up to thirty calls to Maggot's number from the same mobile in the space of a few days. None were answered.

'What day was the first of those calls?' Crowe asked.

'First was May,' her colleague paused, 'the thirty-first.'

'Time?'

'Ten p.m.'

Two hours after the shooting, she thought. 'How many that day?'

'After that, two more that night. Next day looks like five or six, same the next and so on.'

Crowe looked around at her search team. They had been busy going through their finds at the house. Their eyes told her they were thinking the same as her.

'Seems they were very eager to talk to him,' she said. 'Which phone belongs to who?' she asked the guard going through the phone. 'We need to find Jig's.'

'The one we just went through has Jig's name and Hunter's on it, as well as Maggot.'

'So that's the mother's,' Crowe said.

'This one has Jig, Maggot and The Moth,' another guard said.

'Okay, that must be her charming husband,' Crowe replied.

'And this has Maggot, Ma, Da,' a third colleague said.

'Okay, so that's Jig's. Let's double check and ring those names from each of those phones, see what caller ID comes up. But do one phone at a time, yeah? And put in a request for subscriber details and billing.'

Crowe smiled at Jig as she walked back in, clasping a can of Fanta and a Mars bar in her hand. She let them down on the table and busied herself with her file. The dad was brought in and resumed his seat. Crowe could see him glancing around.

'Right, Jig. Can we continue?'

She flicked through sheets and images in her file, sensing Jig's eyes on the can. She let some moments pass.

'Oh, by the way, I got you a drink. Nice and cold. Here,' she said, sliding it across. 'There's chocolate too, if you're hungry.'

She saw his arm raise, but his da let out a loud cough, and his arm retracted.

'Well, it's there,' Crowe said, 'if you want it later, Jig. Okay? No catches.'

She switched on the recording and stated the time and the fact that the interview was restarting.

'Now, Jig, what were we talking about? Oh, football, wasn't it, and your future?'

Crowe spent the next thirty minutes probing and pushing the issue, but Jig just shrugged and nodded, not in any difficult way, just as he would normally, Crowe thought. Through it all he teased himself by eyeing the Fanta and the bar.

Time for a different tack.

'What about your friends, Jig? Any of them into football?'

'Yeah,' he replied.

'All boys? Any girls play?'

'One or two.'

'Yeah, camogie seems to be the big thing now with girls, isn't it?'

'Suppose,' he said.

'Like your friend Sharon?'

She saw something dance fleetingly across his face at the mention of her name. He couldn't disguise it.

'She's probably not much good though, is she?'

'She'd leave ya on yer arse any day.'

Crowe smiled.

'And what about Taylor? Did she play?'

It was like a slap across his face. His body jolted.

The dad slammed his hands down on the table and yawned. But Crowe pushed on.

'Well, did Taylor play camogie?'

Jig nodded.

'She any good?'

The boy dug his chin into his chest.

'Jig?'

'Yeah,' he said, but Crowe barely heard him.

'Her mother told me,' Crowe said, 'God help her, she's in an awful state, that Taylor loved the majorettes the most. Been going to them since she was five years old.'

Jig slid down in his chair.

'The poor girl won't be going to the majorettes again.'

Jig closed his eyes as she spoke.

'Only ten years old. Same as yourself.'

Crowe let that lie for a while. She could feel the dad stare her out, but she ignored him.

'You'll miss her, I'd say,' she said.

Jig seemed to shrink under his T-shirt as he stared down at his legs.

'Of course, I'd imagine, like us all, like his poor mother and sister, you'd want the people who did this caught?'

He twisted in his seat. Crowe could sense he felt he needed to reply to that.

'Yeah,' he said, but avoided her eyes.

'Good, Jig. Good. So, what can you tell us about the shooting?'

She knew not to ask any leading questions. Not until she needed to anyway.

'Just a bang. And me falling, smacking me head and going into the water.'

Okay, Crowe thought, that sounded true. But he must have seen more.

'Did you get to see who was in the car, where the shot came from?'

'Jesus, it's fucking boiling in here,' his dad shouted. 'Can youse not open that bleeding window.'

'Mr Hunt, you are not to –'

'Not right ya know, these conditions are inhumane for people being interviewed and all. Kids particularly.'

On he went. He only stopped when Crowe threatened to throw him out and get a different adult to take his place.

But it worked. He had tripped her up and snapped Jig back into place. The boy simply refused to respond to anything else she asked and kept his gaze pinned in the direction of the floor. Crowe could see the dad smirking. He knew he had got to her. She tried to remain composed by flicking through her file.

'You know, Taylor's ma is down at that canal every day, several times a day. And, her other daughter, Megan, won't walk the dogs any more. In fact, she barely goes out. That's not right, Jig, is it? That the scumbags who did this could get away with it? Surely, you want to show me, and everyone, that you want to help?'

Jig kicked at the bolted table leg, twisted his face from side to side.

'Jesus, you're a great friend, aren't you?' Crowe said, putting an edge into her voice. 'Taylor was shot dead and all you can do is squirm when I ask you for the tiniest bit of information about the lowlifes that did this.'

She stopped for a moment, but there was no reaction. She could feel her heart thumping.

'She had the bottom half of her head blown off.'

Jig buried his head into his chest.

'Ya want to watch yer tongue there, garda,' Hunter said. 'He's a child.'

Crowe looked at Hunter and wondered, just for a moment, what it would be like to drive a fist into his rotten face.

She tried to blank him from her mind. She turned back to Jig, and took an image from her file, of Taylor on the ground post-shooting, and slid it over the table.

Jig sneaked a look. His eyes widened, then looked away.

Hunter said: 'That's out of –'

Crowe cut him off. 'I am cautioning you again, Mr Hunt, not to interfere or I will have to remove you from the interview. Anyway, Jig knows what happened. He was there. He saw his friend's face being blown off.'

That shut him up.

'Now the question is, Jig, are you going to stand up for your friend and help catch her killers?'

'I didn't see who done it,' Jig muttered.

'What? What did you say?'

'Nothing.'

'Nothing, eh?' Crowe said.

'I said I didn't see who done it,' Jig said, louder.

'You know,' Crowe said, leaning forward, 'I find it hard to

believe that you were almost directly opposite a parked car, from where the shot was fired, on a bright sunny day, and you can't give the slightest piece of information about who was inside it, how many, or even the slightest description of the vehicle?'

Hunter shifted in his seat. Jig slunk down.

'You know, you could get the impression, you want to protect the killers more than protect Taylor. I wonder what her family would make of that, if they knew.'

Jig shot forward.

'I didn't fucking see who done it, right!' he roared, his cheeks flushed. 'I just heard a bang and saw Tay's head going sideways. I saw no one.'

Jig folded his arms and tucked his chin back in, breathing hard.

Crowe felt a bit derailed. She had pushed a wedge in, but it just popped back out. The boy seemed genuine. His dad even appeared taken off guard by the outburst. After a moment, he nodded at Crowe, as if to say end of story.

'Jig, where's your brother at?' she said, undeterred.

Jig shook his head.

'He's probably off riding some young one,' Hunter said. 'Bit of a ladies' man. Like his da.'

'That must cost,' Crowe said.

Her colleague muffled a laugh. It wiped the sheen of smugness off Hunter's face. Crowe enjoyed that, even if the interview was going nowhere.

'What about the calls from your phone to Maggot's phone?' she asked.

No response.

'There were ten calls from your phone. Starting after the shooting.'

Crowe leaned forward to Jig.

'Well, why were you ringing him?'

'Just was.'

'Tell me, Jig, how would you feel, if it turns out that Maggot was in that car where the shots came from, and your friend minus her head.'

Jig squirmed on his arse.

'Were you ringing him because you saw him in that car?'

No response.

She could feel Hunter staring at her, probably taking a mental note to add her to his shortlist of detectives to hate. To keep there for the rest of his toxic life. That was the lot of a real detective. She knew that now. She always thought she lacked the hardness to take on scum like Jig's dad, the likes of the Canal Gang, face to face: that the hardness just wasn't in her bones. But she was wrong. It just needed enough reason to show itself.

'You need to understand, Jig, the situation you face. It wasn't just a girl that was killed, as horrendous as that was. A garda was too, only twelve years older than Taylor. Another young garda is in a coma with a severed spine. Anyone, and I mean anyone, who is linked with the gang behind this will have the gardaí on their backs for the rest of their lives. You need to realise that, if you insist on keeping your mouth shut.'

Jig didn't look up, so she fixed her gaze on Hunter. He was struggling to maintain that layer of smugness on his face. Even he knew what it meant for his son.

'Jig?' Crowe said, leaning her head low and trying to look up into his eyes, 'you need to realise that anyone associated with the gang, say to Ghost, is included in that.' She noticed Jig reacting to Ghost's name and continued. 'No matter how young they are. They are marked for life. You hear what I'm saying, Jig? Help me. Then, I can help you.'

She thought she saw Jig dart his eyes up at her from under his thin eyebrows.

'Jesus, me T-shirt is stuck to me,' Hunter muttered, picking the edges of it and pulling them out, his arm brushing off Jig's shoulder.

The boy looked down, and was silent.

Crowe leaned back and tidied her file. She terminated the interview. Jig was brought away.

'Nice try, garda,' Hunter said, as she went for the door, 'but even if Jig knew anything – and he doesn't – the Hunts are no rats.'

34

Shay cut the engine, silencing the radio.

Jig had only been released from custody the previous day. When Shay made his daily call to Hall, he told him about Jig. Then Shay hid the phone, in a ziplock bag, at the dry end of a gutter in his shed that wasn't overlooked by neighbours.

In all the years before the shooting there was hardly ever direct phone contact with Hall. Shay went to the college most days for his course, which provided him with a cover for going to the place. Every Monday, at 1.30 p.m., after the morning classes, he went to the allotted room and Hall would be there. Shay couldn't figure out the connection between the unit and the college, but Hall had free use of it and could go in and out without anyone noticing. It was a great cover for the meeting, Shay thought. Hall took notes in a hardback book during the meetings: the only record of their dealings and Shay's connection with the force. Shay kept no records, nothing that could ever disclose anything about him. Hall, he was sure, kept that book 'offside', outside formal Garda records.

Shay got out and stepped past the rubbish and bicycles. He gave the door a good rap. Inside was the faint scuff of slippers on lino.

The door opened slowly. Jig's ma gazed out, struggling to focus. She looked like she had swum up and down the canal and had swallowed half its contents.

'Look who it is.'

'There's a match on today.'

She didn't respond, just shuffled back down the hallway, leaving the door open. Shay followed her to the kitchen. There was some celebrity dining thing on the box. Jig sat at the kitchen table, his arms stretched out and his head lying sideways. Shay thought, just for a second, Jig's face lightened on seeing him.

'Hospital United today, Jig. Best get going.'

Jig slouched off his chair and passed him without a word and went up the stairs. Shay was about to follow.

'What does be yer story?'

'What?' Shay replied, turning to face Jig's ma. She seemed to have woken slightly and was lighting a cigarette.

'Ya training Jig for the Premiership or something?' She laughed, short and hard.

'He's got talent. I want him to stick at it, not like . . .' Shay struggled for the right words, as out of nowhere Maggot came into his mind. He was just about to say his name when Ms Hunt stuck her neck out towards him, as if she smelled something.

'Like who?'

'Like other good young fellas that dropped out. Happens loads of times.'

'Ya were about to say Maggot, weren't ya, ya bollix?'

Shay stood there, waiting for her to bite off the side of his head. Instead she blinked and looked up to the ceiling. Shay figured a stray thought had entered her head. Her mouth opened and the cigarette hung between her fingers, smoking away. Feet thundered down the stairs, but the sound didn't rouse her. Shay slipped away.

Outside, Shay opened the car door and got in. He glanced down the road at two boys, no older than four or five, who were clambering on top of a huge skip and flinging items off. Shay hit the ignition. The radio came back on.

'And what about this story here about pipe bomb attacks on headshops, which have mushroomed across the country in the last two years . . .'

Shay glanced over at Jig as he entered.

'How you feeling?'

No answer. The boy began to finger his phone.

'Your ma, she looks ...'

'That mad bitch. She's grand.'

'Another crime story in the papers that caught my eye is the investigation into those awful, awful double murders of Garda Ciara Grant and ten-year-old Taylor Williams. Gardaí have released fifty people, arrested as part of that investigation ...'

Shay looked at Jig. He was staring at the radio.

'The story quotes garda sources as saying that the arrests were a massive shakedown of criminal gangs in the area. It says those arrested – which included children as young as ten, could you believe it – were detained for withholding information ...'

Shay made a show of turning off the radio as the car pulled away.

'Guards rough you up?'

Jig shook his head and looked out his window.

'How you dealing with ... what happened on the canal?'

'I don't know nothing,' Jig shouted, swinging towards him. 'I didn't see nothing. Right.'

Shay flinched at the edge in the boy's voice, the gleaming white of his eyes.

'I meant Taylor,' he said.

Jig sank into his seat, his eyes betraying confusion and, Shay thought, pain.

'How you coping with that?'

Jig scratched at the side of his neck and looked down at his phone.

'I saw you at her funeral the other day,' Shay continued. 'Must have been hard on you.'

Jig tapped at his phone and a game sprang to life.

'Did Ghost get trials in England when he was thirteen?'

Shay was taken aback by the change of topic. But he grasped the opportunity.

'Yeah. Before my time. Was a top-class centre back, by all accounts. Tall, wiry. Took no prisoners.' Shay laughed. 'No surprise.'

He could see Jig looking over at him, with what he sensed was a smile.

'He could have gone to any of the big clubs in Dublin when he was young,' Shay said. 'He would have been a few years older than you. He was approached loads of times, but he stayed with us. All through, till thirteen, then got the trial with Arsenal.'

'How'd he do?'

'Good, for a while anyway.'

Shay had heard that when he hit fifteen, Ghost went a bit wild, drinking mainly, then coke. He got himself thrown out of the club. He transferred down the leagues, to Bournemouth, and played with them for a year or two.

'Jig, it's very hard to make it in England. Harder than ever now. Talent isn't enough. You have got to have dedication, discipline. Not get distracted by . . . other things.'

'He smack some guy?' Jig asked. 'Kill him?'

Shay had heard that Ghost did almost kill someone, glassed him in the head at a pub. He had to scarper after that and came home, rejoining his old club.

'There might have been a scrap,' he said, 'but, I don't know what happened really.'

Shay moved the conversation on.

'He coached at the club before I joined. Your brother played under him, then me, before he gave it up.'

No response. Shay probed more.

'You think Maggot will ever pick it back up?' Shay asked. He knew he was pushing it.

Jig played away at some game on his phone.

'Say it to him. See what he says.'

'How the fuck am I supposed to say it to him?'

Shay didn't rush in and let the silence settle.

'Ya think Maggot was good?' Jig asked.

Shay turned to him and nodded.

'Yeah. A tough defensive midfielder. He could lay on beautiful passes too. But he couldn't keep his cool. Why?'

'Just wondering.'

'Sure, bring him down sometime for a tap around.'

Shay turned a corner and swerved just in time to avoid a smouldering car.

'If I ever see him again.'

Jig said it so softly that Shay wasn't sure he heard him properly.
'What?'

But Jig was out the door, clutching his bag, running off towards the pitch, disappearing behind the smoking wreck.

35

The handshake was firmer than it needed to be.

'Great game, Shayo. Jesus, youse were flying today. What ya fucking trying to do, stop us from winning the league?'

Butch slapped him across the shoulder, forcing Shay to adjust his footing. Butch was built like the proverbial. Shay could hear him shouting and roaring like a madman on the other side of the pitch as the game slipped away from them. Which it did. Canal United won, 3–2, thanks to Jig, who scored one and made one.

In between the cheering and roaring at the end of the game, Shay could see the face of Butch as he kicked a water bottle a good twenty yards. Fucking furious he was, like he'd swallowed a carton of sour milk. Now, here he was all matey in front of him. Shay waited for what he really came over to say.

'Listen, that number nine of yers. What's his name, James or something?'

'Jig.'

Butch nodded his head, but his face gave his interest away.

'His folks here?'

Shay slapped a few of his team on the shoulders as they passed, enjoying Butch's obvious discomfort.

'Nah. Never are.'

'Right,' Butch said, walking away slowly.

The rules were clear, Shay reminded himself. Either the boy's parents or the coach had to be present if the manager of another club wanted to ask the boy to join them.

Shay cast a quick look around at the kids. No sign of Jig. He scanned the area, missed him at first and only spotted him when he stepped from behind an adult. Butch.

The cunt.

He was about to roar but, instead, strode over.

Butch glanced over his shoulder in Shay's direction, handed Jig something, and walked casually away.

'What you up to?' Shay shouted, passing Jig.

Butch turned around, any pretence of friendliness vanished. 'What?'

'You know full well what,' he said, pointing back at Jig. 'You approach a boy, their parents or the coach have to be present.'

'Don't start crying, Shayo. Just gave him my card, asked him to tell his folks to ring me. That's all, pal.'

Shay's head began to swim as Butch strode off.

No fucking way Jig is going anywhere. Not now.

He turned back and grabbed Jig by the arm.

'What that prick say to you?'

Jig wrestled his arm free. 'Lay off.'

'You know he's not allowed to approach you like that?'

'So?'

Some of the kids nearby listened in.

'Jig, that fucker cannot be trusted. He shouldn't even be talking to you. What did he say?'

'Nothing.'

'Don't give me shite. What did he say?'

Jig looked up at him, confused and annoyed.

'Just said to get me da or me ma to ring him, and gave me this.' He held out the card in his hand.

'What else?'

'Said I was the type of player they wanted, that some other guys they took in had gone on for trials in England.'

Jig walked on and added, not looking at Shay: 'He said no one in our club has in years. They have a thing with clubs over there, scouts and stuff.'

Shay leaned back, his mind racing.

174

'You know what's going on here, Jig,' Shay said, following the boy, hearing the emotion in his voice. 'He signs up talent from other teams, fills you with shite that such and such played for them, that he ended up in Man United or whatever. But what really happens is they sign you up and put you on the bench. Why? To remove you as a threat to them. I've seen it loads of times.'

He could see Jig was listening, as he twirled the card in his hand.

'Show us that,' Shay said.

'No, fuck off.'

Shay stared at Jig as he walked away.

Jig is my ticket out of here. I can't let anything stand in the way of that.

He stood still, labouring over what he could do, who he could turn to to nip this in the bud. There was definitely one person.

36

Something clicked at the back of Crowe's mind as she studied the geezer. She recalled details from his Garda Pulse file. Jason Stone, Downall Road. Convictions: possession, supply, theft, burglaries. He had stored stuff for the Canal Gang. And one of his former associates was Leo King.

God, the King investigation, she wondered. It seemed like ages ago.

She pulled her car into a space.

Stoner was hopping from one foot to another outside a row of disused shops fronting Canal Shopping Centre. His thin legs bent out, then in. It reminded Crowe of how a cowboy walked. The elasticated ends of his tracksuit bottoms were pulled in tight, revealing bright white socks and fluorescent green runners. The hood of a blue raincoat dug into his face. Not that it was raining. He seemed to be singing. He fancied himself as a rapper, Crowe recalled. In an elaborate movement of arms and hands, he brought out a rollie and swung around against the wind. He cupped his hands and, with the skinny rollie in his mouth, spent what seemed like ages trying to light it.

Crowe laughed. That was something she hadn't done in a while. She felt drained from the last few weeks, with the murders, the round-the-clock CCTV investigation, the two funerals, the raids and the questioning. There were conferences every couple of days and Tyrell was on everyone's back to have their jobs submitted. There was a growing unease that the Canal Gang was getting away with it. The interviews had thrown up little or nothing. That was the impression she got from Tyrell. He wasn't happy with the mass arrests in the first place. It was too soon, he said. And he was right. But they had to plough on. She was heading back to the station to resume her search for CCTV of that articulated truck. But, first, she'd see if she could get any scraps from Stoner.

She beeped the horn and waved over at him. He jumped forward, raising his hand in salute. It was only as he approached the car that his face narrowed. But before he could turn around, Crowe slid down the passenger window.

'How you doing there, Stoner? Putting on a one-man show for the local community?'

'Ah, Garda, Garda ...'

'Crowe, Jason. Detective Garda Crowe.'

'Garda Crowe. Yeah. Right. What's smoking in the cop shop there, Crowe, I mean Garda Crowe?'

She could see he was monged.

'Anything happening?' she asked.

He leaned back out and started rapping.

'Never know what ya don't know. Only know what ya do know.'

'Stoner?'

'She wants what's in me socket, but I'm keeping it in me pocket.'

'What charges do I have on you?'

'She's wrecking me head, spitting out words like lead.'

'Okay, if that's your attitude,' Crowe said, revving the car.

Stoner tilted his head as if he had something in his ear.

'I'm just hanging out, minding me ownie,' Stoner said, stretching his hands out in a gesture of an innocent abroad. 'All I'm doing is having a little smokie, dropping a few raps. *Pap, a pap, pap,*' he sounded, boxing the air.

'You're a model citizen, Jason. Don't you have a long list of break-ins up in court soon?'

Stoner twisted his head again. Crowe knew she was wrecking his buzz.

'And there's loads of handling charges too ...'

'Yeah, yeah. Don't know, garda. Don't really give a –'

'What, a shite, is it? You want me to tell the judge you haven't come to my attention since those crimes? Play down your previous convictions?'

He dragged hard on his miserable rollie and leaned in.

'How's the drought hitting you?' Crowe asked, changing tack.

One thing the clampdown had done was end the Canal Gang's operation. They weren't moving anything around.

'It's a fucking bitch, garda. But, I have my own ways and means.'

'A resourceful fella like you, Stoner. Don't doubt it.'

Stoner laughed at that.

'I knows,' he said, the words dragging out, 'with what happened with the little girl and all, that youse have to come down heavy.'

'And the two guards, Stoner.'

'Yeah, the garda. Absolutely. It's fucking headbanger stuff.'

'You hearing anything on who was involved? Or where they might be?'

Stoner stood back and looked at her as if she had just flashed her boobs at him.

'Youse want to find me plugged and floating on the canal? Youse haven't a clue.'

Crowe nodded to herself. No one knew anything. And even the scraps they had, they were keeping to themselves. Even half-decent addicts like Stoner.

Her mind turned to Ms King. She might get something on that.

'You ever hear anything from Leo King?'

His eyes looked like a slot machine whirring away.

'Leo the Lion,' Stoner said, 'a good skin, like his ma. God bless her.'

'Ever hear from him?'

'Na, he's long gone. They had a fucking army of little ants looking for him. But now,' he said with a smirk, 'they have other, what ya call them, concerns.'

'Who's they?'

'Santa Claus and the elves, who ya think?'

He leaned back out, waving his hand in dismissal. He walked

away towards the rear of the car. Crowe lifted the handbrake and reversed.

'Got some important business to attend to?'

'Pressing. Going home to have a wank and a nice toke. Can join me if ya want?'

'Come here,' she said.

Stoner spat on the ground and leaned back in.

'You hear anything, a whisper, about the shooting, about the gang, or Leo for that matter, give me a shout.'

She rummaged in her bag.

'Here, take this,' she said, handing him her card.

Stoner looked at it as if it was a filthy bone.

'What do I want this for?'

'I want more from you, Stoner. I think your burglary charges are all being held together, in a couple of months from now. In the Circuit Court. Could be a substantial sentence.'

Crowe shoved the gear into first and moved off. Glancing at the rear view mirror, she smirked as Stoner gave her the finger.

37

'Take off your shoes,' Shay shouted. 'Molly, Charlie, come back, they're all wet and muddy.'

'Ha!' Molly shouted, running into the sitting room, little Charlie scampering after.

'Back. Now!' Shay roared. 'Alright, nothing nice for lunch.'

Molly ran back out. 'Ham, I want ham.'

Shay leaned down and tried to unravel her shoes, wet from the downpour that came about half way through the walk home.

'You too, Charlie, take those shoes off.'

'I want melon,' Charlie said.

'Let's take these off and get lunch ready.' Shay pulled back the straps on Charlie's shoes, grabbed them from underneath and felt something soft.

'Jesus Christ,' he shouted, knowing what it was before he looked. 'Bloody dog shit.'

'Uugh,' Molly uttered.

Shay tackled the stairs and washed his hands. He peeped into his bedroom; it was empty. At least Lisa had got up and gone to work, he thought.

Bangers exploded outside. He gave his ears a good shake. He went back down and dumped Charlie's shoes in the back porch, reminding himself to clean them later. The wind was picking up and rattled the front door.

'Why growling outside, Daddy?' Charlie said, standing near the door.

'Ah, it's just the rain and wind,' Shay said, walking into the sitting room, which was a mess. 'Right, clean this up or there'll be no lunch,' he said.

The kitchen was in a worse state. Lisa had left dishes piled up on the sink. The dishwasher hadn't been working for ages. Dirt marks from the kids' shoes ran all the way into the kitchen. He grabbed some kitchen roll and bent down to clean it.

He was still thinking about what he had done. And wondered what else he would end up doing before all this was over.

'Molly took my car,' Charlie shouted.

'Molly, just give it fucking back, will you,' Shay roared, uttering the word before he even knew it.

He wiped the floor and threw the tissue into the overflowing kitchen bin as the fight resumed. He turned on the tap. Everything was just dumped into the sink. He took out the bigger items and placed them on top of wine glasses, knowing the pile might not hold. The tap ran as he recalled the words of Hall.

'We want ears on the priest and Leo.'

'How?'

'That meditation room for starters.'

'But he might be meeting Leo anywhere.'

'You said yourself that's where he talks to people in private. You said there's a corridor from the priest's house to the centre. We want you to look after that room. You have access to it.'

'You won't get approval for that, will you?' Shay said. 'Bugging a priest's room where all sorts of people come in and out.'

'Let us worry about that,' Hall replied.

'This,' Hall said, holding a small ziplock bag, with what looked like a thick black button inside. 'Put it somewhere it won't be seen. Peel the back off it and push the adhesive hard against the surface. Can you think of anywhere to put it?'

I can think of somewhere alright.

Hall handed him the bag. Shay got the feeling Hall just knew he was going to do it.

'Ham. Ham. I want ham,' Molly shouted, rousing him from his thoughts. She was standing beside him, hopping up and down. She pulled at the fridge and rummaged inside.

'In. Now,' Shay shouted through gritted teeth, reefing her back hard and slamming the fridge door.

She protested at the rough treatment.

'Mean Daddy,' she said.

'Melon.'

Shay looked down at little Charlie's face.

'You can see Daddy's busy. Go inside.'

The plates on top of the pot went first, sliding and clattering into the sink. Then the glasses buckled under the weight of the pot, one falling out to the ground. Shay managed to break the fall with his foot. More clattering followed, as everything else fell off the draining board. Knives and cutlery spilled out through the gaps. He felt like screaming.

The priest had agreed to meet him that morning. Shay rang to say he needed to talk, said it was to do with their last conversation.

'Daddy? Daddy?'

Shay swung around. 'What, Charlie?'

'Molly gone toilet,' Charlie said, pointing into the sitting room.

Shay marched in. Molly stood over by her princess castle, one leg bent in towards the other, a puddle at her feet.

'Jesus, Molly, what are you doing? You know not to leave it to the last second. Up to the toilet, now.'

Molly burst out crying.

'Come on. Up.'

'No. I don't want to.'

Shay grabbed her arm. She continued to cry and fought against being pulled. Somewhere his brain told him to stop pulling her, but he wouldn't. He pushed her up the stairs. Shay took off her leggings and underwear, washed her down and told her to go in to her room and put on another pair.

'Can't ... find ... any,' she said from her room, between sobs.

Shay went in to see her sitting on the floor, her knees pulled in to her chest.

'Here,' Shay said, pulling out leggings from her drawer.

'Don't like those,' Molly said, digging her head into her chest.

'They are the only ones there. The rest are in the wash. How about jeans?'

'No.'

'Fine, do what you want,' Shay said, throwing the leggings at her face, closing the door behind him. He could hear more crying, but followed his legs and hard mind down the stairs.

'Daddy, melon,' Charlie said.

'Jesus, bloody fucking melon.'

He pulled the melon out of the fridge and hacked off a slice.

Shay had taken up the priest's half-hearted offer of a cup of tea when he called up. That would give him time. He had figured that under the front of the altar would be good. He peeled back the tape and pushed the device up hard.

'Charlie has melon. I want some ham.'

Molly was back down, a tiny skirt on and bare legs.

'Could you not find something else to put on?' Shay said to her.

Molly shook her head.

'Ham,' she said.

'Jesus,' he said, pulling out a slice from the fridge and giving it to her.

Shay's head was spinning. In the distance he heard the Luas rattling.

The peace in the sitting room didn't last long.

'Daddy, Charlie ate some of my ham. I didn't eat his melon.'

'Right, I'm turning on the television,' Shay said, 'until we have lunch and then I'll turn it off.'

He went up to the toilet, locking the door behind him. The roaring kicked off again and little feet came pounding up the stairs. They were shouting and screaming. They pushed and shoved at the door. They banged their fists against it. Shay tried to roar above them, telling them he was in the toilet, that the door was locked. He was half way through. The screams and banging got so bad he had to get up and shuffle over. He pulled the bolt back and reversed.

'What the fuck is going on?' he shouted as he sat back down. 'Can ye not give me a second to go to the toilet?'

'Molly said ghosts are outside,' Charlie said, upset.

'No I didn't,' Molly said. 'I said, there are ghosts at Halloween.'

'Out!' Shay roared. He clenched his fist and banged it against the tiles. 'Out.' He could feel the throbbing from his fist. Charlie's crying became more hysterical. Molly joined in.

'Go into your room.'

'Lights ... no ... on,' Charlie said.

'Get in and leave me fucking alone. In, in.'

The kids stared at Shay, their eyes swimming in tears. They pattered out of view.

Shay sat there, his chest straining. He finished off. He stank out the place. He reached up to open the window. When he went into their room, Molly was under the blanket and Charlie was behind the board at the end of his bed, a nervous, giddy smile on him.

'Do you hate us, Daddy?' Molly asked, peeping out from the blanket.

Shay fell down on his knees.

'No, of course not. I'm sorry, little ones.'

He reached for their hands, feeling weak and drained, wincing as he recalled what Pat had said when he came in with the cups of tea.

'Everything you say to me, Shay, is in confidence. You can trust me.'

38

The screech of metal from the Luas on Harcourt Street distracted Tyrell from the question. He was struggling for an answer.

'I'll repeat myself, detective inspector,' Commissioner Harte said, raising his voice and straining his neck up like an ostrich, 'have we anything we can go to the DPP with?'

Tyrell looked at the commissioner straight and, maintaining his cool, waited another second.

'No. Sir.'

He heard the Chief, who was sitting beside him, adjust himself in his seat as if to interject. 'Not at the moment,' Tyrell added. The Chief unstiffened.

The commissioner pulled his bottom lip up over his top lip, forcing his cheeks to puff out and his chin to protrude. Tyrell knew his brevity and honesty rankled Harte, but Number One couldn't take him to task on being evasive.

'Nothing,' the commissioner said, leaning back into his seat. The tone of his voice reflected disappointment and blame in equal measure. 'We have one of the worst gangland crimes on record, and Christ knows there have been many, and we have ... nothing.'

'If I may,' the Chief said. 'We have a number of good leads and the arrest operation did throw up some additional information. Detective Inspector Tyrell has identified the criminals who are unaccounted for and who they work –'

'Yes, I know we have suspicions,' the commissioner interrupted, 'but do we have any evidence? The type needed in court to convict the bastards?'

The shakedown was never a good idea, Tyrell thought. He was against it from the off and had told the Chief that. It was too early. They hadn't enough evidence gathered yet. But the Chief was under severe pressure from the Puzzle Palace at Phoenix Park to put on a show.

'I told the parents of Garda Grant and that little girl that we would get the people behind this,' the commissioner continued. 'The Justice Minister wants to see charges and the opposition want war. The gutter press are running stories on the new generation of untouchables, complete with blurred photographs of them. I'm the one who's getting it in the neck.'

When he finished there was silence, disturbed only by the soft metallic sound of the Luas.

'Sir, if I may?'

Tyrell looked over to see Hall, touching the tip of his pink tie.

'While Inspector Tyrell ...'

Detective Inspector you fucker.

'... has listed suspects, we have intelligence – from an asset – that Darren Hunt, alias Maggot, was in the back of the car.'

Tyrell bit his lip. He knew not to lose his composure. The seat the Chief was sitting in groaned from the strain.

The commissioner's face freshened with interest.

'We know that Maggot was part of a canal crew with Shop, who we suspect was also in the car.'

Yeah, we know they're in the same crew.

'... In addition, our intelligence indicates a number of old Provos have offered their services to a group called Republican Communities Against Drugs. This outfit is threatening drug gangs in that area, but unlike the Reals and the Continuity, they are not extorting them for money. We suspect one network – and our best guess is the Canal Gang – intended to strike first. We suspect that the car which Garda Grant and Peters stopped may have been transporting a cache of weapons for that purpose.'

Tyrell tried not to show his exasperation.

186

Fucking speculation.

'We are currently trying to place additional surveillance on key targets, budgets permitting . . .'

That's what the fucker wants, more money for his black ops. What about overtime for the actual fucking investigation?

Tyrell watched Hall pat down his tie as he finished and put on a show of looking impassive. Tyrell saw the commissioner nod again, clearly impressed. He braced himself as Number One looked at him.

'Inspector?'

Even the commissioner's calling me inspector now.

'Either you were aware of all this, but decided not to tell me – which is pretty fucking bad – or you didn't know, which is worse. Which is it?'

Tyrell had hoped the Chief might actually step in. No such luck.

'Superintendent Hall, for reasons best known to himself,' Tyrell said, 'decided not to share this apparent intelligence or speculation with us. If the intel is not shared it is of little use.'

The commissioner eyed him up.

'Do you have a problem, Inspector, with Detective Superintendent Hall?'

'No, sir. He seems to have a problem with us.'

Tyrell knew his frankness attracted few friends, but Hall needed to be shown up for the selfish, slimy bollocks he was.

'Let's make things crystal clear here,' the commissioner said. 'This is no time for egos or turf wars between garda units. I want whoever's behind these murders cornered. If we can't get charges against them for murder, I want them on drug charges, fucking traffic violations, battering the missus, anything. I am not going to have this as my swan song after forty years.'

Tyrell understood the commissioner now.

This is what's making the commissioner's arse bleed. His reputation. And his hopes for an extension to his term.

He watched the commissioner point his finger around the room.

'I want a plan to get these pricks,' he said. 'Even if it takes time to hatch.'

39

Jig listened to his ma's broken wails.

When she was down in the kitchen, between the moans and the filling and emptying of her glass, he watched as she jabbed at her mobile. Her face twitched as she held the phone to her ear. Then she slammed it down on the table and pulled hard on a cigarette.

Yesterday was Maggot's sixteenth birthday, almost four months since the shooting. Still no sign of him.

Jig watched her from the hallway, peering around the doorway. He wanted to say something, but she would have bitten his ear off.

Wayne and Crystal watched TV in the front room all night. Jig gave them biscuits when they were hungry. Sometime around 11 p.m., he pulled them up to bed, and rather than face going back down, lay down himself and played games on his phone.

She had dragged her drunken grief upstairs, and set up base inside Maggot's room. She shrieked and coughed through the small hours of the morning.

His ma's outbursts were getting louder. He heard what sounded like a light swoosh, and knew it was the liquid in the bottle swishing down and back again.

'Ah, give over, for the love of Jaysus.'

His da. He had walked out last night. Said she was wrecking his head. Jig smelled whiskey and chips off him when he came back in. The bastard had eaten all the chips on his way home and went straight up to bed.

'Fuck off, ya stinking ...'

His ma trailed off. His da's words would usually have been enough for her to go in and hit him a couple of slaps and there'd be war. But his ma was weak. His da knew that.

'Is Ma alright?' Wayne piped up.

'She's crying,' Crystal said from the bed above him.

'Go the fuck asleep,' Jig told them.

'Jig?' Wayne asked. 'What's Maggot doing up the mountains?'

Before he stormed out of the house, their da had shouted back at their ma: 'He's not going to fucking answer the phone. He's never going to. He's in the fucking mountains.'

Jig got up out of his bed and looked over at Wayne, who was peeping his head out from under the blanket.

'Go to sleep.'

When his ma kicked off again, he found himself standing at Maggot's door. His ma was sitting in the shadows, on the far side of the bed, with her back to him. A cigarette flared red and light grey smoke funnelled towards the window. With her other hand she lifted the bottle and took another swig. Jig could gauge from the sound there was only another mouthful left.

'What?' she said.

Jig didn't think about what he was going to say. He just felt he should go in. He forced his feet to shuffle along the carpet, glancing up at the side of his mother's face as he moved. She pulled her head up and snorted, rubbed a hand across her nose, and spluttered again. A dim light from outside slid across her face.

'What do ya want?' she said, just as he got to her side of the bed. 'Go back to yer room.'

Jig stood for a moment. He began to turn around. She grasped his arm hard and pulled him down beside her. She dumped the fag into a can. Her mobile was on the floor, the screen still lit up. They sat in silence for a few moments. She took a final swig of the bottle, dropping it on the floor, landing with a quiet thud.

'They killed him, Jig. Our Maggot,' his ma said finally, as if it was the last word on a long discussion they were having.

Jig guessed he had been killed, kind of anyway. The guards

kept saying it to him on the road. Anytime they passed in their cars, they shouted out the window trying to rise him: 'Ye know them mountains are full of maggots,' or 'Has Maggot burrowed to the surface yet, Jig?' followed by thick stupid country laughs.

Even his own da had said it.

But it wasn't until his ma said those words that it was real. Like a nail being hammered in. Jig's eyes peeled back. He imagined men with thick shovels over a big grave and a body wrapped in bin liners being kicked into it. All the maggots eating the skin.

His ma hugged him, rough and tight. Unfamiliar emotions seized Jig. He struggled to free himself, but her bony grasp held him firm.

'Fuckers, wouldn't even let me have a body.'

She pushed Jig back.

'Can't even give him a proper church burial.'

'Why don't ya talk to the coppers, Ma?'

It was the only thing he could think of, to get Maggot's body back.

The darkness could not hide her eyes. Beady little black pebbles pierced into him. He stiffened for a smack.

'No fucking way I'm going to the filth.' She jerked her head towards the window.

He should have known better. It was the same with his da, when he was questioned by that garda months ago. Better dead than a rat, his da always said.

The garda had been right. He did see something. He saw Shop in the car when they were pulled over, before the shooting. He didn't see Maggot, but guessed he was in it, if Shop was. They did everything together.

His ma pushed her face up against his, forcing him to recoil.

'You'll do it,' she said, clasping his wrist.

'What ya mean, Ma? Do what?'

'Get our own back. The Hunt way.'

Jig felt he had to do a piss, but she tightened her grip.

'Not now, yer too young. But down the road, years from now,' she pointed her finger at him, 'when they don't expect it.'

40

The women swiped their phones as their children crawled over the seats.

'Look at this one here,' said one of the mothers excitedly, lifting up her phone and turning it to her two friends sitting facing her.

'These leggings only cost me twenty euro,' the woman said almost spelling out the word 'euro' she emphasised it so much. 'Been delivered and all for that.'

Crowe looked at the women again. High platform heels, hair freshly straightened, fake eyelashes, manicured nails and layers of make-up. In sharp contrast to herself.

I probably look like I've been dragged arseways through a ditch.

She hadn't been to the hairdresser's for half a year. She hadn't bought clothes or underwear in she didn't know how long. And she had still not got around to buying make-up. She had cut her make-up tube in half and had scraped each end dry. The past months were just a blur.

'Sit the fuck down,' the first woman roared at a girl, her daughter, Crowe presumed.

Crowe looked out the window as the Luas glided to a halt. A group of young fellas and girls were messing on the platform. Just as the Luas door closed, one of them lunged for the door, forcing it to open. They all piled in. Just like her thoughts.

She had gone to visit Garda Peters that morning. She tried to get to the hospital every fortnight or so. His mother was there, as always. Although they lived in Tipperary, she drove up every morning, after the traffic, and didn't go back until the late after-noon, before the evening rush. Her husband worked the garage back home and came up at the weekends with her.

Crowe felt stabs of pain in her heart as she watched Peters' mum fuss around the bed, tidy the side tables, straighten the pillows, smooth out the sheets and share small talk with the nurses. On the bottom of the bed lay a tabloid newspaper, which she bought every day for her son.

'A lot of the news is too grim: murders and the like,' she told Crowe, 'so I read him the sport. Mind you, I'm sure I'm not pronouncing all them foreign names right.'

She laughed and Crowe shared the moment with her. She twisted inside at the woman's anguish. She dreaded being asked about the investigation, but knew it was inevitable. She wanted to be honest, but didn't want to break the woman's will completely.

'We are trying hard, Ms Peters,' she said. 'We are doing every-thing we can. We won't give up.'

Ms Peters looked at her, nodded and smiled. She placed her hand on her son's wrist and rubbed it back and forth. Crowe knew Peters could stay in the coma indefinitely. If he ever did wake up, he would be paralysed from the neck down.

The Luas shuddered slightly, rousing Crowe. The women and the kids were gone. She caught sight of impressive graffiti deco-rating some dilapidated buildings.

'Ya know she gives great head,' a boy said loudly.

Crowe turned around. It was the youths that had jumped on a few stops back. One of the young fellas stood in the aisle, his hands down the front of his tracksuit bottoms.

'Shut the fuck up,' a girl replied.

'Don't tell me to shut the fuck up or I'll slap ya one, bitch,' the young fella shouted, pulling one of his hands out and pointing at her.

Crowe could sense other passengers tensing in their seats. She fought her instinct to intervene. She just wanted to get home, though she wasn't sure if Tom would be there. Invariably, he was out these days. She didn't know where. He'd just say he was out,

192

having a pint or watching 'the match', which seemed to be most nights. He'd have a smell of drink off him alright. Some of the nights she came home she found porn on his computer. He didn't bother wiping the history. But could she blame him? They hadn't had sex in ages.

She was always tired and couldn't get in the mood. She had been working non-stop for nearly four months, going through hundreds of hours of tapes to locate that truck. But it was a proverbial needle in a haystack job. And she had built up a backlog of other cases, which she was struggling to work her way through. She didn't know when Tom and her last sat down together for a dinner. But she couldn't sit at a table, have wine poured out for her, eat a nice meal and share small talk, with the killers still out there, sticking their two fingers up at everyone.

She wondered if Tom would do the dirt on her if he got an offer. He was handsome enough and had a weakness, like all men, if an available woman came his way.

She looked out at the grim Bridewell District Court as the Luas stopped and recalled her first cases at the chaotic Court 44. It was like being thrown into an urban jungle, without a map or the language. No one seemed to know what was going on. And you couldn't hear a thing. It was sink or swim.

That was only five years ago. But it seemed like a different life.

There were more shouts behind her.

'My God, be careful. My daughters.'

Crowe saw the young fella pretending to throw a bottle of beer against the window. She looked through gaps of people and made out a woman sitting opposite the youths. She had children with her.

'Sorry there, Winnie,' the youth said, to hoots of laughter. 'What's their names?'

The woman did not reply.

'Ya not understand English, Winnie?'

'Angel. And Precious.'

The kids laughed and repeated the names, ridiculing them.

Crowe sighed. She opened her bag, to check the pepper spray

was near to hand. She took out her badge. She heaved herself up and negotiated her way through people that were getting off. The young fella eyeballed her as she approached. Both his hands were shoved down his grey tracksuit.

'Sit down and leave the woman alone,' Crowe said.

The young fella laughed, surprised by her audacity.

'Listen, love, best thing youse can do is turn yer pretty ass around, yeah, and fuck off.'

'I'm a garda,' she said, holding up her badge. 'If you don't stop harassing this woman I will arrest you under the Public Order Act. Now, sit down.'

Crowe noticed she wasn't the slightest bit nervous.

'We're just messing with Winnie Mandela here,' the boy said, leaning in towards the woman. 'Aren't we?'

The woman clutched her two girls.

'Would you like to sit down with me?' Crowe asked.

The woman nodded and pushed the girls out. Crowe looked at the youth again and down at his friends, two boys and two girls, all around thirteen or fourteen.

'What's this, garda?' the young fella said, pretending to be offended. 'Can't we even have a laugh with them foreigners now? That a fucking crime now, is it?'

She watched his hands move inside his tracksuit.

'Do us all a favour and take your hands out of there,' Crowe said. 'It might be the only way you get any action, but the rest of us don't want to see it.'

His mouth pouted, like a fish. He searched for words, but none came out. Muffled laughs from his friends broke the silence.

Crowe walked slowly back to her seat and acknowledged the woman's thanks. She stared at the big, beautiful smiles of her children.

She wanted to smile back, but dark thoughts pulled at her.

41

Shay heard the sound. But he kept his gaze on the game. Out of the corner of his eye, he saw Ghost zip off his jacket and let it fall to the grass. It was an Indian summer, and the hot September day had everyone stripping off.

The ball had gone out for a throw. Shay could see Ghost jogging down to get it. He seized his opportunity. He picked up his holdall and dropped it beside Ghost's jacket.

He turned to the game. Jig took the ball and swerved around a player and curled a pass in front of Bishop. Shay ran down the sideline, catching up with Ghost. Without even touching the ball to control it, Bishop belted it first time, powering over the head of the goalie and smacking the back of the net.

'Yesss,' Shay shouted and hopped into the air, clapping Ghost's shoulder as he landed.

'Good man, Bishop. Absolute cracker. Great move, Jig.'

'That Nigerian lad can smack the ball given half a sniff,' Ghost said to him.

Shay nodded and ran back up to the half way to push the team on. He looked at his phone. Only seven minutes left. He glanced at the holdall.

I need to get that jacket into the bag before Ghost notices or the sun dips.

Four swans swooped over, their wings stretched right out,

blocking the sun briefly, their great big 'woo' sound softening as they headed for the canal.

The words of Hall rang in his ears.

'Get your hands on Ghost's jacket,' he'd said.

Shay had told Hall some weeks ago that Ghost was back after his summer away. Then at their next Monday meeting, Hall unveiled his plan.

'Bring Ghost's jacket to us,' Hall told him.

Hall knew from Shay's reports that Ghost tended to wear the same jacket to matches and training.

'We'll put the bug in,' Hall said. 'Tell him the jacket got mixed up with the gear in the holdall.'

Shay didn't like the idea. It was risky. Ghost was no fucking fool. Shay knew he could be spotted shoving his jacket into the holdall. What then? And even if he was careful, Ghost would be on the hunt for his jacket. He was a suspicious fucker. These guys would put a bullet into someone's ear for less.

Shay knew the force had hit a brick wall over the summer – and everyone was tetchy. Ghost and Cracko had disappeared when the round-the-clock surveillance ended, a few weeks after the shakedown. They had gone to the final stages of the World Cup in South Africa. After that, the south of Spain. Now they were back in action, as if nothing had happened. Ghost's skin had the same grey-white colour. Not even the African or Iberian heat could breathe life into it.

But the unit was not giving up. Shay had previously supplied them with car registrations so they could put trackers on them. But Ghost was only using his Cayenne sometimes and was more often than not renting cars, as was Cracko. And they seemed to be sleeping in different places. Which was why Hall said they needed to try something else. Their clothes, anything they wore a lot. And Ghost's favourite jacket was a good one.

The final whistle went. Shay called some of the team over. He told them to head back to the centre and to tell Ghost he had to head off. He looked down the pitch, but couldn't see him. He threw down his own jacket on top of Ghost's, picked them up and shoved them into the holdall. The boys walked on ahead, the clippety clack sound of the cogs echoing on the road. Then he spotted Ghost, chatting away to Jig.

Back to normal, Shay thought grimly.

Another figure, sporting a baseball cap, caught his eye across the road. Something about him, or was it a her, looked familiar.

42

Shay welcomed the warmth of sunlight as it cut through the branches. Shafts of yellow illuminated the path in irregular patches; shards of broken glass shimmered ahead.

Molly threw the packet she was eating from on the ground.

'Pick it up,' Shay said.

'Everyone does it,' Molly said, running off towards the playground.

Shay kicked at a sodden Budweiser box and scanned the playground.

'Fucking great,' he mouthed.

There was a fresh scorch area under the last remaining swing. The seat was completely burned. The two chains were blackened by smoke and fire. A dirty crater soiled the rubber surface.

'Look what bold boys did, Daddy,' Molly shouted, pointing at the swings. 'This is junk town now.'

'What can we play?' Charlie asked.

Shay's stomach cramped as he glanced back at Lisa. She sauntered towards him, looking swamped in a baggy tracksuit and a zip-up, both his.

Months had passed, and they were still no closer to leaving. No matter how he spun it, she didn't listen any more. He was stressed, she was fed up. Things were just getting to them. Which meant more bickering and snapping and fights.

'Erm, go over to the climbing frame there.'

Lisa slumped down on a seat outside the playground. He took out his phone and dialled Ghost's number.

'Yeah?'

'You lose your jacket?'

'I did.'

'Found it this morning as I was about to throw the gear into the wash. Must have got mixed up.'

'Must have.'

Ghost was being his typical suspicious self. He better not find the device. Hall had told him he wouldn't. They had experts at this. Hope so, Shay thought.

Otherwise I'll end up like one of those swings.

'Where ya at?' Ghost asked.

'In the playground with the kids. I'll drop it round later or give it to you at training.'

Silence.

'I'm on the road. I'll swing by yer gaff.'

'Na ...'

But the phone had gone dead.

Shay thought he'd better tell Lisa now, rather than wait till they got back.

'Ghost might be at our house.'

Lisa shook her head ever so slightly.

'Right,' she said.

'I said I'd drop something over to him, but he said he was passing and that he'd wait at our place.'

She turned to him. Red circles ringed her eyes like bruises.

'Could you not have rung back and said, "No, I'll call up to you." Do you always have to be such a pussy?'

The road ahead went blurry for a moment as Shay felt the words slice into him.

He heard Molly whisper to Charlie: 'Mommy called Daddy a pussy.'

With his mind the way it was these days, he couldn't take it. It was like Lisa was hammering splinters of wood into his head. For

the briefest of seconds he had an urge to ram into the car in front
of him and if the driver got lippy, he'd punch the fucking head off
him.

He gritted his teeth all the way home, barely managing to keep
it together. Ghost's Cayenne was docked outside their gate. It
blocked most of the road.

'Look,' Charlie said, excited. 'A tank.'

'Is the Ghost man in there, Daddy?' Molly asked nervously.

In their years here, there was never much of a need before for
Ghost to be at their house. Given how the kids were reacting, it
was clear to him why he wanted it that way.

He slowed to a crawl to get past the Cayenne. He scraped the
alloy on the wheels against the footpath, Lisa cursing, as he inched
forward.

'I'll go in and get his thing,' Shay said. 'Stay in the car until he
goes.'

Lisa was looking out the window at the green. A group of kids
gathered around a half-melted plastic bin. They were stuffing it
with newspapers and making laboured attempts to light it.

Shay casually walked past Ghost's car and into his house, grabbing the jacket.

He got a start when he went back out. Ghost was rapping on
the window of his car, waving in at the kids.

'Here,' Shay said, holding the jacket and walking to Ghost's
car.

'Kids love the beast,' Ghost said, bending back. 'Ya not going
to let them out and have a look.'

Shay could see Charlie's mouth wide open. Shay kept his cool
and stayed where he was.

'Bit of a domestic,' Shay whispered as Ghost neared.

'Tell me about it, Shayo,' Ghost said, taking the jacket. 'Fucking
high maintenance the lot of them.'

'Right there,' Shay said.

'Ya got to show them who's the fucking boss,' Ghost said,
pointing his finger at him. 'Ya don't do that, ya might as well
castrate yerself.'

Shay nodded.

Ghost pulled back the huge door and stepped in. The engine boomed, growling like a forest demon, competing with blaring rap. The window zoomed shut.

A door opened in his own car. Lisa got out. She didn't look up and walked quickly to the house. Ghost's window pulled down.

'Don't ya be busting his balls now, Lisa,' Ghost shouted out.

Lisa stopped. Shay turned to her and waited for some drama, but she walked on. Cursing Ghost, he looked back, but Ghost had moved off.

Charlie's face was glued to the window as the Cayenne purred past.

43

The little circles of green light running down the middle of Millennium Bridge distracted Crowe from her thoughts. She skirted around a paper cup in front of a hunched body and thought of that joker, Stoner, again. She'd got a call a few days ago, and knew it was him.

'*The G Man is back, back in the game, still the same,*' he rapped, before hanging up.

And there Ghost was, just the other evening, on the sideline. Back to normal.

Waiting at the pedestrian lights to the Italian quarter, Crowe looked down towards her apartment block, partly obscured by two big posters on a lamppost. One screamed 'Burn the Bondholders', advertising a march to mark the second anniversary of the Bank Guarantee. The other proclaimed 'Jesus Lives', beseeching sinners to repent. She flicked between the two posters, only noticing the beeping of the pedestrian light as it slowed to a stop, then she ran across the road.

Crowe thought Shay was acting odd at the match: as if he was a bit distracted, shifty even. It was the way he kept glancing away from the game, in Ghost's direction. And then he marched off at the end.

There was only darkness and silence when she opened the apartment door. She hit the main light and stood in the sitting room with her hands on her hips. It was almost as if she was in someone else's home. The feeling unsettled her and she fought an urge to head back to the station. She stepped into the kitchenette and dropped her bag on the counter. There was no sign of food, just hardened cheese and cans of beer in the fridge. Plates and cups cluttered the sink. All she could find was a tin of beans. She hacked at it with a dodgy opener and emptied the contents into a pot.

After a search, she found the TV controls. If anything, she just wanted the noise to cut through the silence, and distract her from thoughts of where Tom was spending all his time.

'*Sorcha, this government is not going to allow terror gangs, as I would call them, to do as they want.*'

Crowe opened the fridge again, half looking at the news. The beer called to her.

'*We saw the depths of depravity they went to only months ago when they gunned down one of our children and one of our guards.*'

'*Yes, Minister, but these new laws being considered that were leaked to a newspaper . . .*'

'More laws. That's what we need alright,' Crowe said, stirring the pot. 'Not more actual guards and overtime to sit on these fuckers. Ask him why Operation Swamp was quietly axed.'

'*They will reportedly allow gardaí to apply to the Special Criminal Court to hold specified individuals in preventative detention. Myles Caufield of Lawyers for Civil Rights said this is contrary to European law.*'

'*Sorcha, the civil rights people are great at talking about protecting criminals, not about protecting society.*'

'*But is it not just internment, Minister? We had that in the North.*'

'*Sorcha, this is premature as we have not brought forward any such proposals. But speaking hypothetically, any such law would be targeted. If gardaí had intelligence that individuals were planning a shooting, or a tiger kidnap, they could present their case to the courts, requesting they be detained, for a short period. Only in these situations.*'

'*Myles?*'

'Sorcha, I have already laid out the legal and human rights reasons against any such move.'

'You really know what it's like on the streets, Myles, I'd say,' Crowe said, taking a long swig from the can.

'Groups other than ours, such as garda associations and community groups have said the way you beat this is by good policing and investment in local services.'

Crowe took another gulp. God, she was gasping.

'You don't do it by slashing garda overtime in units tasked with tackling these gangs. And you certainly don't do it by cutting funding to drug projects, employment and youth groups.'

Crowe was agreeing with the lawyer now.

'Minister?'

Crowe poured the beans on a plate and curled up on the couch. She zoned out from the minister's meandering response and heaped the beans into her. She didn't realise how hungry she was. Cleaning her plate, she turned down the volume.

The minister's reference to the murders brought her mind back to the investigation. She went over to the counter, carrying her can, and pulled out a notepad from her bag. She sat on a stool and scribbled down words.

No car. No weapon. No CCTV. No sign of suspects. No sighting of truck. BIG FAT NOTHING.

She circled the last words.

There was no more on the movements of the truck. She had contacted hauliers, garages and trucker pit stops. She sent them images of the truck, but to no avail. The thing seemed to have disappeared. But she would keep going. Something might turn up, eventually.

The best the rest of the investigation team could get after almost four months was a file on Cracko for assaults and drug charges against some kids street dealing.

Crowe didn't think the DPP was going to take the cases against Cracko. Few of the witnesses who gave statements would actually give evidence in court. Even if they did, they weren't reliable, as they were all addicts. Some of the statements were made as they were coming off whatever cocktail of drugs they were on. Other statements were made under duress. Most of the addicts were facing charges themselves. Make a statement or we'll prosecute you, they were told.

Some of the street dealers got a few digs, in the toilets and stairwells, and in the garda cars, out of sight. Crowe had heard the roars and saw the prisoners clutching their ribs afterwards.

She stared blankly at her can.

She baulked at the behaviour of some of her colleagues and thought about going to Tyrell, the Chief even. But she knew they wouldn't appreciate her bringing her precious concerns to them. Attitudes had hardened, lines had become blurred. She never would have accepted such behaviour when she joined.

She swished the remnants of the can around, pondered how things, how she, had changed, then swallowed the dregs.

44

Hall looked at the audio clip on the screen again. At the back of his mind, thoughts were massing.

'Play that again,' he told his DI.

DI Slavin dragged the cursor back and clicked. Hall looked out the big sash windows across the plaza at Garda HQ in Phoenix Park.

'Father, I'm going ahead with it.'

'What do you mean? Going ahead with what?'

'Told ya, there's no way, on me ma's life, those cunts, sorry Father, are getting away with it.'

'Leo, we've been through this many times over the last months. You must find a way of dealing with this that doesn't result in more violence. You know these guys, you know what they are capable of.'

There was a slight noise, as if someone had got off a chair.

'I don't care if I does die, Father, not if it means I can get one over on them . . .'

'I've said this to you, Leo, that if you are going to hurt another person I am obliged to inform the guards.'

'Father, ya swore to me ya wouldn't go to the garda. Ya told me ya swore to me ma ya would look after me.'

'Yes, I did, God bless her. But this is not what she would want. We can't give in to these baser instincts, Leo, no matter how much you have been hurt, and I know you have.'

'Ya seen what they done to people round here. Ya said they

were back as if nothing had happened, even after all the deaths and all.'

There was a moment of silence. Hall could hear the baying of sheep from the city farm in the zoo on the other side of the road from HQ.

'Leo, if they hear you're around ...'

'My life is over, Father. I don't give a fuck. Anyways, I'm working on something.'

'How do you mean?'

'There's others out there, Father, who want to take the war to the Canal Gang.'

'What are you talking about?'

Another break. Slavin looked up at Hall.

'Leo?'

'The RCAD.'

'Republicans? Are you serious, Leo?'

'They know me old uncle, Finbarr. He ran with the RA in the eighties. I've got a meet arranged with a contact. I've been off the gear now for more than a month. These guys have it in for the Canal Gang over the drugs. I heard Cracko assaulted one of their members and they reckon the gang also burned alive a horse of theirs in O'Donovan flats months ago.'

'Leo, you are way out of your depth here. For your mother's sake, don't go down this road.'

'It's for me ma I'm doing it.'

Slavin hit pause.

'That was half an hour ago,' Slavin said. 'The exterior cameras will pick him up if he leaves the church complex.'

'Get onto subversive intelligence and ask them about this Finbarr and get an update on the RCAD,' Hall said. 'I'll talk to Nessan and let him know. What are Leo's general movements again?'

'He leaves the priest's house twice a week, Monday and Friday, before 7 a.m. and heads down to South Road. He meets this old junkie he knows, scores and walks back. He's still off the gear, but buys benzos and weed. On his way he picks up cigs and Coke in the shop at the junction and is home by 7.40 a.m. He rarely comes out otherwise, during the day at least.'

Hall nodded. He knew the RCAD wouldn't take a junkie seriously, even one off the gear, not unless he had something really useful. He took a moment to consider the possibility.

Hall assembled and reassembled strategies in his brain, distracted only by the noise from the zoo as feeding time for the monkeys kicked in.

45

Jig stood on his toes on the edge of the planks and, holding onto the bars, leaned out as far as he could. Underneath, the water poured down the lock, crashing onto the chamber, creating a big bubble bath of foam against the rusted metal gates.

The spray came high enough to kiss his face and hands. The whoosh sound from the water made him feel light and giddy. He smiled out to where Micko and Stu were, but they were looking at their phones and talking, loud enough for him to hear bits.

'I'm telling ya,' Micko said. 'His days are numbered ... fuck up ... seizure ... Cracko ... take over ... set up on our own.'

'And,' Stu said, 'the RA are out to get them. That's the word.'

'Here,' Micko said. 'Little ears.'

Jig sensed them looking over at him, but kept staring at the waters, smiling as the memories soaked into him.

'The chips nice?'

'Lovely, Granda. Ya get fish supper?'

'Ah yeah, I loves the old fish supper.'

They sat on the edge of the canal, their legs dangling over the water. Jig kicked the back of his heels against the huge granite slabs. The chips were deadly. He sucked the salt from his fingers and licked the vinegar inside the big brown bag.

'It's nice for a child to have a treat,' his granda said. 'Not that there was much in the way of treats over there.'

Jig looked up as his granda nodded across the canal.

'What happened there, Granda?'

'Children were treated like dogs in there. By the nuns,' he said, shovelling in chips.

'In them apartments?' Jig asked.

'No. The industrial school's gone now,' he said, pausing as he went for the fish. 'Was a bad country for a lot of children then.'

'I'll be okay, won't I, Granda?'

He gave him a bear hug. 'So long as I'm around, no one will fucking dare harm ya, Jig. Now eat up them chips before they go cold.'

A huge spray roused Jig, his face tingling at the cold water.

'Jig, ya dope.'

Jig looked over at Micko. He was leaning over the balance beam and motioning at him to come over.

'Yer the doziest cunt going, ya know that?'

Jig stepped sideways across the wooden walkway.

'Take this over,' Micko said, handing him a bundle of notes, an elastic band tight around it. 'What do ya be fucking dreaming about anyways?'

Jig stood there, looking at him.

What the fuck is it to youse?

'Don't ya be given me the fucking eyes, Jig, or I'll slap ya right into that canal.'

Micko reminded him of Maggot. That same madness buzzing around inside his head.

'Ya heard anything from Maggot?' Stu asked.

Jig's right eyelid twitched. He was just thinking about Maggot. He saw Micko smile back at Stu.

Cunts.

'Still up the mountains, is he?' Micko said.

'Ya fucking bastard!' Jig roared and heaved forward, but Micko shoved him back.

'Ya want to cool the jets there, little Jig,' Micko said.

Jig was steaming, but Micko was a nasty fucker.

'Sorry,' Jig said. 'Just hate people talking about Maggot and the mountains.'

'Alright. I won't smack ya one,' Micko said, 'this time.'

210

Jig got on his bike and cycled down the path. He curved around a bevy of swans grooming themselves on the grass, their orange beaks nibbling and cleaning their wings and backs. Jig cycled straight across traffic, forcing a car to brake suddenly.

Five minutes later he dumped his bike outside the bookies. He dipped under a man at the doorway having a smoke and entered. He looked around for them, but only saw men studying their racing pages or straining their necks at the screens, armed with their slips and their little pens. The floor was covered in discarded dockets.

They were seated in the corner, with an invisible cordon of space curved around them. Ghost was reading the sports pages. Cracko was looking down at a little notepad, a can of Red Bull on the counter.

'Little J,' Ghost said, looking up. 'How are ya?'

'Good.'

Ghost's shoulders looked slanted to Jig. His chest was sunken, as if something was eating him. Ghost was wearing that T-shirt he liked. *Planet of the Apes.* Ghost told him it was a classic. Jig didn't know what he was talking about, but he liked the image of the man kneeling down and banging the ground with his fists and a big statue out in the sea, toppling over.

Jig turned around, but no one was looking at them. He handed Cracko the wad. Cracko pulled off the elastic with a snap and flicked at the edges. He slapped the band back on and slipped it into his pocket. It took just a second or two. Jig liked the way he did it.

'Fifty short,' Cracko stated.

'Ya what?' Ghost said.

Cracko nodded and scribbled on his little notebook. Jig had heard Ghost call it a 'tick list' the last time. There were numbers and letters on each line.

'Go back and tell that cunt,' Ghost said to Jig, a pointy grey finger poking out at him, 'that I want that fifty plus fifty extra tomorrow. Or I'll rent that patch to someone else. Maybe get my friend here to pay him a visit,' he said, with a look at Cracko.

Jig nodded.

'Ya could be running that bridge in a few years. How about that, little J?'

Jig smiled at the thought. Being a little boss of his own, having little rolls of cash. But, he had something else on his mind.

'Ya ever hear anything about Maggot?'

Jig stood there, knowing he had just said something he shouldn't have. Ghost glanced over Jig's shoulders, then at Jig.

'Why would I?' Ghost said, his voice drowned out by the racket from the screens. 'Yer his bro?'

'Just, Micko and Stu were asking?'

Ghost leaned closer to Jig, his eyes as black as a crow's.

'Don't worry about it, Jig,' he said quietly. 'He had serious charges coming to him, so he could have legged it to Spain or something, to lie low for a while. What ya think, Cracko?'

'Yeah, could be lying low alright.'

Jig looked down at his feet and swiped at the floor.

'Micko said something about someone's days being numbered after some fuck up or seizure or something.'

Jig watched Ghost stiffen, like a rope being twisted. His cheek-bones jabbed against his skin; his jaw protruded. Ghost glanced at Cracko, who was staring at Jig and biting down on his bottom lip. Jig didn't know which one of them scared the shit out of him more. He could see Ghost was trying not to let rip.

Jig wanted to go for a piss.

'Anything else?' Ghost said through clenched teeth.

'He said about Cracko taking over.' Jig could hear the nerves in his voice. 'And said about them setting up on their own.'

Ghost didn't look at Cracko this time. Jig thought he could see colour, like a dull red, on Ghost's yellowy cheeks. He hadn't seen that before.

'They said something about the RA out to get youse as well.'

'Did they? They know ya were listening?'

'Nah, I was pretending to be away with it looking down on the canal. They didn't think I heard nothing.'

Ghost stared at him.

'I went at Micko after he said about Maggot being in the mountains and he shoved me back.'

'Did he, the prick?' Ghost said.

Jig could feel Ghost's brain was spinning.

'That Micko is a fucking runt,' Cracko said. 'His whole family are headbangers. They are going to be serious fucking trouble down the line.'

Ghost didn't speak for a while.

'Don't say nothing to no one about this,' Ghost said, eventually.

Jig was looking down at the floor. Ghost tossed a pen at him, hitting him on the head.

'What did I say?'

'Say nothing to no one,' Jig replied, rubbing his head.

'Except for the cash that's short,' Ghost said. 'Tell the fucker that alright.'

Ghost strummed the counter with his fingers, the nails clipping hard against the wood. He pulled his arms up and folded them on the back of his head.

Jig turned his head to look at the inside of Ghost's lower arm. He had only half seen it before. It was a tattoo of horses running away from each other, pulling something on ropes. Jig blinked as he made out two arms, a head and shoulders at one end and legs on the other. He scrunched his face when he copped it.

'Keep those little ears wide open down on the canal, with each of them crews,' said Ghost. 'Things are getting way too loose around here. There's no fucking respect any more. We'll have to work on that.'

Jig nodded.

'And I'll tell ya what,' Ghost added. 'I'll lob a big chunk off that bill of yers. Keep it up, and it will be paid off in no time.'

That's that bill for the woman, Jig reminded himself. The bill was unfair; he was only doing what Ghost had told him. But he felt good cos he was 'taking it like a man', as Ghost had said.

46

Hall tapped the side of his cup and appraised the recent successes against the Canal Gang. A second major drug haul last night; two in a week. Both of them thanks to the bug Shay planted in Ghost's jacket. Both hauls were conducted by ISD units, not local gardaí, further boosting his standing.

The hauls would have cost Lock Man hundreds of thousands of euro. That would hurt. And being such a paranoid bastard, Lock Man would suspect a rat. That would hurt even more. All of which fitted in to the second part of Hall's plan.

He grabbed a seat inside the door of the coffee shop facing the window. It was just after 7 a.m. Through the steam he watched a geezer scarper across the busy junction and stride down towards the hospital. He had the typical gait of an addict on his way to score, like a man late for a flight. He had a hoodie pulled up, but Hall knew it was Leo.

Not long after, Leo skipped around the corner heading in his direction. He was making his usual pit stop. Pushing open the door, he strode past Hall, who bowed his head.

'Four packs of twenty blue there, bud. Hold on, I wants me Coke as well.'

Hall heard a fridge door open and close and a can land on the counter. As Leo headed back out, Hall shoved his hand out, blocking him.

'Hey, hey, coming through there, pal,' Leo shouted.

Hall didn't move his hand. He sensed Leo leaning down towards him.

'I can help ye,' Hall said, keeping his face looking straight ahead.

'Don't need Jesus, pal. Have me own God in me pocket.'

Hall smirked.

'Thought you were off the gear?'

Leo bolted still.

'Do I know ya, pal?' Leo said, an edge to his voice.

'It's about your mother,' Hall said quietly.

That was met with silence, broken only by a bus horn beeping outside.

'Sit down,' Hall said.

Leo shuffled behind him and took a seat. He placed his smokes and Coke on the table. He tried to edge a look at Hall, past the cap, shades and high collars of his coat.

'Don't be sneaky,' Hall said. 'You don't need to know who I am. All you need to know is I can help you.'

'Don't know what buzz yer on, pal,' Leo said, pulling his hoodie tighter. He cracked open his can and took a swig.

'You want revenge for your mother,' Hall stated.

'Don't be talking about me ma, right, or I'll slap ya one.'

Leo leaned closer, but Hall didn't budge.

'As I said, I can help you.'

'Help me what?'

'I know you want to get the Canal Gang,' Hall said. 'I can help you do that. But I need to know you're serious.'

Leo shot up, forcing his chair back, metal end scraping hard on the floor.

But before he could say anything, Hall added in a controlled voice: 'You walk out of here and your chance is gone.'

Hall knew it was a gamble, particularly with an addict gunning to get high. They knew he had given up the gear alright, but he was going through trays of tablets and bags of weed. Hall put out his hand, gesturing to Leo to sit down. Another moment passed. Hall knew he would sit. He would have been over the bridge by now otherwise. Leo slumped down.

'Who the fuck are ya?' Leo said, leaning towards him, whispering. 'The Garda?'

'Who I am is not important. What is important for you is that I can give you the bait.'

Hall could see from the reflection in the window in front of him if anyone was around, but it was still quiet.

'What bait ya on about?'

'You tell them the garda have them compromised.'

'Yer a copper alright.'

'Just listen. You tell them the garda have inside info on them and you know who the rat is.'

'How the fuck do I know that? Anyways, they'll tie a rock around me neck and fuck me into the canal as soon as I says that.'

'You tell them you know because the gardaí had to throw you in a cell as you were raging to go after them, over your mother. To calm you down, a detective let it slip they had someone on the inside and they were working on that.'

'What ya think I am, the dope of the year?' Leo said. 'Ghost won't fucking buy that and he'll have Cracko pour acid down me throat.'

'Maybe, if it was their call, but it won't be. Ghost will have to send it up the line. I know the boss man. He'll want to know.'

That was what Hall had said to Nessan. Both of them calculated that Lock Man would not be able to resist this one, despite the risks, particularly given their recent successes against the Canal Gang. Anything sniffing of a rat would override the rational part of his brain.

Leo took another swig.

'What's in it for youse?'

'Don't worry about that. We need to know you're serious?'

Leo tapped his smokes on the counter.

'If you're not,' Hall said, 'we'll leave it.'

'Yeah, I'm fucking serious.'

Hall mentally ticked the first box.

'Now, do you know when you're meeting your contact?'

'What contact?'

'In the RCAD.'

'How the fuck do youse know all this?'

'We just do. Well?'

Leo was tapping his feet.

'Haven't got the word yet.'

'Okay, they'll put holes in your knees for wasting their time if you go in half-cocked. Even with your uncle.'

'Ah here, how do you know about me fucking uncle?'

'Never mind. With the bait I've given you, they might, just might, go for it.'

Hall could tell Leo was taking in what he was saying. Second box ticked. Leo was an addict, but he had brains.

'Now, another thing you can tell the Provos is this, that you heard Ghost was back. He's up at the soccer training. You go up to Ghost –'

'Hold on, he'll fucking shove a knife into me head …'

'It will be out in the open and there'll be other people there, so he won't do anything, anything serious anyway. And when you tell him there's a rat, he won't chance it. As I was saying, tell the Provos that you'll say to Ghost you want to meet all of the gang, that you'll say it to their faces and in return you want your debt cleared.'

Silence again. Leo was hopping his legs and tapping his smokes in unison.

'This is your best chance to get revenge, Leo, for your mother,' Hall said.

'Fuck it,' Leo said, nodding.

Hall got Leo to go through it all several times, so he knew it backwards. Third box ticked.

'What do I do next?' Leo asked.

'That's up to your Republican friends. If they bite, they'll devise a plan. But we'll be watching, from a distance. When you know the plan, repeat it back in your room in the priest's house, like as if you are trying to remember.'

'Youse have me bleeding room bugged too? Jaysus. This is fucking mental.'

217

Leo was nearly jumping out of his seat.

'You clear on everything?' Hall asked again.

'Crystal.'

He could see Leo was fingering the drugs in his pocket.

'Don't fucking OD on the tablets,' Hall said.

He got up to leave, telling Leo to wait a few minutes.

'Last thing,' Hall said. 'Don't let anything slip about this conversation to anyone. You do, not only will your plan be history, so will you. And not at my hands.'

47

Jig looked over his shoulder as the BMW revved behind him.

'Just give us the fucking money, or I'll call him over,' Jig said, nodding over to the car.

The woman cursed and gave him the wad of cash and the card.

That was the last one, Jig said to himself. He ran back and hopped into the front passenger seat.

'Got it all,' he said, giving Cracko the mound of cash. 'They all gave me shite about leaving them some of their children's allowance, but I just said they could talk to ya and they handed it over sharpish.'

Cracko held the cash and the cards in his hand, but didn't bother counting it. Jig could see he was looking at some text on his phone.

'Fucking bitch,' Cracko said.

He put the phone away and quickly counted the cash. He took out his little notebook and jotted an amount beside some initials and slotted the cards into a flap at the back of the book.

'Listen, I need to make a house call,' he said, driving off. 'Me moth is at the tanning salon, so I needs ya to watch Seb.'

Jig looked into the back seat. Sunlight flooded through the Ninja Turtles blind and swam over the toddler's face.

'Ya still got those tickets?'

Jig looked at Cracko, confused.

'What?'

But Cracko didn't reply. Jig knew he didn't like repeating himself. So he thought about what he said.

Oh yeah, them tickets. Ghost was asking me about them at the match.

'I still has them in the same place, since before the summer.'

He had put the bags in a neighbour's shed. The neighbour was old. He hardly ever went out and never into his back garden. Jig only had to hop over the low railing into his garden. He left the bags in there, behind a press.

Ghost had said to him at the game about giving Cracko a hand from time to time. Said it be all part of the money he was putting aside for him, on top of minding the tickets and being his gofer. Ghost said he would be like 'the credit union'; he'd have his own account and all. Jig imagined big wads of notes in a safe. But Ghost said that first he still had a bit to pay for the old dear. That was the agreement they had. And a man had to keep his word, he said.

Cracko pulled to a halt.

'Ya able to look after Seb here?' he said.

Jig shook his head.

No fucking way.

'Okay, follow me, but don't touch nothing, don't do nothing. Just keep an eye on Seb.'

Cracko opened the glove compartment and took out pairs of transparent latex gloves and gave one to Jig. He looked at them, then copied Cracko and slapped them on.

They motioned to get out. Cracko opened the back door and lifted out the car seat. Jig pulled up his hoodie. Cracko strode ahead in his bright white Tottenham FC T-shirt. He carried the car seat in his left hand, his right arm swinging back and forth. His chain jangled under his top.

Jig tried to figure out where they were going. They passed some homes with neat front yards, with trimmed grass and flower pots. Jig spotted a house with a shopping trolley inside the gate, stuffed with bags and bags of rubbish. The windows were smashed in downstairs, the upstairs one was boarded up. Cardboard covered over holes in the glass in the front door. The step at the door had some sort of white paint all over it. It looked dark inside.

Cracko banged on the door with his fist and handed the car seat to Jig. He adjusted his feet at the weight.

A scrawny thing, all grey in the shadows, opened the door slowly. Before she could react, Cracko shoved her back into the little hall. She fell like building blocks, down on her arse. She sat there hunched and braced herself for further violence. Cracko stepped over her. Jig waited till she got up before carrying Seb in.

'Wait out there,' Cracko said back to him.

Jig put the car seat down and tried to close the door separating the tiny porch area to the front room, but the top hinge was off and the door wouldn't quite shut.

The place smelled worse than his gaff. There were bags of stuff in the room and wrappers, foils and cans. The curtains were closed, casting the room in a greyness, apart from a narrow shaft of light running across the middle of the floor.

Jig looked down at a long streak of a guy stretched out on a sofa. His right leg was in a big plaster cast and he had a can of beer in his hand. Jig thought he looked familiar. His mouth looked like someone had reefed it open when he saw Cracko. He tried to pull himself up a bit, but he was monged and couldn't with the cast.

'Jaysus, Cracko,' the woman said, as she followed them in, bent over, 'he's just out of James's.'

Cracko lashed her. The woman grasped her face. Jig backed out of the gap in the door and looked at Seb. He was playing with a little mobile hanging off the seat.

'He's out two days,' Cracko said, pointing at her, 'so don't fuck with me.'

There was a creak from the ceiling. Cracko looked out at Jig and nodded at him to go up. The woman motioned to move, but pulled back when Cracko slapped her. She bowed her head like a dog.

'Go up,' Cracko said to Jig, 'and see who's snooping around.'

Jig ran up the stairs. There was a big black bolt across one of the doors, a noise inside. He heaved on the bolt and pulled it back and pushed open the door. A little boy, about three, with scruffy blonde hair looked out at him. He had nothing on apart from a T-shirt. The boy smiled at Jig.

'Down,' Jig said, pointing to the stairs.

Jig watched the boy toddle down and into the front room, stopping still when he saw Cracko.

'It's okay, chicken,' the woman – his ma – said.

'How's the leg,' Cracko said to the man.

'Bad. Broken in two places.'

'Yer lucky I left ya with a leg at all,' Cracko said, his face curling at the edges into a smile. 'Ya have to pay for that seizure.'

'Yeah, I knows, Cracko, I knows.'

'We're going to sell all these,' the woman interrupted.

'So, why haven't ya?' Cracko said.

She began to say something, but didn't. Jig could see her swallowing back down whatever words she had been thinking of.

'Anyways,' Cracko said, 'with the value of that haul, ya want to be shipping this stuff like Argos. Ya dopey bitch.'

Jig wiped his forehead with his sleeve. It was getting sticky.

'But youse know what does be itching me balls more than the money,' Cracko said, 'is how did the filth knows about the haul in the first place?'

'I didn't fucking tell them nothing,' said the man. 'That's straight up, Cracko. On, on, me son's life.'

Cracko nodded. He grabbed an unopened can of cider beside the sofa. Pulling back the opener he took a swig, licking small drips on his lower lip. With a little smile he stepped towards the boy.

'No, leave him,' the woman said, but was rewarded with a dig into her ribcage.

'Fancy a little drink?' Cracko held out the can to the boy.

The boy shook his head and looked over at his ma, his eyes welling up.

'Here, a swig.'

The boy lowered his eyes and pulled his shoulders tight.

'I'm telling ya, Cracko,' said the man, 'I'd never tell the garda nothing.'

Cracko stretched his hand out and poured the cider onto the boy's face. The boy coughed and spluttered. Liquid ran down his top and onto his chubby legs.

'Ah, ya bastard!' the woman roared, as the boy began to cry.

Cracko elbowed her in the side of her neck. The man tried to pull himself up, but screamed in pain and slumped back down.

'Christ, Cracko, I swear,' he said, 'I said nothing to the filth.'

'Tell youse what,' Cracko said, finishing the dregs of the can, 'make us a cup of tea and we'll have a chat about it.'

The woman's eyes darted from Cracko to her fella and even out to Jig in panic. She crawled towards the kitchen, dragging her son with her. Cracko stood in the middle of the room, his thick tattooed arms dangling at his side. He winked over at Jig. From the kitchen came the sound of the kettle.

'Wash out them cups now,' Cracko shouted, with a twisted smile. 'I don't wants to be catching the virus.'

'No problem, Cracko, no problem.'

Jig could see the woman swinging around the kitchen, like a hunchback, and heard the noises of cupboards opening and closing. The little boy pattered after her.

The whistle was building.

'Bring them cups out and I'll get the kettle,' Cracko said.

As she came out, with the boy, Cracko went inside. He came back in carrying the kettle, and some sort of cloth.

Jig jumped at a yelp. But it was just Seb playing with his mobile.

Cracko put the kettle on some boxes and grabbed the woman by her hair. She roared. He yanked her closer. She roared louder. Cracko forced a brown rag into her gob. He elbowed her in the back and she slumped forward on her knees.

'Jaysus, Cracko,' the man shouted. 'I fucking didn't rat. I'm telling ya.' He forced himself up.

Cracko leaned forward and smacked him in the nose with his left fist, sending him slamming back.

'Don't say another fucking word, or I'll do it to the kid.'

The woman whimpered.

'Things have gotten too lax around here since we were away. And the fact youse didn't even offload most of this stuff by now shows a lack of respect.'

Cracko straightened himself up.

'And I'm a killer for respect.'

Jig tilted his head around at the faces and bodies. The boy cried from the kitchen door. Jig got up on his toes and pushed his head in. The boy's little penis was dribbling into a small pool at his feet.

Jig looked back at Seb. His mouth was open and his eyes darted from side to side at the boy's crying. Jig lifted up the seat and turned it around so Seb faced the front door.

He looked back in. Cracko lifted his arm up. Jig saw the kettle raised high. Cracko's face tensed and his mouth tightened as he tilted the kettle forward. Jig saw water pour out. There was a noise, like a fire crackling. A big cloud of steam rose up. Jig jolted at the muffled sickening screams. The woman's legs hopped up and down on the floor, like in those films showing someone being electrocuted. Her waist writhed. She gagged on the rag. The man roared. Cracko flung the kettle at him, smacking him in the chest.

Jig looked at the little boy. His eyes jumped out from his face. He was trying to breathe and scream at the same time, making a sound like he was choking.

Jig lifted the car seat and waited for Cracko. He thought they'd be legging it. But Cracko, his forehead glistening, just stood there, staring at his handiwork.

'Rat or no rat,' Cracko said, after a moment. 'Let this be a warning to youse, and to everyone – don't fuck with us.'

48

Crowe eyed the bare-chested man, as he swayed to some personal silent reverie. He stood at his doorway, his head angled up towards the morning sun and his eyes shut. A cigarette flopped in his mouth. Another client of Ghost's and Cracko's, she guessed.

She pulled her jacket tight and walked to her car. She had wasted her time. The partner still wasn't talking. And never would by the looks of it. Same for his girlfriend most likely. The doctors had told her the woman was in no condition to talk and was on heavy pain relief and tranquillisers.

When Crowe got to the house yesterday, there was pandemonium. There had been an anonymous call about a disturbance. An ambulance had just left with the woman. At first, Crowe thought the partner had done it, but he was in bits too. He had massive bruising around his eye and was clutching his chest. A second ambulance was coming for him. Their toddler, naked apart from a filthy T-shirt, was hysterical. Now and again, he'd gasp out the words, 'Bad man.'

A kettle was on the floor. The partner wouldn't say who did it and refused to give a formal statement. Crowe bagged the kettle and took it away for examination, just in case the couple changed their mind.

The neighbours saw nothing, though one of them had obviously rung 999.

When Crowe checked the partner's name at the station, she discovered he was on bail in relation to a recent drugs haul, reputedly belonging to the Canal Gang. It dawned on her pretty quick who the bad man was. And why no one was talking.

Leaning on the wall outside the house, she thought about the little boy again. She made sure the hospital would check him out when he arrived with his dad, and suggested to staff that a social worker be consulted. In addition to all the drug paraphernalia, she didn't like the look of that upstairs room with the bolt on the outside.

Poor thing. What chance does he have?

She pushed herself off the wall and strolled up to her car. As she did, a passing car slowed down and the driver looked over in her direction. The figure was on the heavy side, Crowe thought. A woman probably. The car, a bit of a banger, came to a stop. The driver had a hoodie pulled up now and didn't budge. Then she turned back and nodded to Crowe as if to get in.

She approached the vehicle, carefully, touching her hip, to make sure the Sig was there.

The woman leaned over and opened the door. Crowe saw it was the manager of the Oasis Community Centre.

'Go on, will ya, sit in before anyone clocks us,' Lynn said.

Crowe complied. The chance that someone like Lynn wanted to talk to her might mean she had something useful to say. In an area where no one volunteered information, what had she to lose?

She pushed off an empty packet of John Players onto the floor. The quality of the air suggested the very bones of the car breathed tobacco.

Lynn drove off, the engine grinding.

They passed the house that Crowe had just come from. She sensed Lynn looking at her.

'Fucking savage that,' Lynn said.

Crowe turned to her.

'You hear anything about it?'

'Just did there a while ago,' Lynn replied, taking a roundabout without bothering to indicate.

'You know them?'

'Yeah. Both of them have been in and out of addiction for years.

Nothing the guy done deserved what they done to his partner, the boy and all watching. Sick fuckers. It's getting worse again, now they're back.'

'Ghost and Cracko's crew?'

Lynn nodded.

'I was thinking of talking to ya,' Lynn said, after a moment had passed, 'and when I just seen ya there, I said fuck it. But don't ever tell no one I talk to ya, right?'

Crowe nodded. Her interest was piqued.

'Ya know about the new Provo crowd?' Lynn said, pulling up at lights and glancing around her.

'The RCAD?' Crowe said, thinking how she had seen a lot more of their graffiti and posters around the place in recent months.

'Well, the upholders of republicanism,' Lynn said, taking off, to career around a roundabout, 'have been going around asking, encouraging more like, local groups to link up with them. All part of a community uprising, they call it, against the gangs.

'I don't be having much truck with them,' she continued. 'One thing I learned over the decades is that, with them, the politics comes first, and the people, second. And they wants to control everything. Having said that, they stood by communities in the eighties and nineties. Anyways,' she said, taking another roundabout, 'it's clear they have their sights on the Canal Gang, now that they're back. And I'm not talking about marching on homes.'

Just as she finished, Lynn turned onto MacBride Road. Crowe knew this was a coincidence, but it sent a shiver down her spine. All her investigations into the Canal Gang had hit a brick wall: the death of Ms King, the murders, and now, the kettle attack. The Canal Gang's reputation as 'untouchables', as the tabloids had termed them, was well deserved. Though the recent seizures had tarnished that. But that was the work of Intelligence and Security.

The disused factory where Grant lost her life was up ahead. As if reading her mind, Lynn took the next turn off.

'As I was saying, garda, I think they might be planning something.'

'Like what?'

'Like, one of them "spectaculars" that the Provos used to boast about. I'm concerned that innocent people in this community are going to get caught up.'

Lynn neared to where she had picked Crowe up.

'Who are you hearing this from?' Crowe asked.

Lynn tilted her head to say she should know better than ask her that.

'Any idea of what kind of spectacular, or when?' Crowe asked instead.

'Definitely something big,' Lynn said, pulling in, glancing around. 'As to when, hard to know, but my gut says soon, like in the coming weeks.'

49

Leo didn't have to be told twice where to meet. St Kevin's Church was one of his ma's favourite chapels. She used to get the bus there for the 10 a.m. mass several days a week.

Sitting at the back of the bus, staring out at people congregated outside a mosque, Leo considered the misery he had inflicted on her. While he was out breaking into houses, robbing women on the streets, she was in Kevin's praying for him, praying for him not to die. That's what she used to say to him when he was in the house, slumped in front of the television, after she came back, always clasping her small black handbag. One day, she left it on the hall table as she went into the kitchen to make them both tea. He had never taken from the house. Not until that day.

Leo closed his eyes. But he couldn't block out the memories. Of what he did to his ma, and his da. He pressed the bell as the bus approached the church.

He dipped his hand into the holy water and blessed himself, a habit ingrained by his ma. He walked over to the far side and sat in the second last pew. That's what a voice on a phone told him when he met his RCAD contact in a pub the other night. The contact handed him a phone and there was a voice at the other end telling him where they would meet, when, and where to sit.

Leo scanned the church. There were a handful of people, lighting candles, bent forward in prayer. There was another one or two scattered at the back. It was dark and brooding, like he remembered it. He checked his phone. Half nine. Bang on.

Hall looked at the laptop screens in front of him inside the van. One captured the front entrance and the road outside. A second covered a side entrance on another road. A third camera captured the road on the far side. Three mobile teams – two cars, one motorbike – were in position. They had another surveillance officer in the church.

'9/2. Bait confirmed,' said their man inside.

'5/0 to 9/2. Over,' said DI Slavin, seated beside Hall.

Behind them were two note-takers, documenting everything.

Good, Hall thought. Leo had sat where he was told by the Provos. The bug was in place and should capture any conversation.

The job was giving Hall the nervous shafts of raw adrenaline that he loved. Mixed in with the excitement was anxiety. He was most concerned about not blowing their cover and had directed everyone to play this one loose.

The meeting two nights ago between Leo and the RCAD in the pub had gone well. They couldn't get ears on the conversation as it was arranged suddenly and was way too noisy. But Leo had remembered to repeat the details back in his room. And while they didn't have ears on the meet, they had eyes. They got photos of the contact when he came out. Fintan Sutcliffe. An old Provo, active in the early eighties with the Concerned Parents Against Drugs and on the fringes in the mid-nineties with the Coalition of Communities Against Drugs, or COCAD.

Hall knew his face and it didn't take long to jog his memory. Sutcliffe had dropped out of active republican circles in the late nineties. He was now touching sixty. He had nothing to do with the new breed in the Reals or Continuity. To veterans like him, they were just criminals. He had come out of retirement, voluntarily, Hall discovered. It turned out he'd lost his granddaughter about a year ago to drugs. The RCAD greeted him with open arms. Since the late nineties, local people wouldn't go to community drug meetings. They were too terrified. But since the start of the year, the RCAD group was having local meetings across south-west Dublin and was beginning to attract a smattering of people. Sutcliffe and his like were wanted again.

The RCAD, it turned out, had links with a sister anti-drugs group in Belfast, manned, in part, by former members of the Provisional IRA. A so-called 'military crew' had reformed in Dublin, like in the days of COCAD. They operated behind the scenes and were the muscle for RCAD, if needed. The ISD's Subversive Intelligence Unit was piecing together who Sutcliffe was associated with. A few knee-cappings, an old Provo favourite, had taken place recently around the canals, of street dealers mainly. There had also been a couple of armed robberies, which seemed to be well planned and executed. There were unconfirmed reports that serious firepower was being acquired with this money, to be used against the Canal Gang, if the opportunity arose. That was where, Hall predicted, Leo fitted into the RCAD plan. And the Canal Gang was already getting jumpy, if the attack on the junkie and his girlfriend over the drug haul was anything to go by.

'9/3. Possible target on move. Wearing blue jeans, black jacket, cap.'

'5/0 to 9/2. Be ready.'

Leo heard the rustle of clothes and feet adjusting to walk sideways into a pew behind him. He didn't turn to look. He knew not to. Whoever it was sat behind him, slightly to his right. The man kneeled down and put his hands over his face as if in prayer. The man tapped him on the shoulder and pointed to the seats on the other side of the church.

Leo hesitated. He got another tap, harder this time. He walked over, the man following. The man sat down behind him and leaned forward, his mouth centimetres from his ear. He had a peaked cap on, Leo could tell.

'Take off your jacket. Push it down the seat.'

Leo obeyed. He had a T-shirt underneath, as he was told on the phone. He felt the guy tapping the top of the T-shirt, shoulders and chest, with his gloves. He then pressed his mouth against his ear again.

'Go to Blades on Eamon Street,' the man whispered. 'Ask for a cover. Do it straight after this.'

Leo felt like his bowels were giving way, but held it together. The voice was the same as the one on the phone. Dublin accent, kind of neutral.

'And start growing a beard.'

Leo twisted his head.

What does he want me growing a beard for? And what the fuck is a cover?

'At training tomorrow,' the man continued, 'tell that Ghost what I said on the phone. You have to get them to meet you in person. The lot of them. Say you'll be back at training on Tuesday for an answer.'

Leo nodded.

'Stay put after Tuesday. We'll have eyes on you. When you get back to the priest's don't fucking move. That means no trips for drugs, nothing. If you need cigarettes, get them before. When you do move, we'll know it's on.'

Leo was sweating buckets. The man had almost moved into his ear.

'Don't mention Blades to anyone. Or talk to anyone. If you do, I'll inject a kilo of gear into your fucking eyes.'

Leo tried to swallow the lump in his throat, but it was lodged there. He gagged for air.

'We'll have no contact after this, no mobiles, no nothing. There's a bicycle outside the entrance. Get on it and head to Eamon Street. Don't stop for lights, trucks, the Luas, nothing. Just in case, like, anyone is following you. Yeah?'

Leo nodded.

'If you fuck with us in any way, you won't have a pretty end. Either will the priest.'

Leo sat there shitless, couldn't even manage a nod.

'Stay here for two minutes, then leave. Do not look around.'

Leo's legs were bouncing up and down. He forced himself to stay put and not piss into his jocks.

'9/2 to 5/0. Target leaving.'

'5/0. All units ready to roll on exit.'

Hall told himself they were dealing with a serious outfit here. The counter-intelligence steps inside the church confirmed that. These guys were not taking chances. But at least they had the target on the cameras. The units were on the move.

'Bait is getting on a bike,' Slavin said, looking at camera three. 'He's legging it.'

'We'll catch up with Leo later,' Hall said, glancing at the camera, wondering where the fucker was off to in such a hurry. 'We need to concentrate everything on the target.'

50

Shay was going to let rip with Jig.

He had the boys in pairs, sprinting up and back to the cones.

'Put the effort in, lads, get your breather at the end,' he shouted at them. 'Move it. Sprint back. Push it. This is the time when it counts, when you're tired. Get your breather up into you, stay with your man, keep up with him.'

But Jig was only jogging to the cones and back.

'Jig. This is the second time I have to tell you. Now, do ten.'

'What for?'

'Sprint back, not saunter back.'

'Fuck sake.'

Shay pointed to the ground.

'Ten. Now.'

'That's shite, that is.'

'What's shite is the attitude. You wonder why we're losing games? It isn't because we don't have the skill; it's the lack of effort to get the ball back when we lose it. You should be breaking your guts for the team.'

Shay wasn't sure why he was giving Jig such a hard time. The boy grunted as he half did the press-ups.

Something twinged inside Shay's brain. He didn't want to know what Ghost did when he told him about the other team looking to poach Jig. He did consider ringing Hall, but then thought, what could he do? He didn't want Hall even knowing. Ghost was his only option.

Shay asked Jig if he'd heard from Butch. He said he hadn't. The gnawing feeling that he had betrayed Jig, denied him the possibility of an exit from his life here, away from Ghost and the Canal Gang, festered in his stomach. Perverse as it was, maybe that sense of guilt was why he was coming down hard on the boy.

Shay placed out more cones on the ground for a game, stepping in to avoid a fresh scorch mark. Seven black rings now riddled the green.

He sneaked a look at Ghost, who was busy on the phone. He was still wearing his jacket, which meant Shay was still delivering the goods for Hall. He had heard on the news about the drug hauls, which probably explained why Ghost seemed preoccupied, stressed even.

Out of the corner of his eye, Shay noticed some movement. A figure was striding over to Ghost, hooded and capped. Shay's heart skipped a beat. Ghost had his back to the man, deep in conversation on the phone.

Christ, Ghost's going to be clipped.

Shay let out a sharp whistle. Ghost turned to him. Shay nodded towards the approaching stranger. Ghost faced the man, but didn't move. The fella halted a couple of feet away.

Ghost casually put his phone into a top pocket in his jacket and zipped it closed. The man started talking. Shay stepped a few feet forward to try and get a look at his face, but the cap and hoodie cloaked him. The man was still talking, then stopped. Ghost didn't respond.

After a few moments, Ghost lunged forward and smacked the guy around the ear. The slap was loud and grabbed the attention of the young fellas.

The atmosphere changed like the flick of a switch: now the very air carried the promise of more violence.

Shay watched Ghost lean over the heap on the ground, pointing a finger down at him. Shay couldn't make out all that he said, but he heard 'filthy' and 'cunt'.

The kids ran towards Shay. He held out his hands to stop them in their tracks. The only reason they obeyed was because this was

235

Ghost business and they knew better than to act the bollocks.

Ghost's long arm trailed down his side, slightly out, like a strap, ready to slap again. The man on the ground got up. Shay was surprised he didn't back off. The man grabbed his cap from the grass and pulled his hood up, but not quickly enough.

'Jesus,' Shay breathed. The guy had stubble and thicker, longer hair than the man in the photograph Hall had showed him the other day. But it looked like the Leo fella alright.

'Who's that, Shayo?'

Shay turned to see Jig looking up at him. Shay just shook his head and watched as the man began talking again.

Leo has some balls, I'll give him that.

He watched Leo as he walked off, leaving Ghost standing there. If Shay didn't know better, it was Ghost who looked rattled. Ghost didn't move for a few seconds, then he took out his phone and fingered it, before putting it away. He strode towards the Cayenne.

'Right, lads,' Shay said, 'back to it. Show's over.'

But he had a feeling the show had just begun.

51

They couldn't help but stare. The children particularly. Ghost always got a buzz from the faces of people who hadn't seen him before.

Some of the mas pulled their precious children towards them as soon as he walked into the pool. They stared at his bones, pressed against his face and his chest and recoiled at the mass of tattoos. He gave them one of his trademark smiles and a couple of kids screamed. They thrashed the water when he jumped in and let out a laugh.

He did the dead-man float in the middle of the pool. The water lapped against him from the force of people swimming away. Like fucking lemmings.

When he turned for the deep end, most people had left. Leaning back against the bars, he split a smile. Just as well for them they did leave, he thought, because however much of a scary fucker he looked, Slammer was making his entrance. They'd shit bricks if they saw that beast coming.

He looked at Slammer's great thick skull, bent in on one side, his chunky shoulders and mass of muscle for a body. Slammer eyed Ghost for a second, but didn't acknowledge his nod; instead he scanned the pool to see who was there.

Lock Man followed, his head bowed, tying his shorts as he barrelled forward. He reminded Ghost of a little bull. The way his head swayed gave the impression he was arguing with himself.

Ghost had wondered why Slammer hadn't buried him ten feet

down in the Dublin Mountains by now. He had chosen Jobs and Shop, after all, but Shop, the prick, had, for some fucking reason, brought Maggot along. Probably because Maggot tormented him to do so. End of the day, the boss held him responsible for a fuck up of monumental scale. But here he was, still kicking. Probably because Slammer had cleaned up the mess and the garda had nothing on them. But he knew his cards were marked. Lock Man prized one quality above loyalty: survival. Then there were the two recent seizures. The boss must be chewing glass over that, he thought, and now this Leo cunt comes along.

Ghost rose his head to avoid the wave that came with Slammer's body entering the water. From the far end, the boss swam towards them, like a mini-whale.

'Ya think this guy is setting a trap?' Slammer asked.

Ghost looked at Slammer. There was no fat on the man, just solid bone, layered over with thick muscle.

'That scrawny junkie?' Ghost replied. 'He couldn't set a mouse trap.'

Even Slammer couldn't help but smile at that one, Ghost noticed.

'We know where he's holed up?'

'Na. He be back on Tuesday for an answer. We can follow him then.'

'Don't use any locals. I'll have two lads there,' Slammer said.

Ghost liked Slammer. He just had that no-fucking-bullshit approach about him.

'So, what's the plan?' Ghost said. 'The boss going to take the chance?'

Slammer didn't answer.

The two of them watched as Lock Man loomed, his bald head coming towards them like a torpedo, his arms smashing through the water. He showed no signs of stopping. Ghost moved to one side to allow his considerable mass to touch the bars, change and wobble into a backstroke, the belly undulating away from them.

'Where's this fucker getting his info?' Slammer asked.

'That's the fucking thing. The more I think about it the more it wrecks me head. He could be spoofing, just to clear his debt.

But he knows that, as soon as we know he's spoofing, he's a dead man.'

'Unless,' Slammer said, 'it is a trap.'

They both moved as Lock Man took the steps at the far end and headed for the jacuzzi, his reds togs sagging off him. He hit a button and the jets erupted.

They took the three sides of the jacuzzi, leaving no space for anyone else foolish enough to think they could join them. Lock Man had his back to the pool and Slammer took the side facing the entrance.

Ghost could feel the boss's eyes on him.

'Yer fucking wasting away,' Lock Man said, looking at him.

'All the stress I'm under, boss. Ya should try it on the streets.'

The joke fell flat. Slammer threw him a look that said 'not very smart'.

'Speaking of jokers,' Lock Man said. 'What about this junkie? He on a suicide mission or does he actually know something?'

Ghost held his bruised hand, sore after smacking Leo, against a jet and thought for a moment.

'I don't know, boss. As I said to Slam, he could be bluffing, just to get his slate cleaned, but he knows he's history if he doesn't have something to tell us.'

Lock Man leaned forward and spat out some water.

'So, what the fuck's his game? Ya met him.'

'I smacked him a few and he stayed. That says something?'

'As?'

'Junkies scamper after that. They don't stay for more. This one got up, stood his ground and repeated what he said. There's something up his ass alright.'

'Yeah, what though, and who put it there,' Lock Man said. 'He connected with anyone?'

'He hasn't the balls or the brains,' Ghost said. 'And everyone knows we're hunting for him.'

'What about someone using him? The garda?'

Ghost shrugged. 'Yeah, it's possible. He says a detective told him about us having a rat or something.'

239

Lock Man's face hardened. He adjusted his weight and looked at Slammer.

'Youse putting eyes on this fucker?'

'He's back on Tuesday,' Slammer said. 'So we'll trail him then.'

Ghost knew well that Lock Man had a thing about rats, even the faintest sniff of one. The two drug seizures had got to him. His cheeks were going red.

'Who he say he wanted to meet?'

'Yerself, me, Cracko, Slammer and Jig.'

'Sounds like he wants revenge for his ma,' Lock Man said. 'Why else include the boy?' He turned to Slammer: 'What the fuck could he do, strap a bomb to himself?'

'Could have someone on the outside to take us out at the meet,' Slammer said. 'He'd have to be followed or tracked for that. Either that or he's bugged and cops hope we admit to something or do him in.'

Lock Man kept his eyes on Slammer. Ghost could feel his mind chewing on it all.

'Whatever the reason is, boss, why chance it?' Slammer said.

Lock Man went silent. Ghost could see he was sweating like a fucking hippo in a sauna. His cheeks were shiny red.

Lock Man raised his finger at Slammer, then Ghost.

'The filth didn't make those seizures by chance.' He looked at Ghost. 'What did Cracko say about that junkie who was holding the last haul?'

'Well, he melted his moth's head and he didn't fess up,' Ghost said. 'Cracko thinks the junkie's no rat.'

A blue vein in Lock Man's temple pulsed.

'And what about that Micko Hynes streak of piss? The boy told youse he overheard him and Stu blabbering away down the canal.'

'Yeah,' Ghost said. 'Cracko's paying him a visit as we speak. But that Micko prick didn't know anything about either shipment.'

Lock Man twisted his head from side to side.

'Things have gone way too ragged. I don't fucking like it. The filth are getting info from somewhere, from someone. Rat or no rat, we need to make sure we have a clean fucking house. Arrange a meet.'

Slammer nodded.

'We can make sure Leo is clean,' Slammer said. 'Take extra precautions. We'll use a secure place, somewhere new.'

'Yeah and,' Lock Man said, his eyes widening, 'we leave him to talk. We say fucking nothing. So even if they have a big fucking microphone sticking out of his bony arse, all they'll hear is him talking shite.'

Lock Man looked at Ghost.

'No chance that Jig is talking, after what happened to his fucking bro?'

Ghost hadn't expected that.

'He doesn't know shit,' Ghost said. 'He does what I say. And no matter what, his crowd would never rat.'

But the thought scurried around inside Ghost's head.

'Better not,' Lock Man said, pushing his legs forward and lying his head back, 'cos ya have only one lifeline left.'

52

Shay looked over from where the kids chose to sit on the Luas and predicted there would be some 'colour' any moment.

Molly continued with her Halloween jokes.

'Why did the skeleton cross the road?'

'Why, honey?'

'To go to the body shop.'

Molly beamed, Charlie laughed. Shay managed a smile.

The voices across from them intruded on their moment.

'Ya know when yer legs do be sore and yer trying to turn,' the woman shouted, a big gold chain with a cross dangling from her neck.

'Yeah, yer sore on yer back and on yer fucking side,' the man beside her said, an unlit rollie in his mouth.

'Yeah. I was sleeping, right, then I sneezed. I fucking sneezed about fifty fucking times,' she said.

Shay watched her gesticulate as she spoke, her hands going this way, then that, out of sync with her words.

A jingle rang from a phone. The woman pulled out her mobile.

'Yeah ... What?'

'Tell me another, Molly?' Shay said, turning to the kids.

But Molly, along with Charlie, was staring at the woman, who was mouthing off.

'That one,' the woman shouted, pointing a finger at her phone, 'she's a proper cunt. I'm supposed to meet her to get fucking bogey urine off the ...'

242

'Molly, another one?' Shay said loudly.

'Why didn't the ghost go to the party?'

Shay gave her a quizzical look.

'Don't know. Why?'

'Because he had no body to go with.'

Shay sniffed a laugh. Molly and Charlie joined in.

Shay's thoughts drifted to Lisa. She had wanted them out of the house. She had migraines, bad ones, she told him.

But Shay thought she was preoccupied with something.

Shay leaned back against the wall, his arms folded, transfixed at the painting. Somewhere, he could hear the kids' silvery voices. He had got them to walk to the museum thanks to a pancake and promises of an ice cream after. That, and the fact it was the museum with the speaking phones, the ones they could type in the painting's number and hear about it. They loved that.

Shay felt a pull to see the painting again; out of nowhere, just as they crossed the Ha'penny Bridge. Seeing it didn't make him feel better, as such. But it resonated in ways he couldn't quite understand.

He pored over Louis le Brocquy's painting again.

In it, a dad sat at the end of a thin, sharp bed, the right side of his body facing out. He was naked and hunched: his legs and big feet angled awkwardly, his head bowed. He looked forlorn and beaten. The mum shot up from the other end of the bed. Her eyes betrayed a terrible despair, as if the nightmare of her reality was worse than the torment of her dreams. Her right hand gripped the sheet, as if clinging on to sanity.

Shay looked at her and saw Lisa. She hadn't slept the previous nights because of the bonfires and crowds out drinking on the green. He tried to reassure her: that Halloween time was always like this, that it would pass.

'It's been going on since August, and last year it went on up to nearly Christmas,' she said. 'I rang the fire brigade yesterday and told them about that huge bonfire and all the toxic stench coming out of it. They told me,' she laughed bitterly, 'that they wouldn't come out because there were a load of kids there and they might be attacked. Can you fucking believe it? Basically, to hell with you people living there.'

The pain in her face pierced Shay's heart like a long needle. But he needed her to just hang in, for the final stretch.

He had met Hall the previous day and told him about Leo and Ghost. He could tell from Hall that something was cooking. Not that he would tell him what.

Shay sensed Charlie and Molly were now either side of him. Charlie pointed at the child in the painting.

The naked girl, not much older than Charlie, stood at the end of the bed with eerie, uncomprehending eyes. One hand touched her mother's foot, the other held up a small bunch of pretty flowers, the only colour in *A Family*.

'Girl has colour in flowers,' Charlie said.

'It's hope,' Shay said, clasping his children, 'in the face of none.'

53

The ball bobbed away from Bowie each time he tried to grab it in his mouth. His eyes sparkled as he looked between Jig and the ball, his pink tongue sticking out and his short legs kicking in the waters.

'Go on, Bowie, ya have it, ya have it,' Jig encouraged, crouching down at the canal's edge.

The Luas thundered over the bridge above him. A gust whipped down the waters, under a second, curved bridge and around the gentle bend of the canal where Jig was, near graffiti of a girl fishing. As he watched Bowie splutter and scramble in the waters, he remembered the day he became his owner.

'Ya think ya be able to look after Bowie for me?'

Jig was delighted, but confused.

'Ya mean it?'

His granda nodded.

'Yeah.'

He took Bowie out of his granda's lap. The pup gave him loads of licks on his cheek and ears. Jig burst out laughing.

'Ah Bowie, Jaysus. Bowie.'

Jig patted the dog on his hard little head.

'Is it a present, Granda?'

His granda stared into the waters. He had his pork-pie hat in his hands and rubbed his fingers around the edges of it. Bowie licked Jig on his cheek, but he didn't react.

'Granda?'

His granda sighed and faced him.

'Jig, I have to . . . go.'

Jig shook his head to make the sentence go away.

'I have to get out of here, Jig. I have no choice. If I had one, I'd stay.'

Jig couldn't open his mouth. It was stuck dry. He could hear his breath through his nose.

'And, I won't be coming back. I can't help it, Jig. Sorry.'

What about all the things he did with his granda, Jig thought, things he wouldn't be doing any more. He'd be left with his da and his ma.

He could feel his granda's strong hands on his shoulders.

'Bowie will look after ya now, Jig.'

A big bark roused him.

He never found out why his granda left. His parents would never talk about it.

Jig watched Bowie pull himself out of the canal, the water slick against his muscular body. He dropped the ball on the grass and gave himself a shake. He padded over to Jig and nudged against him.

Jig grabbed him with both arms, not caring he was all wet.

There was a deep growl from nearby.

Jig knew the noise.

It was weird, but as soon as the shape of Ghost and Cracko emerged into view and took the path down to him, things kind of went silent, as if people and sounds had slipped into the waters.

Jig clasped his chain onto Bowie's collar.

'How's the Jigster?' asked Ghost, looking around him, but not at Jig.

'Alright.'

Jig glanced at Cracko. He was biting on his lip, his arms hanging loosely beside him. He twitched at an image of him lifting that kettle and pouring boiling water onto that woman's head.

'Show us Bowie there,' Ghost said, sticking his arm out like a rake.

Jig pulled Bowie in, then relaxed when Ghost gave him the eye.

Ghost clasped the chain and gave Bowie a firm tap on his head. The dog looked over at Jig. Ghost kicked the ball into the canal. Bowie jumped in after it, but Ghost dug his feet in to take the pull on the chain.

'Woo, easy there, Bowie,' Ghost said.

'Hey, fucking watch Bowie,' Jig roared, moving towards him.

He got about a foot. It felt like his right shoulder got jammed in a door. Twisting, he saw Cracko's thick, scarred fingers clamped over his shoulder and felt it would snap if he moved.

Ghost pulled on the chain and dragged the dog along the edge of the waters towards a concrete ledge.

The bridge overhead clanked loudly with the passage of a Luas. Jig saw the top of Bowie's head. He was trying to climb the ledge, but it was too high for him to grab.

'Leave Bowie alone,' Jig shouted.

Ghost wrapped more of the chain around his hand. He pulled hard and rose his hand up, his wiry arm tightening. The collar dug into Bowie's neck as he was hauled inches out of the water.

'Yer going to fucking choke him,' Jig shouted.

Cracko laughed behind him and pressed his fingers deeper into his shoulder. Jig let out a roar.

Turning his head around, Cracko made a sssh sound with a finger. Jig knew not to roar again. Unless someone else came down the path, no one could see him.

He was sweating all over.

What the fuck is going on? Why they doing this?

Ghost lifted Bowie again. The dog struggled for air.

'Tell me, Jig,' Ghost said, clenching his teeth with the strain, before dropping the dog, 'ya know what this filthy canal is full of?'

Jig shook his head.

'Big diseased rats,' Ghost said, the bridge vibrating again with a Luas. 'Some of them are like fucking cats, the size of them.'

It dawned on Jig what this was about.

'I'm not a rat.'

Cracko's grip tightened a notch. Jig was forced to kneel down on one leg with the crunch. Loose stones dug into his knee.

'I'm telling youse!' Jig roared through his teeth.

Ghost pulled Bowie up again, higher this time. Jig could see Bowie's hind legs now dangling. He was desperate for air.

'Ya know, Cracko here,' Ghost said, 'carries a nasty-looking blade, more like a fucking hunting knife. He could slit Bowie's belly and drop him into the waters. Be feeding time for all them filthy rats.'

Jig tried to push forward, but Cracko crunched down on his shoulder hard enough to snap bone. He nearly passed out from the pain, his face wet with sweat and snot.

'I'm ... no ... rat.'

Suddenly, Cracko let him go and he fell face down on the path. He heard a splash and a bark. Looking up, Ghost was leaning down towards him, his cheekbones jabbing against his yellow skin.

'Good. But we have a hunt on for one. Be at yer gaff at eight, Halloween night. Not a second fucking later.'

Jig's shoulder splintered with pain as he tried to get up. He watched Bowie drag himself onto the bank. The dog ran towards him, the chain scraping on the path, and landed big licks on his cheeks.

54

It looked like a big plaza to Shay; a cobbled one, like Kilmainham or Collins Barracks. In front of him was an old ambulance, its exhaust coughing dirty fumes. It was covered in rust and the back bumper dangled. He was inside it now, but couldn't make out the driver. Ahead of them was a gate, its big wooden doors closed. Kids were massed on the wall over it. 'We have to do it. There's no turning back,' the driver said. His voice sounded familiar. The ambulance spluttered as it tried to pick up speed, bobbing up and down. He could hear the back bumper scrape off the cobbles. The ambulance stopped at the gate as it creaked open. Bottles and glasses rained down on them. The roof was buckling. The windscreen began to crack. 'We have to go back,' Shay shouted, covering his face with his arms. The windscreen was collapsing. 'This is where it gets dangerous,' the driver said. Shay turned to him and saw his own face, all burned and scarred.

Shay screamed as he woke.

Heaving in deep breaths, he composed himself.

His senses told him something was different.

Lisa and the kids were downstairs, but the sounds seemed subdued.

He grabbed his dressing gown, tying it loosely. He couldn't find his slippers. Something told him to move. Half way down the stairs he stopped.

Three holdalls were lined up by the door. Molly's favourite

dolly, Izzy, was sticking out of her bag. Charlie's favourite teddy, Alfie the dog, sat on top of his bag.

His body floated as if he missed a step. He clasped the railing to ground himself, as it hit him.

No fucking way. They can't be.

As he reached the sitting room, there was a beeping from somewhere. He looked into the kitchen. Lisa was leaning over the table, her finger pointing, as if issuing instructions to the kids. She halted suddenly. He knew she sensed his presence, but she didn't turn to him.

The kids were drawing.

They beamed up at him.

'We're going on a secret trip, Daddy,' Molly said, pushing herself up out of her chair.

'Nana's having Halloween party,' Charlie piped up, struggling to hold a huge marker in his little fingers.

'Ssh, it's a secret,' Molly said.

Shay looked to Lisa.

She had her back to him. She was sorting out a row of tupperwares, filled with Halloween goodies she had bought for the kids.

'You're not serious,' Shay said, with as much strength as he could, but it was almost a whisper.

Lisa busied herself moving things in and out of the containers and wiping already clean surfaces with a cloth. Shay saw her glance at the kids before turning around and looking at him. There was no anger in her features. But something had changed. Her eyes were clear. They told him she was leaving. She held the contact, so he could be in no doubt.

She turned back to run the cloth around the sink again.

Shay stood there, not able to figure out what words to assemble.

'We're drawing you a scary picture, Daddy,' Molly said, spreading her left hand across her drawing as if to reveal it. 'I have a witch and this is a pot. She puts frogs and legs in to make a potion.'

She smiled up at Shay, who stared at the pot. It had a leg sticking out of it.

'Mine a scary car with a ghost,' Charlie said, all excited.

Shay's face twisted.

They think it's a game, a game on Daddy. What can I do? My beautiful kids.

Maybe they were only going down for the party, for Halloween, he told himself, and would be back when all the madness died down. He looked at Lisa for any signs this could be true, but she was busy scratching dried flakes off the hob.

He thought he heard the noise of a car. The doorbell rang, but it sounded muffled. Maybe his ears were too blocked to hear. Little feet scampered. He sensed Lisa gliding past him. He shuffled after them.

'Granpa, Granpa!' he heard the kids shout.

Lisa's dad stood in the doorway, clasping the two children in a big bear hug. Lisa was gathering up coats. Shay watched the motions and movements, but felt removed in some way. It was like part of his brain had shut down.

'Daddy, someone squashed our pumpkin,' Molly shouted, pointing to outside the front door. 'And someone stole our skeleton.'

The words didn't really register with Shay as Lisa and her dad ushered the kids out. Shay looked down at the pumpkin. The top of the head had been kicked in, leaving just the edge of its twisted mouth.

He stood onto the rough tarmac. A gust of wind whipped around his shins and blew back the edges of his dressing gown.

'Hairy legs, Daddy,' Charlie shouted and laughed.

'You're like a hairy pencil,' Molly said.

The boot of the car was sticking up. Shay could see smoke from the green curling behind it. His nose twitched at the stink. Bags were thrown in and the boot closed. He could see a mass of twisted metal on the green.

'Has Nana got a scary Scooby Doo? Has she?' It was Molly's voice.

'And scary sweets?' That was Charlie's.

The sides of his dressing gown were flapping back, but he didn't notice. He was feeling dizzy, like when he spun Molly or Charlie round and round. His mouth was stone dry. He needed water.

Wake up.

There was another voice. The kids were in the back seats. The window was down. What? They're waving, calling. Someone blocked his vision. It was Lisa. She said something. Was that a kiss against his cheek? When he blinked and refocused, she was in the car.

He heard Lisa's voice.

'Daddy has a football tournament on, kids. Say bye bye.'

'Bye Daddy.' Molly's and Charlie's voices collided and sang. 'Love you.'

There was a noise. An engine.

Do something, for Christ's sake.

He reached out his hand and grasped in their direction, but there was only air.

The wind blew again. It ran up his legs, snaking up into his chest.

His vision cleared. They were gone.

He wasn't sure, but when a door closed nearby, he sensed he had been standing there for a while. Someone looked at him as they passed.

Above him there were claps. An arrowhead of swans swooped low over the house and arced away from him.

He pushed himself inside, forgetting to close the door.

The silence seized him. He shivered at it.

Alfie had been left behind. He lay there at the entrance, his two front paws stretched out. A flame of hope flared somewhere inside Shay.

Charlie will miss this at night. I could bring it down. Yeah.

He brought Alfie into the sitting room. There was that beeping noise again. He looked up and copped it was the battery in the smoke alarm.

'How did it get to this?' he muttered.

He half stumbled into the kitchen. His bones chilled at the absence of noise, of life. His feet recoiled at the coldness of the tiles. He stood there waiting for a smack in the face, something violent to wake him up.

The drawings on the table were all that was left of the kids. He looked at Molly's witch and the cauldron. He didn't like the leg sticking out of the pot.

He looked at Charlie's drawing. There was a massive black jeep, with thick bull bars to the front. They weren't curved, but straight and angular and bent around the bonnet. The jeep stretched back with several doors and loads of rectangles for windows. The tyres were huge. At the back of the jeep stood a figure, oddly shaped, like a thin man with a big head. There was no nose or mouth. Just two crude shapes for eyes. There were lines from each eye going up and right across the face.

What did Charlie say it was? A scary car with a ghost.

Shay fell to his knees. And raged his head off the tiles.

55

Shay was lying on his side when he woke.

He immediately wished he hadn't. His forehead pounded. He felt it would split and his brain slop out if he moved. He winced in agony. His head was all soft and bumpy above his eyes. His eyebrows were matted on one side.

He wondered had pieces of tile crunched into his skull, the pain was so bad.

But the empty sick feeling hollowing his stomach was worse than the riot in his head. He slowly pulled his knees up towards him and lay there, clenching his eyes shut, as the demons swarmed into his mind.

When he opened his eyes again, he saw Alfie: on the floor, facing him. His black eyes were not sad in a cute way now, more indifferent. The sound of the Luas stole in through an open window. It had that ghostly quality to it, like someone blowing a long breath.

Shay summoned the strength and tensed himself to move. On the third try he managed to push himself off the tiles, hoping his head wouldn't explode. He stood, wavering, holding his hand out against the fridge. Taking steps in inches, he reached up at the shelves, pulling containers down, knocking others over. Lids and contents spilled and clattered. He searched and grabbed for paracetamol, but there was none.

Serves me fucking right.

He pressed his hands against the counter top and leaned hard. His head jangled. Something beeped.

He turned and moved, his arms stretched out before him, his flat feet clapping through the silence into the sitting room. He sat on the armrest of the couch. Squinting, he saw Charlie's cars on the floor and Molly's toy kitchen against the wall. Some building blocks lay scattered. His eyes began to well up again. But anger boiled too.

How could she do this to me? After all I have done, done for her?

Small voices told him that wasn't true. He defied them and cursed in hushed spits. Anything louder would make the pounding in his head worse.

He edged towards the door and forced himself to tackle the stairs, stopping at each step.

At the top, Charlie's and Molly's door was wide open. Shay shivered as he entered. Bedclothes, duvets and pillows were scattered. Teddies abandoned. He stood there, for how long he didn't know, surveying the room. He tried to recall moments with the kids, but the pounding in his head denied him that. He shuffled to his own bedroom.

Looking outside, he saw kids examining remnants of a fire. Some were trying to start new ones, raiding bins for supplies. He scanned the green, what was left of it. The individual scorch marks – he must have counted a dozen – had connected up in places. The entire triangle was now one big blackness, with just patches of grass.

He closed his eyes. Moving slowly, he sought refuge under the sheets.

56

Jig ran back to the boys and held the box of matches aloft, triumphant.

'Have them.'

Spikey and Dizzy Dylan stood guard over the mound of old tyres a guy had dumped from the back of a van.

'I got these out of me ma's bedroom,' Jig said, laughing. 'She'll be banging the walls looking for them in a minute.'

'Get some paper,' Spikey shouted.

Dizzy and another boy ran around, grabbing up armfuls of newspapers, cartons and cardboard.

'Put them inside the tyres,' Spikey said.

Jig struck the match. The paper went up quickly. They sat and watched the flame spread and grow. More rubbish was raided.

Jig looked around as kids gathered, jumping up and down at the small curls of flames. The smoke got thicker and dirtier.

Kids coughed and smacked each other on the back, laughing and spluttering. Some hopped from one foot to another, dancing.

The coughing became heavier. The black smoke covered half the green. Jig could see arms reach out through blinds to shut windows, and laughed.

Jig, Spikey and Dizzy moved away from the smoke as it billowed and sat closer to the canal and watched. Their fire coughed away like a dirty old train.

Jig noticed a few people were putting more stuff out. There

were bits of tables and beds, mattresses, bags of rubbish and even a big old television.

He jumped up and the others followed.

They ran from one house to the fire and back again.

The sky opened up just as Jig spotted a three-seater sofa.

'Bingo,' Jig shouted. 'Give us a hand here.'

Kids ran from everywhere. Jig and Spikey marshalled their army, and heaved the sofa towards the green.

There was a stinking wet smell from the fire now and a toxic black smoke.

A man came out and moved his car down the road. Jig led the loud laughs and nodded to himself in satisfaction.

He looked at his phone. It was still only six o'clock.

He had another two hours of freedom.

57

Crowe dumped her bag on the counter. She clipped off her holster and placed it down, exhaling relief and flexing her hip.

She opened the fridge and took out a can and cracked it open. As she savoured a gulp, her eyes rested on a post-it she'd stuck on the fridge door days ago, reminding Tom to buy some fruit.

Where the fuck was he anyway, she wondered.

On Halloween night? He's hardly out trick-or-treating.

She opened her bag and took out her phone, then grabbed the evening paper she had bought after seeing the headline.

Teen beaten to a pulp in drugs row, it said.

Though Micko Hynes wasn't named, she knew it referred to him. The boy ran one of the canal crews. She had gone down to the parents' place in St Frances flats, but was told to fuck off and had the door slammed in her face.

The teenager had his jaw bone and nose broken, had lost sight in his left eye and had severe bruising all over his back. Any more belts to his head, the doctors had told her, he would have been left a vegetable. All at the end of a club. One, Crowe was sure, wielded by Cracko. But no one would talk. Same old story.

She took a long swig from her can.

Another of my investigations going nowhere. At this rate, I'll be clocking up one of the worst detection rates in the station. Some chance of a promotion then.

What the beating was for, she didn't know. The newspaper said it was a drugs row. But, that's what they always said. No, there was something deeper going on with the Canal Gang in the last few weeks: the seizures, the attack on the addict and his girlfriend and now this beating. The gang was under pressure, for sure. But why? And was it connected to this republican threat Lynn was on about?

Tom intruded on her thinking again. She picked up her phone and rang his number. A faint noise went off from down the hall. It seemed to be coming from their bedroom. Maybe he had dozed off, she thought as she headed to the room. Her spirits lifted.

But there was no Tom. Just the screen of his phone lit up on the bed.

Crowe sat down in the gloom and picked the phone up. She took a long drink, as she deliberated. With only the slightest trace of guilt, she began scrolling through his texts. She didn't want to find anything. But, at the same time, part of her did. It would confirm what she suspected. But she found it hard to focus on the names and numbers. She was just too tired.

She tapped in 171 and hit dial.

'You have no new messages. You have one old message. To hear the message . . .'

Crowe hit six. There was a woman's voice. Crowe tugged at the collar of her shirt. The woman spoke in whispered, broken words. She turned up the volume.

'I know you told me not to ring you on your phone because she might be there.'

Crowe felt as if a switch inside her had been flicked.

'I know, but I want your cock.'

Crowe's arms and legs started to shake. The can slipped from her hand. Foaming liquid spilled out.

'I've put on white gym pants. You'll like them. They're really tight and curve around my big juicy ass.'

The voice was breathing into the phone. Crowe tried to pull the phone away, but it was stuck to her sweaty palm. Her mind was screaming. Her heart banged, but she couldn't stop listening.

'My top is cut really low. And I'm wearing six-inch heels.'

This could not be happening.

The bastard. How could he?

'I'll suck your cock, lick it nice and slow. Hmm. Up and down. Kiss it and lick it.'

Crowe dropped the phone. She felt sick. The wall swayed in front of her. She struggled to catch a breath.

She stumbled and opened the window, closing her eyes to the blast of cold against her cheeks. Faint music wafted from an apartment below. Someone plucking a guitar. A soft male voice. The song sounded familiar. Lou Reed. 'Perfect Day.' Crowe's eyes welled up. She clenched her teeth.

I am not going to stand for this.

She made for the door, but she couldn't help but look at the mobile. The screen glowed. The call was still going. She could still hear the whore. She kneeled down and held the phone to her ear.

'Nothing is off limits. Nothing. I know what you want to do to me. She won't let you do it to her, but I will . . .'

Crowe flung the phone away, smacking it against the wall, and screamed down at the carpet.

'You fucking bastard, you complete fucking bastard!'

She sniffed the tears away and wiped her cheeks.

I am not going to break down here in the bedroom for him to find me, a blubbering, pathetic wreck.

She pushed for the bathroom, though it felt like a boulder was strapped to her body.

58

Jig watched one of the older lads pull out a blazing ball of cloth from the bonfire with a golf club. He scooped it up with the head of the club and swung it around. The other lads roared encouragement and the girls shrieked as he pretended to lob it at them, then actually did, just missing their heads.

A banger exploded in the flames, nearly catapulting Jig off the edge of the sofa. Some of the lads had pulled down the back of their tracksuits and were pretending to roast their arses against the fires. The girls laughed and recorded it on their phones.

Jig wanted to stay for the craic, as it was only getting going now. But Ghost had told him to be home at 8 p.m. He knew he'd better not be late. He checked the time on his phone and started running.

When he neared his house, he didn't recognise the car outside. But, he could sense Ghost was inside it.

Before he got to it, Ghost stepped out. Jig saw the side of his face, his sharp cheekbones glistening. His arms swung as he walked around the front of the car. He had a plastic bag in one hand and for a moment Jig thought he looked like he was trick-or-treating. He laughed to himself at the thought of him and Ghost trick-or-treating, scaring the shit out of everyone, filling their bags with sweets and marshmallows and stuffing themselves.

'Go in and put these on, the runners and all,' Ghost said, handing him the bag. 'Take off yer underwear and just put on the tracksuit.'

Jig opened the bag, expecting to see top of the range gear. But it was some grey tracksuit and cheap runners.

'They look poxy?'

'It's not for a fucking fashion show, just put them on,' Ghost said, pushing him towards his house. 'Who's inside?'

'Me sister.'

'Where's yer ma?'

Jig just shook his head. He saw Ghost nod. Jig wondered was even Ghost afraid of his ma? Jig rapped on the door and Donna opened it. Jig could see she tried to smother a smile on seeing Ghost behind him. He dipped under Donna's arm and took the stairs in jumps.

Donna watched Ghost tap out a cigarette. He was about to put it away when he stopped and offered her one.

She remembered the gesture, although it was ages ago now. She took it and accepted his light.

'Yer looking well,' Ghost said.

She tapped her foot against the door, then smiled.

'Off the gear and the tablets,' she said, taking a long drag, 'almost a month.'

'Yeah?'

'Fucking yeah. I'm a government junkie now,' she laughed, 'just the methadone, well, and the weed.'

The door into the front room opened and out popped one little head, then another. They stared at Ghost in the half-light.

'Right, in, watch the telly,' Donna said, pushing them back.

As she turned to her side, she could sense Ghost eyeing her body, lingering on her curves. She kept her pose for a second longer than she needed to. Just for old times' sake.

'What's their names again?' Ghost asked, as she faced him.

She paused.

'Wayne, Crystal, isn't it?' he said, before she could respond.

She looked at him and thought he smiled as he dragged hard. The light from the street lamp spread over his face as he turned. His skin was pulled so thin she could almost see his bones, grey against the yellowy-white. It reminded her of old television pictures from a prisoner of war camp.

'Where's the dragon?' he asked.

Donna was going to tell him to fuck off.

'Out. Just as well for yer sake.'

Ghost snorted.

Donna tried to figure out whether Ghost's presence at their doorstep was a sign he was innocent of Maggot's disappearance or what. The garda kept saying it was his gang. But she didn't trust those fuckers. They were playing their own mind games. They kept pulling her in for drug searches, even now, knowing she was off all of it. They did it to humiliate her and make her say something about Ghost and the gang. But she had nothing to say. She didn't know anything. Maggot was a mad bastard and, truth be told, a bad bastard. Like their da. He was going to be killed or kill someone himself. It was just a matter of time. But she felt bad about little Jig being in Ghost's grasp. She had left him, and the kids, but she had to. She'd risked all she had managed to do in getting clean by coming back to the hole. She only did so because she heard her ma was down the pub all the time and the kids were running wild and going hungry. The da had just fucking disappeared, same as always.

Donna furrowed her eyebrows at the clothes on Jig as he clattered down the stairs, followed by Bowie.

'Where's he going in that get-up?' she said to Ghost. 'It's hanging off him.'

But Ghost didn't respond and looked down towards the canal.

Jig told Bowie to go to the kitchen, but the dog stayed put, giving a loud bark at the door. Jig pushed him down and closed the kitchen door behind him. Bowie scratched and yelped.

Donna put her arm out to block Jig, but he shoved it away.

'Where ya going?' she shouted after him.

'Leave yer phone behind,' Ghost said.

Jig walked back in and dropped the phone down on top of some clothes.

'Why's he leaving his phone here?' Donna asked. 'Where youse going?'

Ghost flicked away the butt of the fag.

'Listen, Don, don't worry. I'll have him back in an hour, two tops.'

He hadn't called her Don since they were teens. It disarmed her. Ghost wasn't going to do anything. She knew that. He wouldn't be here showing his face if he was. But something was up.

Ghost and Jig moved for the car. Donna closed the door slightly, took her mobile out and turned it to vibrate mode.

'Hey, Jig. Come back here and give me a hug,' she said with strained cheeriness. 'Come on.'

Jig lumbered back, pretending to be pissed off. Donna pulled him tight and slipped her phone into one of his front pockets. Noticing Jig's reaction, she kissed him on the forehead and let him go. As she closed the door, Bowie stopped barking and started to whine.

59

Shay sat in the darkness, facing the window. His head cracked with pain as he lifted the glass. He gasped at the rum and Coke washing through him. It was lukewarm, but he didn't need ice.

The doorbell went again, the sound muffled. His ears were badly blocked. He pressed his fingers against them and shook the wax. One of the ears cleared, but only for a second, then closed over again.

Kids had always got decent treats at their house. Not this year, he thought bitterly. He finished the glass and emptied more rum in, with just a dash of Coke this time.

He wondered were Molly and Charlie still out. Molly was going to dress up as a scary witch and Charlie as Harry Potter. The drink swished inside him as he imagined them sorting through their goodies. The smoke alarm beeped behind him.

Through the half-open blinds, Shay watched the shifting blocks of orange and yellow and, in the foreground, dancing black silhouettes.

A white Hiace van drove slowly past his window and stopped. A man got out and swung open the back doors. There was a shout and kids came running. He fucked stuff onto the road – carpets, poles, seats of some sort and loads of rubbish bags. The back doors closed and the van drove off. Shay cursed the fucker. He savoured a passing thought of smashing his bottle over the man's head. The kids milled around, pondering the best bits, and pulled them over to the fire, leaving the rest on the road.

Shay polished off another glass and poured more in. As he

looked up, he noticed the kids' music drum on the mantelpiece.

He pulled himself up, tensing at the pain, and stepped towards the drum. He rotated the lever. It was the 'Chim Chim Cher-ee' tune from *Mary Poppins*. The notes twanged as he turned it. The sweet sound stirred emotions inside him. Images popped up in his mind: of him playing it as he lay down in Charlie's bed, his son's eyes sparkling at the music and his dad's presence.

He jolted as fireworks exploded on the green, and looked out. There was a huddle of kids around a bigger shape. They roared as fireworks sailed up into the air, smacking and briefly decorating the sky. But some went astray, shooting horizontally, zipping over the grass at speed, hitting off houses and roofs. He heard startled shouts from parents and kids and saw some figures diving for cover.

The combination of pain and swishing booze was making him queasy. He placed the music drum down, grim thoughts massing again.

He felt an urge to get out. He grabbed the bottle and opened the door.

His nostrils flared at the cool night air. His eyes shot back as the alcohol, the acrid smell and the cacophony of noise assailed him.

Shay heaved into the canal, just as two swans glided past, blissfully unaware of the madness around them. Their unruffled detachment grated him tonight. He stumbled down to a lock, and fell against a balance beam. He leaned over the inky black water and dropped the empty bottle. It landed with a plop in the chamber below, a good twenty feet down. The sound washed over him. Some of the spray ran up along his face, soothing his aching forehead. The sensation gave him a pleasant tingling. It felt enticing. He wanted more of it. Thoughts whispered inside him.

Lean in.

More spray played with his face and head. Shay smiled. He could feel himself wobble slightly, but he didn't adjust his balance. He wasn't going to fight it.

Soothing water.

He tilted.

The first clap he heard only dimly. He was tipping. Then there was another clap, and another. Parting his eyes, he tried to focus. It was one of the swans. He had pushed himself up out the water. His big wings were unfolded and he was flapping them, again and again. Shay reached to his side. He managed to grab the top of a rack gate and steadied himself, right on the edge. He blinked at the foaming waters and stepped back.

He gasped as he realised what he was about to do. He stumbled away, his mind a crowded boxing arena of half-shouts, ragged fantasies and mocking voices. The clamour of house alarms, dogs barking and bangers exploding muscled their way in.

His attention turned to the clipped noises of heels running. Ahead, a young girl in shiny red trousers tottered across the road, looking anxiously back at a house. Music blared from an open door and bodies spilled out. Dim voices in Shay's head told him to turn around, but he didn't heed them. Youths ran up the road ahead of him shouting at someone. Then they came back, towards Shay. He lowered his head as they neared.

There was movement and he heard a crunch, caught a glimpse of a fist passing his nose and he lurched to the side. He reached out. His wrist broke the fall. He sensed a body circling him.

Get up.

He pushed himself off the ground, and stumbled forward, his vision blurred. A bottle smashed close beside him. He broke into a run around a corner and up to a roundabout.

He threw himself against a low wall, heaving breaths. His wrist throbbed. He felt his nose with his left hand: it was huge and all zigzaggy. His top was covered in blood and was torn, his trousers too. He pinched his nose to try and stop the bleeding.

'Fucking Jesus,' he muttered.

He tore at a tissue in his pocket and put two bits up his nose.

As the adrenaline spent itself, Shay brooded over the attack.

If I hadn't got up, I could have had my head kicked in.

He fought an urge to go back and jump on the guy.

He vented his spleen at the black sky. Just as his mobile rang.

60

Shay wanted the screen to say Lisa. He needed to hear her voice. But it wasn't. It was the priest. He pressed answer.

'Shay? Jig's in trouble.'

Shay snorted as if he'd been told a stupid joke.

Jig. Can you fucking believe it?

'We need to find him ... Shay?'

Shay stopped short from telling the priest to fuck off. Thick blood dripped through the tissues. He spread his legs apart to let it splatter on the ground. He grabbed his bloody rag and held it to his nostrils.

'Can't ... help,' he managed to say between spits and coughs.

'Shay, something awful is about to happen.'

Shay ran his fingers along his nose again. The bone curved one way, then back the other way.

Must be broken. The pricks.

'Shay?'

'Yeah.'

'Leo told me he was going to die tonight and that the crew were going with him. All of them ... including Jig.'

Shay kept his head back and stared up at the sky, which flashed and exploded in colours. He sucked in air, struggling to cope with the choking sensation in his mouth and nose and the battering to his head.

'He said the RCAD are in on it. He got me to say an Our Father with him and do an act of contrition.'

268

Shay leaned against a wall. He felt so weak and sick of it all. His tinnitus rang in his ear.

'I'm at Jig's mother's house, but she won't listen to me. She might to you . . . Shay?'

Shay hung up and dropped his hand down by his side, shoving his phone into a pocket.

Cunts, the lot of them. Fuck Jig. One less runt from a cesspit of a family. If Leo has a big bomb strapped to his bollocks and kills them all, good riddance.

He clenched his right fist and grated his teeth. Sweat ran down his spine.

Everything is fucked. My family. My career. The lot.

He pulled at his hair and scratched his face as he stuttered forward, weak and dizzy. He banged off a car and caught a glimpse of himself in the windows. The face looking back at him was smeared and swollen, bloodied and blackened, like something that crawled out of the mind of Francis Bacon. He laughed bitterly, spitting blood onto the pavement.

A girl and boy walked towards him, circling around as they approached. They looked the same age as Molly and Charlie. Shay bent down and held out his hand. They screeched at the sight of him and tore across the road, their trick-or-treat bags flapping in their hands.

Shay stood there looking at them as they ran away, glancing back at him in terror. He reached for his phone and pressed in Hall's number.

'Yes.'

'Something's going down,' he said.

'What phone are you ringing from?'

'Emergency.'

'You alright? Ring me from the other phone.'

'Priest's been on,' Shay continued, managing to string a few words without spluttering. 'Leo meeting Canal Gang. Tonight. All going to die. Jig even. RCAD involved.'

Silence.

'We're on top of it,' Hall said.

Shay's phone beeped with another call.
'You don't do anything,' Hall said. 'Is that clear?'
'What?' Shay shouted. 'What about Jig?'
'I told you, we're on top of it. Do nothing.'
The line went dead.
The priest's number flashed again.

61

Leo glanced at the three entrances, waiting for a shooter to come in and open up a hole in his head. He sipped on a 7 Up and tried to keep himself occupied. He'd already read the poster for the Karaoke King about ten times. He only glanced at the poster advertising the majorettes. He didn't want people to think he was some kind of fucking pervert.

He scratched his hair and his beard. He smacked his lips as he watched all the golden pints being poured and slurped. He took a gulp of his lemonade. He'd love something with a bit more kick.

He hadn't planned on seeing Father Pat before he left, but if he wasn't coming back he reckoned he owed it to the priest, for all he'd done. And he wanted an act of contrition. His ma would kill him if he didn't.

This spot, at the end of the bar, near the jacks, was where Ghost told him to be, at 8.30 p.m. sharp. Not that he told him as such when he went up to training. Ghost gave him a note with the message on it and then took it back off him. Before that Ghost had searched him. When he reacted, more instinct than anything, Ghost gave him a smack for his trouble.

His head was wrecked, between Ghost, the RA and the spooks. He was as paranoid as fuck in his bedroom, knowing there was at least one bug there. But he'd done what the spook told him. He repeated to himself the where and when of the meet, but in a way you would do if you were reminding yourself. Other than that, he did jack. He had kept off the gear. He wasn't going to spurn

271

his one chance by overdosing. So he spent his time rolling joints, smoking joints, and playing music, and lobbing blueys and yellies into him. He had the last bluey before he left.

Even with the tranquillisers, his nerves were jangled as he tried to keep sketch on the doors.

At first, he didn't notice the tug on his jacket. Looking down he saw a kid. He was munching on crisps.

'Here,' the boy said, putting something into his hand.

Leo didn't take it. Could be anything.

'Take the fucking thing,' the kid said, shoving it into his hand. The boy walked off towards the lounge area, crunching away.

It was a phone. Leo held it to his ear, not sure whether to expect a voice or the thing to blow up and take his head off.

'Yeah?'

'In the press under the sink in the jacks, there's a set of clothes and runners. Go into the cubicle, take all yer clothes off, socks, jocks, the works, and put on the new ones. Leave yer clothes in the bag.'

'Clothes. Right.'

'Take everything off. We'll know if ya haven't when we meet. Make sure there's nothing up yer jacksey either. Clear?'

'Right, nothing up me hole.'

'Don't hang up. After ya change, go out the back emergency door and get on the next Luas. It's due in eight minutes. It's going to kick off in the pub after ya go into the jacks.'

'Fuck,' Hall said, after hanging up.

'Everything okay?' DI Slavin asked.

Only he and the deputy commissioner knew Shay's full identity, Hall reminded himself. Slavin knew Shay only as CIS/3. Slavin was the handler for most of the assets. But the first couple of assets, Hall was still the handler. That was back when Hall set up the unit and before he got promoted.

'That priest has contacted our asset,' Hall said, eyeing the bank of screens in front of him. 'About Leo and the gang.'

'You think they could jeopardise the op?' Slavin asked.

Hall rubbed his chin and stared at the backs of the detectives logging every detail of the surveillance teams.

'We don't have the manpower to go looking for him now,' Hall said. 'Can't see what they can do, apart from saying a decade of the fucking rosary.'

Slavin snorted.

But Hall knew Shay was an unknown factor in all of this. And he hated unknown factors. He was spinning enough plates as it was. They had lost Leo last week from the church. He never said what that was all about, but in fairness, he did what he told him to do and gave the details about the meet, which set this operation in train.

Most important for Hall was keeping track of the Provo who met Leo in the church. It took that fucker eight hours to actually go home that day. They'd put 24-hour surveillance on him since. That had led them to a number of other targets, most of them associates of Sutcliffe. That, together with the work of the Subversive Intelligence Unit, resulted in a list of five targets.

Hall looked up at the screens. Screen one was an audio from inside the Dry Dock pub. Screens two, three and four were visuals outside the entrances. Below them was an array of screens on the five Provo suspects. Three had left their homes straight after Leo moved from the priest's house. The Provos were being careful, though, Hall thought. They had got into vehicles they had never used since the surveillance started. As a result, there was no tracker on them. The gardaí had to do this the old-fashioned way. Eyes and ears. Hall had six teams – three cars and three motorbikes. One car and one bike on each target. Four other teams were still in situ on the two suspects who hadn't budged.

Hall figured the Provos had some sort of tracker on Leo. Where they put it, he didn't know. The Provos knew Lock Man was a paranoid fucker, so wherever the tracker was it better not be spotted. Otherwise, there'd be no final act to this drama.

Hall had wanted to keep the job purely within his Special Research Unit, but given he had eleven surveillance teams in total and three intervention teams, it wasn't possible. Hall had the assistance of the National Surveillance Unit for the operation. The ERU was in three intervention teams: Black 1 for the Provos, Black 2 for the Canal Gang and Black 3 was backup. All of the units came under ISD and Deputy Commissioner Nessan's control. Hall had full operational command and kept information on a need-to-know basis.

The plan was to swoop on the Provos before they struck. They would nail them for possession of firearms, membership of a terrorist organisation and, hopefully, conspiracy to commit murder. It would be the first successful operation against the RCAD.

More than that, this was an opportunity to nail the Canal Gang. For that, Hall had to wait until the meet, when Leo was with them. That way they could do them for false imprisonment, assault, if they roughed him up, and firearms, if they had any. Or they could get Leo to testify against them, about the drugs he was caught with before he disappeared. It would be a double victory for ISD and for him.

Hall had quietly considered the scenario of it all going tits up: of the Provos succeeding in taking out the Canal Gang before they could pounce. Questions would be asked, he knew, but, given the outcome, it would be lost in the praise. They would have a prompt arrest afterwards of the Provos. And no one would mourn the Canal Gang. Hall's status as a rising star in the force would be confirmed and promotion would be guaranteed.

As long as he managed to keep all the plates spinning.

'What's the location of the Provos?' he asked.

'T/1 is still in Ballyfermot,' Slavin said, 'T/2 is moving this direction from Tallaght and T/3 is driving around the Coombe.'

'We still got nothing on the Canal Gang?'

'No.'

It was the one loose thread: they had no eyes on the gang. They had bugs in some of their homes and trackers on many of their known vehicles, as well as Ghost's jacket. But all was silent. They were obviously being extra careful. Hall told himself he simply hadn't the resources to conduct physical surveillance on them round-the-clock as well. They had concentrated on the Provos and Leo. His thinking was that they would bring them to wherever the Canal Gang would be.

'8/0 to 5/0. Bait is on the phone.'

Hall listened to the audio from the team inside the pub.

'He's turning and going to the toilets, I think.'

'5/0 to 8/0,' Slavin said. 'Keep your distance, but get sight on the bathroom. Make sure you pick him up when he comes out.'

Slavin looked at Hall.

'He's going to move,' Hall said. 'We'll have to be on our toes, from here.'

'5/0 to 8/1, 8/2,' Slavin said. 'There could be movement soon.'

Hall looked up at the feed on the Provos. No change.

Right then, all hell erupted. Hall and Slavin pulled the bluetooths from their ears at the screeching and feedback. On the command centre audio they heard shouting and roaring. Tables and chairs scraped against the floor and women screamed.

'5/0 to 8/0. Report,' Slavin said. 'What's going on?'

'8/0 to 5/0. Fight has broken out. We don't have sight of the toilets.'

'5/0 to 8/0,' Slavin shouted. 'We need eyes on Bait. Do we have eyes?'

Hall could hear an alarm going off, adding to the racket.

'8/0 to 5/0. No.'

Hall clenched his fists.

Shit. We've lost him.

'5/0 to 8/1, 8/2,' Slavin said. 'Bait is 5/7. I repeat, Bait is 5/7.'

Leo pushed through the emergency door, still holding the phone, nearly shitting himself at the blaring alarm. A mass of punters streamed out, screaming and pushing behind him. He moved among them and headed for the canal. Bangers and fireworks were going off all around. He saw a Luas coming. At the green by the canal, near the flats, a fire was blazing. A car was heading slowly towards it. A shape jumped out of the driver's seat and rolled onto the green. Leo ran to the Luas stop, surrounded by others, and hopped on. The car exploded and a massive flame erupted into the sky.

Leo slipped down low on a seat, shaking, and pressed the phone to his ear.

'I'm on.'

'Get off at Smithfield stop. Someone will meet ya there.'

62

Shay ignored the priest's call. He grimaced at the pains in his head and wrist. His nose was a swollen mass and blood had hardened around his mouth, making it difficult to breathe. His jeans were ripped at the knees and his top was streaked in red and black.

People looked at him as he stumbled and ran; splutters of adrenaline pushed his hollowed body forward. Shay's stomach knotted the more he battled his thoughts.

What was Hall fucking up to?

He knew he couldn't trust him.

I've no choice but to play ball. If I intervene now, I could kiss everything goodbye. I'd be blacklisted for good.

He wondered if Leo was talking through his hole to the priest. But he sensed otherwise. The RCAD were serious heads and were gunning for a spectacular. And what bigger prize than the Canal Gang?

There was a bang from the direction of the canal. A fireball rose over the houses and a huge cheer went up.

Shay's ribs ached at the strain from running. His balance was disorientated from his blocked ears.

Jig's house came into view. He saw Father Pat pacing outside.

'My God, Shay, what happened to you?' Pat's eyes widened as he looked him up and down. 'You look like you've been run over.'

Shay struggled to talk, with all the blood and tissue up his nostrils.

'Were you assaulted?'

'You should have been a detective, Pat,' Shay said, stumbling to Jig's door and banging it.

All he could hear was a television blaring inside.

'They're not answering,' the priest said. 'Jig's sister Donna is in there and the mother. Shay, you have to go to hospital. Your nose and your head . . .'

'I'll live.'

'You hear that explosion?' the priest asked, after a moment.

'Dante seems to be out tonight, Father,' Shay said and he kicked the door.

There was stomping on the stairs. The door opened.

Shay remembered her face, though she looked better now than when he last saw her.

Donna reared back, opening her mouth, as she surveyed Shay.

Bowie barked down the hall, behind the kitchen door. The sitting-room door swung back, the white of a television glaring in the darkness. Jig's ma appeared. Her two little ones popped out behind her, sucking on chips. The ma held an arm up to the frame to steady herself. Shay reckoned she had a tankful on board – vodka, tablets, God knows. Strings of greasy hair hung down the sides of her head.

'I'm trying to watch the fucking telly,' she said, shouting every second word, 'and me head is wrecked from youse banging –'

She stopped as she focused on Shay.

'Jaysus, Shayo, ya out trick-or-treating or what?' she said with a rough laugh. 'Or did that dozy wife of yers finally smack ya one for being such a sap.'

Shay clenched his fist.

Christ I'd love to punch you right in that miserable face.

He felt a hand, that of the priest, on his shoulder.

'Jig could be, is, in danger,' Pat said. 'We need to find him.'

The ma's face twisted in exaggerated concern.

'Jig, in danger? Sure, what's new. He's probably down by the bonfires. Thought ya be down there, Father, hanging out with all them little boys,' she said.

Shay looked at Donna.

'Donna, you know where Jig is?' Shay asked. 'Who he's with?'

She shook her head, biting her lip.

The mother reached over to the door and rammed it shut, nearly taking Shay's head off. Pat supported him as they walked to the gate.

'Fuck them, Pat,' Shay said. 'His own family don't give a shite. Why should we?'

His head was banging. He felt near to collapse.

'It's easy to do the right thing for good people, Shay. The real test is doing it for the bad ones.'

'You're a good man for the old quotes, Pat. You should write them down. For all the good it would do.'

Shay leaned against the pillar and concentrated on staying upright.

'What about that detective, Shay?'

Shay slipped and smacked his shoulder hard off the pillar. The priest grabbed him and stopped him from hitting the ground.

'Jesus, Shay.'

The priest groaned as he heaved Shay up. Fresh blood dripped from Shay's nose.

'Here, take this.'

Shay took a tissue from the priest and leaned back again. Out the corner of his eye, he spotted movement from a window above.

'It's all fucked up, Pat.'

'What you mean?' the priest asked, moving closer.

'I'm not who you think I am. I'm a sham, a sad joke of a man.'

The priest furrowed his eyebrows.

'Shay, a lot of people, good people even, are twisted by troubles, tormented by demons. But we have a child here who is in danger. And we are the only people that can help him. If we don't act now it will haunt us.'

The door behind them creaked. A gap opened and Donna stepped out. She walked out to the gate, clasping a cigarette.

'Youse didn't hear this from me,' she said, scuffing a foot against the ground. 'Jig left with Ghost in a car. Over half an hour ago.'

She glanced over her shoulder.

'Ghost told him to leave his phone here, but I slipped my phone into his pocket. I've been trying to text and ring him after youse came, but nothing.'

'What's the number?' Shay said.

She told him and he typed it in and rang it. No answer.

'Any idea where they were going or what for?' Shay asked, still holding the tissue to his nose.

'Haven't a clue. Shouldn't have let him go.'

'We'll have to call the guards,' the priest said.

'She'll go fucking ballistic,' Donna said, nodding to the house. 'If the cops come here, I didn't tell youse nothing.'

She flicked the fag past them and slipped back inside.

Shay slumped against the pillar and reflected on his options.

Better ring the unit and give them this number. Let them trace it. But they've already told me to back off, to do nothing.

He knew, in his bones, they had their own plans.

Pat was beside him, but didn't say anything. He didn't have to. Shay knew they were thinking the same thing.

Spitting blood, Shay pulled out his wallet, his wrist complaining at the strain, and tugged at a card.

63

The noise of the door didn't register. Neither did the voice. Crowe could hear the sounds, but it was like the hum of distant traffic. Coming to, she realised she was sitting up straight, rigid, on the toilet seat. Her hands were clasped, resting on her thighs. She mustn't have moved for ages.

The words of that bitch swirled around her mind.

A dull thud at the side of her head intruded. She heard Tom's voice.

'Tara? You in there?'

The doorknob curled and it inched open. Crowe searched for some strength, to look at Tom's face.

'You alright? I was calling you . . .'

'Well, you fuck her?' Crowe spat.

Tom had stepped into the room by the time she spoke. He frowned, his thick eyebrows, which she used to think were handsome, arched.

'Don't,' was all she could say, sickened at the pretence.

'What you on about?'

His voice was sheepish. Crowe looked back to the tiles. Tom stood there. She could feel him thinking. His search for some sort of excuse just made it worse. The thud in the side of her head was spreading.

'Tara, what's going on?'

She didn't move her mouth, but inside she chewed.

'I'll get you some paracetamol,' he said.

Crowe bit down on her lips as she thought.

What a pathetic excuse for a man. I've been living with him all these years and now I find out, like this. And to think I was going to have kids with him some day, get married, and now ...

She recalled friends where boyfriends or husbands had done the dirt. She used to pity them.

Now it's my turn. I am the one to be pitied. At the hands of a layabout, who lives off my money.

She snuffled and wiped her nose as footsteps returned. Tom walked over, two white tablets nestled in one of his hands, a glass of water in the other.

'Here.'

She recoiled. She couldn't look at his face. She should have told him to ram it up his arse, like he did with his dick and that whore. But the pain was growing. She picked the tablets up without touching his skin and took the water. Swallowing, she dropped the glass onto the tiles, cracking loudly, but not breaking.

'What are you doing?' Tom shouted.

'What? You're worried about some crappy glass?'

He didn't reply, picked up the glass and walked towards the door.

'Go on, crawl back to your dirty slapper.'

Tom stopped. She was a bit surprised when he turned back around, thinking he would just walk off. It was the first time she actually looked at his face properly. He looked like he hadn't shaved in days. Irregular patches of hair sprouted from his cheeks, marooned from his rough beard. Everything about him grated at her now, particularly the baffled, wounded look on his face. She sprang up. He pulled back as she approached and rose his arms to protect himself.

'Well? What exactly did you do to her?' she said, smacking his arms. 'How long have you been doing it?'

The blows were limp. She just didn't have the strength.

'Are you on about that ... that phone call?'

'At last, you fucking stop pretending.'

'It's not what you think, Tara. It's not.'

'It's not like what? That you are fucking someone. Indulging your fantasies on her. Oh, don't tell me,' Crowe laughed bitterly, 'that it's just sex and you don't really love her.' She pressed her finger into his cheek. 'How could you do that to me?'

Her chest stretched tight with the strain.

'I didn't do that, Tara. It's a ... it's a phone sex thing.'

'What?'

'It's a sex line. You ring the number and they ring you back. It's a fantasy thing. That's all.'

'That's all,' she thumped him. 'That's all. You bastard.'

She turned her back to him as the tears massed.

'Tara.'

'Get out.'

She kept her back to him, trying to hold it in.

'Jesus, Tara, it's just –'

'Out.'

The door closed, just in time. She banged down hard onto the toilet seat. The tears ran. She sat there as thoughts collided off each other.

He didn't have sex with her. But he did as much. He let me believe he did. And I did believe it.

She could hear Tom pacing in the hall. In the sitting room her phone was ringing.

She looked at the bath. They'd made love in it, she recalled, the first night they moved in. Tom had put candles circling the edges. She told him it was a bit tacky, but part of her melted inside at the time. They stayed in the waters clutching each other until their skin shrivelled. They both had to work the following day, but stayed up in the bedroom, wrapped in dressing gowns, drinking wine and talking. That morning they made love again, then rang in sick and spent the rest of the day curled up in bed. He was so happy, she remembered, his face one big boyish smile. She was happy too. She curved in on herself at the memory.

Minutes passed. She was getting stiff leaning against the toilet. She pulled herself up and ran the cold water in the sink, throwing it over her face and head. She looked at herself in the mirror. Her hair was all scraggy and knotted at the ends, wet with water and sweat. Her lips were pale.

Look at the state of me.

'Tara? You okay?'

The anger and hurt that had subsided rose again. It wasn't so much what he had done, but the fact everything they had was tainted now, sullied. She could hear her phone ringing again. She pulled the hair behind her ears and wiped her face clean. She studied herself, as if looking for signs of strength. She wasn't going to stay holed up in the loo. She pulled back the door with a bang and stormed into the sitting room, passing Tom. Behind him the kettle was on.

'It's just a phone thing, Tara, that's all.'

She turned to him sharply.

'Stop saying "that's all". You're ringing these lines, fantasising about fucking these women. Do you know at the other end is some skanger? You're pathetic, that's what you are. I'm living with a pathetic little man.'

She looked at him. He looked like a beaten dog.

'But the worst thing was me listening to that and thinking you had gone out to shag some tart. How do you think that makes me feel? You're fantasising about cheating on me.'

'I know, I'm sorry, but . . . but things haven't been easy.'

Crowe pointed her finger at him.

'Don't you weasel your way out of this. Don't.'

Her heart was pounding, waiting for him to say more.

'Well, we haven't had sex in ages.'

'Ah, so this is my fault.'

Her phone was ringing again and she turned to the sound.

'I didn't say that.'

Crowe grabbed at cushions, throwing them around and scoured shelves, knocking things over, looking for her phone. Her mind was racing.

So because we haven't had sex he's allowed to ring sex lines and I'm supposed to be okay with that?

She located the phone. She didn't recognise the number.

'Yes?'

'Detective Crowe. It's Shay.'

She let him speak, but just wanted to hang up. Shay sounded a bit unhinged and there was a racket behind him.

'Have you tried to ring the number the sister gave you?' she asked, composing herself.

'It's ringing out. Can you trace it?'

Tara watched Tom skulking in the kitchen. He clicked on the kettle again and placed two cups on the counter.

I should stay and save what's left of our relationship. This is the last thing I need right now, heading out to some madness. I'm not up to it.

'Detective Crowe? We need to act, quickly.'

The whistle from the kettle screeched. She thought back to Lynn's warning in the car. Was this it?

She held the side of her head. The pain throbbed as she wrestled with her thoughts.

Why should I give a flying fuck about the Canal Gang? They killed Grant and the little girl and left Peters a living corpse. Jig's a little scumbag, like all his family. He sows, he reaps. It will happen now or in five years' time, like with his brother.

She watched Tom fill one cup, then another. She needed to stay here. She was about to tell Shay to just ring the station.

But he spoke first.

'I know what's going through your mind. I've thought the same. Who cares what happens to them? Why should we? But Jig is just a boy.'

64

Crowe watched the steam from the cups swirl and evaporate. Tom stood there, uncertain whether to bring the tea to her or wait for her to come over. He settled on pushing the cup across the counter top.

'Work?' he asked tentatively.

Crowe looked through him.

'Yeah, shit on top of shit,' she said, dialling a number.

She didn't hate Tom. He was just a man, a weak fool of a man. No, it was more she resented him. Not just for what he had done, but how he made her feel about herself and her own part in their relationship.

'Crowe.'

'DI, we may have a situation with the Canal Gang.'

'Is that right?'

She filled Tyrell in on what she knew.

There was a pause on the line.

'Give me the number and we'll try and get a trace going. Go to the house and assess the situation.'

Crowe gave him the number, then stopped, hard thoughts creeping back in.

'Some people would say leave them at it,' she said, 'after all that they've done. Even the boy. You said yourself, it's already too late to save him.'

Another pause.

'Yeah, I did,' Tyrell said slowly, 'but, that was based on my experience, not yours.'

She needed more. She thought she heard something tearing on the line and a soft sucking sound.

'Crowe, some might well say, "Fuck them, let them wipe each other out, after everything." And they might be able to live with that. But,' he said, tossing something in his mouth, 'would you?'

She felt a rip of electricity down her spine, like a zip opening.

'Give us a ring, Crowe, when you're there. I'll see about the trace.'

Tyrell hung up. Crowe was still vibrating from being reminded who she was.

She went over to the counter, fastened her holster and grabbed her bag, ignoring the steaming cup.

'Hey?' Tom called.

'I have to go,' she shouted over her shoulder.

'Be careful.'

Crowe crossed the Liffey and sped down the quays. Whatever was going to happen tonight, what home was she going back to? She pushed out thoughts of Tom masturbating as he listened to his fantasy woman breathing at him to fuck her. Nothing would be the same again. She had to summon strength to keep going. She took a short cut through the narrow cobbled streets under the shadow of John's Lane Church. He'll have to move out, she told herself.

But he's got no money. He'll be living on the streets.

Blocks of flats flanked her as she accelerated. She sped past flames and blurred silhouettes. Approaching the canal, she blinked at a bonfire, the blazing hulk of a car inside and a mass of figures circling it.

Kids scampered in all directions, forcing her to break. Some were dragging bins out of driveways, the bins twice the size of most of them. She manoeuvred bends and roundabouts until she came to Evergreen Close.

She pulled up outside Jig's house. Getting out, she caught an eyeful of Shay. He looked like he'd been hit by a bus.

'Who did this to you?' she asked.

'Myself.'

She tilted her head at the reply. Shay looked half-deranged. But she didn't have time to dwell on him.

Fireworks and bangers exploded from all directions. She scrunched her nose at the toxic stench in the air. She walked up to the door and banged hard.

A blonde woman opened it.

'Donna, is it?' Crowe asked.

The woman nodded, her arms tight across her chest.

'I'm Detective Tara Crowe. These gentlemen,' indicating behind her, 'have reason to fear for Jig's safety.'

'Jaysus, this is for fucking real.'

'You speak to Ghost?'

'Yeah.'

'What did he say about where they were going and why?'

'Nothing. He gave Jig a set of clothes to change into and told him to leave his phone here. I got worried at that, that's why I slipped my phone into his pocket.'

'Ghost see you doing that?'

'No. But Jig's not answering. The phone's on vibrate, though. Jaysus, maybe I put it on fucking silent,' she said, holding a hand to her face. 'No wonder he's not picking up.'

'You did well,' Crowe said.

But Donna didn't hear, her face twisting with another thought. 'Don't fucking tell Ghost any of this, right, or the gaff will be torched, with all us in it.'

'Don't worry about that,' Crowe assured her.

'I'm fucking serious, he would.'

'Okay. I hear you.'

Jig's ma emerged, her hair trailing wildly down the side of her face, her eye sockets all red. She pushed Donna back and stiffened when she saw Crowe.

'Ya know what? Yer like a bad fucking penny.'

'There's reason to believe your son may be in danger –'

'What?' she shouted. 'Yer concerned for his welfare all of a fucking sudden.'

She pointed her finger at Crowe, jabbing her in the chest.

'If anything happens to my Jig, it's on yer head.' She slammed the door.

Before Crowe could say anything, her phone rang. It was Tyrell.

'We're trying to get a location. Get ready to move.'

'Okay.'

'Guess you're getting the usual five-star reception.'

'She's off her rocker,' Crowe replied, 'but her daughter, Donna, seems reasonably sane. She confirmed what Shay said. Ghost brought over clothes and got Jig to change into them. Told him to leave his phone behind.'

'I see.'

A crunch at the other end.

'Remember I told you about what that source had said to me?' Crowe asked. 'She said the Provos were going to carry out a spectacular. Maybe this is it and the Canal Gang is walking straight into it and Leo is in on it.'

'Very possible,' Tyrell replied. 'The precautions the gang is taking on phones and clothes supports that. Lock Man is a cute bastard.'

'We got backup?'

'I notified the Chief. He's requested the ISD to mobilise the ERU. We're scrambling the helicopter ... There's a call coming in. I'll get back to you.'

Crowe looked at Shay.

'The phone is still switched on. We're trying to triangulate it.'

'We're going with you,' Shay said.

Crowe baulked, just as a big drop of rain landed on her face, then another.

'No way,' she said.

'Listen, you might need to talk to Jig,' Shay said, shouting over the bangers. 'He won't talk to you, but he might to me. Same with Leo and Pat.'

Her phone rang.

'Crowe, we have a general location.'

65

Jig dug his fists into his hoodie.

It was freezing in here. Wherever it was. Ghost had got him to pull the hoodie up and lean his head against the dashboard with his arms around his face all the way in the car. At one stage he heard a gate open and they drove up a bumpy path. Ghost got him out and told him to keep looking down until he opened a big metal door and pushed him inside some building. When he looked around it was a warehouse, full of echoes and rattles.

Jig stared at the men. Ghost was in a huddle with two others. One was a mini Incredible Hulk. He had a battered head that looked like the side of a car that had been smashed in and someone had tried to beat it back out. The other man was bald and built like a barrel. He didn't seem to speak, just looked on as the others talked. He gave Jig a hard stare when he fell off a pallet. Must be the boss man, Jig told himself.

The door opened with a clang and Cracko strode in.

Everyone was wearing new clobber, even if it was poxy, he thought, as he tried to balance on an iron bar.

Must be the gang meeting about the rat.

He twitched as he remembered Ghost at the canal with Bowie and Cracko crunching his shoulders.

But what are they going to do? They going to torture some fucker, to find out who the rat is?

There were sounds of bangers in the distance. Jig wondered what Spikey and Dizzy Dylan were up to. He wished he was with his mates, messing. He looked up at the windows that ran along the top half of the walls for fireworks, but the windows were covered with grilles. There were a couple of big metal doors, but all, apart from the one they came in, were bolted and rusty. There was a tapping noise as he walked back the far side, towards the others. Drops fell from holes in the roof. It took seconds for them to hit the ground. He watched them sail down and plop, bang off the metal poles.

There was a noise from outside. Another car was stopping.

Hall heaved in a breath, held it for a few seconds and exhaled slowly. Between the fight in the pub and the explosion at the bonfire, they had lost Leo in the pandemonium.

They only had the targets now. He looked at the feeds on the screens.

'T/1 is on the move, heading north, into Clondalkin,' Slavin said. 'T/2 has gone Rathfarnham direction. And T/3 is driving down the canals, towards Ballsbridge.'

All going in different directions. Hall leaned against a desk and studied the screens, examining the routes of the targets up to this point.

'Decoys,' he said, in a whisper. 'Two of them are sending us in the wrong direction.'

He clasped his chin in his hand and rubbed it, squinting at the screens. Something else dawned on him.

'Or,' he said, looking at Slavin, 'all three of them are.'

'All?' said Slavin, confused.

'Have the two targets who were still in their homes moved?'

'No, they haven't stirred.'

Hall looked at the detectives logging those teams for confirmation and they nodded.

'Mackin was seen going into his apartment last night and hasn't come out since,' Slavin said, reading the logbooks. 'The other guy, Roberts, was last seen going into his house just before 5 p.m. He hasn't budged.'

Hall ran his tongue against his front teeth. Something was up.

'Hold on,' Hall said, 'did one of the teams not report a utility van arriving at Mackin's apartment just after Leo left the priest's?'

Slavin flicked through the sheets.

'Yeah, we have a guy, wearing a yellow hi-vis Irish Gas jacket and cap, carrying a holdall, calling to the apartment block,' Slavin said, reading from the log. 'He examined a box outside for a while. He then entered the building. We got a good look at him when he arrived. No one we knew. He exited,' Slavin said, reading the notes, 'some five minutes later and left in a white van with the Irish Gas logo.'

Hall looked at Slavin.

'Was it the same guy who left, as entered?' Hall asked. 'Tell me it was.'

Slavin looked at the notes.

'Just says Irish Gas guy exited. Nothing else.'

'Get onto 9/0 and check.'

Hall listened to Slavin. The team didn't know for sure if it was the same guy or not. They only had a partial image of him when he left.

'This is the best picture they have of the guy after,' Slavin said, opening up the photograph on a screen.

All Hall could see was a guy in a cap and a yellow hi-vis jacket. His face wasn't visible.

'Call up the images when he arrived?'

Slavin searched for a few moments. He opened up the images separately. The man's bulk and clothes looked different, Hall thought. It wasn't the same guy.

'Circulate the photo of the guy leaving to the other teams and the description of the utility van. Tell me we have the reg?'

Slavin shook his head.

'Fuck,' Hall roared. 'Right under our noses.'

He needed to regain control of this.

'Organise search patterns for teams 9/0 to 9/3. Bring one team back from each of the three mobile suspects. And bring in 8/1 and 8/2. We'll need as many as possible.'

He walked over to the map.

Lock Man would have kept this meeting local, he said to himself, somewhere secure.

'Okay, we have nine teams to find this van,' Hall said, running his finger in circles around the map. 'Get three teams into the Coombe, Rialto and Inchicore, three into Crumlin and Drimnagh and the last three into Bluebell, Ballyfermot and Ballymount. Surely, between them, they can find a fucking white gas van.'

Slavin gave the orders, directing the teams and devising search patterns.

Hall got on to the ERU intervention squads.

'5/0 to Black 1, Black 2, Black 3. We have new locations.'

Jason Mackin pulled the van in near the back entrance to the War Memorial Gardens, his wipers creaking back and forth. He looked at the red dot on his tablet. Leo had gone all the way from the canals into the city centre, across the Liffey, back down the quays and out towards the canal again. He smiled at the gang's attempts to shake off company.

Shoving the van into first, he kept glancing at the map. The vehicle was on the Naas Road now, about a mile from him.

Not only had they bettered the Canal Gang, he thought, but they had also fooled the spooks. They were about to take out the gang right under the noses of the garda. That would put them on the map for sure.

He looked down at his holdall and practised the drill again in his mind.

Jig and the others stared at the door as it clanged open. In walked some hoodie. There was a big guy with him, who nodded to the hulk and shut the door behind him. The bang echoed around the warehouse and there were darted looks back and forth between the hoodie and the crew. Jig felt his body shake a bit. He needed to go for a piss.

The hulk motioned to the guy, who pulled his hoodie down. Jig sneaked up a few steps to take a look.

Is this guy the rat? He looks like a junkie.

He was wearing the same type of tracksuit, it was hanging off him.

The hulk strode over. He told the man to take his clothes off. The man pulled off his top, then, hesitating for a second, took down his bottoms.

Jig muffled his laugh. The guy was bollix naked. He was all black and purple and bones. He had little craters on his legs and arms.

A junkie alright.

The hulk leaned in and examined him, got him to hold up his arms and spread his legs. He pointed at the guy to turn around and bend over.

Jig stared at the hulk looking up the man's arse and burst out laughing. The boss man glared. Jig nearly shat himself and swallowed the rest of the laugh.

The hulk strolled back and nodded to the boss man. The junkie pulled up his tracksuit. As he threw on his top, he spotted Jig and his face darkened.

Jig wondered if they were going to kill the guy.

Are they going to get me to do it? Is that going to be my initiation to the gang or something?

No one spoke. The hulk stood in front of the boss. Ghost was off to the right, near the door. Cracko stood closest to the man, his arms tight against his T-shirt.

Jig watched the junkie shift where he stood, exposed in the middle of the warehouse, standing under a bright light.

The hulk said: 'Well?'

Jig barely heard the reply, the voice was so shaky.

'I wants me debts written off.'

No one said anything.

'Talk,' the hulk said.

'I wants guarantees first.'

Hall's mobile vibrated. He cursed as Deputy Commissioner Nessan's number came up.

'Sir?'

'Why has Detective Inspector Tyrell put in a request through his Chief to trace a phone linked to Jig. And a request to have the ERU on standby?'

'What?'

'They have reason to fear for this boy's safety,' Nessan said. 'They have information that the Provos are going to take out the Canal Gang.'

Hall's mind spun.

Fuck you, Shay, if you're behind this.

'You need to get on top of this, Hall,' Nessan said. 'Quick.'

'Yes, sir.'

'The phone company is locating the boy's phone. Get onto Comms and tell them to keep you informed. I hope this op of yours doesn't backfire on you.'

Nessan hung up. Hall chewed over the use of 'yours' and 'you' and knew what it would mean if it all went pear-shaped. He dialled Shay's mobile.

You're fucking history, Shay, if you've fucked me over.

Cracko laughed when the junkie said 'guarantees'.

'Just get on with it,' the hulk said.

The guy shifted on his feet and scratched at his head.

'Listen, I wants to know I'm safe if I tell youse this? That's fair enough.'

Cracko turned to the hulk. Jig could see him almost begging for a lash at the guy.

'Don't waste our time,' the hulk said, 'or I might allow my friend here,' nodding to Cracko, 'to ask the questions.'

The guy starting shaking.

Jig smiled.

Ya better fucking talk.

'I wants to know why youse killed me ma.' He glanced over at Jig. 'Why?'

Jig stumbled back and fell over a pole. He looked at Ghost, who shook his head to say nothing and looked at the man again.

He's that old woman's son. He wants to kill me.

295

There was silence. Jig heard rain beat against the sheeting on the roof. Big drops fell, making a loud tapping noise as they hit the metal poles. He pushed himself up. He felt something in his trousers and remembered the phone.

'Don't be wasting our time,' the hulk said, with a deliberate nod at Cracko.

'The cops have an inside line on youse,' he blurted out as Cracko moved towards him.

The boss man stepped forward. Jig saw all of them turn to face him, then back to the man.

'I got this off a garda,' the man said, 'when they were actually fucking investigating me ma's murder.'

Jig heard more strength in the man's voice now.

'The copper told me to lie low, not to do nothing, that they had a source.'

The man stopped talking. Jig scanned the faces. The boss man looked like he was chewing on a wasp.

'And?' the hulk asked.

'What I knows is the garda said yer gang is compromised. Her words. She said they mightn't have enough on youse for me ma, but that they're playing the long game and all that. Youse have a rat.'

The boss man tilted his head from side to side, like a boxer in his corner.

'Spit it fucking out,' the boss man said. 'Who?'

Jig shivered at the change in atmosphere. Everyone seemed to stop breathing. No one moved. The hair on the back of his head prickled. Save for the dripping there wasn't a sound.

The man scratched his head, harder this time.

Jig sneaked around the back of them, stopping behind a wooden box. He shoved his hand into his pocket and grasped the phone.

They'd kill me if they knew I had this.

But no one was looking in his direction. Jig blinked at the screen. Fifteen missed calls. A text came up.

Get out Jig. Danger.

He felt warm liquid run down the inside of his right leg. He looked at the message again. He dropped the phone back in his pocket.

'I'm after pissing in me tracksuit,' he said, looking towards Ghost. Tense faces swung around at him, annoyed by the distraction. Jig ran to the door, but didn't know how to open it. He banged on it. He felt eyes staring at him now. He turned and saw the boss man looking at a mobile phone.

'It's a trap,' the boss man roared. 'Out.'

Shay held Crowe's phone and put Tyrell on speaker as she careered down by the canal towards the Naas Road. The wipers swung hard as the rain smacked against the windscreen. Shay shook at his ears to try and hear what he was saying.

'It's off the Naas Road. They're trying to triangulate it as best they can,' Tyrell said. 'Units from the area have been dispatched.'

Shay could hear what seemed like other voices at the end of the phone and guessed Tyrell was still talking to someone else.

'Looks like it's one of the industrial estates, on the Bluebell or Ballyfermot side.'

'Almost there,' Crowe shouted above the metallic noise of the Luas running beside her, the silver tram glistening in the heavy rain.

She put the foot down, passing the Luas, and flung the car around a tight turn across the tracks, horns beeping from all sides. Crowe had to break hard at a steep speed ramp, the front bumper banging loudly.

Shay reached for his pocket as his own phone vibrated. There were two missed calls. A text had come through.

Ring. Now.

He sensed Crowe glancing over, her eyebrows knotting with suspicion.

'What's that?' she asked.

'Nothing,' he said, putting his phone away.

Crowe flew across a junction.

Shay's head smacked against the passenger window when the explosion went off.

The car vibrated off the road and skidded hard against the footpath.

A massive fireball filled the sky ahead.

'Jesus fucking Christ,' Shay roared before the pain from the bang kicked in.

'Explosion?' Tyrell said.

'Yes,' Crowe shouted, fighting to regain control of the car as it slid across the road, 'explosion at one of the industrial estates, not sure which, beside the canal. We need fire crews, ambulances. Now.'

'Oh my God,' the priest said from the back of the car.

Shay stared open-mouthed at the blaze shooting up into the sky. He could see bits of material, sheets of metal, catapulting upwards, and shuddered. He banged the dashboard with his fist, cursing.

'Too fucking late. I'm too fucking late. It's all for nothing.'

Blood ran from his nose and gathered on his lip.

'Fucking go, go!' he shouted, slamming his hand down.

Crowe tore over ramps, the chassis crunching and sparking. The rain hammered against the roof and the windscreen. The yellows of the street lamps blurred in the rain. But behind that was a display of oranges. Shay twisted his head at thoughts of what they were going to find. Bodies blown to bits. Little arms and legs. The priest whispered prayers behind him.

Crowe catapulted them forward at breakneck speed. She narrowly missed a van coming towards them, skidded around a bend and halted.

Shay jumped out before the car even stopped and kicked back the gate to a unit, his arm over his face.

'Shay, wait,' Crowe shouted behind him.

He sprinted up the lane towards the blaze.

I've killed the boy.

Shay ground his teeth at the realisation.

The side of his head throbbed from the impact of the explosion, and, with his nose split and swollen, he struggled to breathe as he ran.

Orange flames danced against a canvas of black. On the other side of the perimeter wall, he heard the canal waters hiss as crackling debris hailed down.

If the gang was inside the building they were blown to pieces, Jig with them.

A sheet of corrugated roofing slammed down in front of him, searing his shin. He winced, but forced himself on.

So, this is how it fucking ends: risking my life searching through rubble for bits of the boy. After everything I've sacrificed.

Somewhere behind, the detective shouted at him to come back. But, ahead, Shay thought he could make out screams. Distant sirens echoed along the warren of Dublin's streets.

The remainder of the warehouse heaved and groaned. He was out of time.

Fuck it, I've nothing to lose.

He stumbled forward, his face bubbling with the heat. His ankle twisted over something loose on the ground, tipping him off balance. Spitting blood from his lips, he looked down and followed the forks of yellow light.

Something small was smouldering.

It looked like a runner.

A child's runner.

'Jig?' he roared. 'Jig?'

66

Tyrell was facing the open window in his office when Crowe entered. A takeaway coffee steamed on the sill.

Crowe clicked the door closed behind her, but Tyrell didn't respond. He'd told her to call in at the end of her shift.

The sounds of traffic and people about their business spilled in from the street.

She looked over to his desk, where the radio was whispering. Her eyes lingered on the wall beside the desk. Grant's smiling face beamed out from a frame.

'You hear the Kremlin has taken over the investigation?'

When she looked back, the DI was facing her.

The Intelligence and Security Division was still called the Kremlin by some of the older crew. She wasn't surprised they had taken over. Their role in the whole thing stank. No better way to manage the situation than assume full control.

'They say why?' she asked.

'Nope. The Chief got a call. He was told Nessan's lot were taking charge and to hand over all files.'

Crowe clasped her hands in front of her.

'Because of the Provos, it's a security matter, we're told,' Tyrell continued. 'Number One says it's their area. Nothing us local detectives can handle. It's not like having multiple murders on our own patch is something we should be investigating.'

Tyrell reached for his coffee and walked to his desk, slipping into his chair. He nodded to Crowe to sit down.

'You not wonder, Crowe, how they arrested all those Provos straight after the bomb attack?'

'They had them under surveillance all the time?' Crowe said, taking a seat. 'Before we alerted them?'

Tyrell nodded.

'But what happened? A fuck up on their part?'

Tyrell looked up at her as he sipped. Crowe wasn't sure if he was smiling behind the steam.

'Did they know the boy was there?' she continued.

Tyrell put his cup down. It was a smile okay. But she couldn't tell if the smile was saying 'you're right' or 'we'll never know'.

Tyrell drummed the side of his cup, a faintly mischievous look on his face.

'Then there was this tracking device, inside Leo's wig,' he said. 'And the message on Lock Man's phone.'

Crowe cocked her eyebrow. She knew about the wig that Leo wore. Ingenious. The Provos had stitched a tracker into the back of the wig. Fooled the Canal Gang. But what was this about Lock Man's phone? She could see Tyrell noticed her reaction.

'The tech guys examined the phones found at the scene,' he said. 'There were two. One, we know, was Jig's. But there was another phone found in Lock Man's hands. It was damaged, but they retrieved a text sent at the time of the bang, telling him it was a trap. They couldn't trace the number, apparently. ISD have it now.'

Crowe clasped the underside of her chair.

'A mole?' she said, more in a whisper, leaning forward. 'Like with Ms King and our search on Jig's house. The gang always seemed to be one step ahead of us. Fuck. Excuse me.'

Tyrell leaned back and held the coffee to his lips.

'Are we all under suspicion?' she asked. 'Are they going to be snooping on us?'

'Safer to think they already are,' Tyrell said, raising his cup to the ceiling.

Crowe followed his eyes. They wouldn't bug their own offices, would they? She noticed Tyrell's head tilt at the radio. He turned up the volume.

'*The news at five. Gardaí are to get increased emergency surveillance powers to allow them to covertly bug gangland suspects for a period of ten days before they need to get court permission. The radical move follows the Halloween rocket attack on a criminal gang by a new dissident grouping which left three dead and four seriously injured. Garda security units have arrested and charged six people.*

'*And the government confirmed it is considering proposals which would allow gardaí to hold crime bosses in so-called preventative detention.*'

'Wow,' Crowe said. 'That's some shopping list of powers.'

'Yeah, I wonder whose,' Tyrell said, still listening to the news bulletin.

'*Meanwhile, government ministers have again rejected reports from Brussels that Ireland has applied for a bailout of up to ninety billion euro . . .*'

Tyrell snapped the radio off and closed his eyes.

They both pondered for a moment.

'By the way,' Tyrell said, 'what you make of this Shay fella?'

Crowe's mobile beeped. She looked over at Tyrell.

'Go on,' he said.

'It's probably Tom,' she said, reading the message. 'We're thinking,' she said, hesitating, 'of going out.'

She saw a little smile on Tyrell's face, but he pulled it back quickly. She typed in a message. She and Tom had promised to make an effort to work on their relationship.

'I suspect you'll get the nod now, after all your heroics,' Tyrell said, straightening his back.

'What about the ban on promotions?' Crowe asked, feeling some heat on her cheeks.

'I think they'll make an exception for you. They should anyway.'

'Thanks. Any chance they'll fill the DS job? Maybe they'll give it to you?'

Tyrell scoffed.

'Even before the canal murders, they said it was a top priority, but the DS office is still empty. As for me, that ship has long sailed.'

Crowe nodded, but wondered why Tyrell didn't think he'd get promoted. Suddenly, she remembered to thank him. She had never got a proper chance to up till now.

'DI, that night, when I rang you on the phone, about leaving the Canal Gang, and the boy, to their fate. I never said thanks for what you said.'

Tyrell opened a drawer.

'You knew what was the right thing to do,' he said, reaching for something. 'You just needed a reminder. We all do, from time to time.'

Crowe got up and walked to the door.

'You were asking about Shay?' she asked, turning around.

Tyrell waved his hand in the air, a packet in his fingers, as if to say it didn't matter.

'Another time,' he said. 'Interesting guy, though.'

Tyrell was right there, she thought. Shay was a strange fish.

'And do us a favour, Crowe.'

She half-turned to face him.

'I don't want you in early tomorrow and full of beans. Come in with a decent hangover for once, yeah?'

Crowe smiled brightly and closed the door, just as she heard a mint crack.

Through a gap in the clouds, Shay watched the sun send a shaft of clear light dancing down the water. The blonde reeds at the edge of the canal bent in the soft wind, their brown flowers shaking their heads.

'Daddy, the reeds are dancing,' Molly said, running her hands through them.

'Something nice after walk?' asked Charlie, who was holding Shay's hand. His son looked up at him, all hopeful.

'Sure we will, after we feed the swans and walk around the canal. Okay?'

'Something nice, something nice,' Molly shouted, skipping up the path.

Shay rubbed his thumb along the top of Charlie's hand. Charlie rubbed back with one of his soft fingers. Shay felt a warmth inside his heart from the gentle sensation.

Shay watched the cyclists and the joggers, glimmering in the late light. For mid-November there was still some warmth in the sun, although there were reports of bleak conditions descending the following week.

The leaves on the trees on the far side shone in a leisurely show of oranges, browns and yellows. In the distance, the two white lights of a Luas approached, accompanied by the sound of smooth metal sliding against metal. Shay closed his eyes, embalming himself in the moment.

When he opened them, Molly had stopped up ahead, at the shrine to Taylor Williams. Shay noticed the Dublin GAA top had been washed again and folded neatly where it had been since the day of the shooting. Three red night-lights rested on it. Beside it, a gleaming glass vase was dug into the earth, white lilies gracefully curving out.

Shay pushed out the image of the girl's shattered face, her sister screaming and jumping, of the dogs barking, of Jig dripping as he stood in the waters.

'Do children get shot on the canal, Daddy?' Molly asked.

'What? No. It was just an awful,' he struggled for words, 'thing to happen.'

'Does girl still have hole in face?' Charlie asked, feeling his own cheek.

'No,' Shay said, rubbing his hands over his son's hair.

'Does it heal in heaven?' Molly asked.

Shay went silent. His children waited for an answer.

His phone vibrated.

Probably Lisa checking up, he thought. It was his first full day with the kids on his own since she left with them.

'Unknown' flashed on the screen.

He sighed. It wasn't the first time they had rung. Sooner or later he'd have to answer. He tapped a button.

'You decided to pick up?'

Shay said nothing. His heart was racing at the sound of Hall's

304

voice. Every night since the explosion he had waited for his door to be kicked in and for him to be dragged away in a black van.

'You there?'

'What do you want?'

'Just touching base.'

'Is that right?'

'Given your solo run, you should be glad that's all.'

'Daddy? Can I have the bread?' Molly asked. 'For the swans and ducks.'

Shay let go of Charlie's hand and pulled out the packet and handed it to Molly. Their little legs scurried off, their feet crunching on bits of glass.

'I'm with the kids.'

'I know, I see you.'

'Fuck you.'

'Only wrecking your head. We need to meet for a debrief.'

'Two weeks on? What you want to debrief me about? I was fucking there. Or is it to tell me how fucked I am? Well, given the shit I've had to go through, put my family through, for fucking years, I don't really care.'

Shay was pissed with himself getting all riled like that, but fuck them and their games.

'You sure about that?' Hall said, his tone sharpening.

'What, the friendly chit-chat is over, is it?' Shay replied. 'You remember me ringing you that night? Not that you did much.'

'You went behind my back. You ignored a direct order. And you jeopardised the op.'

Shay didn't respond. Hall was right.

'Anyway, it's in the past,' Hall said. 'There's a lot of stuff in the past people are not proud about, don't want people to know.'

Fucker.

'You threatening me?'

'There are some things better left buried, is what I'm saying. For the greater good.'

'The greater good, eh? Was it a fuck up or did someone want the crew taken out, and if the boy was collateral damage, well, tough?'

Shay scrunched his nose at the smell of burning flesh and plastic. It happened sometimes when he recalled that night. He was convinced there was some bit of flesh stuck up his nostrils. He had shoved all sorts of nasal sprays up there, but he could not shift the smell.

'This is not a conversation to have over the phone. You need to come in. Get yourself sorted out. Think of your future.'

Shay was caught by a silhouette of the children by the waters' edge, leaning back and throwing the bread in as far as they could.

'My future. Right.'

He hung up and dumped the phone into his pocket. He ran his finger along his nose and felt the zigzag of the bone. The smell had gone.

Swans, ducks, waterhens and seagulls jostled in front of Charlie and Molly, competing for the scraps. Shay stood behind the kids.

That familiar sick feeling spread across the pit of his stomach.

How blinkered I've been for so many years. Obsessed about getting back into the force, thinking it would get my life back. And I was willing to put my family at risk for it. What a fucking idiot.

Shay closed his eyes and felt the warmth of the sun on his cheeks and willed the heat to melt his demons away.

He placed a hand on Charlie's head and looked ruefully at the scars cutting across the back of his skin.

A swan cast its wings up like a cupped hand and glided over to the far side. Shay watched it float away, his focus turning to the right when a dog barked.

Shay was startled when he looked over.

A slight figure leaned back against a concrete base under the bridge. His legs were stretched out straight, one wrapped in a big cast. Two grey crutches lay against him. Bowie at his side.

The kids were shouting, but it sounded like their voices were inside a glass bottle.

Shay looked at the cast again.

He jolted at the images. Jig's small black hand sticking up in the air from behind the block of a wall, the tips of his fingers on fire. The heat of the block as he forced himself against it, cutting his hands deep with the effort. The terrible crunch and screams as he heaved and pushed the block away. The state of the boy when he saw him: passed out, scarred in black and red, parts of him smouldering. He'd shouted at Jig to rouse him, thinking he was dead. And, as he lifted and dragged the boy away, a sheet of roofing cut into the ground, right where Jig had been.

Shay's eyes blinked and his mind shuddered as the images evaporated like spirits. But the smell was back.

Jig had survived. Unlike Leo and two gang members.

The bruising and burn marks on Shay's palms and fingers ached.

'Lads, let's cross over,' he said.

He felt like he was weighed down as he pushed himself across the bridge. He hadn't seen Jig since that night.

Coming down the far side, Shay was taken aback as Jig shifted himself around. He was still badly scorched. His face and neck, the only skin visible, was red with a dark black tinge. There were scars, a right big one on his forehead. His whole left side looked thinner, as if it had been flattened.

Bowie barked and came over to Shay, nuzzled his hard head against his leg and waddled back.

Jig shifted his weight to his right side. His left hand was covered in a padded glove. There was a cast of some sort on his left arm bulging under his top. His right hand was bandaged. The big cast on his left leg was emblazoned with graffiti and images. 'I Beat the IRA Rocket' boasted one.

'Shayo.'

Shay saw Jig's lips move, but didn't hear the words.

'Alright?' Jig added.

Shay didn't respond and scowled at the boy.

'Thanks for ... that night,' Jig said, faltering, lowering his face.

Shay blinked. Everything had changed. There was a deeper connection now with the boy. What kind, he didn't know.

'Thought you were still in hospital,' Shay said eventually.

'Got out, just yesterday. Couldn't wait.'

'How's the ...' Shay said, pointing to the leg.

307

'Docs said the breaks will heal. Eventually anyways.'

Shay nodded.

'And the burns?'

'They does be killing me. Might need grafts or something.'

Shay struggled to identify what emotions he was feeling.

'Good,' he said. 'Good.'

Shay stood there, just looking at Jig. He looked older.

The night was still a blur. His brain seemed to play it back to him in sections – when the explosion went off, the chaos at the scene, Jig in his arms and the mad journey to hospital.

'Ya not coaching no more?' Jig asked.

Shay came to. He shook his head.

'I'm giving it a break, Jig. I'm not sure about going back.'

'Ya should. Spikey was in with me in hospital, says they miss ya wrecking their heads.'

Shay smiled. He watched Jig shift and use his crutch to pull something out from behind the concrete base. He laughed when he saw a football. Bowie barked at it.

Jig tipped it with the crutch over to his right foot, pulled himself up with the second crutch and side-footed it over to Shay, directing it bang on to Shay's feet.

Shay brought the ball out and tapped it to Jig's right foot. Jig trapped it neatly, though Shay could see him grimace at the strain.

'See you down at training then,' Shay said. 'When you're healed.'

Jig looked down at the ball and nodded.

Shay wondered, would Jig ever play again?

Football was his best ticket out of gangland. What's his future now?

But he couldn't dwell on such things. He just wasn't up to it.

'Come on, kids,' Shay said, feeling a need to keep walking.

'I owe ya one,' Jig called out.

Shay looked over his shoulder. He stared at Jig, who held his gaze, then he nodded to the boy.

He walked on with the kids in silence for a few seconds, under the protective cover of the rustling branches.

'Is he going to die too?' Molly asked.

'Jig? No, he'll be okay.'

Charlie tugged at him.

'Look at swan.'

The swan had only a small patch of brown and grey feathers left. The rest of him was silky white.

'Dad?'

'Yes, Molly.'

'You said daddy and mommy swans stay together for ever.'

'Yeah.'

'Will you and Mommy stay together?'

Shay bent down and pulled them close. He wanted to reassure them. But what could he say?

'I don't know, lads. Daddy thought he was looking after you and Mommy, but he wasn't. We'll just have to see what happens. But we both love you. Remember that.'

He kissed them on their foreheads and stood up, clasping their hands.

The light was being sucked back up the canal as the evening folded. The sparkling oranges and yellows overhead dulled to a browny grey.

Shay's shoulders ached at the sudden drop in light and temperature. His cheeks stung at the cold.

He heard a noise behind. A growl.

He stopped, his body tensing.

Behind him, stones and glass crunched and split under the weight of wheels. He heard a window slide down.

Shay gripped the kids' hands tight.

There was no mistaking the voice.

'Alright, Jig. How's me little soldier?'

ACKNOWLEDGEMENTS

Firstly, and most importantly, a big thank you to my wife, Jacinta. She has had to put up with a lot over eight long years. But she has always given me full support, particularly when I needed it. She picked me up, gave me a hug and pushed me on.

My children too have suffered, through an often absent/absent-minded father or, as they sometimes described me, "a grump with a hump". They too encouraged me when I needed it.

A big thank you to my mother, Mona. I used her dining room on and off, for periods of days, over the last eight years, which also enabled me to spend time with her. A thank you to my late dad, Donal, whose love of Agatha Christie has stayed with me.

In terms of practical support, top of the list is publicist and agent (though not my agent), advisor, fellow boys' football manager and friend, Peter O'Connell.

From early on, when he offered to read the first few chapters, all the way to reading 120,000-plus words of a late draft (and giving direct pointers on a major structural edit) and advising me about agents and publishers, Peter has been there throughout. Thank you, Peter.

Other people who provided significant support include readers of the novel. These include crime author Andrea Carter, who has continued to offer me advice. Also thanks to Dearbhail McDonald for reading the novel and offering her support.

Fellow Black & White author and *Irish Examiner* journalist Ann O'Loughlin has been a constant source of support and advice. Thanks, Ann.

Huge thanks must go out to those gardaí – of all ranks – who provided me with their time, knowledge and insight, particularly the one who read the entire novel for me.

I want to acknowledge community workers and drug project workers who I have been fortunate enough to know over many years. My experiences with them influenced this novel considerably. One of them, Graham Ryall, read part of a very early, and very rough, draft.

Major thanks to the Irish Crime Fiction Writers' Group and all its members. I want to give particular thanks to Laurence O'Bryan, who organised both this group and another one I attended. Thanks to Carolann Copland, who also helped organise the meetings.

Thanks to others who, at differing stages, read chapters, including Seán McCárthaigh, Caroline O'Doherty, Nicole Jagusch and Sinéad Crowley and to the advice of Louise Phillips.

Thanks also to Conor Kostick and his 'Finish Your Novel' course I attended at the Irish Writers' Centre.

Thanks to the Arts Council of Ireland, who saw enough promise in my early work to give me an emerging writer literature bursary.

All of which brings me to key people in securing publication: scout, author and publishing guru Vanessa O'Loughlin and my agent Ger Nichol, whose belief in my novel and professional assistance has been invaluable.

Last, and definitely not least, thanks to all the team at Black & White Publishing.